LAGO

Books by John Lee

LAGO
THE THIRTEENTH HOUR
THE NINTH MAN
ASSIGNATION IN ALGERIA
CAUGHT IN THE ACT

LAGO

John Lee

DOUBLEDAY & COMPANY, INC.
GARDEN CITY, NEW YORK
1980

ISBN: 0-385-12993-9
Library of Congress Catalog Card Number 78–60293

For James W. Williamson,
who spent World War II in a strange outfit
called the Combat Propaganda Team,
Psychological Warfare Branch,
and who was in northern Italy
when it happened.

FOREWORD

The Dongo treasure is real. It first came to light in the final days of World War II, when Mussolini and his Fascist hierarchy fled north from Milan in an attempt to escape the onrushing Allies. With Mussolini's arrival on Lake Como, the treasure exploded into view, spewing gold bullion, precious stones and millions in currency across a war-impoverished Italian countryside, spreading death and destruction as surely as if they had been shrapnel.

Though this is a novel, and therefore fiction, it is based on true people and true events. I say quickly that the Lake Como partisans and the American Liaison Officer Team whom I have placed in Mussolini's path are my own inventions, and not meant to represent any of the actual World War II participants. But remember, for every Italian or American who lives and dies on these pages, a flesh-and-blood person prowled the enemy-occupied lake before him.

—John Lee

LAGO

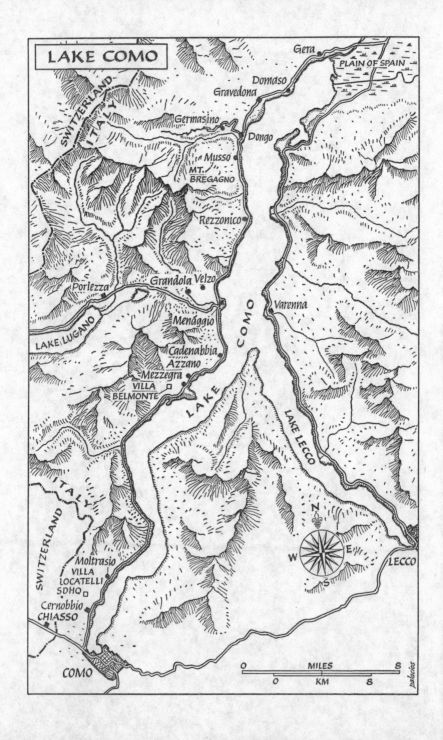

Prologue–1945

The Hour Before Sunrise

Fa cor: Della tua patria
i lieti eventi aspetta;
per noi della vendetta
già prossimo è l' albor.

Take heart: From your homeland
will come glad tidings;
for us the sunrise of vengeance
is already at hand.
— Verdi, *Aïda*

1

Midday sunlight pressed down on the narrow mountain trail above the lake, turning the dog's flanks to mangy gold. The dog ranged happily from tree to bush, ignoring the three men who labored up the trail behind him. Gualfiero Lusso let his rifle dangle and watched the brownish-yellow mutt dart erratically for a bird, which just as erratically took flight and fluttered squawking through the treetops. The dog sat down on the trail, mindlessly content in the warm sunshine, and began to scratch.

Like the dog, Gualfiero luxuriated in the feeling of sun-warmth, but he didn't think either of the other two men even noticed it. Didn't they know that spring today had set her foot upon the land? Oh, it wasn't yet spring by the calendar. Gualfiero and his dog had no use for calendars. Nature was a far more reliable timekeeper, and nature told both man and dog it was spring by the fragrance of pine resin that filled their nostrils, by the upstart breezes that buffeted their ears, by the new leaves on a thick growth of Alpine honeysuckle that crowded the trail.

The dog ceased his scratching and padded curiously to inspect something unnatural, a weatherbeaten sign that tilted from the honeysuckle. Gualfiero, also curious, let his gaze wander to the sign. The letters were faded and the panel only partially visible through the greening leaves, but the message was clear. The sign was a warning. It said, "ACHTUNG! BANDENGEBIET!"

Gualfiero frowned at the German words and shifted his guitar strap farther up on his shoulder so he could take hold of the dog. "Tuono, quiet," he whispered. He held the dog still for a moment, listening, hearing nothing but birdsong and the tentative chirp of insects, then he patted the dog and turned him loose and gestured for Luchino and the American major to come on up the trail.

Partisan country, the warning meant, to be avoided. What insult. These mountains above the lake had always been home to Gualfiero. As agile as a mountain goat, he had climbed them since boyhood, herding his father's sheep, sleeping with his back against sun-warmed boulders, breathing in the perfume of cedars and pine forests and wildflowers. Partisan country. Until the Germans came, these heights and the lake below had been an earthly paradise. And would be again. The Germans would be driven away, perhaps soon, and the sign would decay and fall, but the mountains, as timeless as eternity, would remain.

Moving quietly up the trail, Gualfiero stole a quick look at the lake below. Lake Como, his lake, the most beautiful of Italy's Lombardy lakes. Perhaps the most beautiful lake in all the world. Strings of villas and hovels clung like tiny sunlit boxes to its wandering shoreline. Steep wooded slopes and towering peaks rose on all sides into a cloudless blue sky. On a map, to an outsider like the American officer who trudged along behind Gualfiero and the other partisan, Luchino, Lake Como might look vaguely like an upside-down Y, or perhaps the stick figure of a running man, fifty kilometers tall from head to toe, legs spraddled in midflight with the crotch hovering some eighty kilometers north of Milan. But seen by someone who loved the lake as Gualfiero did, it could never resemble anything so frivolous. Running man vanished.

Lake Como became a shimmering blue jewel in the sunlight, set in emerald mountains. How brutally inappropriate, Gualfiero suddenly thought, that a weathered sign should be left there to remind one that partisans and Fascists and Germans had been killing each other in these rocky heights above such breathtaking splendor.

"Slow down," the American complained. "I can't catch my breath."

Gualfiero looked back at him. A tall man, breathing hard from the climb, the American carried a bulging satchel, which he hugged close to his chest. Gualfiero had warned him about the satchel, about the extra weight and the difficulty it would add to the journey up the mountain, but the American had refused to leave it behind. The man had developed an almost irrational concern for the satchel since the fight with David Landry. The man never went anywhere without it now. Gualfiero knew it contained money. Perhaps that was the reason for the American major's odd behavior. Many men were peculiar about money.

"You didn't tell me it would take this long," the American said. "How much farther? Aren't we almost there?"

Gualfiero cocked his head, trying to sort out the American officer's words. The officer was often hard to understand. For one thing, he spoke an arrogantly bad Italian—mostly infinitives, atrocious pronunciation—as though he thought it enough to make the effort and let the listener work it out on his own. For another, he wore a bandage across his nose, a heavy packing of gauze and adhesive tape, which tended to give his speech a whining, nasal sound.

When Gualfiero was reasonably certain of the American's meaning, he gestured up the trail beyond the ranging dog and said, "Not far now, maggiore. The point of rendezvous is about three hundred meters beyond those trees. I'd say another ten or fifteen minutes. Let Luchino carry your bag for you. That will make it easier."

The other partisan shouldered his rifle and reached for the satchel, but the American snatched it away. "Keep your hands to yourself," he said nasally. "Come on, hurry it up. Let's get moving."

Gualfiero sorted out the meaning again, and though it contradicted the officer's earlier demand that they slow down, he accepted it and moved on up the trail, increasing the pace. Luchino slouched forward and fell in beside Gualfiero. The American struggled to keep up, breathing noisily through his mouth.

"He's in a foul humor today," Luchino muttered.

"The major?" Gualfiero said. "He's just a little nervous."

"So am I," Luchino said uneasily. "I don't feel right about this. We ought to be down on the lake with the others, in position to help with the rescue attempt, instead of up here with *him*."

"No one expects help from us," Gualfiero said. "Our orders were to stay with the American major, to keep him safe."

"Yes, *stay* with him, but on the lake," Luchino objected quietly. "Not go wandering through the mountains. I tell you, Dante is going to be pissed when he finds out we sneaked the major up here."

Gualfiero grinned. "I sent word to Dante. He'll understand."

"Maybe," Luchino said. He glanced furtively at the American. "How can you be so nice to that ass? Especially after what he did to David? And leaving Luisa and the others to rot in that Fascist cell. Even his own men dislike him. I've seen the way the other Americans look at him."

Gualfiero's guitar slipped as they climbed over a break in the trail, and made soft thrumming sounds against his hip. He hitched the guitar back to his shoulder. "The man is frightened, Luchino. You can't blame him for that."

"I blame him for everything," Luchino grumbled. "You mark my words. He'll get us all killed."

Gualfiero opened his mouth, hesitated, then said, "Perhaps he won't be with us that long."

Luchino looked up sharply. "What do you mean by that? Do you know something I don't?"

"No, of course not," Gualfiero said. He chewed his lip, worrying that he'd said too much. His left hand moved to his pocket, feeling the slim shape under the cloth. A gift from the American major. A gift of fear. Luchino would never understand the fear. To him, a man was a man, or he was a coward, and like the others, Luchino had detected the smell of fear that clung to the American. He had assumed an instant dislike for the man, without trying to understand the complexities that ruled his actions. But Gualfiero understood. At least he thought he did. Gualfiero himself had been afraid, deathly afraid, many times. He knew how it could eat at a man's confidence.

"You must know something," Luchino said. "Is that why you agreed to bring him up here on such short notice?"

"I brought him because he asked it," Gualfiero said. "You don't have to stay with us much longer. After we keep the rendezvous, the major wants me to accompany him on another mission. You can go back to Dante's camp, if you want. Would you take Tuono with you? He'd be safer back in camp."

"You and that damned mongrel," Luchino said.

The American, now lagging several paces behind, raised his voice and said, "What are you two talking about?"

"Dogs," Luchino said shortly.

A low whistle drifted down from the trail above them. Gualfiero raised his eyes. He could see a man up ahead, emerging from the underbrush. Gualfiero turned to the American and whispered, "Maggiore, we are here."

"It's a damned good thing," the American grumbled. "I'm surprised we haven't run into a German patrol instead, the way you two waste time talking when you should be keeping watch." At least that's what Gualfiero thought he said.

The man waiting up on the trail waved down at them, then stood quietly, hand resting on a hip holster. Tuono burst through the bushes and started up toward him, tail wagging happily, but then the dog skidded to a halt and the fur rose on his neck. Gualfiero blinked and said, "Wait. Something may be wrong."

"Don't be foolish," Luchino murmured. "What could be wrong? We're here on time. He's waiting for us, like he said he would. Here, let me take the lead." He ducked under a pine bough and moved around Gualfiero to clamber on up the trail.

Gualfiero braced his guitar to keep it from bumping his hip and followed, but his eyes continued to scan the underbrush. Tuono was close to the ground now, his belly only inches from the dirt and he was whining. Gualfiero couldn't understand what was troubling the dog, couldn't isolate anything unusual about the trail or the heavy brush that overlooked it. Perhaps it was all in his mind. Thinking about fear, that might have done it. Fear was contagious. Some people said animals could pick up on things like that, pull it right out of the air, without a word being said. Particularly from their masters.

But then, suddenly, when Luchino was only a few meters below the rendezvous point, the man on the trail threw himself to the ground and covered his head with his arms. At the same moment, Gualfiero caught sight of movement in the bushes, and field-gray uniforms. Two uniformed men parted branches and aimed automatic weapons. Perhaps there were other uniformed men, as well. Gualfiero didn't wait to find out. He shouted, "Luchino! Duck!" Then he whirled and tried to run back down the trail.

A blast of gunfire split the silence and he felt something slap against his head. He fell against the rocks, his scalp stinging. Bullets chewed up the ground around him and his guitar twanged. He took two more hard blows to the leg. Blood streamed from his hair and ran into his eyes, and for a moment he thought he'd gone blind. He groped for his rifle, but the guns continued to hammer at him and something banged into his throat. He choked and fell back into the dirt. He lay still as death, thinking they were shooting only at him, but then, through the film of blood, he saw poor Luchino sprawled on the trail, one eye staring at the sky, with geysers of dirt spouting up around him. Somewhere to the rear, the American officer's voice rose, wailing repeatedly, "Ow, ow, ow."

Then, as quickly as it began, it was over. The hammering guns ceased. The silence rushed in. Gualfiero could hear distant echoes of the guns tailing off through the mountains. Then an even deeper hush. Metal clicked as magazines were removed and bolts slid home. Voices murmured. Someone swore in German, then laughed.

Betrayed. They had obviously been betrayed. Their companion on the trail, pretending to wait for them. He surely must have known. But why? Gualfiero could hear the Germans now, stepping gingerly from the underbrush. He shifted his head minutely toward his elbow, trying to rub the blood from his eyes. As they came closer, he heard a dazed whimper. He thought for a moment it was Tuono, but it was the American major lower on the trail. The American should be quiet. He should feign death. Gualfiero felt he should call out and tell him, but he didn't dare give himself away.

The voices moved nearer yet, and he heard at least two of them speaking in Italian. Who? Was there more than one traitor? Willing himself to move, Gualfiero lifted his head slowly, a millimeter at a time, until his line of sight rose above his elbow. He blinked away the blood and saw feet. German boots. Four Germans. No, six. One was an officer, immaculately dressed for such bloody work in these rugged heights. Tuono lay cringing on the ground at the officer's feet, his thin tail trying nervously to wag, but the German officer kicked at him and Tuono yelped, then scurried away with his tail between his legs.

Another figure appeared behind the officer, wearing shabby civilian trousers. Civilian clothing? Could this be the other voice that had spoken Italian? Gualfiero fluttered a half-lidded eye and tried to see who it was, but the officer stepped between them and Gualfiero could see only the German's face. It was Richter, bloody Richter, chief of the German SD, a man whom the partisans called "The Drowner."

Horrified, Gualfiero shut his eyes and held as still as he could. Don't breathe, don't moan. Let them think they have succeeded. He could hear them move closer, stopping only to prod poor Luchino's body. Then boots crunched on the trail near Gualfiero, and he felt the guitar being tugged from his shoulder. It must have been too badly smashed to be of interest, for it was quickly discarded, broken strings whispering in the dirt near Gualfiero's head.

Richter's voice murmured and moved past, and the other Germans followed. They continued down the trail to check the American. Gualfiero heard the American's voice, choked with fear or pain or perhaps both. He whined something at the foes standing above him, and they spoke back to him. Their voices mingled in anger. An argument of some kind. What were they saying? The satchel? That was it, the satchel. God above, the American was screaming at them, refusing to give it up. How could he be such a fool?

Careful, someone was coming back. Keep playing dead. No matter how much it hurts, don't moan, don't move. Strange, it was so much easier to play dead than he'd ever realized. Almost like dreaming. One merely closed one's eyes and drifted, and the pain

seemed to lift. Even their voices sounded farther away. So easy to
pretend. So easy.

Or was it? Was he pretending? Somehow the thought held no
special horror for him. Not anymore. The pain was gone, and the
fear, and he realized absurdly that he might already be dead. A
dead man, pretending to be dead. It was almost funny. His body
relaxed and he felt queerly light. He drifted deeper into the sanctuary that was buoyancy and silence.

2

On April 18, 1945, some weeks after the coming of false spring
and the mountain ambush above Lake Como, an OSS operational
director named Cornfield hurried through Swiss streets to a staid
old apartment building on the outskirts of Bern. He was admitted
to a third-floor apartment by a husky young man in civilian clothing, one of the Marine guards from the American embassy. Inside,
a handful of middle-aged men talked in hushed tones across a dining table on which a map of northern Italy was spread. From the
looks of the sandwich crusts at their elbows and the drained
brandy glasses, Cornfield could only assume they had been at it
for some time. Off in a corner of the room, apart from the murmuring men and the map, sat Cornfield's superior, OSS mission
chief Allen Dulles, head wreathed in pipe smoke. Dulles was
deeply involved in a whispered conversation with a thin, gray-
haired man whom Cornfield recognized as chief of the British intelligence group in Switzerland. A younger man, a stranger, stood
between Dulles and the Britisher, listening intently to what they
were saying.

Cornfield surveyed the faces around the dining table. With the
exception of the young stranger standing near Dulles, they were
all men whom Cornfield knew. A couple of them were military,
American generals in mufti. The others, like Dulles and the
Britisher, were intelligence people. There was Scibbert, the OSS
Italian expert, on the far side of the table, sipping his inevitable
glass of cassis. And Hobart, the political analyst, with his high

forehead and far-off, thoughtful look. Their presence signaled a problem with Sunrise, most likely. Particularly Hobart. Hobart had been in on Sunrise from the beginning.

As chief operational director, Cornfield was fully aware of the Sunrise project. Dulles talked about little else these days. And perhaps with reason. Hitler's Third Reich was on the verge of collapse. British and American armies were sweeping across the industrial valleys and forested mountains of western Germany. The Soviets had finally launched their all-out attack on Berlin. Within days or weeks the last smoking brick would fall. Peace, an end to dying, the sunrise of sanity would surely follow.

Or would it? Here below the Rhaetian Alps waited half a million German fighting men, veterans all, dug in along the fortified Gothic Line. Even if the German homeland were to fall, the war might well go on. Italy could become Europe's last and bloodiest battlefield. But Allen Dulles had hope that the Germans in Italy might be persuaded to lay down their arms. For the past two months, he had been conducting secret surrender negotiations with an important German SS general, Obergruppenführer Karl Wolff, perhaps the most influential German officer in all of Italy. Sunrise, Dulles called the mission, this slender operation to salvage peace. Sunrise, a name well chosen if it succeeded.

Dulles still hadn't noticed Cornfield. Scibbert, standing at the table, cleared his throat helpfully, and Dulles finally looked up. "Ah, here is the man who can answer our questions," he said. He rose, smiling, and beckoned Cornfield to the table.

Dulles was a mannerly man with close-cut gray hair and a small, bushy gray mustache. He wore rimless spectacles and a tweedy coat that made him look more like a colorless college professor than America's No. 2 spy, second only to the original architect of the OSS, General "Wild Bill" Donovan himself. Yet, in spite of his bland appearance, Dulles was a strong-minded man, and his mere approach caused the figures at the table to part, like the Red Sea opening for Moses. Dulles slipped in to take his rightful place at the head of the table with Cornfield in tow.

For some reason, the British intelligence officer and the lean, young stranger followed only partway, then drifted to stand at the wall some feet beyond the table, close enough to listen, but not close enough to be included in the conversation. Cornfield sneaked a look at the stranger. Angular, raw-boned, he appeared to be in his late twenties or early thirties, with hard eyes and a taut, charged look of readiness, like a knife half out of its sheath or an unholstered gun with the safety off. Cornfield marked him instantly as a field man, probably also British, certainly not one of the scotch-and-water-softened, rear-echelon warriors like the others, and he wondered why the young man was here.

"Gentlemen," Dulles said, "if we're to act quickly, we'll have to work with elements already in the area. I've asked Mr. Cornfield to join us because he knows more about the Lake Como situation than anyone else."

One of the generals, a florid man with a whiskey nose, pinned his eyes on Cornfield and said, "You know about our negotiations with General Wolff?"

"Yes, sir," Cornfield said.

"Good," the general said. He picked up a sheet of flimsy. "Wolff is in Berlin for some kind of conference, but this just came in from his Fasano headquarters. We decoded it only an hour ago." He handed the flimsy to Cornfield. It read:

THE PARCEL LEAVES TODAY FOR MILAN, BEARING FUNDS
FOR VALTELLINA REUNION. GARDA ROUTES APPARENTLY OUT.
SUGGEST OTHER ROADS BE DENIED HIM. CROSSWORD.

It was about Sunrise, as Cornfield had guessed. And this was one of the possible pitfalls which had worried them all. PARCEL referred to Italy's aging dictator, Benito Mussolini. Only last month, intelligence reports had painted the Duce as a dried-up shell of his former self, mired in deep depression at the changing state of the war, holed up in a villa with his wife and two of his children near Wolff's Lake Garda headquarters. But that had apparently changed. Mussolini, who knew nothing of Wolff's Sunrise negotiations with the Americans, had recently confided to the SS general over breakfast that he was considering a withdrawal to the north with fifty thousand Italian volunteers into the Valtellina stronghold, a narrow valley near the Swiss and Austrian borders, still ringed with World War I fortifications. There he hoped to organize a last-ditch stand against the Allies, so that he and Fascism might at least die a heroic death. General Wolff, horrified by Mussolini's unexpected revelation, had quickly passed the word to

Dulles. Such a desperate enterprise, if Mussolini actually gathered the nerve to try it, could wreck Sunrise.

"You can see our problem," the general said. "This switch to Milan has gummed things up for us. We know Mussolini has accumulated a hefty war chest to finance this Valtellina venture. We expected him to take the money and head straight north from his villa on Lake Garda. We've already dropped a couple of OG teams up there to cut him off. But if he's in Milan, that puts him in a position to come up the back way, by following one of those roads along the shores of Lake Como. We want those roads blocked."

Cornfield leaned over the map. "You can forget the road to the east of the lake," he said. "It's little better than a mule track. If Mussolini tries for the Valtellina, he'll have to come up the western shore. Especially if he intends to head up a military convoy."

The general nodded contentedly. "Good. That's the kind of thing we need to know. So let's get on with it. We want Mussolini stopped, and we want his war funds either confiscated or diverted. We've got a man to mastermind it. One of my people, a Major Rossiter. He's with my staff at this very moment, working out the strategy. Now we need to know what kind of tactical assistance he can get from your clandestine people in the Lake Como area."

Cornfield glanced at Dulles, then said reluctantly, "We really don't have much on the lake at the moment. Wouldn't it be better to cut the road below the lake? I could put you in touch with a good agent team down at Saronno, or another at Tradate. If you're willing to cut the road closer to Milan, I might be able to scrape loose a field unit near Voghera to act as backup."

"Too far south," the general said. "The countryside down there is too flat, too easy to bypass. No, it's got to be the road along the lake." He frowned at Dulles and said, "I thought you told us there was an American intelligence team on the lake itself?"

"There is," Dulles said. "We sent an American Liaison Officer Team, what we call ALOTs, to Lake Como about three months ago. They're working out of a partisan camp in the mountains." He gave Cornfield an encouraging smile, the kindly professor urging his pupil to come up with the right answer. "Isn't that right, Mr. Cornfield?"

Cornfield hesitated. "Yes, sir. But I really couldn't recommend them."

The general raised an eyebrow. "Why not?"

"They've been having problems," Cornfield said. "They lost their commanding officer a few weeks ago, and they've met with nothing but bad luck since. Several dead. Supplies shot. Difficulties with the local partisans. They're a crippled team."

Scibbert looked up. "Is that the Holloman group?"

"It was until Major Holloman disappeared," Cornfield said. "The second-in-command, a Captain X. B. Kavanaugh, has taken over. I'm afraid he hasn't done too well so far."

Scibbert set down his cassis thoughtfully. "I seem to remember a report on the Holloman group. They had problems from the beginning, didn't they? Wasn't there some interference from an American officer when they first arrived? A man living among the partisans?"

"An irregular named Landry," Cornfield said. "He and Major Holloman didn't get along. Two of the partisans were captured on a field mission along with one of our ALOTs, and this Landry blamed Holloman for it. They locked horns, and we had to order Landry off the lake. That was a mistake. The partisans resented it."

"I don't give a damn about their personal problems," the general said. He spread his hand across the map and thumped the bluish outline of Lake Como. "Rossiter and my staff people say the best place to cut the road is here, right on the lake. I have to agree with them. Mountains rising all along one side of the road, deep water on the other. There should be any number of strategic points where an armed body of men could take cover in the high ground and block the road. All we need is the manpower. What's the partisan situation? Are there enough friendly Italians in the mountains to do us any good?"

"There should be," Cornfield said slowly. "At last count, we were supplying at least eight detachments of the 52nd Garibaldi Brigade, scattered along the length of the lake. I'd say upward of two hundred men, if you can get them to co-operate."

"That shouldn't be a problem," Dulles said.

Cornfield squinted at him, then said, "It may not be as easy as you think, sir. We shut down most of our aerial supply missions during the winter, and a number of the detachment leaders were very upset about it. They may not be willing to work with us."

"Isn't there some central leader we can talk to?" Dulles asked. "Someone who can force the others to go along?"

"I suppose so," Cornfield said. He touched the map again. "If we really hope for help from the partisans, our best chance is to clear it with a man up here at the northern end of the lake, a partisan chieftain who calls himself Captain Pietro. He controls the Puecher detachment, but the other partisan chieftains consider him the nominal leader of the entire brigade. If we can get him to agree, the others should fall in line."

"Maybe our ALOTs can help set that up," Scibbert said. "Where are they on the lake?"

"Down here," Cornfield said. He ran his finger south along the western shore. "They're hiding in the mountains above the village of Rezzonico with a lesser chieftain named Dante. He's a Communist, but we trust him. The problem is that he may not trust us anymore. Holloman apparently screwed things up for us."

"How?" the general asked.

"Well, it boils down to money. We sent Holloman in with a satchelful of funds, which he was to deliver to the National Committee of Liberation in Milan, but he got a little too zealous about politics and put some important noses out of joint. The money was never delivered. No one knows what happened to it."

"How much money?"

Cornfield's cheeks colored. "A hundred and sixty thousand dollars," he said. "Some gold sovereigns, but mostly Swiss and Italian currency. We had a hell of a time explaining the loss."

The second general, a stout man with the face of a forlorn frog, blinked sad eyes. "You say your Major Holloman disappeared. What happened to him?"

"We don't really know," Cornfield admitted. "The possibilities are endless. All we know for certain is that Holloman was in trouble with some of the partisans, partly because of his own inflexibility, and partly because of our decision to pull Landry off the lake. Holloman took temporary refuge in a safe house while the partisans and the rest of our ALOTs began trying to effect a rescue of the three who were captured, but we understand he walked away with two partisans about a week later and disappeared. Captain Kavanaugh found the two partisans the next day, shot to pieces. There was no sign of Holloman."

"You think the Germans got him?"

"It's possible," Cornfield said. "We think it more likely that he was betrayed by someone in the partisan organization. Probably for the money."

Scibbert shook his head. "Cornfield could be right about the lake," he said. "If there's a traitor among the partisans, we don't dare use them. Remember, we estimate Mussolini's Valtellina war chest to be somewhere between fifty and sixty million dollars in bullion and currency. If someone has turned traitor for a mere hundred and sixty thousand, think of the risk when we send word about Mussolini's millions."

"It has to be the lake," the first general said impatiently. "If there's a traitor up there, we'll just have to rout him out. We can send a CID team in with Rossiter, or maybe investigators from the CIC."

"Excuse me," Cornfield said. "Not if you want the partisans to co-operate. The lake partisans are a proud and independent bunch. You send a team of criminal investigators in there to poke around, and they'll cut you dead."

Dulles still didn't appear to be greatly concerned. "Let's not worry about the traitor," he said mildly. "Steps have already been taken to see that any possible informers are neutralized. Let's get on with the discussion, gentlemen, and wrap this up."

Cornfield shifted uneasily. "Sir? Steps? May I ask what kind?"

Dulles took the pipe from his mouth and waved it casually at the two men standing against the wall. "Our British MI-6 colleagues have agreed to lend us one of their field representatives," he said. "Captain Willoughby here will accompany Major Rossiter and anyone else we decide to send to the lake."

Cornfield's eyes swung to the silent young man, who returned his gaze calmly. Cornfield said, "Meaning no disrespect, sir, but if you send an outsider to the lake, the ALOTs are apt to consider it an indication that they're under suspicion as well."

Dulles puffed quietly on his pipe. "They don't have to know about it. Captain Willoughby will go along as a military observer. No one but Major Rossiter need be told his true purpose in being there. That way he can check into things quietly, without arousing any fuss among either the partisans or the ALOTs. He can decide for himself if and when to tell anyone else."

"Good," the general said. "That does it, then. Any questions?"

Cornfield frowned uncertainly. It was going too fast. They all seemed determined to ignore his objections. He said, "Maybe I haven't made myself clear, sir. If you want the partisans to co-operate, you're going to have to send them someone they can trust."

The general narrowed his eyes. "Are you suggesting they can't trust Major Rossiter?"

"No, sir. Not at all," Cornfield said. "But your man would have to prove himself to them. That would take time. If I read the purpose of this meeting correctly, you don't have much time."

The general grunted, but he seemed to accept Cornfield's explanation. "Well, what about an intermediary?" he asked. "Can't we send someone as a spokesman? Someone they know? This fellow you mentioned earlier. The one you pulled off the lake. What's his name?"

Cornfield swallowed. "Landry, sir. Captain David Landry."

"Do the partisans have confidence in him?"

"Yes, sir, I suppose so. He lived with them for a year and a half. He even helped them get organized."

"Okay, so what's the problem? Get him."

Cornfield hesitated again. "He, uh, he doesn't exactly belong to us. He's regular Army. Air Corps, I think. Or maybe Engineers. I'd have to look it up."

The general actually looked pleased. "Regular Army, eh? One of our boys? What was he doing on the lake?"

"He was a passenger on a reconnaissance flight in '43, the way I understand it," Cornfield said. "His plane was shot down over northern Italy by a flight of Messerschmitts, and he headed cross-country, trying to make Switzerland. Lake Como is as far as he got. Some woman took him in and hid him."

"Good for him," the general said. "Well, let's get him. And fast. The sooner we bring him in and brief him, the sooner we can get this thing started. How quickly can you put them on the lake?"

Cornfield thought it over. "I'll have to check with our flight people," he said. "If you can deliver everyone to Cecina for briefing and outfitting within twenty-four hours, we should be able to put them on the lake the following morning, under cover of darkness."

"We'll have them there," the general said.

"Uh, I'm not so sure about Landry," Cornfield said. "As far as I know, he wasn't attached to any unit once we pulled him off the lake. No one knew quite what to do with him. After so much time in the mountains, he didn't seem to fit in anywhere. I'm not sure you can even find him."

"Don't worry about that," the general said. "If he's regular Army, we'll find him. You just get the plane ready."

3

Near midnight of that same day, a lean, bony man with tousled hair and a rumpled khaki uniform shifted his shoulders more comfortably against the splintery wooden hull of a beached fishing boat and listened to its Italian owner yarn, ". . . but when the Fascists took the great golden krater away to Rome, do you think they turned it over to the national treasury? No. The minister's brother-in-law sold it to an antiquities dealer, who sold it to a collector in Switzerland, who promised it to a museum in the United States, just as soon as the war is over. The Americans will pay a fabulous price. My uncle's friend will never get a lira, yet he was the man who plowed it up."

"What'd he say?" asked the private from Dallas. "What'd he say?"

David Landry took a careful swallow from the second fisherman's bottle of grappa and passed the bottle along. In turn, he was handed a quart of Ancient Age that the sergeant from Oakland had stolen from the officers' club and contributed to their private fraternization session on the sands. Landry skipped the Bourbon. He passed it to the older Italian on his right, figuring that while Bourbon would be rare in the lives of a trio of Livorno fishermen, it loomed pleasantly on the postwar horizons of his own.

Landry said, "He says if the Italian Government doesn't

confiscate a treasure, the crooked politicians will. So if you really turn up anything with those mine detectors of yours, you'd best keep it from official notice."

"Damn right," chimed in another private, this one from Pittsburgh. "That goes for the Army brass, too."

"Che ha detto?" asked the first fisherman eagerly. "Che ha detto?"

Landry duly translated, although they didn't really need his services. For that matter, he thought it doubtful that any of them really believed the treasure tales they'd been swapping. The fishermen enjoyed thinking that every abandoned villa, every ancient grave held its secret treasure. The GIs countered with the usual rumors of payroll treasure buried by retreating Germans. Gold bullion and Reichsmarks totaling two hundred thousand dollars this time, although a corporal named Cohen insisted it was more like four hundred thousand. It was in the churchyard, said one faction, while another favored here on the beach. They were all just enjoying a chance to yammer, lounging on sand that still retained a hint of warmth from the afternoon sun, exchanging liquor and dreams.

Landry shouldn't have been drinking with a group of enlisted men on a deserted Italian beach. Technically, in the ordered military world to which he had returned, captains should drink only with fellow officers. The acceptable alternative was to sit by himself in a narrow, bleak room with a single window overlooking a row of garbage bins behind the officers' mess, a room that had been assigned him as quarters almost two months back. But Landry's war had given him a taste for lawlessness, and tonight Landry had wished for a deserted beach, some harsh grappa and raw, red Bardolino and a share in someone else's dreams.

His own dreams hadn't been that pleasant lately. Hardly a night passed that he didn't wake up in a sweat, vividly aware of gray-green German field uniforms working their way up the slope below Pietro's camp. The dreams were all in brilliant color, and fear was there, thick enough to slice. Landry found it odd, since fear had been a familiar enough companion in all the months he had spent with the partisans of Lake Como. But it was never this night phantom, this nocturnal visitor. In a way, fear had spiced days in which the only duty was to kill off your enemies whenever you got the opportunity. A simple, anarchistic approach to life. Almost pleasant. Unless, of course, the enemy got you first.

Sometimes Landry's sweaty dreams came from an earlier period, and instead of German field uniforms he saw parachutes popping out of a smoking B-25 Mitchell. It was a falling dream, naturally. Only three chutes, other than his own, out of a crew of six, then falling, falling. Landry had seen the other chutes come to ground, scattered over a wide area skirting the marshes below Ferrara, but he never saw the men again. Members of the Italian resistance found him hiding in the marshes two days later and sneaked him off along an underground chain toward Switzerland. The last link in the chain had been a partisan collaborator named Viviana, a blue-eyed beauty who lived in one of her father's big houses on Lake Como, just a hefty day's hike from the Swiss border. Landry could have taken that last step to Switzerland and spent the next year and a half in comfortable internment, but Viviana introduced him to a young medical student who called himself Pietro, and Landry elected instead to join an embryo resistance movement that was forming in the mountains above the lake. He told himself it was only to help the young partisan, Pietro, but he knew better.

Harass German detachments on the lake. Swoop down from the mountains to sabotage their supply lines, then flee. Spend wet days, some days, crouched over the best weapon Pietro's small band could spare, an ancient Mannlicher rifle with a rusted rear sight, and spend warm nights, some nights, in a bedroom with purple wisteria blooming outside a shuttered window. Pick up the language with unconscious speed, not just totally immersed but utterly blitzed.

Landry had found his partisan war arduous, but so compatible that he'd almost resented the sudden appearance of military order in the persons of an American Liaison Officer Team whose commander, a major carrying a satchel filled with money, seemed not a little surprised to find a misplaced American in the partisans' midst. Within hours, Landry discovered that even the other ALOTs regarded the major as a sonofabitch. Within a month, Landry and the ALOT major had quarreled so bitterly that the officer radioed his headquarters and demanded Landry's removal from the lake, back to a great war machine that apparently couldn't be bothered with a mere erratic cam with war's end so near. Particularly a cam that had been missing for a year and a half.

Landry was billeted in Livorno, then ignored, but it wasn't so bad. There were magazines to read, genuine food three times a day, plenty of home-front comforts available at the PX. There was ample time to think of home and the future. Home for Landry was Baltimore, though he no longer had any family living there, and training was civil engineering at Penn State. He had always thought that once the shooting was done he might try to tie in with one of the aspiring international engineering firms, maybe an up-and-comer like Brown & Root out of Houston. Build roads in Siam, or airports in Egypt, or dams right up the road in Switzerland. Build for a change, instead of tearing down. And, of course, he'd come back to Italy someday, when his own bad dreams had faded. And they would fade, now that he was done with warring. He'd done everything he could to bother the Germans, and his government had rewarded him by tearing him away from his friends, away from the tall, elegant Viviana, away from his personal commitment. Well, to hell with them and their oh-so-important rules and regulations. If they liked him better sitting on his ass doing nothing, then he would sit and do nothing. As far as he was concerned, the war was over and they could do with him what they wanted. He was comfortably out of it.

Very comfortable indeed. The splinters of the fishing boat scratched Landry's shoulders gently if he leaned just so and wriggled. He'd watched a pair of pigs, staked out on the beach by some Livorno family, perform the same act, and he concluded the pigs knew what they were about. He yawned, wondering if he were sleepy enough yet to meander back to his quarters and go to bed and face the dreams.

These would be the last minutes of serene laziness life would offer Landry for a long time, though he didn't know it. Five minutes later, while one of the Italian fishermen described once again the hasty withdrawal of a German Panzer unit from the area, flashlights suddenly winked on at the far side of the beach and MPs' voices could be heard over the restless surge of the sea, calling Landry's name, and David Landry went back to war.

Book One

THE PARTISANS

Day One

Correte allor soldati
In Italia, dov'è rotta la guerra
Contro al Tedesco.

Soldiers, go quickly
To Italy, where war has erupted
Against the Germans.
    —Verdi, *La Forza del Destino*

1

Settling in the darkness, cutting into the water, the amphibious
hull of the Grumman Goose sent a V-shaped spray past the cockpit windows. David Landry clung hard to the back of the pilot's
seat as metal rattled and the plane bumped and shuddered through
the water. The two Pratt & Whitneys surged and the stubby plane
heeled to starboard, dipping a wingtip float into gentle swells. The
pilot throttled back. "You sure this is the right place?" he asked
Landry.

Landry swallowed. God, how he hated flying. "That's Rezzonico, up along the shoreline," he said. "They should come for
us any moment."

"I can't give you more than five minutes," the pilot warned.
"Talk about sitting ducks. Every German for miles is probably

awake by now, wondering what plane was fool enough to land on the lake. I've got to get out of here."

"We'll hurry," Landry said. "Thanks for the lift."

The other two members of the Lake Como landing party had already cranked open the hatch. The Britisher, a lanky captain named Willoughby, leaned his Thompson against the bulkhead and helped the regular Army man, a small, tough, fighting cock of a major named Rossiter, transfer duffels of demolition equipment and personal kits to the hatchway. Landry pitched in. When they were done, the Britisher reached for his weapon and crouched by the opening, watching the dark shore. Rossiter and Landry leaned to stare over his head.

They were all three togged out to look like Italian peasants, thanks to an OSS supply specialist in Cecina, but they had been so heavily armed that Landry felt like a parody of a superkiller commando raider, even in the darkness. Knife handle sticking out of his right climbing boot, Army-issue .45 automatic bulging in a shoulder holster under his shabby civilian coat, Thompson submachine gun resting in the crook of his arm. Rossiter, who had exuded authority at the briefings, looked just as silly, but it went farther with him. He seemed lost and uncomfortable somehow without his uniform, as though authority had to be underlined with khaki and brass. On the other hand, the Britisher, similarly outfitted and similarly armed, looked quite natural.

"See anything?" Landry asked.

The Britisher looked back with an expression Landry couldn't read. Maybe it was just typical English reserve, but the man had been standoffish from the moment they came together at the Cecina briefing center. "Not yet," he said. "I thought I spotted a light beyond that near promontory, but it disappeared."

Landry waited. When they'd told him he was coming back to the lake, he expected to feel some overwhelming emotion. Warmth, concern, a little nervousness, like a prodigal and profligate son come home at last, uncertain of the reception he would get from his stay-at-home family. But he felt nothing so far except a kind of deep uneasiness at being in the cramped hull of the Grumman, mixed with a testy resentment at the strong-arm tactics used by the Army brass to force him into this mission. They hadn't asked him if he wanted to go, or if he was willing to go. They'd only told him what would happen if he didn't go. After the boredom of Livorno, Landry had found only pleasure in the prospect, though he had no intention of admitting it to anyone. Least of all to these two unknown officers.

The Britisher jerked his head and hissed, "There. Something coming. From the south."

Major Rossiter leaned closer, champing nervously on an unlit cigar stub. The smell was foul. "Are they our guys?" he asked.

Above the burble of the idling Grumman engines, a faint knockknock echoed across the water, an ancient gasoline engine straining through the darkness. Landry shifted his Thompson and primed it. The engine sound chugged fitfully onward. Across the moonlit gloom, barely visible against the black backdrop of mountains that crowded in to cradle the lake, a thin spume of white froth peeled back from the prow of an approaching shape. It was a fishing boat, a first cousin to the one Landry had leaned against only forty-eight hours earlier, but smaller, squatter, one of the hundreds built to ply the waters of Lake Como in daily search of trout, perch, pike and tench. It chug-chugged straight at them. A light blinked briefly from the bow. Three shorts. Darkness. Another. Then another.

"It's ours," the Britisher said unnecessarily. His tone was flat, but his shoulders relaxed visibly. Landry eased the actuator knob forward on his Thompson and locked it, then leaned toward the cockpit to tell the pilot. The man seemed grateful.

When the fishing boat was closer, the feeble engine shut down and the distance narrowed in silence. Two men took up oars to bring her in. A third knelt in the bow and used his hands to guide the boat past the wing struts. As they drifted to the hatch, the man in the bow whispered in passable English, "Ehi, you looking for a ferry ride to shore?"

Now one welcome feeling came, a great gladness. The voice and figure were immediately familiar to Landry. It was Piccione, one of the unfortunate trio whose capture by Fascists some two months ago had cost Landry his place among the Lake Como partisans.

"Hello, you Marxist brigand," Landry whispered back. "When did you get out of jail?"

The man twitched at Landry's voice, then leaned forward, peering through the darkness. "David?" he said. It came out *Dah-veed*. "Maledizione! Is it you?"

"Esattamente," Landry said. He couldn't help grinning broadly. "Who else would they send to nursemaid a bunch of crazies who can't even stay out of Blackshirt prisons?"

"Maledizione," the man said again. He glanced over his shoulder. "Lucertola, tenente Tucker, look who is here!"

The boat thumped against the Grumman and both Landry and the Britisher grabbed it and held tight. The two figures in the stern dropped their oars and came forward. One of them, an American ALOT named Harry Tucker, a pale, quiet man with a chronic case of jitters, stopped short and whispered a greeting too low for Landry to hear. The other man came all the way, throwing open long, muscular arms in a far warmer welcome, for he was a better friend. Everyone called him Lucertola (the Lizard) because he liked to sit in the sunshine, eyes half closed, and bask, sometimes for hours on end. At that, the Lizard was lucky in his partisan nickname. He was so squat and ugly that more muscular comparisons to an ape inevitably came to mind, and he stuttered, the only Italian Landry had ever met who did so. He pounded Landry on the back and his mouth worked and stammered words finally popped out. "Eccolo! David! Come va?" It sounded like someone trying to sneeze. Eh-eh-eh-*EC*colo.

"Bene, Lucertola, grazie," Landry said. "Was all quiet on shore?"

"As a tomb. No one stirs this night but we. But we shall hurry a little, eh?"

Landry translated for Major Rossiter and the Britisher. "He says everything is okay, but they'd like to hurry."

"God, yes," Rossiter whispered around his cigar. "Let's get this heavy stuff into the boat."

They made the transfer rapidly, with duffels of primacord, plastic, fuses and timers passing from hand to hand. When the supplies were stashed, Landry and the British captain scrambled onto the boat. Rossiter came last. As soon as the Grumman hatch was closed and bolted, Landry slapped his palm against the fuselage to tell the pilot they were clear. The Lizard and Tucker took up oars again and pushed against the hull, shoving the boat free.

The two Pratt & Whitney radial engines snorted and the Grumman leaned back on its haunches. Landry watched the plane lumber across the dark water, slowly at first, then picking up speed. It quickly fused with the night, almost impossible to track except for the trail of white foam skimming past the hull. Then the foam disappeared and the twin engines groaned more heavily, rising, rising.

A figure came to squat beside Landry, and Piccione's voice murmured, "He wasted no time, this pilot of yours."

Landry glanced at the young partisan. This peasant's son had a face that was astonishingly handsome, but he looked much thinner than when Landry had last seen him. Drained somehow. His eyes were weary, young in years, but old with premature knowledge. "When did you break out of jail?" Landry asked him.

"Thirty-seven days ago," Piccione said softly. "Exactly thirty-seven days. I count each one. Life has turned sweeter."

"And the others?" Landry asked. "Lieutenant Creedmore and Luisa? Did they get out as well?"

There was a delay in Piccione's answer, only a moment's hesitation, but it was noticeable. "All three of us," he said. "One of the Americans found where the Fascists were holding us. No one told you?"

"They didn't tell me anything," Landry said. He wanted to ask more, but the Lizard cut off conversation by cranking away at the ancient boat engine, filling the silence with stubborn coughings and chokings. The engine sputtered and died.

"Come on, get us moving," Rossiter hissed. He sounded tense.

The Lizard kept cranking and the engine finally caught. It began a methodical thrub-thrub-thrub. A solitary searchlight, some four miles up the lake, switched on in the darkness and probed from the shore, fingering the lake.

"Oh my God, they're on to us," someone whispered. It sounded like Rossiter again.

"Don't worry," Piccione assured him. "It is only the Fascist garrison at Musso. We are far out of their range."

Nevertheless, there was a general stir, an almost audible easing of tension as the boat began moving. Landry felt it, too. He knew water confused direction of sound, but it also carried it like an amplifier. It was good to be under way.

Dogs began to bark as they neared shore, and the Lizard shut off the engine to let them coast. They silently took up oars, listening and waiting. The village of Rezzonico had taken shape in the darkness ahead of them, and Landry found himself straining forward eagerly, hoping to make out one particular house among the buildings that jostled along the water's edge, dreaming in the predawn moonlight. The red tile roof of this special house was a brighter red than most, being newer, and from his one-time eagle's nest on the mountainside, Landry used to think he could spot it. But moonlight turned all colors to shades of gray, and at this hour he could only guess. There, those tall shadows rising above the roofs—the cypresses whose shade smothered every new camellia Viviana planted in her tiny garden? That dark cascade on a back terrace—the wisteria that tried to thrust its rampant clusters through the shutters on her bedroom window? He turned to ask Piccione, for Viviana was known to all of them, although to some less intimately than others.

"It is the house beyond the point," Piccione whispered, reading Landry's mind. "The one with the wide chimney." He grinned at Landry in the darkness. "She is still here, on the lake. Her father ordered her to join him in Switzerland again last month, but she prefers to stay and help us. She will be much surprised when she learns you are back. Happily so."

Landry ducked his head and pulled on the oar, hoping Piccione was right. The recall from the lake had been enforced so suddenly that he'd never even had a chance to say good-by to Viviana. The houses became more distinct as they rowed in from the lake, and Landry took a longing look at the chimney Piccione had pointed out, then forced his mind back to business. "Who's waiting on shore for us?"

"One of the Americans, il capitano Kavanaugh," Piccione said. "And a newcomer, an old man we call il Veterano. He joined us shortly after you left. He's from Sicily, very strange, very quiet, but Dante trusts him."

"Dante didn't come?"

Piccione shook his head. "He was not eager to meet the plane. He stayed in camp with Luisa."

From the dark shoreline, a flashlight blinked abruptly through a grove of almond trees, a short followed by two longs. Landry knew the trees were almonds. He had walked there with Viviana when their blossoms, earliest to bloom, were barely swelling on the trees, winter's promise of a spring to come.

"There, that is our signal," Piccione murmured. "It is safe to put in."

Landry feathered his oar. "What about Pietro? Didn't you bring him?"

"Not yet," Piccione said. "Two of the Americans went across the mountains to fetch him just before we came down. They should be back in Dante's camp tomorrow."

"Why the delay? We're supposed to talk to Pietro as soon as possible."

Piccione shifted restively. "We tried not to tell too many people you were coming, David. Not until the last minute. There have been difficulties. We think we have an informer among us."

Landry frowned. "An informer?" He sneaked a look at Rossiter and the British captain. No one had mentioned the possibility of an informer during the briefings. "Are you sure?"

"It must be so," Piccione said. "The Germans have been very lucky lately. Wherever we go, they seem to be waiting. Ambushes. Raids. Roadblocks. Dante thinks the American officials blame him for the trouble. We've had no supplies since February. Dante is very angry."

The boat nudged sand, and both the Lizard and Piccione jumped into knee-deep water to pull her in closer. Two more figures appeared from the cover of trees and plunged in to help. One of them, a big, long-faced man with a nose so imposing that it cast its own shadow in the moonlight, grabbed the prow and tugged. He was strong. The boat instantly lodged itself on the sandy bottom. X. B. Kavanaugh. No one else was that big-nosed or that powerful. A nature photographer before the war, Kavanaugh was perfectly at home in underbrush or rough terrain, through which he managed to move with unbelievable quietness for such a big man, but in water he splashed as noisily as a robin in a birdbath. Behind him, Landry heard both Rossiter and the jittery ALOT, Harry Tucker, gasp at the unexpected noise. Landry grinned down at the big man and said, "Hello, X.B."

Kavanaugh stepped forward awkwardly in the water and splashed noisily again. He peered up at Landry and his deep voice rumbled, "David? David Landry? I'll be a sonofagun. What are you doing back on the lake?"

"I'm not absolutely sure myself," Landry said.

"Quiet up there!" Rossiter rasped. "You want to bring the Fascists down on us?"

Kavanaugh looked past Landry. "Who's that?" he asked.

"His name is Rossiter," Landry whispered. "*Major* Rossiter, and he's feeling a little nervous."

Kavanaugh reached out a vast hand to help Landry from the boat. Amiable as always, he tried his best to keep quiet, but he pulled Landry into the shallow water clumsily and splashed with him toward the shore, and neither of them achieved silence until they were on land.

An old man with gray whisker stubble on a stubborn chin and a cloth cap pulled low over the eyes, a stranger to Landry, turned away from the boat and stepped into the trees. In a moment, he reappeared with two mules, leading them down to the small, sandy beach. That would be the newcomer, the Sicilian. Il Veterano, Piccione had called him. The Veteran. Probably because of his age. Landry offered him a silent smile. The old man didn't respond.

Things went swiftly now and the heavy duffels began thumping down on the sand, but not swiftly enough for either Rossiter or Tucker. A pair of nervous Nellies. "Hurry," whispered; "Yes, hurry," echoed, while Piccione and the old man tied duffel after duffel onto the pack saddles of the mules. The last of the duffels was hoisted into place and one of the mules snorted loudly, registering resentment at the weight of its load. The old man clamped calloused hands over its muzzle and stroked it to silence, but someone stirred in a nearby house and a window creaked open.

"Chi è?" called a sleepy voice.

"Go back to sleep!" Piccione whispered hoarsely. "This is partisan business."

The window quickly closed.

"Okay, let's get moving," Kavanaugh said. "We'll take the goat trail back of the church as far as the scree, then peel off through the rocks. You take the lead, Tucker." He switched to Italian. "Piccione, you and Lucertola spread out and give us cover. The rest of us will follow with Veterano and the mules."

Tucker vanished into the darkness, followed by Piccione and the Lizard. The old man paused only long enough to withdraw an old shotgun from beneath the pack saddle of the lead mule, then clucked the mules into motion.

The cobbled streets rose at sharp angles, climbing from almost the moment they left the beach, and they followed them toward the rising mountains, guns ready, passing beneath closed shutters. They could hear movement in some of the houses, but no one seemed eager to open windows and look out at them. The mules moved quietly, and Landry realized that someone with foresight had booted their hoofs with felt.

Only once did they falter. When Harry Tucker reached the narrow highway that ran parallel to the shoreline from the town of Como in the south all the way to Gera in the north, he stopped and held up his hand. He squinted both ways along the dark ribbon of road. Landry felt his own mouth go dry.

Kavanaugh waited patiently, then finally called out, "What is it, Harry? What's the holdup?"

Tucker glanced back at them. "Nothing," he said. "I . . . I thought I saw something."

Kavanaugh whispered to Landry, "Nothing ever changes. He's as jumpy now as he was the day we arrived." Then, louder, he said, "Come on, let's get a move on. There isn't a German within five miles of us."

2

On a wooded hill above the landing party, standing in deep night shadows, three men waited patiently beside an open Mercedes command car. One of them, SD Sturmbannführer Ernst Richter, senior German security officer on Lake Como and the man known to the partisans as "The Drowner," trained a pair of binoculars on the darkened village of Rezzonico. "They're crossing the road now," he said calmly. "I count seven . . . no, eight men. How many did we see coming down? Five, wasn't it, Lieutenant?"

"Yes, sir," murmured Richter's adjutant, Untersturmführer Gunther Stenzel. "And two mules."

"Ah, yes, the mules," Richter said. "And heavily laden, from the look of them." He shifted the field glasses farther up the hill, toward a bell spire set among dark cypresses. "They appear to be making for the church. I believe there's a trail in back of the cemetery, isn't there?"

Stenzel gestured to the burly sergeant standing next to him, Scharführer Fritz Knaust, and the sergeant unfolded a map and shielded it with his body while Stenzel hurriedly traced a line with a pencil-beam flashlight.

"Yes, sir," Stenzel said. "There appears to be a trail that climbs about a quarter of a kilometer or so, then veers south." He flicked off the thin beam. "Shouldn't we alert the garrison at Gravedona? We could still catch up with them. They'll have to move slowly with the mules."

Richter lowered the glasses. He stared at the darkness beyond the church, his eyes opaque. Then he smiled at some inner thought and stuffed the binoculars into a leather case. "No, we'll wait," he said softly. "I would rather know what this is all about. It must be urgent, for them to put a plane directly on the lake that way. We'll wait a day or two until we hear more about it. Then we'll see."

Lieutenant Stenzel cleared his throat worriedly. "What if this time we hear nothing?"

Richter waved the doubt away with a finely manicured hand. "You underestimate my powers of persuasion, Lieutenant. We will hear, and keep on hearing, until we are ready to stop listening." He studied the church for a moment, then climbed into the back seat of the car. Making himself comfortable against the deep leather cushions, he said, "All right, Sergeant Knaust. We've seen enough. As soon as they are out of hearing, you may drive us back to Cernobbio."

3

Landry believed in rewarding himself for unusual effort such as climbing mountains, even if he had to withhold a desirable act to serve as the reward, and he had deliberately refrained from looking back all through the morning. It wasn't until they puffed their way to a dead cedar tree he'd set as his goal that he stepped out of the column of climbers and turned. There, finally, from a vantage point even an eagle would envy, it stretched out below him—a full view of Lake Como, his lake, home, a rich, deep blue, peaceful in the noonday sun.

He wanted to stand for a moment to savor the sight, but the column continued to move, and abruptly, something changed. There was no movement other than that of the climbers, no sound except the hard breathing of the men and the buzzing of flies around the lathered rumps of the mules. But Landry sensed a presence, someone hiding in the thick underbrush, watching the approach of the column. Above the gully a rock thrush cursed in birdlike irritation, flitting in a brown blur from limb to limb. Landry glanced an urgent question at X. B. Kavanaugh and got a reassuring nod in answer. A picket protecting the partisan camp. One of Dante's men.

The British captain, climbing a few paces ahead of Landry, was apparently aware of the picket as well. His hand eased the Thompson from his shoulder almost nonchalantly, and Landry saw him pluck the cocking handle out of the safety slot. Major Rossiter, on the other hand, trudged among the rocks in complete innocence, apparently without the vaguest notion that they were no longer alone. It wasn't until Rossiter saw the Britisher's move that Rossiter also looked up sharply and began to scan the brush.

"You'd better call him out," Landry suggested to Kavanaugh. Landry nodded at the Britisher's Thompson, now cradled in the crook of his arm and ready for firing, then at Rossiter, who was still inspecting underbrush. It wasn't a fair test for Rossiter, of course. He was a tough, sharp little man, but he was dead tired. The party had climbed for hours, first through the cold darkness of the terraced vineyards on the lower slopes, then through the chill gray of dawn. Now the sun was high and hot and even the tough partisans, accustomed to mountain climbing, breathed like an assortment of broken bellows.

Kavanaugh grinned and cupped his hand to his mouth. "Ehi, paesano," he called in Italian. "You would be wise to show yourself. We have strangers among us with eager trigger fingers. They just might shoot your ass off for sneaking up on us."

The bushes parted slowly and a man slipped into view. He was an older man in his forties, wearing a sweaty Luftwaffe cap stripped of its German insignia. He smiled sheepishly and sat down on a rocky overhang above them, his legs dangling. He laid an old Scotti Brescia rifle across his knees. Landry recognized both man and rifle. Its stock was broken, and Landry, no gunsmith but good enough with his hands that most of the partisans brought him their repair work, had helped the man invent new ways to tape the stock together many times.

"I had you in my sights the whole time," the man said.

"You're lucky to be alive," Kavanaugh said. "We heard you thrashing around in the bushes for almost a mile. The noise was deafening."

"You never heard me," the man said. He produced a stained, pitted pipe, which he stuck between his teeth. "Not once. It was that damned bird that gave me away."

"Ehi, Salvo," Landry called up to him.

The man shaded his eyes, peering myopically down at Landry. The man's smile broadened. "Ehi, David? Non e possibile. It was for you that these clowns went to the lake? Wait until Dante hears. We thought we had seen the last of you."

"As did I," Landry said. "But my government decided I needed a quiet vacation, so they sent me here to rest, along with two fresh companions." He nodded toward Rossiter and the Britisher.

Salvo regarded the two new faces with minimal interest. "That one looks like a little Napoleon," he said, squinting at Rossiter. "What's he good for?"

"He's a pezzo grosso from the American Army," Landry said. "And you'd better be careful. If he knew what you were saying, he'd tie your legs together in a knot."

Salvo shrugged. "Other things can be more important than new faces. I hope your government also sent you with a little meat?" He gestured hopefully with the pipe. "And perhaps some tobacco? I'd give my soul, if I had one, for some tobacco."

"Some may have fallen by accident into my supplies," Landry said.

"In that case, you may pass without pause," Salvo said. "Tell the comandante to save a share of your delicacies for me. I'm on lookout until four."

As the column moved on, Rossiter hung back and studied the surrounding terrain, but it was apparently only an excuse. He waited until Landry came abreast of him, then slipped back into line. He walked in silence for a moment, chewing his cigar, then said, "For what it's worth, Captain Landry, I speak a little Italian."

"Oh?" Landry said. He kept his tone noncommittal, but his mind raced, going back over anything he might have let slip on the boat or during the long morning's climb. Fortunately, the necessity to hurry had left them little breath for speech, and nothing seemed too gratuitously insulting.

"As for Willoughby, I'm told his Italian is quite fluent," Rossiter continued. "Your partisans have some mighty strange names here, but I'm damned if I'm going to get stuck with something like 'Napoleon.' I don't want Willoughby offended, either. You know how touchy the British are."

Piccione and Kavanaugh saw them talking and drifted over to walk with them. Piccione said, "Is anything wrong?"

Rossiter plucked the wet cigar from his mouth. "No, no, nothing at all. We were just talking about names. Piccione, that's yours. That means Pigeon, doesn't it? And the others. Lizard. The old guy, just Veteran. Don't any of you have real names?"

"Not that we use," Piccione said. "Most of us have families down on the lake, or at least nearby. If any of us are to be caught by the Germans, we would prefer that they know only partisan names. That way, the families stay safe."

"That makes sense," Rossiter said. "I understand you were caught a couple of months ago. Is that what you told them? Only partisan names?"

Piccione's face stiffened. "I told them nothing," he said.

"Oh come on," Rossiter said. "Not even a couple of names?"

"I told them nothing at all," Piccione insisted. He turned and marched away.

Rossiter stared after him. "What'd I say?" he asked. "A man falls into German hands, he tells *something*. It's nothing to be ashamed of."

Kavanaugh pushed stiff black hair from his forehead. "I should have warned you. Piccione has changed since we broke them out. He's edgy most of the time. Temperish. I can't say I blame him. Things were pretty hard for all three of them. The Blackshirts had them locked away in Tremozzo, but the German SD visited almost every day. Creedmore and Luisa, well, the Germans kind of messed them up during interrogations. They didn't even touch Piccione. Didn't ask him any questions, either. He seems to think the rest of us blame him for not getting knocked around, too. Hell, I figure the Germans just hadn't got around to him yet."

Rossiter looked thoughtful. "That, or maybe they left him alone on purpose. They do that, you know. They bust up one prisoner and leave the next alone. Play one against the other. Should I apologize? I don't want to start out on bad terms with any of the partisans."

"I'll talk to him," Landry said.

Landry climbed to the head of the column, where Piccione had taken position, and fell in beside him, matching strides. "The major didn't mean anything by his remark," Landry said.

"I know," the young partisan murmured. He glanced at Landry. Worry and doubt were written plainly on Piccione's face. "I don't know what's wrong with me, David. I'm too quick to take offense. Exhaustion, Dante says. He says it will pass. You must think I'm a fool."

Landry shook his head. "Kavanaugh explained it to us. A man has a right to be temperish after what you and the others went through."

"The others, perhaps. Not me. Did Kavanaugh tell you what the Germans did to Lieutenant Creedmore and Luisa? Especially to Luisa?" Piccione's jaw tightened. "You remember how pretty she was. No longer. The others pretend not to hold me responsible, but I know better. Wait until you see her. You should prepare yourself, David. You mustn't act shocked. I will never for-

give myself for what happened to her. Dante says after all we are
alive, we escaped, all is well. But I say the price was high."

"I have to agree with Dante," Landry said. "Being alive is more
important."

The young partisan climbed in silence for a while, then said,
"Thank you, David, for understanding. And belatedly I thank you
for your help. Had it not been for you, we might all be dead by
now."

"Me?" Landry said. "I didn't do anything."

"You strengthened Dante's heart," Piccione said. "After Major
Holloman forced you to leave the lake, Dante refused to have any
more to do with him until he agreed to send his men down the
mountain to help search for us, as you had insisted. It was a wonderful argument. Get Salvo to tell you about it when he gets off
duty. Salvo tells it splendidly." His tone, though cheerful, sounded
forced.

"How did they find you?"

"One of the Americans, Harry Tucker, learned where we were
being held. He told Lieutenant Stefanini and they smuggled a gun
to us. We were to escape at nightfall, but there was some
difficulty. I think the Germans were warned of our plans. They
sent an officer and two guards to remove us to the SD headquarters in Cernobbio. We had to shoot our way out."

"That sounds messy," Landry said.

The coolness returned. "They deserved to die," Piccione said.
"I would have killed them myself, had the gun been in my hands."

The gully climbed another hundred yards between steep rock
walls, then opened into an earthen bowl. Water seeping underground must have collected in it. The ubiquitous pines and cedars
gave way here to wild chestnut trees. A chasm, no more than
twenty feet deep but wide enough to slow any German or Fascist
patrols, separated the bowl from a boulder-strewn encampment
just barely visible through the foliage on the far side. A narrow
rope bridge hung across the gap. It wasn't the camp Landry remembered, but he had known for the past several hours that they
were headed for different, higher ground. He couldn't help wondering when and why Dante had seen fit to move. To locate an encampment so high, so far from the lakeside, surely limited Dante's
effectiveness.

The two mules snorted skittishly at the mere sight of the rope bridge, and the partisans stopped to tie and unload them on the near side. Kavanaugh waved the others across. The bridge swayed under Landry's feet, then he was on firm ground, and an emaciated dog, more yellow than brown, met them. It neither growled nor barked, but wriggled at their feet, teeth bared in an ingratiating grin, as though it hoped to prove its harmlessness before someone chanced to hit it. "That's Tuono," Kavanaugh told Landry. "You remember. He used to belong to Gualfiero."

"Used to?" Landry said.

Kavanaugh looked away. "Gualfiero is dead now."

"When?"

"Couple of months ago. We found him on the trail above Acquaséria, him and Luchino, shot to pieces. The dog was the only survivor."

Landry reached to pet the dog, but his shocked eyes were all for the camp. Apparently Gualfiero and Luchino weren't the only casualties during his two-month absence from the lake. The camp itself was large enough. It consisted of a scattering of rough stone huts tucked under the trees. Two of the larger huts toward the center appeared to be old, perhaps constructed by goatherds or prewar cigarette smugglers who worked the mountains between Lake Como and Switzerland. The other huts, newer and smaller, were put together loosely, open to the wind and the elements. A couple had been patched with hammered tin. But few of them seemed to be occupied. A man squatted in front of one, cleaning a weapon. Two more men leaned through the low entrance of another to look them over. Dante's group had numbered almost forty when Landry left them. From the looks of the empty huts, Dante would be lucky if he could muster ten or twelve now. The casual but effective disorder of the old days seemed to have slid rapidly toward chaos.

"What happened to Dante's outfit?" Landry asked. "He used to have four times as many people."

Kavanaugh shrugged. "A lot of them are dead," he said. "We've been hit pretty hard lately by the Germans. Some of the others quit and went home when the weather turned bad and the planes stopped dropping supplies. That's why we moved up here.

Dante figured we were too weak to do much damage until good weather brings us fresh recruits."

A woman's voice hailed them from the far side of the clearing. Kavanaugh swung his head toward the biggest hut. "That's Luisa," he said. "Come on. I'll introduce everybody." He led them toward the hut. The dog, which seemed to have attached itself to the Britisher, followed closely behind.

A man slipped into view as they approached and stood by the woman, waiting. It was Dante. Tall, wiry, mustachioed, with unblinking eyes, he was dressed against the mountain chill in faded Zouave trousers and a dark brown pullover sweater. At least three pairs of socks showed above the leather tops of his boots. Luisa was also outfitted against the chill. She wore corduroy trousers and carried a sheepskin jacket about four sizes too big. Her free hand slipped shyly into Dante's as Landry and the others drew near.

The big chestnut trees cast a heavy shadow over her face and Landry was only a few feet from her when he saw what Piccione had been trying to tell him. His breath caught in his throat. He remembered her as a pretty, dark-haired girl with an obvious crush on Dante. High cheekbones and a sensuous, well-formed mouth. That was changed now. There were burn scars across her forehead and under her eyes, splotches with dark centers, and one of the formerly handsome cheekbones had been smashed and had healed slightly lower than the other, impairing the symmetry of her face. She smiled shyly and Landry saw dark gaps where four of her teeth had once been. The shock must have shown in his eyes, for the smile faltered and she looked away.

"Luisa. Well met," he said, trying to make up with warmth of tone what his unconscious expression had already spoiled.

Without meeting his eyes, she said, "Hello, David." *Dah-veed* again, softly, like sad music. "I'm glad it's you. Welcome home."

"Thank you," Landry said. He offered his hand to Dante. "And you, comandante. It's good to see you."

"Is it?" Dante said. The dog, which had clung close to the Britisher's legs, switched his attention to Dante. Tuono jumped up, an ungainly tangle of long, awkward legs, and shoved his forepaws against Dante's chest. Dante pushed him away with a gesture that was apparently well practiced, and ignored Landry's outstretched hand in the process.

Disturbed by Dante's frosty greeting, Landry stood back while X. B. Kavanaugh tended to the formalities, introducing Rossiter and Willoughby. Dante dipped his chin politely at each of them and said, "I welcome you." But his voice was emotionless, almost perfunctory.

Veterano and the Lizard came across the clearing during the introductions, each bearing duffels from the mules. They drew up beside Dante's hut and Veterano said, "Where shall we put their supplies?"

"Ask them, not me," Dante told him.

Unfriendliness oozed from every syllable. Landry's apprehension mounted. Something was badly wrong. Rossiter also shot a keen, searching look at the tall partisan chieftain, but he apparently decided not to be offended. "With your permission," Rossiter said, only a trifle stiffly, "we will excuse ourselves and choose lodgings now. I hate to admit it, but after that stroll up your mountain, I'm a little tired."

It was a plea for hospitality that no Italian could have resisted. Dante thawed partially and said, "Yes, of course. We are low in strength, as you can see, so most of the huts are empty. If there is no bedding on the floor, you may take what you wish. There is hay for the mules behind the other large hut. I suggest you put a layer on the floor before you make a bed. This high, the ground gets very cold at night. Luisa, please accompany our guests and help them select what they need." To Veterano he added, "I would suggest the radio hut for their supplies. It leaks less than the others."

The old man hesitated, then took a yellow flower from his vest and offered it on the flat of his calloused palm to Luisa. She took it with delight. "A leopard's-bane?" she said. "Oh Veterano, where did you find it?"

"On the scree above Rezzonico," he muttered, almost too low for the others to hear. He backed away in embarrassment. "It's nothing. Only a flower." Then he tucked his chin to his chest and hurried off toward the radio hut at so fast a pace that the Lizard had to trot to catch up with him.

The others turned to follow. Dante put his hand on Landry's

arm. "Stay with me a moment, David. I would have a word with you."

Landry felt quick relief. He waited until Luisa and Kavanaugh led the others away, then asked, "What's going on, Dante? What's bothering you?"

Dante's somber eyes studied him. "I should have known it would be you, David. For your government to show us sudden attention after ignoring us so long. Who are these men you have brought? Are they here to investigate us?"

Landry was surprised, and he let it show. "What in God's name for? Why should anyone want to investigate you?"

"You think we are responsible for the recent difficulties, do you not? For the disappearance of Major Holloman? For the loss of the money?" His eyes narrowed. "Of course you do. It is natural that you would suspect me, an admitted Communist. You Americans are all so unwilling to accept anyone who believes differently from yourselves."

He sounded bitter. Landry frowned in exasperation. "Come on, Dante. You know me better than that. I don't give a damn about your political beliefs, as long as they don't interfere with your abilities. You could be a Russian in disguise and I wouldn't care."

"Whatever happened to your Major Holloman, it was not our fault," Dante said. "Ask your own countrymen. It was an American who was assigned to watch over him. It was an American who abandoned him. Two of my best partisans died as a result. We found them in the mountains, one dead, the other dying. There was no trace of your Major Holloman or his money."

"He's not my Major Holloman," Landry said. "Believe me, Dante. Our presence on the lake has nothing to do with him. Just be patient. Major Rossiter will explain everything when Pietro arrives."

"I would expect you to say that," Dante murmured. "We have been friends, David. But friendship no longer matters when one is determined to shield a loved one. If you feel compelled to protect Viviana, then by all means . . ."

Landry cocked his head. "Wait a minute," he said. "What has Viviana got to do with this?"

Dante ignored Landry's question. "You need not hide your feelings from me, David. I feel a similar affection for Luisa. Perhaps it is natural in such times of stress. One sees so much death, one turns instinctively to the promise of life. Very well, I accept that. If you wish an option to present to your government, I will give you one. Your countrymen seem convinced that the increased German activity is the responsibility of an informer. Why must it follow that there is an informer? Blame instead the rescue of our three compatriots who were imprisoned by the Fascists, a rescue arranged by your own people. Blame your American friends, the two lieutenants Tucker and Stefanini, for resorting to such a crude scheme. Blame Lieutenant Creedmore for losing his head under pressure. He shot and killed a party of Germans, one of them an important officer, during the escape. The Germans have increased their raids and their antiguerrilla activities? Of course they have. Not because of an informer, but because they were infuriated by the murder of their men. It need not have happened. We could have rescued all three of them without bloodshed, if only your men had trusted us."

"You're still over my head," Landry said. "How does Viviana figure into this?"

Dante took a deep breath. His expression said he didn't believe a word of Landry's professed confusion. "I don't accuse her, David. But you must agree that her culpability bears examination. She was, after all, in a better position to betray Major Holloman than any of the rest of us. You know this is true."

"No, I don't. I don't know a damned thing. I didn't even know I was coming back to the lake until the day before yesterday."

Now it was Dante's turn to look confused. "Are you serious? No one has explained the situation to you?"

"No one has explained anything, Dante. I told you, we aren't here because of Holloman. Now what's all this nonsense about Viviana?"

"I'm sorry," Dante said. "I thought you knew. Major Holloman moved into Viviana's house shortly after you left. It was from her house that he disappeared."

4

Several hours later, some seventy miles east of Lake Como and Dante's mountainside camp, a twin-engined Heinkel 111 bearing an important passenger from Berlin rolled to a stop on darkened tarmac at the Brescia fighter strip, and German ground crews, mindful of prowling Allied night fighters, hurriedly doused the landing lights. The Heinkel, a cigar-shaped medium bomber converted to transport service, ran up its engines in a final sputter of defiance, then shut down. Propeller arcs glistened and slowed, and a hatch swung open in the belly.

First out of the Heinkel was a tall, white-haired SS general in a leather greatcoat, carrying a slim valise. No sooner had the general's feet touched the ground than a brown-and-gray sedan sporting SS runes on the front fenders sped across the runway and pulled up beside the plane. The driver of the sedan, an SS major with a noticeable limp, hurried forward to greet the general. "Herr Obergruppenführer," the major said warmly. "Welcome back to Italy. How was your trip?"

"Regrettable," the tall, white-haired general said. He handed his valise to the major and stepped wearily into the car. The major hesitated and leaned in after him.

"Did you see the Führer?" the major asked nervously.

The general nodded. "Yes, I saw him."

"Was it . . . difficult?"

"Extremely difficult." SS Obergruppenführer Karl Wolff, Höchster SS und Polizeiführer of all Italy, unbuttoned his greatcoat and sighed. His survival, until forty-eight hours ago, had been in doubt, resting solely on the tenuous balance of Adolf Hitler's deteriorating sanity.

"Did he know?" the major asked. He glanced at the Luftwaffe crewmen stepping from the plane and lowered his voice. "About Sunrise, I mean."

General Wolff's eyes closed. "He knew. Kaltenbrunner told him everything. Sunrise. Switzerland. Dulles. Everything."

"Oh my God," the major said. "What will we do?"

"Nothing," Wolff said. "I may have talked us out of trouble. At least for the moment." He leaned back. "Take me to Fasano. I want to rest."

As the major climbed under the wheel of the sedan and started the engine, Wolff rested his head against his gloved fist and relived those terrible hours in Berlin. It had been touch and go. Reichsführer Himmler had accused Wolff of treason, shouting at him across the room while Kaltenbrunner watched and listened. Wolff had denied the accusation, of course, and had demanded an audience with the Führer so he could defend himself, even to the point of insisting that Himmler accompany him to the Chancellery and repeat his charges. It was a poor bluff at best, but it quieted Himmler. The man had turned positively pale at the mere suggestion of a confrontation with Hitler.

But it didn't stop Kaltenbrunner. On the afternoon of April 18, only two days after the Russians opened their assault and began to press toward Berlin, Wolff found himself being delivered to the bomb-shattered grounds of the Chancellery and a fateful life-and-death meeting with the most powerful man Germany had ever known.

It started poorly. The splintered trees in the garden, the bomb craters, the smoke-blackened buildings. Then down those awful stairs to the grim, gray underground bunker. Hitler, in his tan jacket and black trousers, sitting quietly in the conference room, his pale face twitching, his blue-gray eyes seething. "Why have you deliberately disobeyed me?" were his first words. Not even a greeting. Just the accusation.

Wolff, with his heart in his throat, talked fast. Never once removing his eyes from the Führer's face, as though to lose eye contact might mean to lose his life, he talked and talked. Using every ounce of persuasion at his command, he told the Führer that he had made independent contact with the Allies in Switzerland for one reason alone. So that if he were to fail, or if the terms proved unacceptable, the Führer could then disown him. But he had not failed. By his secret visits to Switzerland, he had succeeded in opening doors that were thought to be impenetrable. It was now possible, through the American representative Allen Dulles, to speak directly to the new American leader, President Truman, and to Hitler's old enemy, Prime Minister Winston Churchill. All

Wolff needed were instructions from the Führer. Should he proceed?

Hitler listened silently until Wolff finished, then sent everyone but Wolff from the room. When they were alone, Hitler said, "I accept your presentation. You are a lucky man. Had you failed, I would have had you shot."

Later, on a rainy afternoon when no Allied bombers could be expected over Berlin, they had walked together in the ruined garden above the bunker. Hitler told Wolff in confidence that he expected new miracle weapons to be ready at any moment. In the meantime, Wolff's initiative in Switzerland could be used to widen the chasm between the Eastern and Western Allies. If Wolff could keep the British and Americans dangling, Hitler was certain he could hold out in Berlin for another six to eight weeks. By then, the Allies would surely be at each other's throats. The only stipulation he made was that Wolff must try for better terms than unconditional surrender. And with that, Wolff was given permission to return to Italy.

Now, as the darkened sedan came to a fork in the road that led north to Lake Garda and Wolff's private villa in the town of Fasano, Wolff opened his eyes and asked the major, "How goes the war?"

The major glanced in the rear-view mirror and said, "Not good. The British have taken Argenta and are moving on Ferrara. The Americans have cut off Bologna. Our troops are resisting magnificently, but if the Allies break through to the Po Valley, I fear a rout. That's good tank country, and we have nothing to stop them."

"It was raining in Berlin," Wolff said. "If the storm should move south, perhaps heavy rains could turn the Po Valley to mud and mire their tanks. Maybe even ground their aircraft. But we rarely have such luck. Are things quiet on Lake Garda?"

The major stared hard at the road. "I am sorry, my general, but I fear not. I have disturbing news."

"Oh?"

"With the Allied offensive beginning to make gains and the front threatening to collapse, the Duce gathered his ministers three days ago and fled. He is now in Milan."

Wolff's mouth drooped. "Did you notify the Americans?"

"Yes, sir. As soon as I heard. I also tried to replace the Duce's Waffen-SS guard with one of our own, but Lieutenant Häger refused to relinquish his command without written orders. I didn't press the issue."

"Then there is nothing more we can do," Wolff said. "It's up to the Americans to stop him."

"Yes, sir. Do you think they can, sir?"

"I don't know," Wolff said. He massaged the bridge of his nose. "The Americans expect me in Switzerland on Monday," he said. "Perhaps while I am gone, you should crate our files and move our own headquarters north, to Bolzano, nearer to General Vietinghoff's Army Command. We don't want to be cut off by the Allies, either."

"Yes, sir. I'll make the arrangements tomorrow. What stance will you take when you next meet with Herr Dulles, sir?"

"I fear I have no option," Wolff said. "If the offer is still open, I shall sign the surrender particulars no matter how harsh the terms. This abomination has gone on long enough."

Day Two

Sunday—April 22, 1945

Era un esercito contro un manipolo,
un contro quindici . . .

An army against a handful,
fifteen to one . . .
—Cilea, *Adriana Lecouvreur*

1

If Captain Victor Willoughby found any dog more disappointing than an ill-trained brute that liked to rush a stranger with all teeth bared, it was a dog that approached each newcomer with cringing belly and hopefully wagging tail. When one of the partisan mules began to stamp on the other side of the rope bridge, Willoughby knew automatically that someone was coming up the slope through the early-morning mist. He called to him the yellow mongrel that had greeted them with far too much friendliness the previous day. Apparently the pet of a partisan who had been killed, it was ownerless as far as Willoughby could divine, and it needed someone to take it in hand. He would keep the dog by him until whoever was coming up the trail had arrived, and teach it a little dignity.

At least two minutes passed before Rossiter and Captain Landry and the partisans sitting around the small, almost smokeless cook fire began to eye the bridge and reach for weapons.

Foolish of them. If they ever bothered to watch a pair of mules, they would have learned that one was assigned to sentry duty at all times, ready to warn its napping or grazing workmate of any approach that might mean danger. But, then, men so rarely realized that animals were worth watching.

"Sit, Tuono," Willoughby instructed the dog. He smiled to himself at the resounding name, Thunder, given to this thin-flanked specimen, and he pushed firmly on Tuono's haunches to enforce the command. The dog stiffened nervously and turned to lick his hand. "Sit," Willoughby repeated patiently. This time, Tuono allowed himself to be pushed to the desired position. Willoughby decided he would have to ask the local dialect for a few simple commands. For all he knew, the dog was unable to understand his own formal Italian.

Seated off to himself on a pine log, Willoughby progressed to "Stay," holding the dog in iron hands when the human lookouts appeared among the trees, followed by a clot of ragged men and two men who were obviously American. Seven of them in all. One of the Italians, a young, bearded, slender man with a look of quiet strength about him that Willoughby instantly liked, detached himself from the group and strode across the bridge to greet Landry like an old friend. They clasped one another and pounded backs lengthily before the bearded man turned to greet the others. Rossiter watched it all with a rather grim look about him.

An odd lot, these Americans and Italians. Either given to outward displays of fawning comradeship and affection, or downright rude. Somehow, between their early-afternoon arrival in camp yesterday and last night's communal meal, an edginess had developed. Landry, so full of smiles on the way up the mountain, had turned into a thoughtful brooder, spending the remainder of the day off to himself, scarcely responding to even the most polite of inquiries. Apparently it had something to do with the missing officer and the trio of victims who had been captured by the Fascists. No point in wondering about the missing man, Holloman. He was dead, no doubt. Betrayed, most likely, as Dulles and his operations chief had suggested back in Bern. Unless Holloman had opted on his own to walk across the mountains to the safety of Switzerland. And the three who were captured? Willoughby had noted already a seemingly general hostility whenever the Holloman chap's name came up, as though everyone in camp, including Landry, blamed him directly for the capture of the threesome. Why were they so quick to direct censure at a man who was no longer here to defend himself? It seemed obvious to Willoughby that any number of variables could have entered into the capture, including the same possibility of a traitor.

"No, stay," Willoughby warned Tuono, who had begun to wriggle his whole bottom and struggle against the restraining hands. The sight of the new arrivals shedding their weapons and sinking around the tiny fire was almost too much for the dog to bear. Of course, Tuono was only a cur, with no generations of breeding to stiffen his backbone, like Willoughby's magnificent Airedales, but any dog could learn.

Now introductions were being made. Willoughby rose politely and headed for the circle of partisans and Americans, bringing Tuono by the ragged rope that served the poor creature as a collar. One of these people gathering around the cook fire was very probably the traitor whom Willoughby had been sent to find. It was conceivable that the source of the treachery came from outside the camp itself, but more likely that it festered from within. He looked at their faces guardedly, wondering which of them he would have to kill.

In fairness to the dog, Willoughby allowed Tuono to greet each man. Willoughby listened carefully to the names being passed around, but he looked hard at only one man. The bearded young partisan with intense eyes and the look of strength was Pietro. The man they had been sent to see, the leader of the partisan bands. Captain Landry seemed to have overcome his temporary moodiness of the night before. The American's smile was as broad as Tuono's, the major difference being that Landry kept his tongue from lolling out and fired questions instead. "And Oreste?" Willoughby heard him ask the bearded partisan. "He didn't come?"

"Alas," Pietro said. "He was killed two weeks ago in a raid on the Liro garrison. Poor Oreste. He was wounded in the leg, and when he stopped and tried to bind the wound, they caught up with him and split his head open with a rifle butt."

"What sorrow," Landry said. He looked as if he meant it. "What about Romolo? Don't tell me Romolo . . . ?"

Pietro nodded. "Captured almost a month ago and tortured by

The Drowner. Ah, my friend, there have been many changes. Many old faces gone. But let us not mar this reunion with ill-timed sadness. What is that marvelous fragrance, that forgotten incense that my unbelieving nose picked up as we crossed the bridge? Can it be coffee? No, I'm surely imagining things. The only coffee my men and I have known for timeless ages is that foul spilth one brews from barley. Even if what I smelled were genuine coffee, you couldn't have brought enough for us all to have a sip?"

Captain Landry had, of course. The man could scarcely have included more than a change of clothes in his personal kit, so loaded had it been with tobacco tins for the partisans, two American hams, a dried salami from Siena, and a huge slab of bacon, which the salami-chewing Dante group had voted last night should be saved for the arrival of Pietro's band this morning. All very nice of Landry, but there was such a thing as being too friendly. What was he trying to prove?

Willoughby regarded the muscular young American and wondered if *he* could be the fount from which betrayal had flowed. True, he had been away from the lake during most of the severe setbacks, but that didn't necessarily exclude him from the list of possible traitors. Holloman had disappeared only a week or two after Landry's removal from the lake, and if the reports from the ALOTs were accurate, Landry had been allowed to make his way alone from Dante's camp to the clandestine aerial pickup zone north of the lake on the broad Plain of Spain. Couldn't he have used that time to advantage, seeking revenge on his enemies by striking a bargain with the Germans, or perhaps colluding with one of the partisans?

It seemed none too likely. And yet, like a sycophantic dog, like poor Tuono, a man who appeared to want everyone to like him was open to suspicion in Willoughby's mind. Willoughby's sister always claimed that he took as his model for human behavior that of the strong, valorous Airedales, whose deep-voiced barking had rung from spacious runs in the days when Willoughby's kennel and the show ring had commanded his every thought. That was before the war, of course. Before his kennel had become the all-but-empty home of only the four brood bitches Willoughby had refrained from selling when he realized war was coming. Only three of them left now. His sister had written less than a month ago that Nellie Melba, the oldest bitch, had died of a stroke. Willoughby would miss her.

As to behavior, well, Willoughby had to admit that his sister had a point. Dogs were often more loyal than people. His Airedales were as alert as mongooses, as brave as lions, afraid of nothing that walked, and Willoughby tried to be worthy of them. They were also gay and affectionate, as perhaps he was not. That was the fault of the wartime job he had been given. Suspicion had become a way of life, and friendship with men under suspicion was out of the question. Someday, God willing that it came soon, the war would end and Willoughby would try to repopulate the kennel and try to find room in his own life for gaiety and affection.

Willoughby realized that he was frowning. He arranged a less forbidding expression on his face and watched the partisan girl, Luisa, refill a huge, blackened coffee pot and measure out the brown richness that all the partisans and even a few of the Americans crowded around to inhale. One of the newcomers stepped on Tuono's foot, and, when the dog cried out, bent to pet him. Tuono forgot pain for delight. Willoughby began once more the process of attaching names to faces. This was Stefanini—Freddy, they called him—one of the two American ALOTs who had gone across the mountains to fetch Pietro. With a name like Stefanini, he surely had an Italian heritage, and his dark eyes and wavy, dark hair said the same, but it was interesting how different he looked from the other Italians. Bigger. Heavy in the chest and arms. The chief difference, though, was the way he moved. Standard American slouch, but long strides, and he had none of the Italians' grace, much less their expressive gestures.

Soon the bacon was frying and the coffee gently boiling, their combined odors apparently a happy torture to the starved young partisans. Major Rossiter brought out his inevitable unlit cigar and came to stand over Landry and Pietro. Willoughby drifted closer to listen. He heard Rossiter ask in his halting Italian, "How is it with the Puecher detachment? Are you at fighting strength?"

Pietro seemed to find it difficult to take his eyes from the cook fire. He said distractedly, "Our numbers are improving. I have twenty-two men now, and every week we add two or three more."

Rossiter frowned. "So few? We thought you would be in better shape."

"No, no, that's good," Pietro said. "For a while, during the early days of March, there were only sixty-eight of us on the whole lake, all eight detachments combined, scattered from Como to Ponte del Passo. But the warm weather will increase patriotism. Another few weeks and we should be strong enough to mount some good raids."

Rossiter shook his head and squatted beside the bearded young leader. "No more raids," he said. "No more minor harassing operations. I bring important news. We're going to cut the Como road."

Pietro's eyes swung around, the bacon and coffee smells forgotten for the moment. "Cut the road?" he said. He looked at Landry. "Why, David? What is happening?"

But Landry gestured, open-handed, to Rossiter, tactfully giving him the question. Rossiter picked up a stick and began to draw in the dirt. Pietro hunched forward to watch as Rossiter sketched the upside-down Y of Lake Como, and then, two feet to the right of it, added the elongated porkchop shape of Lake Garda. A few of the partisans wandered over to stand above them curiously, as did Dante and most of the Americans.

The major mounded dirt between the lakes to suggest the Bergamo Alps, then built another ridge of mountains to the north, along the hypothetical Swiss and Austrian borders. What remained was a long, narrow valley stretching above the two lakes, a ribbonlike depression that ran east to west on a scale that equaled some forty to forty-five miles.

"That's the Valtellina," one of the standing partisans volunteered. It was the pipe-smoking sentry they had encountered on the trail yesterday, the one whom Landry had called Salvo.

The major shifted his cigar. "What do you know about it?"

Salvo said, "Only that it is surrounded on all sides by mountains. There are fortifications there from the last war. And some electrical stations."

"Exactly," Rossiter beamed. "This whole valley is like a fortress. If I were a Fascist looking for a place to set up defenses, I couldn't pick a better site. Difficult of access. Except for the roads at the two ends, completely protected from mechanized armor by mountainous terrain. Put a small army in there with enough money and arms to keep them going, and they could defend it for months. There are TB hospitals—at least a couple of them, we're told—that could be converted to take wounded, and two outlets for escape in case things heat up—off to Austria through the Stelvio Pass, or to the safety of Switzerland through the Bernina Pass."

Pietro seemed puzzled. "You expect a Fascist army to move into the Valtellina?"

"That's exactly what we expect," Rossiter said. He chewed his cigar for a moment, then said, "Landry tells me I can trust you, Pietro, so I'm going to tell you and your men something that is considered extremely sensitive. There's a peace initiative from the Germans in Italy. They may agree to lay down their arms in the next week or two. If they do, the war here will be over, and you can all go home."

There were appreciative murmurs from the partisans, and Pietro said, "That is truly splendid news."

"Yes, it is," Rossiter said. "But there's a problem. That's why I came to Lake Como to talk to you. We have information that Mussolini may retire to the Valtellina with an army of fifty thousand Blackshirts. If we don't stop him, we can forget about the peace. It would take months to dig him out."

Pietro still looked puzzled. He studied the crude map in the dirt and said, "But the Duce and his ministers are situated here, on Lake Garda. If they intend to move an army to the Valtellina, the most logical route would be the roads running north from Garda or Lake d'Iseo. Why come to us?"

"That's what we thought, too," Rossiter said. "The American OSS have already taken steps to close those two roads. They dropped a pair of assault teams on the eastern end of the Valtellina almost a week ago, one to close off Route 38 below the Stelvio Pass, and the other to shut down the bypass route east of Sondrio at Colle d'Aprica. But now we have evidence that Mussolini has abandoned his quarters at Lake Garda and moved to Milan."

"I see," said Pietro. "So the focus shifts to the west and the most logical route becomes our own Como road."

Rossiter said with satisfaction, "You've got it."

The coffee was ready. One of the American ALOTs brought the first steaming cup to Pietro. The American was a stranger to Willoughby, an athletic fellow with more than a touch of the Irish apparent in his own background. Dark hair, but candid blue eyes, a ready smile and skin so light that there was a peppering of freckles all over his face. He looked lighthearted, too, perhaps because a dimple in his right cheek deepened with each smile. Presumably the other ALOT who had accompanied the young Italian-American, Stefanini, to Pietro's camp. What was his name? Creedmore. Wesley Creedmore. Not an Irish name at all, but probably named after John Wesley, the Englishman. Or wasn't there an American badman named John Wesley Hardin? Did American parents name children after outlaws?

As the freckled American handed the coffee cup to Pietro and stooped to stroke Tuono, the American asked in an excruciatingly twangy accent, "That's the big secret, then? The old rooster is in Milan?"

"Unless he's already on his way here," Rossiter said.

Willoughby raised an eyebrow, but not because of the exchange between the two men. The American was busily scratching Tuono's ears with thoughtless kindness, and Willoughby's eye had fallen on his left hand. Willoughby felt a sudden crawling sensation in every vein, the body's automatic empathy with someone else's injury. The fingers stroking Tuono's spiky fur were badly mangled. All five nails were gone, ripped out by the roots, and rough scabby tissue, still healing, had covered the tips. On impulse, Willoughby looked toward the cook fire and sought out the unmarred visage of the handsome young partisan who had met them at the plane. Piccione, smiling cheerfully, stood near the battered partisan girl, Luisa, helping her with the heavy coffee pot. Even in a nation where great physical beauty could be seen on any country lane, any city street, Piccione's looks were startling. His nose and mouth, hinting of princely disdain, might have been carved from Carrara marble. Magnificent dark eyes gazed out at the world from a palisade of thick lashes. Even his hair was so lustrously black that in the sunlight it gleamed with the blue sheen of a blackbird's feather. It seemed strange that the Germans would mistreat only two of their prisoners while leaving such an obvious target untouched.

Pietro sipped cautiously from the cup of hot coffee and said to Rossiter, "You ask a great deal of us. To close the road to an army would take many men. Many of us would surely die. The Fascists would outnumber us at least fifty to one."

"Yes, I know," Rossiter said. "But it's important. And we don't have to hold off the entire army. If we can keep them busy long enough to figure out which part of the convoy contains their war funds, we can swoop down and grab it. An option is to divert the vehicles carrying the treasury, maybe turn them back. Without funds, Mussolini can't stockpile medical supplies or food or even ammunition. The whole Valtellina business would become unworkable. I've got a pretty good strategy worked out. We still have the advantage of surprise and mountainous terrain, so if you'll consent to gather the Garibaldi detachments, we can . . ."

Pietro stopped him with a gesture. "Things are no longer that simple, Major. I do not command on word alone as I once did." He leaned past Rossiter toward Landry and said, "How do you feel about this, David? Do you believe in it?"

Landry's eyes met Rossiter's, then Landry said, "Yes, if it will bring peace. I guess I do."

"In that case, I will give you my own unit for the fight," Pietro said. "I will alert them as soon as I return to camp and we will be ready to move any time you say. I might even be able to persuade a half dozen of the boys from the Cravero and Gramsci detachments to join us. But if your major wishes the entire 52nd Garibaldi, it will have to be cleared through the Como Federation. They make all political decisions now."

Rossiter said, "This isn't political. It's military."

Pietro shrugged. "The Committee of Liberation in Milan now considers any requests from the Americans to be political." He sounded uncomfortable. "For that you can thank your Major Holloman's refusal to distribute his funds in an equitable manner. He made many enemies among the important members of the CLN."

"Damn it, I can't block the road with a handful of men," Rossiter said. "How long would it take for us to get clearance from this Federation of yours?"

"I can arrange a meeting," Pietro said. "Dante will send a man down this very morning to call them together. Let David name a place and they should be able to meet with him by tomorrow afternoon."

"Landry?" Rossiter said. "Why not me? I'm the one in charge."

Pietro was silent for a moment, then said tactfully, "Yes, I understand, Major. But to be frank, I don't think they'll listen to an outsider. The Como Federation members are not fighting men. Some of them are old, and all are cautious. They would be more comfortable with someone they know."

X. B. Kavanaugh said, "It's dangerous to send either of them. Everyone on the lake must know about that seaplane landing by now. The Germans will have patrols all over the place. You let Landry go down to the lake and he's apt to get his tail shot off."

"No, I'll go," Landry told Kavanaugh. "That's what they sent me back for." He looked at Pietro. "Where would you suggest the meeting take place?"

"Why don't you meet them in Rezzonico?" Pietro said. "It's the closest point for you, and the Federation people can travel up the lake without causing suspicion. We have a friend in Rezzonico who permits us to use the room above his bar."

"Rezzonico," Landry repeated. He hesitated, then said, "Why not? Rezzonico is as good as any place."

"Excellent," Pietro said. "Then it's settled. This will work just as well, my friends. You will see. Even if I were allowed to give the command myself, it would take time for my men to carry the word to all the encampments. This way the word will go out more rapidly. Once the Federation representatives hear David's explanation and agree to help, runners will be dispatched immediately to all detachment leaders." His eyes sought Dante. "You, comandante, it is your camp. You should select the man to arrange the meeting."

"Salvo," Dante said. He nodded toward the pipe-smoking partisan. "He knows the trails better than anyone."

"Then Salvo it is," Pietro said. "Move as swiftly as you can, Salvo. Stop for nothing. Make certain the Federation members understand the urgency of the meeting."

Salvo shifted uncomfortably. He turned hungry eyes to the cook fire. "I had hoped to sample the bacon," he said.

Pietro grinned up at him. "Very well. I suppose Mussolini and his army of Blackshirts will wait five minutes."

As if to speed Salvo on his way, Luisa declared the bacon ready, and the partisans abandoned the circle to crowd around her. Salvo was awarded the first rasher, and he stepped away from the skillet, bouncing it hotly from hand to hand, his whiskered face split in unbelieving glee.

Willoughby looked down at Tuono. Long ropes of saliva drooled from the dog's mouth and his tail had begun a steady, rapid beat at the sight of Salvo's bacon. Too optimistic. Not only the dog. All of them, too optimistic. Rossiter with his "pretty good strategy." The partisans with their willingness to mix it up and damn the odds against them. Amateurs, playing at war. And what if they weren't ready when Mussolini came?

But that was Rossiter's problem. Willoughby's job was the simple one of finding out which of these amateurs had gone bad and to excise him as a surgeon might cut away a tumor. Then, if Mussolini appeared, the partisans and the Americans might at least have a chance to stop him, though Willoughby regarded the probability of their doing so about as likely as Tuono's being given a share of the precious bacon. The partisans would no doubt devour even the bacon grease, just as Mussolini and his Fascist divisions would in turn surely devour the outnumbered partisans.

Willoughby patted the dog and was rewarded by an even faster beat of the tail. Willoughby had nothing but American K rations in his own kit, but he rose and led the animal away. After all, optimism sometimes paid. He would check through the rations and see if he could find something Tuono might regard as an equally acceptable feast.

2

Shortly before noon, long after Pietro's ragged, thin partisans had set off across the mountains to return to their own camp, seven older, better-fed Italians entered a spacious ground-floor suite of the Palazzo Monforte, the Fascist Prefecture of Milan, some thirty miles south of Lake Como.

It was an ornate chamber, full of mirrors. At one end of the

room, two Fascist officers stood stiffly when the seven solemn men
entered, as if expecting to be dismissed at any moment, but afraid
to make a move until ordered. Two more men stood outside tall
windows. They were Waffen-SS sentries, part of the German guard
complement that had followed Mussolini from Lake Garda four
days earlier. A reflection of pigeons whirling outside stirred in the
mirrors, but otherwise the room was quiet. Sunlight streamed
through the windows onto a thick carpet interwoven with the bundled ax and rods of the Roman fasces. Gaily painted frescoes of
the Romulus and Remus legend looked down from a lofty, gilt-
edged ceiling, and Roman statues stared with stony disapproval at
the mirrored flutter of the pigeons. Across from the windows, resting on the carpeted floor in hastily constructed piles, were row
upon row of shiny gold ingots, hundreds of them, sparkling with
yellow brilliance in the reflected sunlight, caressed by the shadows
of flickering wings. Near a marble fireplace, wooden benches had
been set up and were smothered by stacks of foreign currencies,
fresh new bills straight from the vaults of Fascist banks, crisp
mounds of lire, francs, dollars, pounds sterling, Reichsmarks,
some in square bundles two and three feet high. The two Fascist
officers had been counting currency, banding stacks with bank
wrappers and stuffing them into open cardboard boxes on the
floor.

The touch of gaiety in the chamber's appointments and the
massive wealth stored along the mirrored walls provided no cheer
to the seven men spreading around a mahogany conference table.
To the head of the table, slumped in the gray-green uniform of the
Fascist militia, tasseled cap clutched tightly in his hand, jackboots
on his feet, came the discouraged figure of Benito Mussolini. His
eyes were downcast and he seemed to be avoiding the bright yellow glitter of the gold. Around him, faces long, shoulders sagging,
clustered six of his most trusted military and ministerial advisers.
Contrary to the belief of the OSS and now of the partisans on
Lake Como, the Valtellina decision was not yet a concrete one.
The war was lost, as far as the men in the mirrored chamber were
concerned, and defeat already hung heavily over their heads. Now
they had assembled to consider their shrinking options. The final
stand in the Valtellina was only one of the possibilities, and far
from the most popular.

Fernando Mezzasoma, Mussolini's youthful Minister of Popular Culture, stared disconsolately at the mounds of colorful currency, then gestured for the two Fascist officers to leave. Both men fled on tiptoe. Mezzasoma waited until Mussolini and the others took their seats, then removed his glasses and began to clean them with a wrinkled handkerchief. "Why are they always so close?" he asked wearily. He gestured at the Waffen-SS sentries outside the window.

"They are always there," Mussolini murmured. "Like the spots on a leopard."

"They'll leave us soon enough," Nicola Bombacci said. "They care about nothing but themselves. If we are to survive once the Germans abandon us, we must begin to act independently now. The important thing, of course, is to save the Duce." The gold gleamed merrily behind his words.

Fernando Mezzasoma put his glasses on and tucked his handkerchief away. He asked Bombacci with icy skepticism, "Are you so worried about the Duce? Or is it your own neck that concerns you?"

"I worry for my own welfare, certainly," Bombacci admitted. He was an older man with a short, graying beard, and his voice quavered with strain. "Only a fool would deny it. But the Duce is my primary concern. We must provide for his safety."

"And how do you suggest we do that?" Mezzasoma asked.

Bombacci hesitated. "Well, I've been thinking. Perhaps we could fly to Spain. I am told there are Italian torpedo planes at Ghedi, enough for us all. The Generalissimo would surely offer us sanctuary."

"Don't count on it," said a white-haired man sitting across from Bombacci. He was a military man, Italian Marshal Rodolfo Graziani. He thrust his jaw forward and declared, "Franco is a rabbit. He won't risk offending the Allies. Not even for us."

"It wouldn't have to be Spain," offered Guido Buffarini-Guidi, former Minister of the Interior. "If the torpedo planes are truly available, perhaps we could fly to South America. Or even to Polynesia. We could stage an accident and announce that the Duce is dead. They might not even bother to look for us."

Marshal Graziani made a sour face. "You don't understand the hopelessness of our military situation. The Allies control the air. Try to fly anywhere through the umbrella of British and American planes, and you won't have to stage the Duce's death. They'd shoot you out of the skies before you got fifty kilometers."

"What about Switzerland?" Buffarini-Guidi suggested. "We wouldn't have to fly if we sought sanctuary in Switzerland. We could drive. Put together a motorcade and drive."

"Yes, yes, Switzerland," Bombacci agreed eagerly. "The border is close. We could make it in a few hours."

"And be arrested at the border," Graziani warned. "The Swiss will not risk offending the Allies by allowing us free passage."

Bombacci shuddered. "It's true the Swiss might arrest us," he said. "But surely they would never hand us over to the Allies. It would be a breach of their neutrality, wouldn't it?"

Buffarini-Guidi glanced at the gold bullion and the stacks of currency. "Perhaps we could buy our safety," he suggested.

"Slink away if you wish," Graziani said. "But don't insult the Duce by asking him to go with you. The only honorable path is to fight. We must go to the Valtellina. And the treasury must go with us. Every pound of gold will buy us ten dead Americans. I'm certain the Duce agrees."

Mussolini, sitting with eyes half closed, didn't seem to be listening, but his gaze wandered to the shiny yellow ingots.

"The Valtellina is a noble thought," Mezzasoma said, "but let us not be too hasty. There may still be a chance for an honorably negotiated peace. The ecclesiastics won't want to settle for an Allied victory if it means leaving the partisans in power. There are too many Communists involved at the higher levels of the resistance movement. I think we should approach Cardinal Schuster and ask him to intercede on our behalf with the Vatican. Perhaps we can arrange acceptable terms."

"Peace. Escape. These are pipe dreams," Graziani muttered.

Francesco Barracu cleared his throat. "Marshal Graziani has a point," he said. Barracu was a civilian, undersecretary to Mussolini's Salò cabinet, but Barracu still thought like a military man. On his lapel he wore a gold medal, signifying he had been disabled in battle. "The Church will never help us," he said. "We must fight, my friends. It's the only course open to us. If we wish history to treat us with honor, we have no choice. But why go to the Valtellina? Let us make our stand here. In Milan. Let us turn the Prefecture into an armed bunker and go down in glory."

Mezzasoma reacted with horror. "No, no," he said. "We can't do that. To make a final stand in a heavily populated area such as this would alienate the Milan Curia forever. We must not make enemies of the Church. We may need help when all is done."

"Nonsense," Barracu said. "If we must die, let us die here in Milan, publicly, in the open, where people can see it."

Bombacci's eyes watered. "Need we talk so much of dying?"

A gust of wind rattled the window and a breath of air slipped through a crevice above the sill, stirring the piles of currency on the benches. A few crisp notes fluttered from the top and fell soundlessly on the carpet. No one made a move to retrieve them.

"To fight in Milan is pointless," Graziani insisted. "If we are to have any chance of success, we must go to the Valtellina. Only there can we gather our Black Brigades. Costa, on his own initiative, has already sent two hundred riflemen and some artillery units to prepare the way. Pavolini will see to the rest." He nodded toward a Blackshirt officer, Alessandro Pavolini, secretary of the Neo-Fascist Party. "But we must not delay. We must make our decision now."

Alessandro Pavolini said, "There will be no delay. I've already dispatched orders to our best Black Brigades in the provinces of Liguria, Veneto and Emilia. I have instructed them to fall back to the Po Valley and make their way to Lake Como. Within a week, we will have twenty thousand men ready to join us in the Valtellina."

Mussolini, who had remained silent through most of the discussion, finally stirred. "Twenty thousand?" he murmured in a deep voice. "I thought you expected fifty thousand?"

Pavolini shrugged apologetically. "We have been forced to revise our estimates. But I can guarantee twenty thousand, Duce. And with twenty thousand men, the Valtellina will hold firm."

Mussolini's left eye twitched and his face turned gray. He shifted his eyes once more to the stacks of gold bars, gleaming invitingly in the reflected sunlight, but he didn't seem to see them.

Buffarini-Guidi, who had been busily making notes on the back of an envelope, now looked up and said, "I think I may have the answer. All we need is a submarine. It wouldn't have to be a big one. If my figures are correct, we could construct a fifteen-man submarine for something in the range of three billion lire. We have the money. And we can get more."

"A submarine?" Graziani scoffed. "Even if we had the time to build one, what would we do with a submarine?"

"We'll use it to flee," Buffarini-Guidi said. "It shouldn't take us more than three months underwater to reach some small island in the Pacific. We could take the rest of the gold with us. Bombacci, get a map. I'm certain there are some small uninhabited islands east of Borneo where we could . . ."

Graziani rolled his eyes. "Spain. Polynesia. Now, Borneo? Such foolishness. My God, what will you think of next?"

Mussolini moved uncertainly in his chair. His eyes flickered nervously toward Marshal Graziani. He said, "It wouldn't hurt to look. Get the map, Nicola."

3

The difficulties of lugging a set of Chinese checkers up and down a mountain had not diverted Landry from bribing a friendly corporal to swipe one off a table in the flight-standby room at Cecina. The moment his idle glance settled on it, he knew he had to have it for Viviana. Chinese checkers were a craze, and Viviana loved both the very newest thing and the very old.

Crouching over his pack, Landry hefted the bag of colored marbles and tried once again to decide. Tuck the awkward pitted board with its six-pointed star in the front of his sweater, kangaroo-style? Tuck the marbles in the pack? Or jettison them? Three pairs of nylons were already in the pack. They took up so little room that there was no problem in taking them with him to the village of Rezzonico, even if he were to conclude that he would avoid Viviana, cut her dead, refuse to have anything further to do with her.

The Chinese checkers were to have been the really special present, a proper hello in lieu of the proper good-by he hadn't said. A peace offering to assuage the guilt he'd felt, realizing how difficult the good-by would have been. How could he have said a proper adieu to the best-loved component of happy anarchy? So long, Viviana. It hurts like hell to think I'll never see you again, but there was never much of a future for us, was there? You love gleaming new satins and antique bibelots too much ever to be happy in a construction shack in Siam. By-by, lovely dilettante, up to your smooth, soft neck in war but unable to take even war seriously. You belong in an airy villa by a blue lake, or, siren that you are, sunbathing on a rock off Capri. When this dreary war ends, given the lucky men who always flock around you, you'll probably never give another thought to me.

Thinking now of the men, thinking more precisely of Holloman, Landry tossed the marbles aside. Dante's news had been bitter—to think that Holloman, a man Landry disliked thoroughly, had moved in with the woman he thought he loved. Not that it should have come as a total surprise. Holloman had shown an instant fascination for Viviana. In fact, Holloman, who seemed to think he had something special to offer sexy ladies, had insisted on "consulting" with Viviana on the very day Luisa and the others were caught. Landry figured he was as broad-minded as any member of his generation, but wasn't possession a part of any love? And to have a possession manhandled by a lousy sonofabitch who . . .

Shadow fell across the opening to Landry's hut. In the instant before he looked up from his pack, Landry began to whistle. He was afraid hot jealousy might be painted on his face, or some angry word framed on his mouth, and he tried to pretend he'd just been absently whistling a song, singing a word or two, certainly not sitting and growling jealously to himself over memories better left untapped. Then he did glance up, and it was with pleasure that he saw Freddy Stefanini leaning through the gap. Behind Stefanini, standing with the slightly shy smile of a person who is eager to see you but doesn't want to intrude, was Wesley Creedmore. Stefanini said, "May we come in?"

"Sure," Landry said. "I was hoping I could grab some time with you two before I head down to the lake." In their brief time together, Landry had come to think of Wesley Creedmore and Freddy Stefanini as buddies, if not fast friends. Freddy Stefanini had struck Landry as a kind of displaced person, much like himself, which was the first bond. Stefanini was a demolitions expert, though he also served as the ALOT unit's radio officer, and he had apparently come to Italy with an outsider's sense of coming home, only to discover he was still an outsider. He'd joked about it. "In Queens, everybody called me an Italian, when they were being polite about it, but do you know what these damned Eyeties call me here? A foreigner. I guess that makes me a man without a country, doesn't it?" But Landry could see that it bothered Stefanini, and he thought he could see other things too—a quick, natural shrewdness and a sensitivity to the feelings of others, traits that Holloman apparently never even suspected were there.

Wesley Creedmore, on the other hand, always seemed too bustling to give much thought to what other people were thinking. It was as though he had so much energy that he had to use it on whatever came to hand. More wood was needed for the campfire? The moment you started out to look for an armload, you met Creedmore already coming back with wood stacked up to his chin. He was as quick with a favor for a friend as he was to fire on a foe, and he always seemed surprised to be thanked for either. The fact that both young men were dedicated killers, that either of them could rake a knife across a man's throat or put knee to back and snap a man's spine without so much as a second thought, bothered Landry not at all. War did much to warp one's values. Killing was not only an occupational hazard, but also a professional duty. Put these same two young men back on the peacetime streets of America, as druggists or shoe salesmen, without changing their newly acquired characteristics and war-deadened regard for life, and you couldn't trust them for a moment. Landry knew there were hundreds of thousands of men like Stefanini and Creedmore, himself included, who would soon have to unlearn the process of killing without passion. In the meantime, in a kill-or-be-killed world, a cold-blooded approach to life and death was not only easy to overlook, it was even a trait to be admired and applauded.

Stefanini bent to squeeze through the narrow opening. Creedmore came after him. They sat tailor-fashion on the dirt floor, and Stefanini cleared his throat. He asked, "When're you going down to Rezzonico?"

"Just as soon as you and Rossiter finish the afternoon radio check and he gives me the word," Landry said.

"We've already done the radio check," Stefanini said. "Rossiter is off talking to Dante now." His eye fell on the abandoned Chinese checkers set. "Crazy baggage you've got there. A present for Viviana?" His question sounded very casual.

"I was thinking about it," Landry said. "But the board is too bulky. Maybe I'll leave it for another time."

Stefanini sat very still for a moment, hands clasping and unclasping in his lap, with nothing but the sound of wind breathing through cracks in the hut wall to fill the silence. Finally he said, "Creedmore and I have been talking, David. We think there's something you ought to know before you see Viviana."

"That Holloman moved in with her?"

Stefanini looked startled. "How do you know about that?"

"Dante told me."

"It isn't like it sounds. He didn't exactly move in. He was just hiding there."

"It's none of my business," Landry said. "She's a big girl. She can do what she wants."

"No, now wait," Stefanini said. "It wasn't like that. She didn't even know he was coming. And nothing much happened, either. I know. I was there, using her place as a radio setup while the others were out looking for Creedmore and Luisa." He stopped and ducked his head. "At least I was there most of the time. I guess Dante told you about that, too. He blames me for what happened. I was supposed to be watching out for Holloman, me and a couple of Dante's partisans. But when I found out where the Fascists were holding our guys, I took off. I guess I blew it."

Creedmore spoke up in his western twang. He was an Oklahoma boy, and although, like Stefanini, he liked to kid himself and bragged he had gone to college on a football scholarship "back East" at the University of Missouri, Oklahoma remained strong in his speech. "You didn't blow anything," he said. "If you hadn't shown up when you did, there wouldn't have been anything left of us but three big grease spots." He glanced uneasily at Landry. "I know it sounds rotten, considering what must have happened to Holloman, but I figure three for one is a pretty good trade."

"There didn't have to be a trade," Stefanini said. "If I'd sent for Dante and the others, instead of going off half cocked and leaving Holloman by himself at Viviana's house, all four of you might have been okay."

"Why Viviana's house?" Landry asked.

"Aw, you know how stubborn Holloman was," Stefanini said. "He got it in his head that someone was going to make a try for that satchel of money he was carrying, and he wouldn't listen to any of us. He insisted he had to hide. I guess he was still pretty mad at you for busting him in the nose, so when it came to picking a hiding place, he wouldn't settle for anything but Viviana's house. He claimed he had some unfinished business."

"Yeah, I can imagine," Landry said. His jaw tightened. He found it a pity to think that Holloman was apparently already dead. He almost wished the privilege of killing the man had been saved for himself.

Landry's conscious mind concentrated on what Stefanini was saying, but his memory, stirred by thoughts of Viviana, was on other things, angry things. Holloman, tall, slightly balding, showing an early tendency toward paunch, suddenly appearing on the lake with the other ALOTs. Holloman, incongruously sporting a slim gold pocket watch with, of all things to wear to war, a Phi Beta Kappa key on the watch fob, brandishing written orders that instructed the partisans to see to his needs. Holloman, instantly arrogant and abrasive, and, worse yet, flashing banknotes and gold sovereigns from his satchel of OSS funds. And then the final act of obtuseness, switching tactics at the last moment on the way to a lakeside meeting with four Milanese representatives of the Comitato di Liberazione Nazionale per l'Alta Italia, ordering the ill-fated Luisa and Creedmore and Piccione to wait in a small albergo while he ran a personal errand, going, yes, to Viviana's house and staying too long, so long that Luisa and the others were spotted and arrested by a flying squad of Blackshirts.

It had turned cold that February day when Landry learned what Holloman had done. Wind blew down from Switzerland just to the northwest, moaning of snow on the high mountains, and its gusts had darkened the lake, always blue, to a deep hyacinth color. Then came Holloman, his nose red with cold, grumbling because no one had advised him to take a scarf and gloves, bustling up the rocky slopes to Dante's camp, alone. He'd missed his meeting, he said, and now he needed fresh escorts to try again. Landry, acting as translator, had stared in confusion at the empty trail behind Holloman. Fresh escorts? What had happened to his first escort? Without the slightest trace of guilt, Holloman had told them. Luisa and the others had gotten themselves caught, he complained. He'd only been off at Viviana's for a few minutes, but they had foolishly allowed themselves to be cornered by Fascist soldiers. Landry and Dante had both panicked. Brushing Holloman aside, they quickly gathered Dante's band of poorly armed partisans and ordered them down to the lakeside to find the missing trio before the Blackshirts got around to handing them over to the German SD. Time was vital. Once the German security people cut through the tangle of Fascist red tape and got their hands on captives, the eventual end was certain: questioning under unmentionable circumstances, then when they were drained, being dropped, hands bound, feet bound, bellies split open so they wouldn't rise, into a hole of deep water known as the Cernobbio vortex.

But Holloman wouldn't have it. He demanded that Landry and Dante give up any idea of a time-wasting search. His orders and his mission, he insisted, were far more important than the fate of any three minor individuals. Landry told him where he could stuff his orders and his mission, so Holloman got huffy and tried to pull rank. When that didn't work, Holloman pulled a gun. In the few seconds that it took for the gun to change hands, Holloman just happened to get his nose broken. He ended on the seat of his pants, staring up at his own .45 automatic, with his life only a hair-trigger pull from ending. It took the combined efforts of X. B. Kavanaugh and Freddy Stefanini to drag Landry away from him. One more moment of time, and Landry might have faced a court-martial instead of merely being yanked from the lake.

". . . almost a week before we heard anything," Stefanini was saying. "Then Harry Tucker dug up some people in Tremozzo who told him about daily German SD visits to a Fascist cell down there. Harry checked it out and found an old woman who cleaned up the cell block every afternoon, and she said the Germans had already started interrogations. You know what that means."

"I understand," Landry said. He glanced at Creedmore's maimed hand and was instantly sorry. Creedmore flushed so deeply that his freckles disappeared, and he hastily tucked the hand out of sight. "So you left Holloman and went to Tremozzo on your own?" Landry asked.

Stefanini's mouth compressed. "I figured I had to. Tucker thought he'd been spotted, and he was feeling kind of chicken about going back. And you know me, I just kind of blend into the surroundings. I figured I could get the old lady to smuggle them a gun, maybe in her wash pail or under her petticoats or something. It never occurred to me that Holloman would go wandering off the minute I was gone. And it isn't like I left him alone. Viviana was there. So were the two partisans."

"Why did he leave?"

"No one knows. He didn't tell Viviana. There was apparently a lot of whispering between him and the partisans, then the three of them just took off. Dante's people found the partisans the next day. Holloman was gone."

"Could Holloman have shot the partisans?"

"I doubt it," Stefanini said. "He was a jerk, but he wasn't that bad. Besides, Gualfiero was still alive when they found him. He wasn't making much sense, but he kept muttering something about Germans. Dante had townspeople from Acquaséria carry the kid up the lake to his family. I guess the trip was too much for him. His cousin brought word that he died a couple of days later."

Landry asked the next question more slowly. "There's been talk of an informer. Do you believe it?"

Stefanini shrugged. "Hell, I don't know. We've had a lot of trouble lately, but that might just be bad luck. The Germans have got a pretty sharp old guy running the security branch down in Cernobbio. Man named Richter. The partisans call him by a pretty mean nickname, because of all the bodies that get dumped in the water, but he's too good to take lightly. He's on our tails all the time."

"He's tough," Creedmore said. "I'll grant you that. But he isn't doing it by himself. He's had help. And from someone close to us, too."

"You sound pretty certain," Landry said.

The two ALOTs exchanged looks and Creedmore said, "Somebody had to warn the Germans that we were about to bust out of that jail in Tremozzo. Okay, Dante doesn't believe it. He claims there isn't any informer, or leastwise if there is, it's someone down on the lake and not up here. He's always going on about how if I hadn't lost my head and shot up the place, the Germans wouldn't be bothering us anyway. All I know is that there were three of them waiting when we busted out. And they weren't there by accident, either. They were hiding. If I hadn't shot them, they'd sure as hell have blown away Piccione and Luisa and me."

Shadow flickered at the entrance again. Rossiter and Dante stood just outside, peering in at them. "What's this?" Rossiter said. "Some kind of private party?" The hut, small and airless already, suddenly seemed to shrink.

"Just catching up on the last couple of months," Landry said. "Stefanini tells me you've finished radio contact. Any news of Mussolini?"

Rossiter nodded. "He's still in Milan. So far, he shows no sign of moving. Maybe we'll have time to get ready after all." He bent over, as though intending to enter the hut, then apparently decided it was too crowded. Still standing outside, he said, "There's something else. You heard what I told Pietro about the money for this Valtellina thing. Now the Germans tell us there's even more than we expected. Somebody, an SS man in Milan or something, has seen maybe fifty boxes of currency and a whole mountain of gold bullion sitting in one of the rooms at the Prefecture. Sounds like they're emptying every bank vault they can get their hands on."

Landry whistled softly. "How much?"

"Hell, I don't know. The original estimate was maybe fifty or sixty million dollars. If it's higher than that, I don't want to think about it. You might keep it in mind, though. If you need an incentive to wave in front of these Federation guys, drop a couple of hints about the money."

"I'll use it if I have to," Landry said. "When do I leave?"

"You might as well take off now," Rossiter said. "Dante wants to send a couple of people down with you. The girl, for one. I okayed it."

"Luisa?" Landry said.

Dante nodded. "If there is to be action, I want her in a place of safety. You will take her to Viviana for me, David. Veterano will go with you. He can put you there before daylight."

Landry raised an eyebrow. "I thought you . . ."

"What I said yesterday has no bearing," Dante told him

quickly. "The situation has changed. I do not want Luisa exposed to any more danger. She will be safer with Viviana."

Landry bowed to fate. Wordlessly, he added the bag of marbles to his pack and tucked the Chinese checkers board under his sweater next to his stomach. Though unanswered questions still nagged at the back of his mind, he would be seeing Viviana after all. He had to admit he was happy at the prospect.

Dante left to fetch Luisa and Veterano, and Landry crawled out of the hut, dragging his gear after him. Stefanini helped Landry settle the pack comfortably on his back and strap it. Landry reached for his Thompson, but the gesture was automatic, absent-minded. He didn't know quite what to think about the obsessive suspicion that there was an informer at work among them. It made so little sense, unless you kept reminding yourself that spies and espionage were the stock in trade of men like the ALOTs, and even of Dante's men, who had a way of seeing a Fascist sympathizer behind every bush. Maybe the suspicion was just a phantom born of too little food and too much time on a chill mountainside; their own nocturnal visitor, like Landry's recurrent dreams. Yet, it would do no harm to be careful.

"Will you guys do me a favor?" Landry asked. He didn't exclude Rossiter, but he directed the words largely to Stefanini and Creedmore.

Stefanini said, "Anything you want."

Landry checked the action on the Thompson and tucked it under his arm. "Keep your eyes open, will you? I'd be just as happy if none of Dante's people goes down the mountain while I'm gone. Or anyone else, for that matter. I'd rather not have any Germans waiting when we get to Rezzonico. Capisce?"

"You got it," Stefanini said.

4

The raven of the night, the black-crowned night heron, had two ripening moons all to itself that night over Lake Como. Flying with long neck curled and head pulled well in, the heron could see both the moon in the heavens and its pallid reflection in the waters below. Dimmer starlight also reflected from a placid surface where the only other glimpse of light was a touch of phosphorescence—fish darting, or fireflies probing the lakeside gardens. All else was darkness. From the villages sleeping along the shore, there were no flaring street lights, no pale yellow above closed doorways, no gleam from tightly curtained windows. The villages of Lake Como, like the rest of German-occupied Italy, were under strict blackout rule, and the land lay dark and quiet.

Had the heron risen on a column of warm air swirling up from the lake, and risen high enough, it could have seen the startling carpet of lights to the west, across the mountains. Neutral Swiss cities such as Locarno and Bellizona and Lugano—especially Lugano, less than fifteen miles from the eerie wartime darkness of the lake—had glittered peacefully throughout the conflict. National borders were seldom so obvious. Yet, in wartime, when belligerent nation stood cheek to jowl with neutrality, the difference was remarkable. One passed from fear and deathly darkness to cities glowing against the sky. Store fronts, brightly lit, jammed with hard-to-find items, lined the streets. Sidewalk cafes continued to operate under strings of carnival-bright lightbulbs. Cars moved openly, headlights shimmering. One could put match to cigarette without cupping hands and worrying that it might be seen by an enemy.

In just such a peaceful neutral city, amid brightly lit store fronts and gaudy sidewalk cafes and headlighted moving cars, the OSS operational director named Cornfield, collar turned up against the evening chill, cupped his hands from force of habit and lit his cigarette. He had been trying for months to quit smoking, but it was a futile battle. Codes and charts and pins on maps filled his life with tension, and tension fueled his need. Perhaps if he had a quiet job, something minor in the Quartermaster Corps or running a unit of Military Police somewhere stateside . . . But he knew better. Tension follows a worrier, no matter what the task, and Cornfield was a chronic worrier.

He inhaled deeply and checked his watch. Almost ten, and still no sign of the embassy car. Dulles had set an immediate rendezvous, as though it were important, and Cornfield had dropped everything to stand on this street corner with his nerves jangling and the litter of half-smoked Chesterfields growing at his feet. Something new to do with Sunrise, no doubt. General Wolff was due back in Switzerland any minute now. Maybe Dulles had heard something. Perhaps the negotiated peace would become a reality after all.

At last, the car. Cornfield dropped his freshly lit cigarette and ground it under heel as he had the others, watching the big, black, chauffeured Chrysler glide through Bern traffic. As it pulled up beside him, he saw the reason for the delay. Sitting in the back, next to Dulles, was Hobart, the political analyst. If Dulles had taken the time to pick him up, it was Sunrise, all right. But it couldn't be good. Hobart's face was tight with worry.

Dulles rolled down his window and Cornfield stepped off the curb to lean in. Cornfield said, "What is it? Trouble?"

Dulles sighed. "I'm afraid so. We just received a coded communiqué from the Joint Chiefs. We've been ordered to break off all contact with the German emissaries. The Sunrise matter is finished."

Cornfield was rocked. "My God, why?"

"It seems the Russians have complained," Dulles said bitterly. "They've accused us of deceit. They claim we're trying to arrange a separate peace with the Germans."

"Only in Italy," Cornfield said. "Italy has nothing to do with the Russians. Why should Sunrise bother them?"

"Who knows what will bother the Russians these days?" Dulles said. "At any rate, the new President and the Prime Minister have decided this is an inconvenient time to anger our Eastern Allies, so we've been ordered to pull in our horns. Sunrise is dead. At least for the moment."

"But General Wolff will be here tomorrow. What can we tell him?"

"We tell him nothing. We're not even to speak to him. The communiqué was quite specific. Hobart and I are on our way to cable Washington and London, to ask them to reconsider. Even if they agree, it will take time. Perhaps as much as a week. I doubt Wolff will wait."

"What about the Lake Como team?" Cornfield said. "Major Rossiter? Do we warn them that things have gone sour and pull them out?"

Hobart leaned across to the window. "I would advise doing so," he said. "They won't be of much use to us, even if Sunrise is reactivated. Given this delay, I'm afraid we'd be in for a clash of wills on Lake Como. The lake is Comrade Ugo's territory."

"Who's Comrade Ugo?" Cornfield asked.

"One of the Communist resistance leaders who sit on the National Committee of Liberation in Milan. He holds political responsibility for the lake region. You've seen the formal complaints from Milan about the nondelivery of the Holloman funds. We think Ugo is behind them. I suppose I've been worried all along that the Communists might get wind of our Lake Como preparations and get Ugo on our tails. I'm told he's tough, even for a Communist."

In a tone as bitter as Dulles's, Cornfield said, "Why didn't you tell us this before?"

Hobart sighed. "I thought you were aware of the complexities of the Italian resistance movement."

Cornfield was silent. He had considered the complexities often, even though he didn't profess to understand them. The Italian resistance was no longer a tightly knit, monolithic organization. It was composed of six different political groups, each with its own ideological persuasion and its own degree of activity, and now with the war winding down, each of the groups had begun to think more about postwar prominence. Ambition and party policy had replaced mutual co-operation, and the result was often chaotic. The situation had created problems for more than one of Cornfield's field teams.

"I'll get on the radio tonight," Cornfield said. "I'll tell them to pack up and pull out."

Dulles stroked his mustache thoughtfully. "No, don't say anything just yet," he said. "Let's carry on as though nothing has changed."

"Sir?" Cornfield said. "Shouldn't we at least warn them? If Sunrise is dead . . ."

"We may yet get Sunrise back on active status," Dulles said. "If we do, I want Rossiter's team in a position to help us. As for this Ugo, he's only one man, fifty miles away. He can't do us any harm. Let's just pretend everything is copesetic, for the time being. You can always warn them later, if it becomes necessary."

"But they could get themselves killed," Cornfield objected. "And if Sunrise is finished, it could be for nothing."

Dulles showed irritation. "We'll have to consider them expendable," he said. "Sunrise is the issue now. If we can't get it back on track, thousands might die. A handful of men on Lake Como become unimportant by comparison."

Cornfield clenched his teeth. "Yes, sir. Very well. Sir."

Dulles frowned slightly, perhaps not liking the unnecessary emphasis Cornfield had put on the "sir," but he let it pass. He said, "Everything will work out. You'll see. Let's just keep our priorities in order." He gestured for the driver to move on.

As the limousine pulled away, Cornfield shivered and tugged his collar tighter around his throat, though the evening was no colder now than it had been before. Without thinking, he reached for another cigarette and stuck it in his mouth. It wasn't until the match flared and came toward his face that he realized what he had done. He plucked the cigarette from his lips and stared at it. He almost threw it away. Then he thought about Rossiter and Landry and the Britisher and the ALOTs and all the partisans above Lake Como, deep behind enemy lines, in constant peril, prepared to sacrifice themselves if necessary to stop an aging dictator and his fleeting dreams of glory. And for what? Perhaps for nothing.

Deliberately, Cornfield stuffed the cigarette back in his mouth and lit it, then puffed furiously, almost greedily, as he headed back toward his office.

Day Three

Monday—April 23, 1945

*Mai non s'è udito
di straniero marito
che sia tornato al suo nido.*

Yet who has ever heard
of a foreign lover
returning once he's departed.
   —Puccini, *Madama Butterfly*

1

Viviana Armellini awakened to the feel of her maid's hand roughly shaking her shoulder, and from the smell of damp earth and crushed mint she knew instantly that Franca had slipped into the garden to meet her newest admirer. Viviana's maid was forty-six, while the admirer, a village mason, was surely not a day beyond his twenty-fifth birthday, and Viviana's first sleep-numbed thought was to wonder, not for the first time, how in the world Franca did it.

"Three partisans have come," Franca said. In the candlelight, Viviana saw that she was smiling.

Viviana didn't heed the words. It couldn't be much past two in the morning, and she was sleep-stupid. She stared dreamily at Franca's old black dress and untidy black hair as if at some somber mystery. Even in the flickering light, two deep wrinkles showed between the maid's eyebrows, and the years had etched sad parentheses around an undistinguished mouth, so surely the attraction didn't lie in Franca's face. Yet the face was always animated, and Franca's movements were lithe and quick. Viviana had seen her dance once, at a village festival, and she was as light as a twenty-year-old girl. What was her body like, under that faded black fabric? Even more mystifying, how did Franca maintain her reputation as a respectable woman in a village where Viviana, who regarded herself as far more discreet about her lovers, caused nothing but raised eyebrows?

"Get up," Franca insisted. "They ask for you."

Franca chattered on about something, but Viviana was busy yawning. She ran strong, nervous hands through her own untidy hair, and gave a moment's thought to Franca's young mason. A fishhook embedded in his right thumb, a clumsily treated infection, had left him the use of only his left hand and kept him out of the war, but he was skillful even with only the one hand. It was well. Viviana had to have a mason in for several days every year. The village houses ran down the hill to the lake, and they were always slipping. Each spring brought new cracks that needed to be plastered. But the young man had worked so quietly, hardly saying a word. When had Franca found a chance to ensnare him? Viviana had known his fate only after all the work had been done, and she'd heard Franca laughing at him in the kitchen.

Reluctantly, Viviana threw the covers back. She was a chronically chilly person, and April nights were cool. "Who waits?" she asked carelessly.

"Three partisans," Franca repeated. "One is il signore. Your American. The one with the shoulders who knows how to fix things. He must try the water heater. I weary of carrying all those buckets."

Viviana stiffened. Then she slipped from her bed and grabbed the candle. In three long strides, she was at her mirror, gazing apprehensively at golden-brown hair cut in a silky pageboy bob and restless blue eyes that gazed back from . . . Holy God, what had happened to the delicate oval of her face? Was that the beginning of two furrows between her own strongly marked eyebrows? The mirror sternly informed her that more than mere months must have passed since the last time she saw David Landry.

The brows drew together as Viviana silently argued back at the lying mirror. It was only a little over two months. She had seen those square, well-set shoulders move out her front door with a feeling of such irritation that only the fact that she loved the old flowered bowl full of potpourri she'd put on a rosewood table by the door had prevented her from throwing it at him. Such a puritan young man. Arguing. Always arguing, this time because his jealousy had chosen one of his own countrymen, Major Holloman, as a target. "Do you think you are my father?" she'd screamed at one point. "He thinks I should be a perpetual virgin. Do you dream what it is to be born a female in Italy?" Later, he'd stormed out, his footsteps fading up the narrow, crooked street, and he'd not even had the courtesy to come and apologize when the Americans had ordered him from the lake. To part, Viviana had thought forever, with a quarrel . . . But now . . . A pink tinge climbed from the collar of her favorite pajamas and gave freshness and bloom to the oval face at which she had been frowning. Viviana turned from the mirror. "I'll dress," she told Franca. "The new silk slacks. Did you sew a button on the shirt?"

"Why dress?" Franca said. "And your ugly slacks, never. They'll be too slow to take off later."

"You have missed your century," Viviana snapped. She seized her hairbrush and began rapidly to tidy her hair. "You should have been a medieval procuress, one of those old women who infiltrated convents under guise of selling thread, and whispered love messages from dubious men into the ears of young schoolgirls. Slut, you didn't sew the button on. Oh never mind. My shoes. Where are my black sandals?"

Within five minutes, Viviana followed her grinning maid to the head of the stairs. Even if Franca had not already told her who waited, her breath would have come faster at the sight of the man who waited at the foot. The hard, confident face. The shock of stubborn hair falling over the high forehead. The casual grace of the tall body, despite the rough peasant's clothing he affected, as, calmly, unhurriedly, he started up to meet her, one hand outstretched. It was Landry, it was sun, it was glorious spring, after gray and dreary winter.

"Why, David," Viviana said in a voice she was gratified to notice was both controlled and cool. "What an unexpected pleasure." Partially but not solely because of the presence near the door of the two partisans who had accompanied Landry, Viviana accepted the hand he held out to her and shook it politely.

Landry was actually turning red with annoyance. His other hand tightened on the heavy submachine gun he carried as if he would like to turn it on her. Delightful.

"You don't seem surprised that I'm back," he said.

"No, I'm not surprised," Viviana lied. "The whole village has been talking about a plane that landed on the lake. Obviously it was neither German nor Fascisti, not the way the Blackshirts have been rushing around seeking its passengers. Ergo, an American plane. Ergo, bringing an American." Maliciously, she added, "Although it had occurred to me that it might be another handsome, agreeable stranger like Major Holloman."

There, Landry's flush was deepening. But why did one take such pleasure in goading him? Cautioning herself to stop it, Viviana crossed to the big, hooded fireplace that occupied one whole side of the room, and gestured for the partisans to come warm themselves by the embers. Only then did she see that one was a woman, and a young woman she knew, Luisa Galeazzi. At the sight of Luisa's ruined face, Viviana felt her superficial poise evaporate. She clutched her black silk shirt—Viviana always wore black; "It's so convenient for funerals," she would say, but she knew that it became her—over her stomach, where the button was missing, and said, "Luisa, my dear, how nice you look. Just let me build up the fire. Franca? Franca, what do we have in the house to eat?"

Luisa quietly introduced an old fellow, and Viviana bit hard on her lower lip to dam her effusions. Poor Luisa. The mere sight of the girl had become so profoundly uncomfortable since she fell into Fascist hands. Viviana snatched up a black cashmere shawl, disturbing one of her pair of spoiled white cats who had chosen it as a bed, and covered her gaping blouse with it while pretending to hug it around her to keep warm. "Sit," she said. "Franca will bring wine. Then you will tell me how I can help you."

The old partisan obviously felt uncomfortable in a parlor. Or perhaps, like the villagers, he had heard cause to disapprove of

Viviana. He waited unsmiling until Luisa was comfortably seated by the now leaping fire, as solicitous as an old shepherd folding an ailing lamb, then followed Franca to the kitchen. Landry sat, too, although with a curious stiffness, and answered Viviana's question.

"Would you mind if Luisa stayed with you awhile? Dante wants her in a safe place. It looks as if we're in for a little action, and Dante doubts the security of his camp."

His tone was businesslike. Viviana tried to match it. "Action, yes. I am told the Fascisti in Como seem to be making preparations of some kind. They are said to be expecting Black Brigade reinforcements from the south. I had hoped to send word to Pietro as soon as I learned more."

"Have you had any word concerning Mussolini?"

Viviana tried to remember. "Only that he is rumored to be in Milan."

"We know that," Landry said. "No mention of his coming here? To the lake?"

"None that I have heard," she said. "Why is Dante worried about the security of his camp?"

Landry sighed. "There's talk of an informer."

"Oh surely that is incorrect. Who among us would help the Germans, with victory so near?"

"No one knows," Landry said. He looked at her hesitantly, as though he wanted to say more, perhaps ask her a question, but then his eyes veered off and the moment was past. He covered by saying, "Dante seems to think the Americans blame him. Because he belongs to the Party."

"Nonsense," she said. She leaned back on an old, rose-colored divan whose priceless brocade she had allowed to become smoke-stained by keeping it too near the fire. "Dante's political beliefs are misguided, and I have told him so. He is an idealistic fool, and he places too much faith in his Communist fellows. I think he will be gravely disappointed someday. But he is no traitor."

Landry's face was impassive. "I'm sure you're right," he said.

"I doubt he appreciated my lecture," Viviana said. "Not only am I a woman, and therefore incapable of political thought, but also I fear Dante holds my father's wealth and position against me. As far as Dante is concerned, I'm the decadent offspring of an exploitative landowner." She laughed lightly.

Luisa's welted cheeks flushed. "Dante has never spoken so unkindly of you," she said.

"Perhaps not," Viviana said. "But he must surely think it. I have little patience with men who treat women as brainless chattels, and I fear I've offended him from time to time."

"He has never treated me as a brainless chattel," Luisa said. "Perhaps what bothers him is that you have chosen to stay here, in the comfort of your home, while others face the war in more austere surroundings."

Viviana felt her own face redden. "Oh my child," she said. "Now I fear I've offended you." She shrugged nervously and leaned closer to the fire. It was so cold. "I cannot apologize for the way I live," she said. "People tell me things, and I pass them on to the partisans. That is my war."

The others now looked as uncomfortable as Viviana felt. A silence fell. Viviana could hear the hiss of resin from a pine log in the fireplace. Franca finally came in with the wine and a warmed-over dish of rice and salt cod, and they made awkward conversation until Luisa rose and asked humbly if Viviana would be so kind as to . . . she felt so tired . . . a little sleep . . .

Viviana was half afraid that Landry would be gone before she got Luisa settled. But he sat stiffly staring into the fire, a thoroughly cleaned and empty plate in his hands, looking so worried and tired that Viviana suddenly cursed herself as a malicious bitch. She rushed to him, stepping on one of the cats in the process, and tried to take both his hands, but the plate got in the way.

"Oh I am so clumsy," Viviana said in exasperation. "And mean. David, I am a mean woman. I should have realized that Luisa might have a more than casual interest in Dante. And yet I insulted him, insulted her, to her face. Why can't I be more careful? Why can't I think before I speak?"

He looked sad. "We all say things we're sorry for later."

"But to belittle Dante, even in jest . . ." She sobered for a moment. "David, has it occurred to you that the informer, if there is one, might be someone who was angered by the way they treated you? Even Dante . . ."

"Dante has lost men, too," Landry said.

"I suppose so," she said. "Anyway, I should never have said those things about him."

"Perhaps you were within your rights," Landry said. "Luisa may not know it, but Dante all but accused *you* of being the informer."

"Me?" she said. Her cheeks reddened again. "How dare he! What possible reason could I have to become an informer?"

"It wasn't a matter of reason," he said. "More of opportunity. Dante told me about . . ." He stopped. "Well, it doesn't matter now. What matters is that you're well."

"Oh David," she said. "I *am* mean. I really am. All this time, I've been wanting to tell you—I am so glad to see you. One is so absurd at times. I suppose I feared I would never in this world see you again."

His face lightened. He looked around, perhaps for someplace to put the plate, and Viviana seized it and threw it in the fireplace. A man's voice spoke questioningly in the kitchen, then Viviana could hear Franca answer and laugh. The man laughed as well.

Viviana sighed and arranged herself comfortably at Landry's feet. Both his hands were available now, eagerly reaching to grasp hers, and Viviana no longer felt cold at all. She freed one hand to draw Landry's face down to hers, but he gasped, and she clambered up to her knees. "David, you're wounded!" she said. "Your poor stomach. Is it . . . ? They've put it all in a cast!"

He grinned and reached under his sweater. The reason for the curious stiffness of his posture appeared. It was a board with round holes all over it. "I brought you a present," he said. "It seems pretty silly now, but there are some nylon stockings in my pack."

"Real stockings," Viviana marveled, but her hands reached eagerly for the board. She turned it around and over to inspect it. "David, what is it?"

"A game everybody's playing. You play it with marbles. I'll show you how."

"Marbles, too?" she said happily. "I warn you, I'll win. I always beat the boys at marbles when I was a little girl." She saw Landry's eyes flicker, a small shadow, and although she wasn't sure why, she sought a safe topic. Laughter still came from the kitchen. "I hope Luisa's friend is only a friend and not an admirer," she murmured. "It sounds as though Franca is working her wiles on him. That woman. No man is safe around her."

The topic proved unsafe after all. In the firelight, she could see a questioning look appear in Landry's eyes, and an unspoken name—"Holloman"—hover near his lips.

But he didn't ask it. Not then. His old jealousy, if that's what it was, slept for a moment, and much later in the morning, when the church bells began to ring for early Monday Mass, Landry slept too. Viviana stayed awake awhile longer, watching his face and listening to the wisteria vine whisper scratchily in a moist morning breeze that soothed her own face. Franca had been wrong. When lovers were reunited, even lovers who spent too much time quarreling, silk slacks were not slow or difficult at all to slip off.

2

Mussolini's presence in Milan had also come to the attention of resistance leaders in that city, and with it, hints of the massive wealth accumulating in Mussolini's Fascist war coffers. While Landry slept on that Monday morning of April 23, 1945, a small company of Communist cell commanders hurried to a drab, unlit garage not far from the Pirelli tire works to discuss plans for seizing both the Duce and his chest of war funds.

The leader of the group was a man with thinning brown hair, a squashed, round face and a wide mouth that almost never smiled. He took his position at the front of the garage and called the meeting to order. He was an important man in the resistance hierarchy, holding as he did a seat on the National Committee of Liberation. His Party compatriots called him Comrade Ugo, but that wasn't his real name. Slight in stature, barely five-foot-five, with delicate, tapered hands and tiny feet, he looked brittle, almost effeminate, but no one who knew his reputation would ever dare challenge him.

Ugo leaned against a greasy tool counter and squinted resentfully at the others, mostly young men in their twenties and thirties. An odd light—some might call it cruelty, others strength—shimmered from his intense brown eyes. He singled out a newcomer sitting on the dusty running board of a Fiat, a recently elected rep-

resentative of the Volunteer Corps, a man who called himself
Valerio. Valerio had come highly recommended to Ugo. A dedicated Party worker, Ugo had been assured, one who would do as
he was told and keep quiet about it. But Ugo found the young
man irritatingly tall, with an irritatingly full head of dark hair
slicked back from his forehead. Valerio also wore a fussy black
mustache that Ugo found irksome. Nevertheless, the young man's
eager face radiated enthusiasm and Ugo thought he might find a
use for him.

"Comrade Valerio?" Ugo murmured. He was gratified to see
the man's spine stiffen. "Have you any suggestions to offer us?"

Valerio's response was predictably adequate but unimaginative.
He, like the others, had heard whispers that non-Communist
members of the Committee of Liberation had been approached by
one of Mussolini's ministers, Fernando Mezzasoma, who was attempting to arrange peace talks through the office of Ildefonso
Cardinal Schuster. Since a peace arranged by the Milan Curia
would not be politically expedient, Valerio favored all-out collab-
oration in a proposed general strike, one that was designed to
weaken government control and hasten the German withdrawal.
The strike, already organized and slated to begin on Wednesday,
only two days hence, might prove the catalyst to Mussolini's
downfall, Valerio suggested. Ugo made a mental note that Valerio
might best be used as a man of action, not for ideas.

One of the others, an ambitious cell commander named Sandrino, raised his hand impatiently and said, "We can't just assume
a passive role, not if we want to get our hands on Mussolini's
funds. We must move in actively. Why don't we organize the railway workers to sabotage tracks and persuade the electrical unions
to cut off the current to German barracks? If we keep the Germans busy enough, maybe we can storm the Prefecture. I could
get you a hundred men who would like to see Mussolini strung up
by his heels."

"What would we do about his German bodyguard?" Ugo asked.
"How do we force our way through them?"

"Twenty Germans at the most," Sandrino said. "He used to be
surrounded by an army."

Ugo appreciated Sandrino's spirit, but condemned his judgment.
"Twenty Germans armed with automatic weapons could present

quite an effective barrier," he told Sandrino gently. "Nevertheless, we'll keep your proposal in mind. If the Germans should choose to retire—and they might well do so in the next few days—we may give your frontal assault a try."

"What about Mussolini's whore?" asked a brash young cell leader near Sandrino. "I hear Clara Petacci has followed him here from Lake Garda. Maybe we could kidnap her and hold her for ransom. We could demand all the money. They say she's a good-looking woman."

"Would you trade a fortune for a woman?" Ugo asked him.

"Me?" the cell leader said. "Hell, no. I wouldn't care if she had boobs as big as di Coca peak." Some of the others snickered.

"What makes you think the Duce is any different?"

"Well, he's old and she's young," the man said. "He's held onto her for so many years, I'd say he's stuck on her." There was more laughter, and the young cell leader looked embarrassed. Defensively, he said, "Well, at least she would be easier for us to get our hands on. They say she's off in an apartment by herself, a couple of blocks away from the Prefecture, with only one or two German guards."

Ugo shook his head. "We're not here to make . . ."

A door opened at the rear of the garage and sunlight flooded in. Some of the men flinched, thinking raid, but it was only one of the volunteers who handled telephone traffic for the Committee of Liberation. The man made his way apologetically across the room and found a space on the running board. He tried to catch Ugo's eye, but Ugo ignored him.

"We are not here," Ugo began again, "to make war on women. Don't misunderstand me. If I thought Petacci would give us leverage, I'd be for taking her this very day. But she's useless to us. The Duce didn't even bother to bring her to Milan. She had to come crying and whining after him on her own. She's a plaything. Nothing more. The Duce has only one thing on his mind now. To save his own head."

"Maybe we could snatch a couple of his ministers," someone else suggested. "He might be willing to trade for someone important."

"I doubt it," Ugo said. "No, Sandrino is right. We must make our move toward the Prefecture and the funds themselves. But not a frontal assault. Perhaps we could . . ." The telephone volunteer tried again to get Ugo's attention, wriggling and snapping his fingers like a schoolboy with a need to go to the bathroom. Ugo frowned. "Yes?"

"If the subject of this discussion is Mussolini," the man said in a high, squeaky voice, "it may already be out of our hands. The Americans think he will soon leave Milan."

Sandrino, seated two spaces from the man, craned his neck and stared. "How do you know what the Americans think?"

"We just got a message from Lake Como," the man said. "An American OSS man named Landry is to meet this evening with members of the Como Federation to ask for partisan help in stopping Mussolini. One of our comrades called to ask for guidance."

Ugo was instantly interested. "And what did you advise him?"

"Nothing," the man said. "I told him instructions would be relayed within the hour by telephone. That's why I was late."

Ugo nodded thoughtfully. "Excellent," he said. "You are certain the Americans expect Mussolini to head for the lake country?"

The telephone volunteer shrugged. "That's what our colleague from the Federation said. He wasn't too sure of the details. Apparently they have only the word of some partisan come down from the hills. But the meeting has definitely been arranged, and they need someone of importance to tell them what to say."

Ugo scanned the faces before him. "What do you think we should tell them?" he asked Sandrino.

"Give them the green light," Sandrino said. "Stop the bastard."

The newcomer, Valerio, frowned. Ugo nodded for him to speak. "Forgive me," Valerio told Sandrino, "but it seems to me that Mussolini is Italian business. Why should we help the Americans?"

"What difference does it make?" Sandrino said. "This is an uncomplicated matter. Mussolini must not be allowed to escape. If we can't stop him here, then someone must stop him there."

"What about the funds?" another man asked. "The hill partisans are country simpletons. You let them help the Americans, and I guarantee the Americans will end up with all the wealth."

"An interesting observation," Ugo said. "But shouldn't we wait to see what the Americans have in mind? Perhaps they are privy to information that has eluded us."

Valerio waved his hand again. "They are still Americans," he said. "And Mussolini, to the disgrace of us all, is an Italian. If anyone writes finito to him, it must be an Italian, preferably a member of the Party."

Sandrino made a noise with his teeth. "We're more likely to screw around and let the bastard get away. A bullet is a bullet, no matter who fires it."

Ugo looked briefly from one face to another and made up his mind. He inclined his head to the telephone volunteer and said, "You did well to bring this to our attention, comrade. I will make the call myself and give them their answer."

3

While the cell leaders huddled together in the garage on the northern outskirts of Milan, a young German Waffen-SS officer walked from the Prefecture to an apartment building in the center of the city. He was Obersturmführer Helmut Häger, and his job was to protect Benito Mussolini. He had been called away from his duties this morning by a frantic note from Mussolini's mistress, Claretta Petacci.

Häger climbed the stairs to her apartment, dreading the storm of tears he was sure would confront him. He hesitated outside her doorway, his black-gloved fist poised to knock, and listened to the gramophone strains of Puccini coming from inside. A thickly Italian voice, marked by the ticks and scratches of many playings, sang:

> *Ragazzi, fate largo!*
> *Salute a Mister Ashby, dell'Agenzia Wells-Fargo.*

She was listening to Puccini's *Girl of the Golden West* again. How typical. Her world falling about her ears, and still she filled her hours with fanciful romanticism. Those sickening love novels that she gobbled by the dozens. Operas that pretended to deal with love and death and betrayal, but that did so with such cloying sweetness as to be unbelievable. Puccini was an ass. How much better her time would be spent listening to someone with power and strength. Wagner, for example. *Die Götterdämmerung*.

He sighed and rapped at the door. A moment passed and the gramophone music dropped to a decent whisper, then he heard the rustle of silks. "Who is it?" Timid, hopeful. Door still closed.

He said, "Lieutenant Häger, madam. I've come in response to your note."

"Oh of course." Rattle of chains. Inner lock turning.

The door opened and she looked up at him, her dark hair perfectly in place, dark eyes and lovely face a carefully prepared mask of sadness. He felt his breath catch in his throat. It always did when he saw her. A beautiful woman, even at thirty-three. How much more beautiful must she have been as a twenty-year-old when Mussolini first met her. One could hardly blame the Duce for being smitten.

He said, "At your service, Madam Petacci."

She pouted, a pretty, girlish moue. "You promised to call me Clara."

"Yes, Clara. I'm sorry."

She beckoned him in, then crossed to a couch ahead of him and offered coffee. Her movements were graceful and fluid, though a bit self-conscious. She knew she was beautiful and reveled in it. He felt color rising in his cheeks as he sat stiffly and took the proffered cup.

"It's so nice that someone at least has come to see me," she said. The practiced sadness returned with a delicate sigh.

"I can't stay long," he said. "My duty is at the Prefecture."

She sat opposite him on a blue-and-green, candy-striped chair, where the morning sun fell softly about her face, doing justice to her creamy complexion. "Why hasn't he sent for me?" she asked.

"The Duce has been extremely busy," Häger said. He sipped the coffee and looked away, trying to busy his eyes elsewhere. His primary duty, of course, was to look after Mussolini, which was why he had been assigned twenty of the toughest Waffen-SS troops in northern Italy. But Claretta Petacci, with all her dark good looks, was also a part of his duty. The German High Command had long since recognized that to keep Mussolini firmly under control, it was also necessary to maintain a watchful eye on the Duce's mistress. At least it had been until this abrupt withdrawal to Milan. For some reason, the Duce had not only abandoned his wife of many years and left her behind, he had also come away without a word to Clara Petacci. Even now, after she had followed him to Milan, Mussolini had shown no interest in seeing her.

"Too busy for me?" she said. "Are you sure he knows I'm here?"

"He knows, Madam Pet . . . Excuse me, Clara. But his time is consumed with conferences. Plans. Decisions. This is a very difficult period for him."

She accepted Häger's words, but there was hurt in her eyes. He wondered again, as he had many times before, if she could really be in love with the man. It was hard to see why. Certainly Mussolini had once been a robust, muscular conqueror, a man of strength and will, the all-powerful Caesar of Fascist Italy. But that had changed. Now he was just a tired, fat old man in poor health. There were those who claimed she maintained her liaison with him merely so her relatives, in particular her brother, could continue to exploit the situation. But Häger found that hard to believe. She had always seemed so genuinely concerned with the Duce's welfare.

Now she stood and wandered to the window. She seemed to be biting back the tears that Häger had feared, but that wasn't necessarily of any consequence. He knew she cried easily.

"A man has been watching my apartment," she said. "Is he one of yours?"

He was, but Häger decided to be magnanimous. "No, madam. He's a Blackshirt guard. The Duce ordered him personally to protect you and see to your safety."

Her hand went to her mouth and a little girl's voice said, "He did? He did that for me?"

"Of course," Häger lied. "You are in his thoughts constantly." Good God, he was beginning to sound like an Italian opera himself.

She raised her eyes demurely. "Will you take a message to him?"

"You know I will, madam. Anything you wish."

"Will you tell him . . ." She hesitated. "Tell him I know a place where we might go. It's a small house high on the Jocherhof peak, hidden in a pine forest. One can reach it by foot, they say, and we could hide there for years. I've committed every detail of the route to memory. If he would send for me, I could show him on a map. We could live quietly there."

"I'll tell him," Häger said. He set his cup down and rose. "Now I must return to duty. The partisans grow bolder by the day. I must see that my men are alert."

She crossed to him and took his hands. "Dear Helmut," she said. "You work so hard for him. I know you must be tired, yourself."

"Yes, madam. I am." He could have added that he was also discouraged, homesick, fed up with Italians and sick to death of the war. But he didn't. He had his duty.

"You will take care of him? You'll protect him at all costs?"

"With my life, if necessary." He didn't mention that he had no choice. It would be the firing squad for him if he allowed anything to happen to Mussolini. His orders were to stay close to the Duce wherever he went, to see to his safety. Not as easy as it sounded. The Duce was behaving so erratically these days. Almost as though the Germans were his enemies, rather than his protectors. Everything was so hectic. Too many ministers and their families gathering. So many valuables being brought. A fabulous treasure of gold and currency massing. Were they planning to flee? Where and when? How could he stop them?

"You're so kind," Clara Petacci said.

He bowed stiffly and snapped his heels.

As the door closed behind him and he carefully arranged his military cap on his head, he couldn't help frowning. The devil with her. He had his own neck to think about. How would she react if she knew his ultimate orders, handed down only a few days earlier? If the war continued to go against them and it appeared that Mussolini might fall into the hands of the enemy, Häger had been instructed to turn the guns of his own men on the Duce. Rather than allow him to be captured, Häger was to see to Mussolini's death himself.

Strains of Puccini rose once more from the room. The chorus

was calling for a necktie party for that poor miserable bandit, José
Castro:

> *Al laccio! A morte!*
> *Al laccio! Legatelo!*

4

Major Peter T. Rossiter, chafing with impatience, clambered over
a rocky ridge to the rear of Dante's partisan encampment and
hauled himself up among dwarf junipers for a better view of the
lakeside below. The water was particularly blue today, though
somewhat obscured by a noon haze. He could see the village of
Rezzonico clearly enough, though some of its roofs were hidden
behind a green-layered hogback, and he thought briefly of Landry,
down there among the enemy, sweating it out, no doubt a bundle
of nerves by now, waiting for the meeting. Farther to the north,
perhaps three miles up the winding lake road, was another fairly
sizable town—no, two of them, separated by the barest minimum
of space. Those would probably be the twin villages of Musso and
Dongo, if he remembered his map correctly. Wasn't there a bridge
between the two? Or a tunnel? If so, it might be a good place to
plant the explosive charges.

Bridges and tunnels. Damn it. He'd been trying to talk strategy
with Dante most of the morning, but either his Italian was insuffi-
cient or Dante was deliberately misunderstanding him. Every time
Rossiter raised a question, Dante would start that non capisco
business. Rossiter had the irritating suspicion that Dante understood everything he was saying, and was just pulling a stubborn
act, probably because Landry was out of pocket. These partisans
all seemed to think that Landry was running things, not Rossiter.
He would have to straighten that out, and soon. Not that he had
anything against Landry. But it was hard enough to run a military
operation without trained troops. To attempt it without a proper
understanding of who was in charge could be suicide.

Rossiter stretched his neck to follow the winding coast south, below Rezzonico. The town of Menággio should be down there somewhere, four or five miles beyond the bend. What had he heard about Menággio? There was a small feeder road that led up into the mountains, wasn't there? A road that wound up eventually at Lake Lugano and the Swiss border? What if they tried to stop Mussolini here near Rezzonico, and the crafty old bastard backed up and took the Menággio feeder road to Switzerland? Could the Blackshirts do an end run around Rossiter's roadblocks that way? Probably not. The Swiss would never allow Mussolini to violate their neutrality without a fight.

Still, it would be worth checking. Rossiter dropped down from his perch and started working his way along the ridge, hoping to get a better view toward the south. It was hot work, clinging to the rocks below the junipers, and he began to wish he'd brought a canteen with him. He was about to drop to a ledge when he heard odd noises coming from the trees. At first he thought it was a beetle or something, but then he recognized the clicking for what it was. Morse. Someone was off in those pines, tapping out a radio message. How could that be? Lieutenant Stefanini and his radio were back in Dante's camp.

He slid down from the rocks and backtracked a few feet to a slot among the boulders and worked his way through. On the other side of the jumbled rocks, a few thin pines wobbled skyward, stunted, as if they didn't get much water up here, and Rossiter paused, listening again for the clicks. Instead, he heard the high-pitched stutter of incoming Morse. Whoever it was, he was getting an answer. Rossiter cocked his ear and listened, but he couldn't make it out.

The incoming di-dits and da-dahs stopped and the hand-clicking started again as more Morse went out, and Rossiter pushed through a clump of bushes to get closer. The sound was deceptive. He made a wrong turn at one point, and when he backed up, he suddenly found himself standing above a narrow trench with a man at the bottom, leaning over a gray transmitter, the kind that had to be cranked to build up a charge. Pine boughs and leafy trash were pushed back, as though the radio had been covered and uncovered.

"What the hell are you doing?" Rossiter demanded. The man jerked around and stared up at him, and the key fell silent. "Oh it's you," Rossiter said. "How come you're way out here, so far from camp?"

The man climbed out of the trench, looking sheepish. He didn't say anything, just wiped his palms down the sides of his trousers, as though to dry away sweat.

Rossiter eyed him suspiciously. "Who were you signaling on that radio?" he asked. He leaned over the lip of the trench and peered at the transmitter, and his gaze fell on the markings below the dials. "That's a damned German radio," Rossiter spluttered. "What the hell are you doing with a damned German radio?"

The man moved slowly toward him.

Rossiter fumbled at his holster and pulled out the big .45 automatic. "Hold it right there," he said. "You better come up with some answers, fella. You've got a lot of damned explaining to do."

The man hesitated, and for a moment it looked as though he was in pain. He doubled over, and his right hand slid toward his boot. He teetered precariously on the balls of his feet.

Rossiter gaped at him and let the barrel of the automatic droop. "What's the matter with you?" he asked. "You hurt?"

Still the man said nothing, but his feet shifted and his chin came up. Too late, Rossiter realized that the man's curious posture was only a crouch before springing. He tried to raise the gun, tried to backpedal, but the man came driving up at him, empty hands swinging at Rossiter's arm. Rossiter felt stinging pain and the .45 went flying away in the dirt. Rossiter stared in bewilderment at his own right arm. A small slash through the wrist tendons suddenly bubbled red. "You crazy bastard," Rossiter cried.

Then he saw that the man's hand wasn't empty after all. He felt the knife going in below his rib cage, felt the white-hot stab of pain, felt great astonishment. A growl stuck in his throat and he tried to reach out with his arms, but the man withdrew the knife as easily as he had plunged it in and stepped away. Rossiter teetered, his eyes locked on the knife blade, shiny only a moment ago, now dulled with a greasy jacket of red, more red, Rossiter's own red. He felt pain again and winced, felt his astonishment turn to frustration, felt growing anger, lost hope, emptiness.

And then he felt nothing.

5

The upstairs room in Rezzonico where Landry was to meet with the Federation members turned out to be a modestly furnished apartment with a window overlooking the street, the kind where housewives lower small baskets on twine so the postman can deposit letters, rather than forcing him to trudge up dark and narrow stairways to make deliveries. The owner of the apartment, a fat, red-faced bartender who huffed and puffed at each landing, delivered Landry to the small flat without comment and opened the door for him, but wouldn't go in. Instead, he puffed back down the stairs and left Landry to make his entrance alone.

Three elderly gentlemen waited inside, seated primly in straight-backed wooden chairs, hands in laps. They offered no greeting. Landry recognized one of them, a cobbler from Como, but when he smiled and tried to say hello, the man looked away.

It didn't take Landry long to discover the reason for their coolness. He'd barely launched into his explanation when one of the men, a thin scarecrow with a beaky nose, shook his head and said, "I'm sorry. We have been instructed to reject your request. There will be no massing of the 52nd Garibaldi detachments."

Landry was stunned. "But why? Surely you see our problem?"

The three men looked at each other, and beak-nose said, "There is a fear in Milan that you will capture Mussolini and dispense American justice. It has been decided that Mussolini is an Italian problem demanding an Italian solution. We cannot help you."

Landry winced. "I'm sure the authorities in Milan have misunderstood," he said. "We have no intention of trying to capture Mussolini. We hope merely to thwart him, to turn him back. If he is allowed to pass unimpeded, the war could continue."

The cobbler seemed uncomfortable with the decision. He said shyly to his fellows, "This man is the American David Landry. He is known to us. He wouldn't lie. Couldn't we check with Milan again?"

The man with the beaky nose shook his head. "We have our instructions," he said. "They are quite clear."

"Perhaps my own explanation was not so clear," Landry said. He tried again, watching their faces for signs of understanding. Clearly they understood, but just as clearly they were not to be swayed. "There may be a great deal of money involved," he said reluctantly. "The Blackshirt Brigades will have a treasury of gold bullion and currency in their possession. Perhaps several billion lire."

It was the wrong thing to say. Though their faces registered interest and surprise, the beak-nosed man stood and drew himself up. "Signore, we are patriots. You cannot buy and sell our loyalties."

Landry frowned. "Please, you have misunderstood me," he said. "I did not intend such an insult. I meant only that with such a treasure at their disposal, once they reach the Valtellina they might even be able to buy their way to freedom. If we don't . . ."

But he had lost them. The man with the beaky nose nodded curtly to his companions and they all headed for the door. Only the cobbler looked back in timid apology.

Landry knew it would be useless to try to stop them, so he followed them to the head of the stairs and watched them tramp down the narrow well in single file. He stood alone in the darkness with his disappointment until their steps faded, then headed down himself.

The bartender must have deciphered the outcome of the brief meeting from the faces of the Federation men. When Landry entered the small barroom at the foot of the stairs, the bartender looked at him across the shoulders of several roughly dressed patrons and shrugged regretfully.

Veterano, standing watch outside, was as good as the bartender at reading faces. He plunged his hands into his pockets and said to Landry, "Too fast. The answer was not good?"

"No, it wasn't good."

Veterano grunted. "It will be curfew soon. We must return to the house of the signorina. We will leave for the mountains at midnight."

Viviana had prepared a small, calm oasis in a world Landry found increasingly frustrating. Its borders were the gentle limits of the candlelight in her dining room, and its concerns were soothingly trivial: Would he and Luisa like the dinner she had arranged? Lake fish, delicately sautéed, with risotto alla Milanese. It wasn't as grand as she would have liked, she lamented, for even the black market had dried up lately, but she and Franca had done their best.

The table was set for four, but Veterano begged off, preferring a quick snack in the kitchen and a post at the garden wall, where he could watch the street. Franca smiled at his decision. She promised to keep him company at the wall once she had finished serving, a promise that brought red patches to his gray-stubbled face and sent him fleeing into the garden without even the snack.

After inadequate fare and tin plates in the austerity of Dante's mountainside camp, Luisa's eyes widened when Franca brought a steaming tureen to the table and ladled chicken broth with delicate little dumplings into fine chinaware. Viviana looked pleased. She looked less pleased later, however, when Landry found his appetite flagging over the fish.

"Don't you like it?" she asked him anxiously.

"It's fine," Landry said. "I was just thinking about the meeting."

"They're fools," Viviana said. "They have little power."

"They have enough. Damn it, I wish I knew how the resistance leaders in Milan picked up on this."

"I'm sure one of the Federation officers called them," Viviana said. "You should have expected it. Our Federation representatives are far too timid to make such decisions on their own."

Luisa tried to help. "Even if the other partisan detachments can't join you, Dante will help," she said. "So will Pietro. I heard him say so."

"Dante has twelve men," Landry said. "Pietro might be able to pick up a few willing collaborators, but even so, I doubt that we can muster more than forty guns. It's ludicrous, when you stop to think about it. Forty partisans against a whole damned army."

"They're good men," Luisa said shyly.

Landry sighed. "I know."

Viviana said, "You mustn't let the Federation decision upset you, David. Let the new American major worry about it."

Landry put down his fork. Even from Viviana, such advice was inane. What do you do when some harmful act, perhaps a fatal one, has taken place? Think of something else? Ponder whether Mozart's parents were kind to him when he was a child? Smile and think, "Too bad, I don't care"? He said, almost to himself, "I just wish Holloman hadn't been so hard-nosed with the people in Milan. Maybe they wouldn't be so quick to take it out on us now."

Viviana put down her own fork. "I'm not sure that's fair, David. Major Holloman told me several times what was happening. They were all greedy, each organization trying to undercut the other, each group insisting that it and it alone should benefit from the funds."

"That's natural enough," Landry admitted.

But she was getting angry. He could tell from the impatient way her manicured nails drummed the tablecloth. It was inevitable. He forked a bite of the fish, not tasting it, to try to make amends, but Viviana's eyes were already to the flashing point. "You're resentful because Major Holloman came to stay with me, aren't you?" she said. "That's what really bothers you about him."

Landry gave up. "No, but I've given it some thought."

"I'm sure you have," Viviana said sharply. "And now I suppose you want to know what happened?" A door opened beyond the kitchen, but Viviana was wound up and ignored it. "Do you want to know every little detail? What he said, and what I said? What he did, and what I did? Every incriminating aspect of our sordid little assignation?"

"No, of course not," Landry said. "It's none of my business."

"Precisely. Nevertheless, to put your mind at ease, you should know that nothing happened. He came here because he was frightened. He had word that some of the Communists in Milan intended to take the money from him by force. He wanted me to get in touch with my father in Switzerland, to arrange help. He had heard that my father has property holdings just across the mountains on Lake Lugano, and he hoped to hide there until he could arrange assistance from his headquarters. That's all there was to it. It was strictly business."

Veterano's voice murmured in the kitchen, speaking urgently to Franca. Landry squirmed uncomfortably and glanced at his watch. "It's midnight," he said. "Veterano and I have to get going."

"Yes, perhaps that would be best," Viviana said. "I wouldn't want to keep you from important matters." She sounded tired and cross, but there was disappointment in her eyes.

Landry said, "Viviana, I . . ." Then, almost as though on cue, Veterano appeared at the door, with Franca at his shoulder. Landry bit off his apology and pushed away from the table. "Is it time?" he asked Veterano.

Veterano shook his head. His face said it was more than the passage of time and the proximity of midnight that had brought him inside. He quickly snuffed the candles and headed for the window.

"Germans," he whispered. "They are surrounding the house."

Day Four

Qualcuno è nel giardino!
Chi è là?

Someone's in the garden!
Who's there?
> —Verdi, *La Traviata*

1

As church bells tolled the hour from the hill, Landry brought his Thompson to the window and pulled back the blackout curtains. Veterano pointed to the corner, where gray figures fanned out from a truck at the end of the street and darted from doorway to doorway in the darkness.

"How many?" Landry asked.

Veterano bunched his shoulders. "Perhaps twenty. Too many to fight. There's another truck at the opposite end of the street."

"What about the garden wall? Have they got it covered?"

"On one side, yes. Perhaps on the other three as well. I didn't wait to see."

Landry spotted two more figures leapfrogging through the shadows. It was the Livorno nightmare come to life. The gray-green German field uniforms. The fear. But as though fear were the catalyst, suddenly everything snapped into place. Landry's war became simple again. The hand holding the Thompson steadied. He found himself wanting to open fire, to cleanse his life of frustration and complications, and it was almost with reluctance that he said, "Let's try the gate in back. Maybe we can sneak down to the beach."

Viviana crowded close to the window and whispered, "You can't use the gate, David. I hired a stonemason last week to wall it up. The bricks are already head high. Let me hide you in the cellar."

"We can't stay here," Landry said. "If they know about the house, they must know about the cellar, too. It's over the wall for all of us. You and Franca as well."

"But Franca and I will be safe here," Viviana said. "They have nothing against us."

Landry shook his head. "You don't seem to understand, Viviana. You've been blown. We all have." He turned to Veterano. "Take the women down through the garden. I'll try to keep the Germans busy up here for a couple of minutes, then I'll join you. Get them over the wall, understand?" Veterano was not a man to waste words. He took Viviana roughly by the elbow and tugged her away. Together with Luisa and Franca, they hurried through the kitchen, heading for the garden.

Landry stared one last time through the blackout curtains and saw that one man now, the vanguard, was edging his way toward the front door while his fellows covered him from the shadows. Landry let the curtain drop and primed his Thompson, then ducked down to the entry hall. Swiftly, silently, he moved to the door and slid the bolt back, unlocking it. Then he pressed himself to the side.

In moments, he heard the man's breath, short, nervous puffs, as though he had been running for miles. Boot leather scraped on stone and the heavy iron handle began to move slowly as the German tested it. It clicked open, and the German, surprised, hesitated. The door stood ajar, not more than an inch or two, for perhaps three heartbeats, then eased wider, slowly, slowly.

Landry held the Thompson at his shoulder, barrel up. Moonlight fell from the street through the narrow opening. A hand appeared, followed by a helmeted head. As the German's shoulders moved warily through the door, Landry grabbed a fistful of tunic and yanked him inside, hurling him in a short arc against the wall, head first. The soldier's neck compacted against the wall and his arms and legs flopped out to the sides. He collapsed in a heap.

The soldier's sudden disappearance brought a shout of alarm from the street. Landry slammed the door and shot the bolt, then grabbed the unconscious German under the arms and hauled him back toward the living room. Someone opened up with a rifle from outside, and it was immediately joined by another half-dozen rifles and at least two Schmeissers. Landry fired a Thompson burst at the door to keep them thinking, and was rewarded by the sound of bodies diving for cover.

Hastily, in spite of fingers that had begun to tremble once more, Landry groped at the unconscious soldier's belt until he found a pair of stick grenades. He wrenched the grenades loose and skipped over the man's crumpled form, heading for the stairs. More gunfire erupted from the street. The stone front of Viviana's house absorbed most of the punishment, but stray slugs began to find their way through shuttered windows and the big, wooden door of the entryway, chewing up Viviana's plaster walls and smashing china in the dining room.

Landry hurried up the stairs and ducked into one of Viviana's unused bedrooms, overlooking the street. He eased to the window and looked down. He could see several soldiers sprawled on the cobblestones, plinking away with rifles, and at least a half dozen more massed next door, getting ready to rush the front of the house. In the opposite direction, maybe sixty feet up the street, three enlisted men wrestled a machine gun from one of the trucks and hustled to set it up.

Landry leaned his Thompson against the windowsill and pulled the window open. He unscrewed the metal caps at the base of the two grenade handles and set one grenade aside. He hooked his finger in the porcelain ring that dangled from the handle of the other and took a last look through the window, judging his distance. Then he yanked the string to arm the delay pellet. Four seconds, more or less. He hauled back and hurled the grenade into the darkness.

He couldn't see where it went, but he heard it clank and clatter against the cobblestones. Apparently the Germans by the machine gun heard it as well, for their heads jerked toward the truck and they threw themselves flat. Moments later, the street lit up with a sizzling flash and the truck rose four or five feet in the air. The eruption of sound reached Landry a split second before the concussion. Windows shattered on both sides of the street.

The explosion stunned the men below, and Landry added to their shock by slinging the second grenade in the opposite direction. As it exploded, he poked his Thompson out the window and sprayed three quick bursts from side to side.

Confused shouts rose from the street, and Germans scattered, convinced they were facing several armed men in different parts of the house. Landry took advantage of the turmoil to break for the rear of the house, racing toward Viviana's bedroom and the window overlooking the wisteria. He didn't waste time climbing down. He threw the window open, clutched his Thompson in both hands, and jumped. He hit the soft earth where Viviana had tried so hard to coax her camellias into life and took off running, heading for the bottom of the garden. A loud roar ripped from the front of the house, shaking the ground, and Landry tripped, falling headlong across a gravel path. His first thought was that the Germans had recovered from their confusion and had retaliated with grenades of their own. But as he scrambled back to his feet, he saw a fireball rolling above the roofline and realized it was only the burning truck. Flames must have reached the fuel tank.

He began to run again, and a figure loomed up ahead of him. "Here," a voice whispered. "The women await us on the other side."

Landry angled toward Veterano, adrenaline pumping. Behind them, the sounds of gunfire were suddenly peppered by sporadic bursts from the direction of the blazing vehicle. Ammunition canisters, heated to the melting point, were ripping apart on their own. It sounded like the start of a whole new war.

"Let me give you a boost," Landry hissed to Veterano. "We've got to get out before they realize the house is empty."

Veterano merely grunted. He scaled the wall as lithely as a fifteen-year-old, leaving Landry to scrabble up behind him. The three women crouched silently on the other side of the wall between two tall houses. Landry and Veterano joined them, and they all hurried toward the down-slope street. As they approached it, Landry heard jackboots crunching along the cobbles. He took the lead and poked his head into the open. He could see the backs of six or seven German soldiers, heads pulled down between shoulders, weapons extended, racing away to join the fight on the upper side of the block. He waited until the soldiers disappeared around the far corner, then whispered, "It's clear. Luisa, you take Viviana and Franca and head for the beach. Veterano and I will provide cover."

Luisa obeyed orders like the soldier she was, and Landry slipped from between buildings with his Thompson low. He had his back to the women, watching the corner. The first hint of trouble came when Franca screeched, followed by the sound of a scuffle.

Landry whirled and saw two uniformed men wrestling with Luisa and Viviana in the darkness. The two Germans had apparently come from the shadows of a recessed doorway, and one had Luisa pinned by the arms while the other, a sergeant, grappled with Viviana, trying to hold onto her and his weapon and at the same time ward off blows that Franca rained at his shoulders, his ears, his bobbing elbows.

"Hold it!" Landry shouted. "Hände hoch!" The two Germans jerked their heads toward the sound of Landry's voice. The one with Luisa turned and thrust her in front as a shield, with one arm hooked around her throat. His other hand dipped to his belt and whipped out a bayonet, which he quickly pressed against the skin below her right ear.

Veterano, frozen against the bricks between Landry and the two Germans, saw Luisa's jeopardy and bellowed with rage. He launched himself across the intervening space with such roaring fury that the enlisted man's knees buckled. The shotgun whirred at the end of Veterano's sweeping arm, and the terrified German soldier released Luisa and involuntarily raised his bayonet arm to ward off the blow. It didn't help. The dark gun barrel went *crackcrunch,* breaking wristbone and slamming into his skull as though the arm had never been there. The force of the blow knocked the soldier flying against the wall.

The sergeant, horrified by what had happened to his companion, shoved Viviana away and dropped his weapon. Franca took two more belts at him before she realized that his hands were in the air and the fight was over.

Landry ran to them, his Thompson leveled at the German sergeant. He took a look at the crumpled shape by the wall, and his eyes bugged.

Veterano shrugged. "Sometimes I forget to shoot."

The gunfire on the upper street subsided, and across the dark silence came the sound of pounding rifle butts and splintering wood. "They're breaking in," Landry said. "They'll be onto us any moment now. We'd better get moving."

Prodding the German sergeant with the Thompson, Landry directed them quickly down the street and around a corner toward the beach. Dark windows opened cautiously above them and pale faces peered out. One man saw the German being hustled along with his hands clamped on top of his head and whispered, "Bene. Viva la Resistenza!"

They were almost to the bottom of the street when a whistle trilled three times back at Viviana's house, calling the soldiers to formation. The German sergeant turned grave eyes on Landry and said in Italian, "Do you hear the signal?"

"I hear it," Landry said.

The German chucked his chin back toward Viviana's house. "They know now that you have escaped. All the roads will be covered. All the trails to the mountains. You may as well give yourselves up."

"Fat chance," Landry said, but it made little sense in Italian and the sergeant looked puzzled. Landry eyed the man's unit patches. He was Sicherheitsdienst, SD. The others had worn Waffen-SS markings. "What's your name?" Landry asked.

"Knaust. Scharführer Fritz Knaust. And yours?"

"Rumpelstiltskin," Landry said. "You're with the security branch. What are you doing here with a bunch of Waffen-SS?"

"My major arranged it," the German said.

Landry's jaw tightened. "Major Richter?"

The German looked surprised. "How do you know my major's name?"

Landry didn't answer. His mind flitted quickly to what Creedmore and Stefanini had told him in camp, just before he headed down the mountainside. That Richter's security people had been getting help. From someone close to the partisans.

As they reached the beach, soft wavelets sighed against the shore. Veterano left the women at a string of fishing boats and whispered, "Americano. Where do we go from here?"

"Into one of the dories," Landry said. He gestured at a blue-and-white, flat-bottomed boat near the edge of the water.

The German sergeant shook his head without removing his hands from his cap. "It will do you no good," he said. "My major wants you badly. And he will get you. There will be patrol boats on the lake as soon as word gets out that you have escaped. Give yourselves up to me. I will see that you get humane treatment."

"Humane treatment?" Landry said. "Your major runs that little chamber of horrors near the Cernobbio vortex. What would you know about humane treatment?"

"Not all SD are alike," the sergeant said.

"Oh?" Landry said. He glanced at Luisa's ravaged face. "And what is the distinction? Some of you torture people only on weekends?"

"I am serious," the sergeant said. "Let me take you in, and I will hand you over to the Waffen-SS. Make them find you, and you will no doubt end up in the hands of my major. He can be a hard man."

The women climbed into the boat and Veterano put his shoulder to the curving bow. Landry handed the Thompson to Luisa and said, "If the German tries to run, cut him in two." Then he gestured for the sergeant to join him and they both helped Veterano push the boat into the light swells.

As soon as the dory floated free, Veterano crawled aboard and hoisted first the German sergeant, then Landry in after him, making it look easy. "Where do we go now?" Veterano asked Landry.

"We row north," Landry said. "There's an inlet south of Musso. We can get there before daylight if we stick close to the shore."

"Shouldn't we try for the mountains?"

"Not yet. They'll be watching for that. We'll lay low for a few hours. If we stay out of sight, maybe the patrols will ease up."

"And the German?"

"He stays with us. At least until it's safe to move on."

"And then what? Do we kill him?"

The German sergeant, though he seemed unable to follow the

whispered flood of Italian, nevertheless understood the sidelong glances coming his way. He said, "You are talking about me?"

Landry shrugged. "My friend wondered what to do with you."

"And what did you tell him? Am I to die?"

"That depends," Landry said.

The German smiled without mirth, a sad, hopeless smile. "And you would give the SD lessons in torture and humane treatment? Perhaps we are not so dissimilar after all, Herr Rumpelstiltskin."

2

In spite of the worsening war news, Benito Mussolini found himself unable to make a simple decision. Was he to lead his Black Brigades to the Valtellina and a gallant last stand? Or was he to forget honor and run for his life? Because he couldn't decide, he preferred not to think of it at all. And so, on this Tuesday morning when Luigi Gatti, his secretary, came to his rooms in the Prefecture to announce that two ministers had begged an audience, Mussolini felt an instant twinge of irritability.

"Which ministers?" Mussolini murmured unhappily. "I don't want to talk about the war today."

"Mezzasoma and Buffarini," Luigi Gatti told him. "They have news from Cardinal Schuster."

Mussolini sighed. "Very well, bring them in." He leaned back in his chair, massaging the bridge of his nose.

They came in together, youthful Fernando Mezzasoma and the elegant Guido Buffarini-Guidi. An air of excitement wafted in with them. "Duce," Mezzasoma bubbled. "We have just talked to the cardinal. He has offered to host a meeting between you and three officials of the Italian resistance, important high-level members."

"I have no interest in meeting with partisans," Mussolini said. "Besides, nothing could come of it. Even if we came to terms, the Allied armies would refuse to honor them."

Buffarini joined in optimistically. "They would have to, Duce. The partisans have already been recognized by the Allies as the only legitimate voice in the occupied areas. If the partisans agree to an armistice, the terms would become binding. Most especially if the Church plays a role in the negotiations."

Mezzasoma agreed. "It may be our last chance for peace," he said. "Think of the good, Duce. Perhaps we can spare our poor people any further sacrifice. And . . . and perhaps save our own lives."

Mussolini stared at his hands. "When and where would such a meeting take place?"

"Tomorrow evening, Duce. At the archbishop's palace. If you are willing, the cardinal will arrange face-to-face discussions for six o'clock."

"I suppose it wouldn't hurt to talk," Mussolini said. "I make no promises, mind you. There are conditions, important conditions, that must be met. But still, if the resistance leaders are willing to be reasonable . . ."

He laid his hands on his knees and breathed deeply. It was the first hint of good fortune to come his way in a long, long time. Perhaps survival would not be impossible after all.

3

During the predawn darkness, Landry's party had taken shelter beneath a railway trestle. They waited with their prisoner, heads low, watching a blood-red sun rise above the lake. The sunrise had a naked, almost terrible beauty. Like gold spangles, a scattering of clouds burned in a hard green sky. The strengthening sunlight caught another object—a solitary Italian scout plane that circled overhead. No sizable German or Italian patrols appeared, but several military cars and troop trucks sped along the road north from Rezzonico. Though the intense color of the sky was ominous, Landry welcomed it. Later in the morning, wind began to gust, and the scout plane gave up and flew away.

"Shall we try for the mountains?" Veterano asked.

Landry surveyed the sky and the steep slopes that rose toward

Bregagno peak. Spring storms could be nasty. "Can you get us to Dante's camp from here?"

"With some difficulty," Veterano said. "It is a steep climb for an hour or so, perhaps troublesome for the women, but after that, a trail leads across lesser slopes."

Landry glanced at Viviana's toggery. Her tight-skirted black suit and her shoes—open-toed, sling-backed, high-heeled affairs—were hardly designed for climbing. He said, "Do you think you can make it?"

"The Germans have left us little choice," she said.

Veterano cast an eye at the prisoner. "What about him?"

"This is where we part company," Landry said. "You take the women on ahead. I'll handle it."

Viviana's eyes widened, but she said nothing, just followed Veterano from beneath the trestle and hurried through a tangle of trees and undergrowth with Franca and Luisa.

The SD sergeant was a big man with slightly protruding ears and deep-set eyes. He watched the women work their way up the slope behind Veterano, then touched dry lips with tongue and said in Italian, "We do not go with them?"

Landry shook his head. "The partisans have no facilities for prisoners."

"I see," said the German. "This, then, is as far as I go?"

"I'm afraid so."

"I understand," the German said. "Shall I face you? Or turn my back?"

"Whatever you prefer," Landry said.

The German swallowed. "If it won't offend you, I think I would rather see it coming. May I kneel?"

Landry nodded.

The sergeant lowered himself to the ground. His hands plucked unconsciously at fresh spring grass and a blade came loose in his fingers. He stared at it in brief surprise, then crushed it between thumb and forefinger and lifted it to his nose. His gaze moved to Landry. "I am ready," he said.

Landry cocked the Thompson. The German watched him steadily, without fear, but unspoken thoughts and emotions were present in his eyes. Regret at dying so close to war's end. A craving to see home again. A silent plea for life, but at the same time a stubborn refusal to beg.

Landry sighted down the barrel of the Thompson and felt sweat break across his forehead. He hesitated, and in the hesitation he discovered that the simplicity of war had shattered once again into tiny, confused fragments. He sighed and lowered the Thompson. "Go on, beat it," he said.

The German blinked at him in astonishment, then in confusion of his own. "You would let me go?"

"Shut up," Landry said. "Just get out of here."

The man needed no further urging. He stood shakily, his hands wiping against his trouser seams. He took a cautious step backward, then turned and scurried down toward the road, stumbling and sliding in the shale. He looked back only once, just before he reached the winding lake road. When he saw Landry by the trestle, still watching him, Thompson pointed toward the ground, he frowned and hurried again, trotting south toward Rezzonico.

Landry shrugged his Thompson onto his shoulder and looked up through the trees. He could see Veterano and the women making minute progress on the slope. Veterano would know, of course, not having heard the shots. It didn't matter. There was no point in trying to hide it.

But as Landry started his climb, he felt drained and miserable. Not because he had allowed an enemy soldier to go free. The German sergeant could do them no appreciable hurt. He was just one man. No, the misery came from something else. A far more harmful enemy lurked somewhere in their midst. That was beyond doubt now. From the moment the Germans had appeared on the street outside Viviana's house, Landry had known the truth. Somewhere, on the lakeside or in the mountains, a turncoat prowled among them, breeding betrayal.

Whoever it was, man or woman, would have to be found.

And next time, there could be no hesitation.

Leaden rain clouds continued to darken the sky as they climbed. Chill wind whipped at Viviana's bare legs, numbing them, and she stumbled often. Landry stayed close to her through the morning and afternoon, steadying her when he could, murmuring encouragement when she wearied. Franca, though equally awkward at the beginning, grew more accustomed to the rough terrain in time and soon began to pull herself hand over hand across rocky embankments and through tangled barricades of Alpine honeysuckle like some young country girl. Franca's resolute assault upon the mountain trails seemed to embarrass and strengthen Viviana. As the day wore on, Viviana's face turned stiff with determination, and she stolidly refused help from anyone, including Landry.

It was late afternoon by the time they approached Dante's high camp, and Landry spent the last several hundred meters of the climb staring at the thickening clouds, worrying about the weather. He knew from the briefings at Cecina that a great storm had been hanging over western Europe for the past several days. Apparently it had exhausted itself over France and Germany and was now rolling past the mountains into Italy, where the spring-warmed lakes of the Lombardy region awaited the depleted air mass with warmth and new moisture. The sky would grow darker and darker. Eventually, perhaps as early as tomorrow, the storm would take on new life and the rains would come. He couldn't help wondering what additional harm a storm might do to their already fragile plans to cut the Como road.

Someone in camp must have seen them approaching, for Landry heard voices calling and several figures rushed down to greet them, babbling excitedly. By the time Landry made sense of what they were saying, it was as though all the threatening thunderclouds had prematurely let loose at once. At first everyone talked simultaneously, Dante's hands chopping the air, Piccione trying to break in from the side, Kavanaugh's and Stefanini's voices mingling and butting against each other. It took Landry several moments to understand. The Army man, Major Rossiter, was missing. He had wandered beyond the confines of the camp before noon yesterday, supposedly to reconnoiter the lake below, but he had disappeared, as though the mountains themselves had opened to swallow him. Not only that, but while everyone was out looking for him, someone had stolen into camp and smashed the ALOT radio.

Landry tried to quiet them, but interruptions and addenda continued to shower from all sides as they walked into camp. Finally, it was X. B. Kavanaugh who raised his voice and insisted that everyone shut up so he could make a sensible report. Rossiter had gone off on his own, apparently, without bothering to tell anyone. Piccione had seen him briefly, picking his way through the boulders south of camp, and had considered challenging him, but decided against it. The others were widely scattered, seeing to their weapons and making preparations for the attack on the lake road, so no one missed Rossiter until Salvo returned from Como at midafternoon to report that he had successfully persuaded the Como Federation members to meet with Landry in Rezzonico. Dante and Salvo had looked for Rossiter, but couldn't find him. On the off-chance that Rossiter might have wandered too far and lost his bearings, Dante sent out a small search party. They were back in an hour, empty-handed. The whole camp then scattered to scour the surrounding territory while there was still light enough to do some good. They stayed out for hours, calling Rossiter's name, prodding through rocks and defiles, long after the sun faded beyond the peaks and darkness settled.

"All but me," Freddy Stefanini interjected. "I came back at sundown to make the regular evening radio contact. That's when I found the radio, busted all to pieces."

Kavanaugh wagged his big head in despair. "And that's the way it stands," he said. "What if Mussolini shows up with his Army? What are we going to do?"

Landry sighed. "I hate to add to your problems," he said, "but I've brought my own share of bad news. Whatever we do, we're going to have to do it alone. The Como Federation has refused to help us."

Dante looked at him in surprise. "They refused? Why?"

"Orders from Milan," Landry said. He told them quickly about the meeting above the bar, the abrupt rejection. He also told them about the surprise raid on Viviana's house, though it seemed less important in light of what might have happened to Rossiter.

Kavanaugh said, "That does it, then. We'll have to give up on this whole roadblock thing."

"We can't," Landry said. "It's too important. There are people depending on us."

"What can we do about it?" Kavanaugh said. "Rossiter had all the ideas. I wouldn't even know where to start."

"If we could re-establish radio contact, someone at headquarters could tell us what to do," Landry said. "Freddy, do you think you can get the radio working again?"

Freddy Stefanini made a face. "No way. Someone made mincemeat of it. The damn thing looks like it was worked over with a sledgehammer."

Salvo said eagerly, "There is a radio in Menággio. Piccione used to use it in the old days, to ask for supplies. The schoolteacher kept it hidden in his cellar. You remember, Piccione?"

"I remember," Piccione said. "But the wiring was old. It never worked well."

Stefanini looked thoughtful. "If it's only the wiring, maybe I can fix it."

"Good," Landry said. "After we've worked out some options, we'll have Piccione take you down to Menággio and give you a crack at it. In the meantime, we're on our own. Without a radio, we're going to need Pietro and his men more than ever. Someone will have to go for him."

Salvo took the Luftwaffe cap from his head and wiped the sweatband. "I'll do it, David. I've been to his camp many times."

"You've just finished one trip," Landry said.

Salvo put the cap back on. "I can use the exercise. Besides, I'm almost out of tobacco again. I fear I was greedy. Pietro has friends on the lake who distribute weekly allotments. Perhaps I will be lucky."

Landry grinned at him. "Okay, but tell him the whole truth. Tell him what happened with the Federation people. If he's still willing to help us, tell him to gather as many men as possible and bring them here. We'll stage in Dante's camp and move down to the lake tomorrow."

"Move where?" Creedmore said. "We don't even know where Rossiter planned to set up his roadblocks."

"We'll have to make our own plans," Landry said. "I'd suggest somewhere near Dongo and Musso. There's a blind curve south of Musso with a wooded overhang. If we can barricade the road with trees, maybe we can take cover up above and hold off anyone who tries to pass."

Dante said, "I know the place you mean, David, but it could be awkward. There is a German garrison at Gravedona, less than five kilometers to the north. What if they come down the road and attack us from behind?"

"We don't have to hold the road forever," Landry said. "I think we could aim at creating a delay. Then if Freddy can get the radio working in Menággio, maybe we can make a pitch for air support. If not, we'll hold on as long as possible, then fade into the trees."

Kavanaugh said, "We can give it a try. But I'd feel a whole lot better about it if Dante hadn't mentioned the Germans at Gravedona."

"Forget the Germans," Landry said. "We'll mine the Vallorba bridge with Rossiter's explosives. Then if the Germans come at us, we can blow it. Not only that, if any of Mussolini's people get past us at the roadblock, the bridge will stop them. We can catch them in between."

Creedmore cocked his head and grinned incredulously. "That's it? That's your idea? Fifty thousand Blackshirt soldiers and a full German garrison, surrounded by little old us? Sonofagun, David, I think you've got it. We'll have those suckers right where we want them."

Landry simply forgot Viviana. By the time the council of war ended, Franca and Luisa had a pot of soup simmering. First one, then more of the partisans and ALOTs drifted over to sniff it. It was then that Landry saw Viviana sitting by herself on a pile of stones. She had slipped off her shoes. Barefoot, her chic black suit and soft shantung blouse streaked with dirt, Viviana looked thoroughly out of place, but her attitude gave no sign that she knew it. She merely looked contemplative, observing the goings-on of the partisan camp as though trying to decide if the strange environment were dull or entertaining. Franca, on the other hand, seemed perfectly at home, surrounded by men hungry for more than mere food, and she traded wisecracks and smiles with them lustily. She soon had at least three men, including the Lizard and a tongue-tied Salvo, convinced they were the sole objects of her attention.

Landry was tempted to go to Viviana, but he knew it would have to wait. He detoured instead to squat between Piccione and Freddy Stefanini near the radio hut. Stefanini had his wrecked ALOT transmitter in the dirt before him and was trying to salvage the tuning coil and odd bits of wiring while Creedmore and X. B. Kavanaugh and Harry Tucker looked on gloomily.

Landry nodded his chin at Stefanini and said, "You and Piccione be damned careful when you get to Menággio. Someone wants us out of touch, and he wants it badly. So keep your heads down."

Stefanini pushed the ruined radio away in disgust. "You don't have to tell me that," he said. "We all know we've got an informer among us." He glanced over his shoulder toward the cook fire, then lowered his voice. "The only question now is who. That British guy, for instance. David, how much do you know about him?"

"Willoughby?" Landry said. "Not much. He's a military observer. They sent him along to protect British interests."

"Military observer, my ass," Stefanini humphed. "Piccione and me, we've been watching him. Something funny is going on."

"Bull," Kavanaugh said. "He couldn't be the one. He just got here."

"I'm not saying he's the informer," Stefanini said. "But I can damn well tell you he isn't what he claims to be. Him and Rossiter, they had their heads together all the time, talking about something."

Creedmore looked around toward the cook fire, where the Britisher stood talking quietly to Salvo. "You're crazy," Creedmore muttered to Stefanini. "Of course he talked to Rossiter. They were probably planning this roadblock business together."

"You think so?" Stefanini said. "Then how come when Rossiter turned up missing that British guy didn't offer any suggestions on what we could do to make the roadblock work? You all saw him. He just stood there with his mouth shut and listened. What kind of a military observer is that? You ask me, he's a phony. He seems a hell of a lot more interested in Dante's partisans than he is in any military stuff."

Piccione nodded. "That's true. He has talked to many of our people. He even spoke at some length to me last evening, after we gave up our search."

"About what?" Landry asked.

Piccione shrugged expressively. "It's hard to put a finger on. He seemed to be speaking of partisan life in general, though there were several moments when I felt he was more interested in our recent problems."

Creedmore hissed, "Knock it off. He's coming this way."

Stefanini turned deliberately to watch Willoughby and Salvo approach, carrying bowls of soup. The young Italian-American waited until they were close enough, then pushed his chin out and said, "We were just talking about our traitor. Who do you think it is?" It sounded like a challenge.

Willoughby sat down in the dirt near Landry, juggling his soup bowl. He spooned a mouthful. "Why should I think it's anyone?" he countered casually.

"Well, you seem awful damn interested," Stefanini said. Again, the challenging note. Willoughby eyed him quietly over the rim of the bowl, but said nothing.

Stefanini stared back at the Britisher for a moment, then seemed to back down. He turned his head and scanned the faces around the cook fire. Veterano stood near Luisa, helping her add firewood to the flames. Stefanini nodded toward him and said, "Well, I don't know about the rest of you, but I vote for the old man. We don't know that much about him. And he's new. He joined us just about the time things started going bad. How do we know the Germans didn't send him up here?"

Creedmore snorted. "You've got more wild hairs up your ass than a shaggy monkey. It couldn't be Veterano. That old guy is pure business. He never thinks of anything but doing his job."

"Yeah?" Stefanini said, bridling. "What the hell do you know about it? He's not even from around here. Sicilian, Dante told me. And he speaks English. How come an old guy from Sicily speaks English?"

Landry looked up sharply. "What makes you think he speaks English?"

"Hell, I've heard him," Stefanini said. "I caught him cussing out the mules one day, and he cut loose with a string of American profanity that would make a dockworker blush. Perfect conjugation, too."

"Aw, come on, Freddy," Creedmore told him. "That doesn't mean anything. Piccione speaks English, too, and I don't hear anyone accusing him."

"Piccione doesn't try to hide it," Stefanini said. "That old guy does."

Piccione shook his head solemnly. "You are wasting your time," he told Stefanini. "It could not be Veterano who is our traitor. He was not in camp when Major Rossiter disappeared, nor when the radio was broken. He was with David."

The Britisher set his soup bowl aside and smiled at them. He seemed amused. "What makes you so sure there's only one traitor?" he said. "With the problems you've been having, there could be more. At least two. Perhaps they're working as a team. Have you never considered that?"

From the shocked silence that greeted Willoughby's quiet comment, it was obvious to Landry that none of them had.

4

Sergeant Fritz Knaust, back at SD headquarters in Cernobbio after hitching a ride with a Fascist motorcycle courier from the Azzano barracks, riffled through a file cabinet and listened to his superior officer, Major Ernst Richter, berating the Waffen-SS commandant from Gravedona. The Gravedona officer was a pudgy, bespectacled captain in a wrinkled uniform. He was white-faced with humiliation, but he didn't dare talk back to a security officer.

"It was a fiasco," Richter said sternly. "My own small force of fourteen men could have done better. Worse, a troop of boys. Have your men no pride?"

"They did their best, Herr Sturmbannführer."

"Their best? Sergeant Knaust reports they fled their posts when the explosions started. Isn't that right, Sergeant?"

Knaust, who had less to lose than the Waffen-SS captain, said, "I wouldn't say they fled. Most of them were diverted to the front of the house in the mistaken belief that they were needed there."

"Nevertheless," Richter said, "they displayed a complete breakdown of discipline. If they'd held their ground, we would be finished with this exercise. I consider the entire episode shameful."

"Discipline is difficult to maintain," the captain said apologetically. "You must understand, Herr Sturmbannführer, morale is quite low. The news from Berlin, the war reports. Most of my men just want to go home."

"How touching," Richter said. "And what kind of home would they have to return to if every German soldier felt the same way? Fortunately, the catastrophe in Rezzonico need not be the end for us. Your men may still have a chance to redeem themselves."

The captain blinked sweatily. "I beg your pardon?"

"You will assemble your complement within the hour," Richter said. "I now have information as to the whereabouts of the partisan encampment belonging to the leader known as Dante. The man you allowed to slip through your fingers this morning will no doubt be hiding there. I expect confirmation this evening. If so, I want him captured or dead before daylight tomorrow. You will lead your men into the mountains and assault the partisan camp at dawn. Do you understand?"

"Sir, my men have been patrolling the lake all day, looking for the American. They are tired."

"They can rest tomorrow," Richter said. "I'm told there are no more than sixteen men in camp, counting both partisans and American agents. Surely you can handle sixteen men?"

The captain sighed. "We can handle them."

"Excellent," Richter said. "Your attitude is improving already, Captain. In the outer office, you will find my adjutant, Lieutenant Stenzel. He will give you the co-ordinates and a description of the camp. Take care, Captain. I will not accept another failure."

The Waffen-SS man's cheeks reddened. "Yes, sir. It will be as you say." He slipped into the outer room and closed the door behind him.

Richter smoothed brownish hair that was already combed carefully over a sloping forehead, and, as if reacting to an unpleasant odor, wrinkled his long nose, faintly crooked at the bridge. Knaust saw that Richter was in an awkward humor tonight. He hoped the major would turn to gaze out the window at the lake. For some reason, merely looking at the Italian countryside often seemed to soothe the man. But the major only leaned back in his chair and murmured, "That officer is a complete fool. Is there any wonder that we're losing the war?"

Knaust said, "He's right about his men. Their hearts aren't in it any longer."

"I suppose I can understand that," Richter said. "There are times when I, myself . . ." He let the words die, and sighed.

Knaust pondered the note of bitterness in the major's voice. Knaust thought he knew where it came from. They had both heard the Swiss and Milanese radio reports. The war, already going badly these past several months, seemed now to be swirling to a disastrous end. Bologna was in the hands of the Americans and Poles. The British had overrun Ferrara. Modena and Reggio had fallen and Mantua had been abandoned only yesterday. German forces were reported to be fleeing toward the Po, leaving their heavy artillery behind, with but two serviceable planes left to give them cover. The door to Milan was ajar, and Clark's American armor was already streaming toward it. To ease Richter's obvious depression, Knaust said, "Will you have a glass of wine, sir? It would refresh you."

"Yes, a good idea," Richter said. "You may join me, Sergeant."

Knaust poured two goblets half full of a rich, red Sangue di Giuda and carried them both to the desk. Richter took one and held it to the light, his hand caressing the crystal. The major seemed to like the wines of Italy almost as much as he liked the scenery. He also apparently had no objection to the superbly chiseled goblets, the gift of a Fascist tax assessor.

"What shall we drink to?" Richter asked. He sounded gay, but the angry look crept back into his eyes. "Indeed, what is left to drink to?"

Knaust watched him, feeling uncomfortable. Major Richter was ordinarily a hard man, with no time to waste on emotion and the frills of self-pity. Knaust had served with him for a long time, not only here in Italy, but also earlier, in better days, and he'd never seen the major so morose. "Shall we drink to days past?" Knaust ventured.

"Why not?" Richter said. "It may be all that remains to us." He tossed the wine down like schnapps, barely tasting it. Knaust sipped more slowly, trying to put himself in the major's place, trying to fathom what terrible thoughts would make the major turn so pensive. Surely it galled the man deeply to see it all slipping away like this. Major Richter was from a working-class background, not unlike Knaust himself. A laboring family in Munich. But the major was ambitious and had risen above his past. Knaust, lacking incentive, had not. The rapidly unraveling war effort must be doubly difficult for the major, having striven all those years to pull himself up from humble origins until he could take his place of honor in the ranks of the new German aristocracy, the Nazi military hierarchy. How would it be to taste those years of influence, of raw power, then to lose it all? For if the war ended badly, and it was now obvious that it would, the major would plunge all the way back to his lowly beginnings. There wouldn't even be a moment for acclimatization. One step and he would reach bottom.

"You're not drinking," Richter said. "What's the matter, Sergeant? Thinking about your close call with the American?"

Knaust had to smile. Truly, it was ridiculous to be worrying about the major's mere melancholy, when the most important person in the world, one Sergeant Fritz Knaust, had come so close to dying that day. "No, Herr Sturmbannführer," he said. "My mind had wandered to other things. But I am happy not to be the latest entry on the partisans' list of victims."

Richter's face changed, became more businesslike. "You will have your revenge, Sergeant. We will not weaken. Not so long as there are still partisans in the mountains. Partisans." He pronounced the word like a curse. "Those filthy butchers. Their methods contradict every principle of soldierly conduct. Like cowards, they strike and flee, strike and flee. Given a free hand, and the time to exercise it, I would cheerfully wipe them out to the last man."

"And yet you told the Waffen-SS captain that our primary concern was for the American. Why single out one American?"

Richter shrugged. "As to that, I admit placing more stress than I really consider necessary. I wouldn't really care about this Landry or whatever his name is, nor about this puerile plan to block the Como road, if it weren't for the pleadings of our squeamish contact." He paused and turned thoughtful. "Actually, I'd prefer to leave them alone for a time," he murmured. "Did you know the Americans expect Mussolini and his entourage to bring a veritable treasure of gold bullion and currency to the lake?

Millions, they say. Absolute millions. I'd almost rather let them make a try for it."

Knaust was puzzled by Richter's sudden shift of thought. "Sir? Let them try for it? What would that accomplish?"

Richter clasped his hands behind his head. "Think about it, Sergeant. We know where the partisans are hiding. Suppose they succeeded in stopping Mussolini and managed to wrest the treasure away from him. We could wait quietly until they conveyed it to their mountain stronghold, then we could set upon their encampment and take it all. A mountain of gold. Riches beyond imagination. Think what we could do with such wealth."

"Then why send the Gravedona garrison to raid the camp now? Why not wait?"

Richter's dream bubble appeared to burst. "Because the partisans haven't a chance in hell of succeeding," he said. "And because our impatient turncoat has gone into a panic and insists that this Landry is dangerous. I suppose we could delay for a time, just to see what might happen . . ." He hesitated, as though tempted to let the partisans come down from the hills to try for the treasure, then shook his head. "No, our turncoat wants the American dead immediately, so dead he must be."

"Perhaps he *is* dangerous," Knaust said.

"I can hardly believe that," Richter said. "The partisans, yes. But this American, Landry? He had you under his gun and let you go, did he not? He sounds a fool to me. A weakling. What harm can he do us?"

Knaust thought back to the trestle, to those numbing moments when the submachine gun wavered at his head. "I don't know, Herr Sturmbannführer. There was something in his manner. I don't think it was weakness. This man may be more dangerous than any of us realize."

5

Harry Tucker slipped to the edge of the clearing by moonlight. He could hear sounds in the camp behind him, some of the people gearing up to move out, but there was no light anywhere. "Are you there?" he whispered.

"I'm here," a voice murmured back.

"Where? I can't see you."

"Here, in the trees."

Tucker peered through the heavy foliage, made out an upright shadow standing in the darkness. "Listen," he said, "the reason I wanted to talk to you . . . we've got to do something about Landry. He'll figure this out if we don't do something. And that Britisher, too. If they do, we've had it."

"They won't find out," the voice said.

"The devil they won't. Landry is stubborn. You remember how he acted when . . . well, you know, back when they yanked him off the lake. He gets an idea and he just hangs on. He's going to find out about us, and so is the Britisher. I should never have helped you in this thing. I . . . I think I want out."

"What about our share of the OSS funds?"

"To hell with it," Tucker said. "What good is it if we don't live to spend it? From now on, you're on your own. You can have the money, too. I don't want any part of it."

The figure stirred. "What's bothering you, Harry? Is it really Landry, or is it your conscience? Maybe you'd like to go back to the way things were. Is that it? You intend to tell them what you've done? What we've done?"

"My God, no," Tucker said. "Don't worry about that. If I said anything, they'd put me against the nearest boulder and shoot me."

Silence, then softly, "You worry for nothing. I've already taken care of Landry. He'll be dead by morning."

"Oh hey, not another killing," Tucker said. "Look, why don't we admit it's over and take off? We could be in Switzerland in a few hours. No one could touch us."

"No one can touch us anyway. Not unless you lose your nerve."

"I haven't lost my nerve," Tucker said. "I just want out." The figure stirred again, and Tucker, suddenly nervous, backed away. "Don't go getting any ideas," Tucker said. "You touch me and they'll start wondering. You couldn't stand up to an investigation, and you know it. So leave me alone."

The voice sounded hurt. "Harry, how can you even think that?"

"Just stay away from me," Tucker said. "I'm going back to camp now. If you're smart, you'll give it up, too. We've had our run of luck. There isn't any more. So just leave me alone."

Tucker hurried away from the trees, slipping from shadow to shadow, but he couldn't help feeling there were eyes still on his back.

Day Five

Wednesday—April 25, 1945

Alla novella aurora assaliti saremo.

At the coming of dawn, we will be attacked.
            —Verdi, *Il Trovatore*

1

Landry lay beside Viviana, only half asleep, listening to the far-off warble of an insomnious rooster. It was the faintest of sounds, eerily distant, like a kitten mewing at the bottom of a well, a tiny, tinny predawn madrigal rising from somewhere far down on the lake.

Viviana had come to him in the night, wearing a pair of Luisa's baggy worsted pants and a voluminous flannel shirt. They had laughed together in the darkness of Landry's hut about the ludicrous look it gave her, then had lain together in Landry's blankets, whispering and telling mild lies about the future, making plans that neither of them had great hopes would ever come to pass. They hadn't made love, at least not this night, but rather, by mutual and unspoken consent, clung to each other until sleep claimed them, each offering peace in place of passion.

And now, with the eastern sky beginning to lose its inky thickness and storm clouds admitting only the vaguest predawn light, Landry lay awake and wondered what it was that had disturbed him. He listened once more to the call of the rooster, fading in, fading out. From the foot of the camp, closer, much closer, he heard one of the mules snort in its sleep. Closer yet, from one of the partisan huts, came a tearing sound, like canvas being shredded. Lucertola, probably. The Lizard had always been a heroic snorer.

Then he heard an even closer sound, the closest of all save Viviana's sleep-soft breath at his side. Footsteps. The cautious tread of boots touching gravel, someone slipping through the trees outside his hut. Coming toward him. He unburdened his arm from beneath Viviana's head and reached silently for his Thompson. As he cocked it, a shadow fell across the ground outside the hut entrance.

"David?" Whispered. Urgent. A head appeared at the opening. It was Veterano, trying to see into the darkness.

"I'm here," Landry whispered back.

"Germans come," Veterano murmured. "Many of them. Creeping up from below."

"The guards?"

"Nunzio and Captain Kavanaugh. I warned them. They are alerting the camp."

Landry rolled upright and shook Viviana gently. Her face came off the blanket in sleep-tousled confusion. "What is it? What's wrong?"

"We have visitors," Landry whispered. "You go with Veterano."

"Go? Where?"

He lifted her to her feet and guided her to the entrance. To Veterano, he said, "Go by the women's hut and pick up Luisa and Franca. Then take them to the ravine at the south end of camp. I'll meet you there as soon as I wake the others."

Veterano gripped Viviana's arm, but she balked like a mule. "My boots," she said. "Luisa loaned me some boots. I'm damned if I'll stumble around barefoot." She dug at the foot of the blankets and quickly located them. She and Veterano went one way, and Landry headed the other, moving quickly through the darkness toward the near sleeping huts. He stopped at the Lizard's hut first and tapped the butt of his Thompson lightly against the stones. The snoring ceased immediately. "Germans," Landry whispered. "Grab your gun."

As soon as he heard the Lizard scramble to his feet, Landry hurried toward the Britisher's hut. But Willoughby, alert as ever, was already on his way out, Thompson dangling from one hand, tugging his knapsack to his shoulder with the other. "Where?" he asked.

"Coming up from below," Landry whispered. He nodded at a pair of partisan huts beyond the trees, and the Britisher understood. They broke apart, each going his own way to spread the alarm.

Landry stopped next at Harry Tucker's hut and again tapped stone with gun stock. No response. No sound at all. "Harry?" he called softly. Still no sound. He ducked through the low entrance. Tucker was lying on his side, his head cradled on a pile of straw that he'd covered with a spare shirt.

"Wake up," Landry said. "We've got company." No movement. Landry shook him. "Come on, Harry, wake up. We've got . . ."

A hushed flutter, like an ax head whistling through the air, slashed through the darkness and Landry threw himself flat on the floor of the hut. A tearing roar erupted outside, flames shooting up through the trees, and the ground wobbled drunkenly. Another roar followed the first, then a rain of explosions crashed to ground, ripping the camp apart, turning the gray predawn into red and yellow day. Mortars!

Landry struggled to rise, one arm flung protectively above his head. Confused cries came from the clearing and shrapnel pinged against the stone walls of Tucker's hut. Some of the larger stones, dislodged by concussion, toppled inward. Bright bursts of light flashed through the gaps. Landry saw, in the pulsating flicker of mortar explosions, a spreading circle of blood soaking through Tucker's blanket and seeping into the straw beneath. Poor sod. Hit already? Struck by a stray fragment before he could even rouse himself?

Landry dropped to his knees for a closer look, touched Tucker's wound, felt for his pulse, but another mortar shell crumped into the dirt outside, only a few yards away, flinging him across the hut, and he suddenly found himself running across open ground a good fifty feet from Tucker's hut, zigzagging wildly through an orchard of bursting mortar explosions. He saw a body, one of Dante's men, tangled around the trunk of a tree. He saw figures fleeing helter-skelter for the boulders, silhouetted against flames. He saw a towering pine tree disintegrate at the base and the bushy top come crashing to the ground. Then, abruptly, his legs were pumping in the air and there was no ground beneath him and he felt himself falling, falling, hands reaching.

His knee struck first as he came to earth in the bottom of a dry ravine, and he tumbled forward on his face. Someone else came flying over the top after him and landed on his shoulder. Landry rolled over, hurting, trying to catch his breath. The light of explosions still flashed above, but here, at the bottom of the gully, there were darkness, shadow, safety.

"Madonna!" a voice stuttered close to Landry's ear. It came out Muh-Muh-Madonna. Lucertola, clutching his side, gasped for air.

"Are you hit?" Landry asked. The Lizard looked blank and Landry realized he had spoken in English. He repeated himself in Italian.

"No, David. Just the wind knocked from me," the Lizard said haltingly. He rolled his head back and sucked air. His mouth worked and more stutters popped out. "God. Where did they come from?"

"Come on, keep moving," Landry said. He lifted the Lizard by the arm. "Stay in the bottom of the ravine."

They followed the winding ravine, running hunched over, hearing shrapnel hiss overhead, until finally the explosions fell behind. Daylight threatened and dark, brooding clouds became more distinct with each jogging step. Even so, the shadows in the gully were so thick that they almost ran into Veterano's shotgun before they saw him. He was poised behind a sandbank with Viviana and Franca, shotgun aimed up the ravine. When Landry called out to him, he lowered the barrel.

Viviana came from behind the sandbank to meet Landry. She reached for his hand and squeezed it, her eyes making quick inventory, as if to assure herself that he was all right. He squeezed back. "Where's Luisa?" he asked.

"She wasn't in the hut," Veterano said. His throat sounded tight.

Something moved in the underbrush above them. Landry raised his Thompson. But when the branches parted, it was the Britisher, with Tuono wriggling under his right arm and a dazed Creedmore hanging onto the other. "Hello, down there," Willoughby whispered. "Has your gully room for a pair more?"

Landry gestured them down. They slipped on loose dirt, sliding down the ravine wall on their backsides. Creedmore hit bottom and muffled an exclamation. The dog squirmed frantically, but Willoughby held him tight. Landry bent over them. There was a streak of blood above Creedmore's eyebrow, and fresh drops of blood welled from his unhealed fingertips. "What happened to you?" Landry asked.

"I'm okay," Creedmore said. "Just a little dizzy. I ran into a damn tree, trying to get clear of the mortars."

"But your hand is hurt, too."

Creedmore tucked it inside his shirt. "I must have banged it on something," he said. "Willoughby says I was crawling in circles on my hands and knees when he found me." He grinned. "I'm fine, Coach. Keep me in the game."

Landry said no more. An old ankle dislocation, a calcium deposit in one foot, a knee that went out on him from time to time—Creedmore had a collection of old football injuries, like many players, that would haunt him the rest of his life, but he apparently preferred to accept both old and new pain quietly, not wanting anyone to fuss over it.

Creedmore spoke up again. "What the devil happened, anyway?"

Willoughby said, "I should think that rather obvious. Your informer has been at work once more. That was no small patrol, happening up the mountain by accident. Someone deliberately led them to us."

"That's the way it looks to me, too," Landry said. "Did either of you see Dante along the way? I didn't have time to check his hut."

Willoughby shook his head.

"What about Luisa?"

Tuono wriggled again as more explosions burst behind them and the Britisher took off his belt to make a temporary leash. "May I suggest we keep moving?" he said. "The Germans will be coming up on camp any moment now. A bit more distance wouldn't hurt."

Landry nodded. "Someone will have to circle back around the camp and try for the trail beyond. We've got to intercept Pietro and warn him off."

"I will do it," Veterano volunteered. "It will give me a chance to look for Dante and Luisa."

"Don't waste the time," Landry said. "The important thing is to keep Pietro and his men from walking into the hands of the Germans. The rest of us will head south, to warn Freddy and Piccione."

"Luisa is important, too," Veterano said.

"I know she is," Landry said gently. "We'll just have to hope she got away. In the meantime, tell Pietro that if he thinks he can set up the roadblock by himself, go ahead. As soon as we can round up our stragglers, we'll join him."

Veterano hesitated, as though wanting to say something, then frowned and clambered up the wall of the ravine. Mortar bursts flickered beyond him, though less intensely.

"Let's get going," Landry told the others. "Menággio is a long walk from here."

The Lizard took the lead, clutching his rifle. As they put distance between themselves and the camp, the gray sky gradually brightened and the mortar explosions petered out. A heavy silence settled across the mountains. The Lizard paused and looked back at the burning camp. His lips pushed in and out and he muttered dolefully, "I wonder how many of us died."

"I saw two bodies," Landry said. "But the only one I'm sure of is Tucker."

Creedmore swung his head around. "Harry got it?"

Landry nodded grimly. "I was in his hut when the barrage began."

The Lizard worked his mouth again. The stutter popped out hesitantly. "He was a good man, David. But don't worry, we'll pay those damned crucchi for it. I promise you."

"The Germans didn't do it," Landry said.

The Lizard's forehead wrinkled in puzzlement and Willoughby stopped dead in his tracks. "What are you saying?" Willoughby asked.

"We were supposed to think it was the Germans," Landry said. "But it wasn't. I saw the wound. He was knifed."

After that, they crept along in silence.

Within minutes, a steady drizzle began to fall.

2

The wholesale retreat from Dante's camp was only the first of many withdrawals that stormy Wednesday. Another had its beginnings that afternoon when factory whistles screeched throughout Milan to proclaim the start of a general strike by the populace. Though German soldiers still occupied the center of the city, armed partisans ventured into the open for the first time on the outskirts and brazenly ranged the streets.

At the Prefecture, Mussolini waited through the afternoon, then nervously gathered a small retinue of advisers and went outside to his tan Alfa-Romeo sedan. His appointment with representatives of the National Liberation Committee was set for six o'clock at the archbishopric, but he fully intended to be early. He, too, had heard the worsening war reports and he knew time was growing short. Not only had the local partisans grown unexpectedly bold, but also there were rumors that Americans, no longer impeded by German defenders, were looming on the horizon and might reach Milan as early as this very evening. Even more disturbing, Alessandro Pavolini, secretary of the Neo-Fascist Party, who had already revised his estimate of Valtellina volunteers downward from fifty thousand men to twenty thousand, had today corrected the figure twice more. This morning he had approached Mussolini apologetically with a new estimate. Ten thousand men. There would be only ten thousand men. It was unfortunate, but time was working against them. Then, later in the day, with a sheaf of papers and reports in his hands, Pavolini reluctantly revised the figure again. With all provinces reporting, he now knew the true number of men to be three thousand. But at least this time the figure was definite. And the three thousand were good men, veterans all. At this very moment, they were being trucked toward Como, at the foot of the lake, where they would await the Duce.

With the estimate of Valtellina volunteers cut in successive bites from fifty thousand to three thousand, Mussolini found himself more agreeable to the thought of a negotiated settlement, even if it had to be with partisans. Perhaps this session with the National Liberation representatives would be the proper route to salvation after all. Clad in his customary militia uniform, black shirt, gray britches, and tunic, he took his place in the rear of the Alfa-Romeo. Mezzasoma and Buffarini-Guidi climbed in beside him and Francesco Barracu sat in front. Together, they drove in silence to the palace of the archbishop.

Ildefonso Cardinal Schuster, his scarlet silk soutane in sharp contrast to Mussolini's black-and-gray military attire, met the Duce in the reception room of the palace. He greeted Mussolini solemnly. The partisan leaders had not yet arrived, so Schuster invited Mussolini and his men to sit at a couch and offered them a tray of biscuits and a decanter of rosolio. Mussolini declined.

Schuster, a thin, gaunt man with wide ears and soft, sad eyes, asked gravely, "What will you do, Excellency, if this meeting fails?"

Mussolini brooded for a moment, then said, "I will retire to the Valtellina with an army of three thousand men."

"You will continue the war, then?"

"Only for a little while," Mussolini said. "Then I shall probably give myself up."

Schuster said, "Do not permit your expectations to delude you, Excellency. The number of men willing to go to their deaths in the Valtellina may be closer to three hundred than to three thousand."

Mussolini scanned the cardinal's face, but there was no rancor in the cardinal's sad, blue eyes. "Perhaps a few more than three hundred," Mussolini said. "Not many. I have no illusions."

At precisely six o'clock, the insurrectional committee of three, appointed for the occasion by the National Committee of Liberation, arrived at the palace and were ushered into the reception room. They were General Raffaele Cadorna, an old soldier with a respected reputation, and two civilians, Riccardo Lombardi, an Action Party engineer, and Achille Marazza, who was a lawyer and a Christian Democrat. Each in turn kissed the cardinal's ring, and then they were introduced to Mussolini and his three ministerial companions. Mussolini surprised them by rising and offering his hand. Cadorna took it uncertainly.

As the two opposing parties stood and stared at each other in embarrassment, the sound of a new voice came from the anteroom, speaking to Schuster's secretary. A brief conversation was followed by an explosive cry of anger. It sounded like Marshal Graziani. Mussolini, fearful that Graziani might try to interfere with the negotiations, said quickly, "Well, gentlemen, and what are your proposals?"

Cadorna and his companions exchanged looks and Cadorna said, "Our instructions are simple. We are here to accept your surrender."

Mussolini's cheeks flushed. "I haven't come here for that," he objected. "I was told we were to discuss conditions."

Marazza, the lawyer, stepped in to soften Cadorna's blunt statement. "I believe the Committee of Liberation had given us authority to settle any details. If you wish to discuss conditions, we are at your disposal."

Mussolini was partially mollified. Each man sought a chair, but like water finding its own level, they somehow ended up carefully aligned on opposite sides of the round coffee table, resistance leaders toward the center of the room, Fascists with their backs to the wall. Graziani bustled in from the anteroom, face red. He stood beneath the chandelier for a moment, staring at the unlikely gathering of contrary ideologies, then took a seat to Mussolini's left. He looked as though he wanted to say something, but Mussolini spoke first.

"You understand, of course, that my only wish is to bring an end to the suffering," the Duce said. "Italians should not be fighting Italians."

"We quite understand," Marazza said.

"Then let us see if we can reach an honorable arrangement. Perhaps we can end the fighting this very afternoon."

Barracu, who enjoyed a soldierly reputation himself, coughed lightly and said, "It might be better if we restrict ourselves to consideration of the terms, Duce. We mustn't sign anything yet. After all, we still have obligations to the Germans. It might not be considered morally correct for us to abandon our allies without first informing them of our intention to negotiate an independent peace."

Oddly, it was Graziani who snorted at the mention of the Germans. "They don't seem to have been bothered by the same scruples," he snapped. "We owe them nothing."

Mussolini was surprised by the abrupt about-face of his militant marshal. "Rodolfo? This from you?"

"And more, if our military brigades were in a position to deliver it," Graziani said. "I have just learned from the cardinal's secretary that General Wolff has been discussing surrender terms with the enemy for almost two months."

As it happened, the surrender endeavor of which the secretary had spoken had nothing to do with Sunrise, but was only a temporary ecclesiastical link that had been set up by Wolff as a smoke screen for his talks in Switzerland. Nevertheless, its mention provoked an electric response. Mezzasoma and Barracu gasped. Mussolini assumed a look of pain.

The three partisan representatives had been advised of the Wolff approach before the meeting, and now they seemed puzzled by the reaction of the Fascists. Marazza said, "You mean the Germans have not bothered to inform Your Excellency of their peace maneuvers?"

Mussolini shook his head. "They did this behind my back," he said. He stood. "I am sorry, gentlemen. We can go no farther with this until I have settled accounts with the Germans. If you will wait for me here, I will return in one hour."

"You're sure you will return?" asked Marazza.

"One hour," Mussolini repeated. He headed for the door.

When the Alfa-Romeo pulled up in front of the Prefecture, Mussolini discovered a crowd of his most faithful hierarchs gathered with their families. Nicola Bombacci rushed to him, whitefaced, and said, "Duce! Armed bands of partisans are shooting Fascists without trial. The Germans say they are powerless to help us."

"The Germans have long since given over helping us," Mussolini muttered. He brushed past Bombacci and headed inside. As he passed Lieutenant Helmut Häger, the Waffen-SS officer entrusted with his safety, Mussolini scowled and said, "Your General Wolff has betrayed us all." Häger blinked at him wordlessly.

Mussolini stalked into the ground-floor suite where the Valtellina funds had been deposited. He stood with fists on hips and stared at the neat rows of golden ingots. Mezzasoma and Buffarini-Guidi came timidly into the room, waiting to see what he would do. Mussolini ignored them for a moment, then picked up a Beretta submachine gun and waved his hand at the treasure. "Have this loaded into the cars," he said. "We will leave Milan immediately. We go to the Valtellina."

Word spread quickly. A larger crowd gathered while Blackshirt guards streamed back and forth with the heavy ingots and bulging cardboard cartons stuffed with currency. Several ministers joined the activity with their families and rushed about in the fine mist, adding their own belongings—clothes, furs, jewelry, paintings, personal art objects of gold and silver—to the growing mass of wealth in the courtyard. By the time Mussolini came out of the Prefecture, a string of eleven cars stood in line, front doors ajar, back seats loaded from floorboard to rooftop. Mist turned to sprinkling rain. Mussolini stood with his chin thrust out while old comrades came to embrace him. Pavolini hurried up to promise faithfully that he would soon follow with the three thousand Blackshirt volunteers. Ministers crowded around Mussolini to reaffirm their allegiance, then herded their wives into the front seats of treasure-laden sedans and limousines. Lieutenant Häger, recognizing that Mussolini's mind was finally made up, quickly assembled his guard detail of twenty men and loaded them into a canvas-covered lorry and two smaller military cars.

A late arrival, Marcello Petacci, who had brought both his wife and his sister, Claretta, in a large automobile that bore Spanish diplomatic plates, ran across the courtyard with a bewildered expression on his face. He rushed to Fernando Mezzasoma and said breathlessly, "Where are we going?"

Mezzasoma shrugged. "Who knows? Perhaps to our deaths."

As soon as the ministers had crammed the last of belongings, family, and themselves into the waiting cars, Mussolini strode to the head of the caravan and stopped by his Alfa-Romeo. He raised his fist with the submachine gun clutched in it. "Forward!" he cried. "To the Valtellina!"

A crowd of spectators roared, "Duce! Duce! Duce!"

Then, at several minutes past eight o'clock, with a drizzly, stormy sky hanging low over the Milanese skyline, the caravan of twelve civilian cars and three German military vehicles pulled out of the Prefecture courtyard and headed north for Lake Como. Well-wishers and Fascist sympathizers waved deliriously from the sidewalks until the last car disappeared. Once the cars were gone, an awkward silence settled. The spectators stood uncertainly for a moment, until they seemed to realize where they were, what they were doing. And that they were now alone.

Within minutes, the street was completely empty.

3

Shortly after nine o'clock that night, a cable reached Allen Dulles in Switzerland. Washington, upon reconsideration, had decided to go ahead with the Sunrise negotiations. To placate the Russians, a Soviet emissary would be invited to sit in on the deliberations as an observer, but would be given no authority to make demands or request changes. Dulles was ordered to carry the peace initiative to a quick and satisfactory conclusion.

But by then it was too late. General Karl Wolff and his adjutants, after three days in Lucerne without any word from the Americans, had finally given up and crossed the Swiss border back into Italy, destination unknown. And the Lake Como team, Cornfield advised Dulles bitterly, had broken radio contact. There had been no word from them since Sunday.

There was nothing to do but wait. With luck, Wolff might eventually contact them again, once he reached his headquarters, and the liaison could perhaps be reinstated. But the Valtellina situation would have to work itself out.

4

German military units were also left to work things out for themselves that night. A war front that had held steady for over a year and a half, resisting the relentless Allied surge from one line of defense to the next, had finally shattered into tiny fragments. Demoralized German troops, no longer able to fight back, lacking heavy artillery and air support, driven from their last line of concrete shelters and mountain bunkers in the Apennines, began to surrender in wholesale lots to advancing British and American armies. Unhindered by organized defenses, American mechanized units fanned across the Po Valley, streaking toward Milan, toward Lake Garda, toward Lake Como.

German support elements in rear areas, realizing they were in jeopardy of being overrun, hastily packed up and began a disorderly retreat, hoping to reach the Alpine passes to Austria before the Allies could cut them off. Dozens of truck convoys, loaded with equipment and downcast men, already jammed the roads north, and more would follow.

One of these fleeing convoys consisted of a string of twenty-six Luftwaffe communications trucks bearing heavy rolls of wire, telephone and radio gear and 150 frightened technicians under the command of a young Luftwaffe lieutenant named Hans Fallmeyer. Fallmeyer and his communications personnel wanted only to see home again, or what was left of it, but they made the mistake of choosing the Como road as one leg of their escape route.

Within twenty-four hours, they would find themselves joining the clutter of confused actors gathering on the Lake Como stage, and a chaotic drama of errors and random fortune would begin to unfold.

Book Two

MUSSOLINI

Day Six

Thursday—April 26, 1945

E avanti a lui tremava tutta Roma!

This, then, is the man before whom
  all Rome trembled!
                          —Puccini, *Tosca*

1

Mussolini and his caravan rolled into the town of Como at the
foot of the lake before midnight, but they didn't stay long. Rain
poured down on them in torrents as they left their cars and sought
temporary shelter in the Como Prefecture, only to learn that villagers and farmers in the area had taken up arms and were beginning to harass local Fascist officials, and that the German garrison
near Como was on the verge of pulling out. Word also reached
Mussolini that his wife, Rachele, had come to Lake Como only
the day before with two of their children and was hiding at the
Villa Montero in Cernobbio, less than a mile from the SD headquarters in the Villa Locatelli. He didn't try to see her, but he did
take the time to pen a last note. In it, he told his wife of thirty-five
years that he had decided to make a final military stand in the
Valtellina, and he advised her to try for safety across the Swiss
border. "We may never see each other again," he wrote, "and I
ask your forgiveness for all the harm I have unwittingly done

you." He gave the note to Buffarini-Guidi, who sent a man off to deliver it by hand.

Because the German troops in the Como region were already leaving, and Pavolini had not yet appeared with the promised Blackshirts, Mussolini decided at two o'clock that dark Thursday morning that he would tarry no longer in Como. A safer stopping place lay ahead. Only thirty-four kilometers to the north, halfway up the winding Lake Como road, was a town that offered access not only to Switzerland via a small mountainous feeder road, but also regular ferry service to the eastern side of the lake, should it become necessary. It seemed a more prudent place to wait for Pavolini and the Valtellina volunteers.

And so, leaving only one man in Como to tell Pavolini and his army where the Duce could be found, Mussolini gathered his entourage and set off again, civilian cars and German military vehicles driving slowly through the rain and darkness, headlights dimmed to avoid aerial attacks by Allied night fighters. It would take them another two hours to reach their new destination.

2

The worst enemy for Landry was the rain. As he and his small band of refugees stumbled down from the mountains, it drummed on his bare head with stinging impact. It drenched his clothes. It peppered directly into his eyes, blinding him, so that he blundered over a rock here, slid into low-hanging branches there. Viviana trudged silently beside him, somehow keeping up, but Landry was so dazed by the constant beating of the rain on his unprotected skull that he could scarcely wonder where she had found the energy for the exhausting descent. It was nearly three o'clock that morning and still raining when they followed the Lizard into Menággio. Mud became cobblestones beneath Landry's boots. The dark streets slept, but he didn't notice. He kept his head down, to keep the rain from his eyes, slogging through the streets to the house of the schoolmaster in whose cellar they hoped to find Freddy Stefanini and Piccione.

The schoolmaster was one Don Ottorino Perfetti, a stout, broad-shouldered man, who nevertheless had an owlish look about him. He answered their knock quickly, but to Landry's racked impatience, he kept his door on chain lock until he recognized the Lizard. Then the door opened and Landry was finally out of the rain. The schoolmaster clucked at the disheveled wet-hen look of the two women, then cringed back in surprise as Tuono shook off his own burden of rainwater. Landry blinked, knowing he looked owlish himself, trying to get his wits about him. It was as if the rain still fell, echoing inside his skull. He managed a grin for Viviana, whose hair was plastered flat against her head, and he felt a little warmer when she smiled back. He felt warmer still when the schoolmaster led Viviana and Franca to a purring fire and pressed glasses of brandy into their hands, but it was quickly back to work for him. Landry and Willoughby, with a soaking Tuono sticking close to Willoughby's legs and Creedmore and the Lizard hanging right behind, followed the schoolmaster down worn steps into a cold cellar filled with boxes of discarded textbooks and a few dusty bottles of Sassella, Inferno and Grumello wines.

Apparently this household had not been sleeping. Stefanini must have been hard at work when he heard the knock at the door and had only just extinguished the light, for when the schoolmaster carried his candle to a kerosene lamp and tried to relight it, he found the glass chimney too hot to handle. As he reached for his handkerchief and worked the chimney loose, Stefanini stepped from the shadows and moved into the guttering candlelight. Tuono, happy to see another familiar face, rushed him and poked wet paws into his stomach. Stefanini pushed the dog aside and said, "What the hell are you guys doing here?"

Creedmore and Willoughby sagged down on textbook boxes. Landry brushed a small river of water from his hair and said, "Germans hit us. They came in at dawn, just a few hours after you and Piccione left, and blew Dante's camp apart."

"My God," Stefanini said. "How many of you got away?"

"We don't know. Veterano spotted them coming up the mountain in time to give us some warning, but we never had a chance to count noses." He blinked and tried to think what should come next. Raindrops still drummed in his head. "Any luck with the radio?"

"Not much," Stefanini said. "The damn thing is older than Marconi. I was trying to bypass some shot insulation when you guys knocked on the door and scared us spitless."

"Maybe I can give you a hand. I don't know much about radios, but . . ."

"What I could use most is a couple of miracles," Stefanini said. He lifted a blanket and exposed a black box lying dismantled on the surface of a table. "Spent tubes, bad wiring, missing parts. I think I can make do with the tubes. They're weak, but we should get a signal. My biggest problem is that both the W/T key and the mike are missing. We've looked all over the cellar, but Don Ottorino thinks maybe they got left behind somewhere. I'll have to improvise something."

"Well, let me know if you need help," Landry said. He slipped out of his wet coat and looked around the cellar. "Where's Piccione?"

"He's out trying to scrape up some copper wire," Stefanini said. "There's a bad coil that needs rewinding." He shook his head slowly. "You guys look like warmed-over death."

"We're bushed," Landry admitted. He sank down between Creedmore and Willoughby and leaned his Thompson against the wall. "Wake us up in about two years, will you, Freddy? That ought to just about do it."

Piccione, unable to find copper wire for the easy taking, had finally settled on an alternate solution. He climbed one of the rough-hewn telephone poles that lined the lake road and cut the telephone wire with his pocket knife. Then, pole by pole, he worked his way back toward town, until he had accumulated a roll of wire almost too heavy to carry. He was ready to return to the schoolmaster's house when he heard car engines and saw dim headlights coming up from the south toward Menággio. He hefted the roll of telephone wire across his shoulder and quickly ducked into wet shrubbery on the side of the road.

It was a long caravan of vehicles. A German Kübelwagen came first, then a line of slow-moving Alfas and Lancias and Fiats, maybe ten or twelve of them. Bringing up the rear was a German military truck. Piccione could see soldiers through the canvas flaps, slumped on bench seats along both sides.

He expected them to keep on going, through Menággio and on to the north, but the lead vehicle, the Kübelwagen, pulled to a stop less than a hundred meters up the road, near the Fascist club house. The rest of the cars slowed and drew up in a line behind the Kübelwagen. Some of the drivers dismounted.

At first Piccione thought it might be a caravan of Germans intent on sealing off the Swiss border. From Menággio wound the small dirt road that rose through the mountains to Lake Lugano and the Porlezza pass, the last point between here and Ponte del Passo where cars could turn away from the lake to cross over to Switzerland. But the caravan seemed to be stopping for the night. Soldiers from the truck crossed the road to a schoolhouse and broke open the doors and set about turning it into a temporary bivouac. People from the cars—Piccione could see now that they were civilians, and Italians at that, mostly men, some women, a few children—stepped wearily toward the club house.

It was curious, and Piccione wanted to get closer, but a handful of German soldiers came out of the schoolhouse and took up guard positions along the line of parked cars. A slender track of light, gleaming through the blackout curtains of the club house, fell on the forward Alfa-Romeo, and Piccione realized there were men still sitting in it. They seemed to be waiting for something, perhaps for the club manager, who came rushing down the steps a few minutes later, stuffing his nightshirt into his pants. A short, stubby man in a militia uniform leaned out of the car. He had a jutting jowl and he murmured curtly to the club manager and was quickly directed toward the Villa Castelli, just up the road, where the local Fascist leader lived. The jowly man pulled his head back into the Alfa-Romeo. As he did, someone opened the car door to admit the club manager and the dome light switched on. Piccione started with the shock of recognition.

Heart pounding, he abandoned his armload of telephone wire and scurried away from the road. He circled up the hill to the schoolmaster's house. As soon as the schoolmaster let him in, he rushed down to the basement, scarcely able to contain his impatience. He saw Stefanini at the work table, then he saw Landry and Creedmore and the Britisher sprawled on the floor, resting. It brought him up short for a moment, and he wanted to ask them what they were doing here. But he couldn't contain his own news any longer.

He waved his arms toward the road and gasped, "He's here! Mussolini! In Menággio!"

3

Veterano spotted Pietro and his men just at dawn, working their way across the rain-swept mountains above Musso. They were strung out on the trail, walking single file, and there couldn't have been more than eight or nine of them, not the twenty that David Landry and the others had been expecting.

Veterano didn't approach them instantly. The sky was gray and they wouldn't be expecting anyone to cross their path this far north of Dante's camp, especially in this kind of weather. To make sure they didn't open fire on him and ask questions later, he took shelter behind a boulder and let them come toward him on their own. Truth to tell, the momentary rest was welcome.

Veterano, whose real name was Salvatore Basevi, was sixty-three years old, though he had told everyone in Dante's detachment that he was only fifty-four, and while he could still outstrip most of the younger partisans at traversing the mountains, he found that prolonged exertion tended to make him more tired and achy with each passing day. Not that it had anything to do with age. Veterano was very sensitive about age. He resented his years, just as he resented the name the partisans had attached to him, Veterano, the veteran, the old man. He could still take any man among them, strength against strength. But his energy, he had to admit, didn't seem to last as long these days. He was convinced it had something to do with these northern climes. Veterano was a Southerner, more than that, a Sicilian, and he wasn't accustomed to the cold and moisture of the North. Paradise, for him, had always been the dry, hot landscape of his homeland, and the smell of the sea blowing across bleak brown rock.

Pietro and his small band were inching their way upward. They

were still too far away to hear a hailing call. He sank back and
rested, waiting. He shouldn't be this tired. Of course, part of it
might have been the worry. Luisa, not in her hut when the Germans came. Worry sapped a man's strength, and Veterano worried
desperately about Luisa. Not as a lover worries about his sweet-
heart, no, of course not. Veterano knew he was too old and too ignorant ever to aspire to that. But Luisa had treated him kindly,
accepted him, a Southerner among these strangers from the North,
and he would gladly die for her, if she cared to ask it. She was, in
her quiet, sympathetic way, much like the woman Veterano had
mourned after twenty-eight years of marriage and childbirth, all
dead now save his two sons in America. The only touch of home
he had on this side of the Atlantic was Luisa. There were times
when she smiled her crooked smile that he was plunged back to
his youth, back to a hot afternoon sun burning his arms brown
and the sound of his wife's laughter on the beach and the creak of
oars in his dory and a looseness at his back when he dragged in
his net with glorious sunset tinting the Mediterranean all brown
and purple and rusty.

He heard voices. Pietro was closer. Strange that Pietro and his
men had taken so long to cross the mountains. Strange that there
were so few of them on the trail. The delay was partially his own
fault, Veterano decided. He could have reached Pietro hours ago
if he hadn't spent so much time scouting the area around Dante's
ruined camp, ducking Germans, trying to find some sign of Luisa.
He thought he'd actually seen her at one point, running through
the trees below camp with her head low, her hand clasped tightly
by another figure, a man. Dante, perhaps. Veterano hoped so.
Dante would see her to safety.

Pietro and his column were almost to Veterano's hiding place,
and he straightened. He called, "Pietro. Do not shoot. It is I, Veterano, from the camp of Dante."

He anticipated difficulty, a moment of awkwardness, perhaps a
serious challenge before they were willing to accept him at his
word, but Pietro surprised him by calling back, "Yes, we were expecting someone to meet us. Come out."

Veterano stepped cautiously into the open, still not sure they
believed him, and talked fast. "Your friend, David, sent me. I
have come to warn you. You must not go to Dante's camp."

"Yes, we already know," Pietro said. He gestured at a man behind him, and Veterano saw the big American, Captain Kavanaugh, standing at Pietro's shoulder.

Veterano felt a surge of hope for Luisa. At least one other had made good his escape. Uncharacteristically, he stepped forward and grabbed the big American in a strong bear hug. "You made it," he said. Then he saw Salvo, the pipe-smoking partisan who had left before the attack to fetch Pietro. He threw his arms around Salvo too. "They told you what happened?" Veterano asked.

Salvo nodded sadly. Though Salvo's face was wet with rain, Veterano thought he saw moisture of a different kind in the eyes. "We were on our way to look for survivors," Salvo said. "The rest of Pietro's men will wait for us on the lake."

"You may as well turn back," Veterano said. "Any who survived will have scattered to the mountains. Perhaps they, too, will go to the lake."

"How many were hurt?" Salvo asked Veterano.

Veterano shrugged. "It is difficult to say. I watched from the trees and saw the Germans bring out four bodies. Baldo, Nunzio, Emmanuele and the American, Lieutenant Tucker. Others may be wounded and hiding."

Kavanaugh's face darkened. "They got Tucker?"

Veterano said, "His body was among the dead."

"'Brave men and good wines last a short time,'" Pietro intoned. He spat to the side of the trail. "Well, what now? What does David wish us to do?"

"You are to arrange the roadblock on your own, if you are able," Veterano answered. "David says he and the others will join you as soon as possible."

"Hey, come on," Kavanaugh said. "Without Dante's people, what chance is there?"

"Dante will show up," Veterano insisted. "Luisa, as well. They all will. With the camp overrun, they have no place to go but to the lake. We must be there when they arrive."

"We will go down and see," Pietro said. "We certainly can't accomplish anything hiding in the mountains." He grinned and clapped Kavanaugh on the arm. "Besides, my oversized friend, today is Thursday. Salvo has reminded me that this is the day they hand out the weekly ration of tobacco. I think we all deserve a good smoke, do we not?"

Kavanaugh swallowed. "Isn't that what they always ask a man before he faces a firing squad?"

4

Mussolini's caravan of cars tarried in Menággio for four hours that morning, then broke up. Shortly after eight o'clock, while weary German guards slept in the Menággio schoolhouse, two of the Alfas pulled away from the parked cars and headed up the small sideroad toward Switzerland. It wasn't a general exodus, just the two cars followed by a half-dozen German escorts in the Kübelwagen, but it triggered activity in the Fascist club house and several ministers rushed outside with their families and piled into cars to hare after them, as though fearful of being left behind.

The cars didn't go far. Landry and his companions, who had been watching from cover, followed up the circling muddy road on foot, and found that the Fascists had only driven a couple of kilometers to a small resort hotel, the Miravelle, near the mountain village of Grandola, just above Menággio.

That the cars should have moved at all was puzzling to Landry. The Swiss border, if that was the attraction, was still twelve kilometers farther up the road. Willoughby thought the move might have been prompted by someone's fear that the parked cars, strung out as they were in front of the club house, might be too visible from the air. Here, at least, they were partially hidden by a thick growth of pines and cedars. Whether Willoughby's guess was correct or not, it was evident to Landry that this was only a temporary stopping place; the German truck and the bulk of the Waffen-SS guards had remained behind in Menággio.

Landry and the others paused in the trees to study the Kübelwagen, nosed in near the entrance of the hotel. It was empty, but Landry could see two German guards loitering near the corner, looking tired and cold in the steady drizzle. The rest of the cars were parked in a semicircle to one side of the hotel.

"Like wagons facing an Indian attack," Creedmore muttered, and Landry spared a glance for his crouching companions. Creedmore and Stefanini looked as miserable as Landry felt. They obviously hated the rain just as much as he did. The others, Piccione, the Lizard and Willoughby, sensible Europeans all, wore caps. But Creedmore and Stefanini, like Landry, were bareheaded, and rain poured down their cheeks and temples and ran under their collars. Landry sighed. Americans, himself included, never seemed to realize that headgear should be worn for utility, not mere looks.

As Landry knelt uncomfortably in the rain, Piccione caught him by the sleeve and whispered, "Look!" Three civilians came out of the hotel and trudged past the German guards to one of the cars around on the side. The civilians stood in the rain beside the parked car for a moment, talking among themselves as though trying to make up their minds about something, then they climbed into the car and backed away from the semicircle. They drove down to the juncture where the hotel drive met the road, then paused. After a moment of indecision, the car turned and headed up the winding road toward Switzerland.

"Did you see him?" Landry asked. "Was he with them?"

Piccione said, "No, not Mussolini. But we are close. One of those men was Zerbino, Mussolini's Minister of the Interior. Another was a man they call Buffarini-Guidi, who once held the same office. I did not recognize the other."

"But two of them were Fascist ministers? You're sure?"

"I think so. I have seen their photographs many times."

"Let's get closer," Freddy Stefanini whispered. "I'd like to see what they've stashed in all those cars."

"Soon," Landry said. "Let's be sure first that Mussolini is really here. We'll split up and try for a look through some of the windows." They had been seeking confirmation of Mussolini's presence for hours now, ever since Piccione brought the word to the schoolmaster's house, but except for the two men Piccione had just claimed to recognize, nothing indicated any connection to Mussolini. There were German guards, of course, but escorts might have been assigned to any semi-official expedition. Also, if this was truly part of Mussolini's expected move to the Valtellina, where were the Blackshirt Brigades? To Landry, there was an opera-buffa touch to the whole scene and he was beginning to doubt Piccione's powers of observation. An Italian tyrant, escaping from war to a picture-book resort hotel high above the lake? It was a little too farfetched for him to take seriously, but he told everyone to be careful as he sent them down toward the hotel. Piccione and Willoughby headed for the rear, while Stefanini and the Lizard moved closer to the cars to provide cover. Landry paired himself with Wesley Creedmore and they circled to the far side of the building to reconnoiter.

The two German guards hovered near the front entrance, trying to stay out of the rain, so it was no challenge to avoid them. The fine gravel of the hotel drive crunched beneath Landry's and Creedmore's feet, then they were across and on soft, muddy ground. Their target was a row of brightly lit windows. They crept toward them through the chill, wind-whipped spring morning.

The first four windows belonged to the lobby, and Landry could see men and women inside, standing in frightened clusters. A nervous hotel manager rushed from group to group, gesticulating, unable to keep still for more than a few seconds at a time. Landry saw no faces he could recognize, so they moved on. The fifth window opened into an empty dining area, as did the sixth and seventh. But the eighth window was different. Apparently an office, probably belonging to the hotel manager, it contained three men. One, sitting at a desk with his back to them, was a heavy-set man in a gray uniform, studying a map. On the far side of the desk stood an edgy civilian with a short gray beard and a young Waffen-SS man wearing the collar tabs of a lieutenant.

Creedmore ducked back at the sight of the German officer, but Landry felt a stir of interest. He realized that Creedmore was pulling at his arm. "Come on," Creedmore whispered. "That's an SS man. He'll see us."

Landry shook him off. "Look at the man behind the desk. Shaved head. Proper size. I'll bet anything that's Mussolini. I wish he'd turn around so we could see his face."

"Sure," Creedmore said. "Why don't you tap on the window and get his attention? Jesus, let's get out of here."

But the inability to control impatience, to move merely for the sake of movement, had lost more than one hunter his prize. Landry held his ground and peered cautiously past the sill.

Then three things happened almost simultaneously, each

equally startling. For one, the Waffen-SS officer made a move around the desk, and Creedmore twitched, sure they had been seen. But the man only reached for a carafe of water on a sideboard near the window. At the same time, two figures appeared at the rear corner of the building, and this time even Landry twitched before he realized it was Willoughby and Piccione, circling to meet them. Then the man behind the desk turned to speak to the German officer, and Landry got his first clear look at the famous face—the heavy jowls, the jutting jaw, the brooding mouth. It was unreal. It was more than ridiculous. But even with reading glasses perched on his nose, the man was, unmistakably, Benito Mussolini.

"Good Godalmighty!" Creedmore hissed.

"Got him!" Landry hissed back.

Creedmore's hand tugged more urgently than before. This time Landry allowed himself to be pulled from the window. Willoughby and Piccione waited at the rear corner of the building. The Britisher shook his head and whispered, "No luck, I'm afraid. Nothing but kitchens and empty rooms back this way."

"We had some," Creedmore said, "but I don't know whether it's good or bad. He's here. We spotted him in an office." Creedmore shot a wondering glance at Landry. "It *was* him, wasn't it? He looked so small. I guess I thought he was a whole lot taller."

Landry had to smile. "I'd bet my life on it," he said. "Come on, let's get back to the trees and tell the others."

"What about the cars?" Creedmore said. "Old Freddy was pretty hot to take a look at what's in them. He keeps remembering what Rossiter said about all that money."

"Too dangerous," Landry said.

"It'd only take a few minutes," Creedmore said.

Willoughby also seemed curious. "It might be rather interesting."

Creedmore urged, "Those German guards are all but asleep on their feet, David. I'll bet we could sneak up around the back and they wouldn't hear a thing. Specially in this rain."

Landry's own inquisitiveness had been aroused as well. He hesitated, then gave in. "Okay, I guess a quick look wouldn't hurt."

They skirted the rear of the hotel and worked their way to the cars in the side courtyard. Stefanini and the Lizard, grown nervous with the passage of time, had edged through the trees and were waiting impatiently some thirty feet beyond the nearest car. They looked relieved when Landry waved them in.

All six men hunched behind a gray Lancia Aprillia, a sedan parked near the trees, and Creedmore peered over the top to make sure the guards were still at the front of the building. Landry and Stefanini pressed their noses against the rear window of the Lancia and looked inside. The back seat was stuffed high with cardboard cartons, clothing. Creedmore tried the door, but it was locked.

"Let me," Stefanini whispered. He handed his carbine to Landry and bent over the car door handle. He took a piece of metal from his pocket and jiggled it in the key slot. The lock knob popped up and Stefanini stood back, grinning. "Product of a misspent youth," he said.

They opened the door and crowded around the running board. Willoughby seemed to see something of interest in the front seat, and he leaned past Landry to inspect it while Landry rummaged beneath furs and overcoats for one of the cartons. The carton was securely taped, but Landry ripped it open. Stacks of brightly colored French currency fell out.

"Whooo-e-e-e-e!" Creedmore said under his breath. "Do these poor old eyes deceive me, or is that the Bank of Paris spilling all over that back seat?"

Landry hesitated with his hand poised over the money. Something flared in his brain. Greed? Temptation? He picked up a sheaf of bills, all large-denomination French franc notes, new and tidy, wrapped in a crisp bank wrapper. He fluttered the edges and sucked in his breath, with Piccione and Stefanini hovering at his shoulders like vultures. Stefanini said in a choked voice, "My God! There must be a hundred thousand dollars in that box!"

Landry was just as impressed. "More," he said. "And there are two more boxes just like it on the floor."

Creedmore leaned past Landry for a closer look, then straightened up so violently that he almost hit his head on the door frame. "Look at that," he twanged. He pushed a carton aside and exposed a layer of shiny yellow ingots lining the floorboard. "Gold! That's gold!" He lifted one of the bars clumsily from the car.

They passed the gold bar from hand to hand, staring first at it,

then at each other. It was incredibly heavy for its size. Stefanini
was the last to take it. He rubbed his fingers across the shiny surface, then raised his eyes and said, "I hope you don't mind, guys,
but I think this would be a nice time to start my retirement fund."
He laid the ingot on the running board, and leaned into the car.
He seemed indecisive for a moment, as though torn between the
bank notes or gold, then reached into the open carton and started
transferring stacks of currency to his pocket.

Creedmore looked troubled. "Hey, take it easy," he whispered.
"You'll make a mess and give us away."

Stefanini ignored him. He filled one pocket and started on a
second. Piccione and the Lizard seemed equally tempted. They
hesitated, then crowded into the doorway beside Stefanini and
started stuffing their own pockets. Creedmore stared after them
and a look of hunger came across his face. He obviously wanted
to join them, but he didn't. He stood back and plunged his hands,
the good one and the maimed one, into his pockets. But the look
of hunger remained.

"That's enough," Landry told Stefanini and the two partisans.
"Cover the rest and let's get out of here. We don't want the Fascists to know we've spotted them."

"They'll never miss it," Stefanini whispered giddily, still stuffing
his pockets.

"Back off," Landry said more firmly.

Stefanini turned his head. For a moment, he stared at Landry,
the kind of surly look when a dog's hackles rise and the muscles
coil for battle. The killer was very close to the surface. Piccione
and the Lizard also tensed, as if ready to take on the underdog.
Then Stefanini looked away, and the danger passed. Landry
stepped in to close the door. Stefanini shifted, as though unwilling
to lose sight of the cartons and the gold. Landry couldn't blame
him, not even for the moment of hatred. The stacks of bills were
so new, so crisp and clean. He saw from the corner of his eye that
Creedmore and Willoughby were craning their necks as well.

Landry heard Piccione and the Lizard sigh. Freddy Stefanini
patted his bulging pockets and lifted the gold bar from the running
board. His anger was past, at least for the moment. "Let's do one
more car," he suggested. "We could take just a little from each,

and they'd never even miss it. We'll never get another chance like this."

Landry was prepared to argue, but the German guards settled it. One of them appeared at the front corner of the building, tugging his collar close to his throat. He began a slow, slouching stroll through the rain, checking each car in the semicircle as he passed it. Landry and the others ducked away from the Lancia and scrambled back into the trees. Stefanini flattened himself beside Landry and held the gold bar close to his face. He stared at it for a moment, then pressed his lips to it. "Bee-yoo-tiful!" he murmured.

"Quiet," Landry whispered.

The guard came down the curving line to the Lancia, then circled it and started back toward the front of the hotel. He didn't appear to notice anything unusual about the Lancia, just moved doggedly through the downpour, staring at each vehicle as he walked. It took an eternity, but he finally returned to the corner and disappeared, and Landry could hear nothing but the drumming rain.

Creedmore raised his head and looked longingly at the cars. "How much do you figure is there?" he said. "Altogether, I mean."

Stefanini caressed his gold bar like a nursing mother and said, "Enough. Couple of million bucks in that one car alone, I'll bet. Twelve cars in all. Figure a minimum, two million per car. That's twenty million bucks. Maybe more. Just sitting there. Only a few feet away."

"Twenty million?" Creedmore said. He licked his lips. "Let's not talk about it anymore."

"Maybe thirty or forty million," Stefanini said. "Think about it. We could all grab an armload of gold bars, if we wanted to, and take off across the mountains for Switzerland. Nobody would ever miss us. We could buy a bunch of villas and live like movie stars."

Creedmore suddenly looked angry. "Shut up, Freddy. You know how much gold weighs? I figure that bar you swiped is worth maybe . . . what? Maybe five hundred bucks a pound. A scrawny punk like you, I figure you could handle about sixty pounds, maximum, if you stopped every twenty feet to take a breather."

"I'm not so scrawny," Stefanini objected. The killer flickered again.

"You could be Charles Atlas and it still wouldn't make any difference," Creedmore said angrily. "We'd have to carry at least two thousand pounds of gold to get away with even a million. That's a whole ton. How are we going to get over the mountains with a ton of gold?"

"Knock it off," Landry told them. "We've got business to tend to. Freddy, you and Creedmore get back down to Menággio and get that radio going. Take Piccione and the Lizard with you to scout up some transportation. Someone has to head north to alert Pietro."

Stefanini eyed both Landry and the Britisher suspiciously. "What about you two?"

"We'll stay here and keep an eye on the hotel," Landry said. "If any of Mussolini's Blackshirt Brigades show up, send either Piccione or the Lizard back up to warn us."

Stefanini said, "You trying to get rid of us so you can glom all the loot for yourselves?"

"Don't be an ass," Landry told him. "Remember what we came up here for. Mussolini's down there in that hotel. Have you forgotten?"

Stefanini clamped his jaw, then clutched the gold bar to his stomach and backed reluctantly from the bushes. As Creedmore and the two partisans started to follow him, Landry reached out and plucked at Creedmore's sleeve. Quietly, so the others wouldn't hear, Landry said, "Thanks."

"For what?" Creedmore said. "I didn't do anything."

"That's the point," Landry said. "If you hadn't held back when the others started grabbing, things might have gotten out of hand."

Creedmore looked startled, then grinned. "Yeah, they were really having some fun, weren't they? Pitching around like blind dogs in a meat house. I was pretty tempted myself. I guess I was just afraid the Army brass would show up and demand it all back, or I might have joined in too." He hesitated, looking as though he wished he had, then ducked away through the trees and hurried to catch up with the others.

Landry leaned against his Thompson, hunching his back against the raindrops that trickled unceasingly past his collar and down his neck. After a while, he noticed Willoughby was staring at him. Almost conversationally, Landry said, "Okay, so maybe I was a little stiff-necked. I did what I had to. Damn them all for making it necessary."

Willoughby said, "Yes, they came down with the fever, didn't they? Especially Lieutenant Stefanini."

"A fever like that could get us killed," Landry muttered. He winced at the self-righteous sound of his own voice, and added quickly, "Ah hell, I felt it as much as anyone. If you and Creedmore had gone along with the others, well, I don't know. Maybe I would have, too."

"But you didn't take anything," Willoughby said.

"Neither did you," Landry said. "Hell, Creedmore had more reason to dig in than the rest of us. His family is dirt poor. He wouldn't have gotten even his first two years of college if it hadn't been for a football scholarship. The way I hear it, his father is the most illustrious drunk in some dusty little Oklahoma town, and when a kid like Creedmore is offered a way up and out, it's like a miracle. How could I start filling my pockets when a guy like that just stands there looking wide-eyed and honest?"

Willoughby nodded. "I felt it rather strongly myself," he said. "I wouldn't have needed much, but I absolutely must find the money somehow for a new automobile after the war. If you've ever had three breakdowns in one day with a carful of overheated Airedales, you'd know what I mean."

Squatting in the rain, Landry felt a moment's closeness to the Britisher. "I would have needed a lot," Landry admitted. "Enough to rent a palace in Siam, if I chanced to end up there. A certain friend might just go with me if I could swing her a palace." He thought briefly of Viviana, hiding at the schoolmaster's house, and wondered if a palace would really be high on her list of priorities. He almost asked Willoughby for his opinion, then decided a discussion of anything so personal would be inappropriate. To cover his hesitation, he said, "I just wish we could have gotten that radio working a little sooner. Not only so we could send word to Switzerland about Mussolini, but also to put their minds at ease. They must be pretty worried about us, not hearing anything."

"I shouldn't be concerned about that if I were you," Willoughby said. "I doubt they've even noticed we're off the air. I had occasion to meet your Mr. Dulles and Mr. Cornfield when this mission was in the planning stages. Mr. Dulles impressed me as a man interested only in overall results, with no time for small fish like us."

"Dulles?" Landry said. "Never heard of him."

Willoughby smiled. "Of course not. Why should you have? You're not actually one of them, are you? One forgets. You handle yourself quite well, you know."

"Oh," Landry said. "He's an OSS man?"

"A very important OSS man," Willoughby said. "I shouldn't be surprised to see him take over the entire American intelligence system someday, especially if he pulls off this Sunrise project."

"You seem to know a lot for a military observer," Landry said.

Willoughby smiled again. "Yes, well, that's what observation is all about, isn't it?"

The Britisher fell silent, but he still seemed to be studying Landry. Landry said, "You got something else on your mind?"

"As a matter of fact, I have," Willoughby said. "I was just trying to decide whether or not I could trust you with it."

"Don't do me any favors," Landry said.

"I doubt you'll consider it a favor," Willoughby said. "I'd like your advice on whether I should wait for sufficient proof, or whether I should kill a man perhaps prematurely."

Landry gawked at him. "You what?"

"The traitor," Willoughby said. "I had an arrangement with Major Rossiter, but I'm afraid that's gone by the boards. I dislike putting a potentially innocent man out of the way, but on Rossiter's dictate it would have been all right to do so. Now that I lack higher authority to decide things, I feel the need for approval. I'd like you to be Rossiter's stand-in."

"What are you talking about?"

Willoughby sighed. "I rather thought you would have guessed by now," he said. "I wasn't really sent here as an observer, you know. I'm a ferret. Your government has authorized me to find and eliminate the person responsible for the systematic betrayals in this area. It's politic that I do my work quietly, of course. I'd appreciate your co-operation in keeping things that way."

Landry found himself groping for words. "How come no one

told us?" he asked. "Okay, so I'm an outsider, and I can see the OSS not wanting to share secrets with me. But you haven't even told the ALOTs. Surely you don't suspect one of them?"

"I suspect everyone," Willoughby said. "That's my job. ALOTs. Partisans. Civilian sympathizers. Frankly, until the last day or so, I even suspected you."

Landry shook his head. "You're wrong. It can't be an ALOT. They've got nothing to gain." He frowned suddenly and chewed at his lip. "It can't be a partisan, either."

"It has to be someone," Willoughby said. "Given Lieutenant Stefanini's convenient absences in times of stress and his rather surprising greed today, he begins to look like the most likely candidate."

Landry found words quickly this time. "Bull!" he snapped. "Freddy is my friend. I'd know if he was the one."

"Your friend?" Willoughby said. "For a moment there, down at the car, I thought the two of you were going to come to blows. Perhaps even worse. What kind of a friend is that?"

"That doesn't mean anything. Just because he got carried away by all that gold and stuff doesn't mean he's a traitor. He couldn't possibly betray anyone. There's no reason for it."

"Even friends sometimes make mistakes," Willoughby said. He seemed to recognize Landry's distress, and his face softened. "You're a sensible man," he said. "That became obvious to me from the way you stepped in and filled the vacuum in Dante's camp after Major Rossiter disappeared. But you have a blind spot. You mustn't let friendship confuse you."

"Hell, I'm confused, but not by friendship. You may as well know where I stand, Willoughby. Don't make a move for Freddy. You'll find me in your way."

Willoughby shrugged lightly. "That's what I needed to know," he said. "Since you feel so strongly, I'll wait for adequate proof. But I warn you. When I feel sure enough, I'll have to kill him."

"Why?"

Willoughby said, "Because treachery is one of the fatal diseases of our profession, and it mustn't be allowed to spread. It's hard on the faithful, don't you see? My job is to enforce the faith. Or to make sure that those who are faithless have only a limited time in which to enjoy the fruits of their treachery."

"Your job stinks," Landry said.

"Perhaps. But it's a necessary one." He peered at Landry for a moment, a deep, searching look, as though trying to read behind the eyes. Then he shrugged again. "Nevertheless, I'll wait until I'm sure. Perhaps you're right about Stefanini. About friendship, too. It must be comforting to be able to put your faith in someone. I've often wished I could make friends more readily."

"It isn't something you have to work at," Landry said.

"It is for me. For example, a man should be completely honest with his friends. I haven't been completely honest with you. I let you think I took nothing from the car earlier. Actually, I did take something." He reached into his canvas kit and pulled out a gray chauffeur's cap. "I found this on the front seat. Here, take it. The bill should keep rain from your eyes, and since it's wool, the cloth will turn water."

It was a clumsy tender of friendship, and Landry didn't know quite how to react. He hesitated, then reached for the cap. "Thank you," he said. "Thank you for backing off on Freddy, too. You'll see you were wrong about him."

The gesture of friendship, once made, seemed to make the Britisher uncomfortable. Briskly, he said, "You'll look a damn fool in the thing, but then we can't have anyone seeing us anyway, now can we? I suggest we forego any further discussion and withdraw to that stand of fir trees. The branches will give us some protection. I predict we're in for a long, unpleasant wait."

5

X. B. Kavanaugh entered the outskirts of Gravedona late that afternoon with Pietro and the Puecher partisans, intending to seek overnight shelter in the home of a partisan collaborator, but a townsman, a local barber, saw them sneaking through the rainy streets and startled them all by rushing out of his barber's stall and shouting, "Viva la Resistenza Armata!"

Kavanaugh was sure it was a trap. The pattern had always been for compliant townspeople to look the other way when partisans crept into town. Pietro must have thought so too, and his mouth opened with what Kavanaugh was certain would be an order to turn and flee, but then the barber's customer, a portly man with lather on his face, came beaming out of the stall and called, "Comrades! Welcome! The Fascists are gone! Our village is yours!"

Word of the partisan arrival spread quickly and shopkeepers, housewives and tradesmen rushed out of nearby store fronts to surround them, babbling of momentous events.

". . . shooting in the streets of Milan . . ."

". . . retreating everywhere . . ."

". . . war is over . . ."

Kavanaugh backed up against a wall near Pietro, trying to understand what was happening. It took a while to sink in. Somehow, in the past twenty-four hours, the slow but steady Allied advance had turned into a rout. German lines had splintered and German troops were fleeing to the north. Partisans in Milan had seized the radio station and announced hourly that Americans would arrive at any moment. Even here, in Gravedona, the small Italian garrison had withdrawn. This very morning, while the local German military detachment was in the mountains on some kind of exercise, every single Fascist soldier in Gravedona had climbed onto a commercial steamer and headed down the lake. The Germans had returned by lorry at midday, only to discover they were now alone, and were, at this very moment, holed up in their barracks at the northern end of town, obviously wondering what to do. A monitor at the town telephone switchboard reported they'd tried to reach the German garrison at Como for instructions, but for some reason the lines seemed to be down somewhere to the south.

Pietro asked, "How many Germans?"

The barber threw out his arms. "Who knows? Fifty. A hundred. It isn't healthy to pay too much attention."

Kavanaugh told Pietro, "More like a hundred. If these are the same troops who hit Dante's camp, there were one hell of a lot of them. We'd better keep moving."

"No, wait," Pietro said. "Veterano, you told us David wanted the garrison at Gravedona neutralized?"

The old man nodded. "Yes, comandante. He said it was necessary."

"Then we must do it," Pietro said. "This may be our best chance."

X. B. Kavanaugh had been the eighth child in a large, exuberant Michigan family, the members of which all habitually talked at once. As a prewar wildlife photographer, Kavanaugh had learned the advantages of working alone, and in the forests had encountered the need for gratifying silence. But he had also learned the habit of prudent caution, and now he objected, "What chance? They outnumber us ten to one. Even if you call in the rest of your people, we'll still be severely undermanned."

Pietro touched a forefinger to his cheek. "Ah but the Germans don't know that," he said. "And if they have listened to the same radio reports as the good people around us, they will be quite low in spirit."

"Arm us," the barber offered. "We will help you."

"Yes," agreed the man with the lathered chin. "Give us guns, comrade. We'll help you bloody their noses."

Pietro's eyes began to gleam. "Perhaps that is a good idea."

"We don't have any extra guns," Kavanaugh reminded him.

"But the Germans do," Pietro said slyly. "Perhaps we can put together an army yet." He called for paper and pen and wrote a stern note to the garrison commander, demanding an immediate audience. If the commander was willing to surrender, he wrote, all Germans would be guaranteed safe conduct to the Austrian border. If they did not, partisan forces would attack in strength and the Germans would be annihilated to the last man. He signed it boldly, "Pietro, Commander of the 52nd Garibaldi Brigade."

The barber wanted to deliver it, but Pietro told him he had another use for him. So a girl was summoned from a silk workroom on the hill and sent by bicycle to hand the note to the German commandant. In the meantime, Pietro sent Veterano with two men to the lower end of the village to avoid any surprises from the south, and set up headquarters in an ice-cream shop. Villagers continued to stream to him, asking for guns, and he assigned the barber as a supply sergeant, though the barber's instructions were to take names only and inform them all that arms were to be distributed just as soon as the Germans agreed to lay down their own weapons.

Kavanaugh still wasn't comfortable with the idea, but if he lacked decisiveness, he had never lacked courage. When the girl returned from the German barracks to report that the garrison commander was willing to talk to Pietro, Kavanaugh matter-of-factly volunteered to go along as interpreter. Courtesy of his OSS training, he spoke more German than Pietro did. They set out immediately on foot, walking openly through the village toward the German barracks. On both sides of the narrow street, red kerchiefs and tablecloths hung from windows, put there by inhabitants to show their support for the partisans.

A solitary German guard, a fuzz-cheeked youth with frightened eyes, peered at them from beneath the lip of his chamber-pot helmet as they approached the front gate, then snapped to attention and offered a military salute. Pietro returned it with aplomb.

The garrison commander turned out to be a pudgy, bespectacled Waffen-SS captain in a wrinkled uniform, sitting behind a cluttered desk. He didn't rise. He looked insolently from Pietro to the large-nosed Kavanaugh. "Who is this man?" he asked in fractured Italian. "He doesn't look like a partisan to me."

"He isn't," Pietro said. "He is a Swiss national, sympathetic to our cause. He is here to clarify any difficulties with language."

"I see no reason for difficulties," the captain said. "Your communication to me was presumptuous and overbearing. Unless you have an adequate explanation for your impudence, this discussion will come to a close."

Pietro smiled brazenly. "How about two hundred loyal partisans, armed to the teeth? Is that explanation enough?"

"There aren't two hundred partisans on the entire lake," the captain snapped.

"They are in the heights above Gravedona at this very moment," Pietro said, "with mortars sighted on your barracks. There are also reinforcements on the way from Val Chiavenna, elements of the 40th Garibaldi Brigade. Within the hour, we shall have you surrounded by a force of almost three hundred men."

The captain studied Pietro's face carefully, as if trying to determine whether he was telling the truth. He even asked Kavanaugh to repeat it in German, to give him time to think, but he couldn't seem to make up his mind. "What would you wish of us?" he asked Pietro.

"It is quite simple. You surely know the situation by now. All German resistance has ended. All isolated garrisons such as yours have surrendered. There is no escape for you and your men. You have no alternative but to capitulate. If you order your men to lay down their arms, my people will guarantee the safety of their lives and their personal possessions. We will offer safe conduct to the nearest border point, either to the Swiss border, where you may give yourselves up to Swiss authorities, or to the Austrian border, where you can rejoin your countrymen."

"And if we refuse?"

Pietro brushed the thought away. "You have no choice. If you refuse, my brigade will open fire on the barracks and level them. You will be exterminated."

"I can't surrender," the captain said. "It is my duty to resist at all costs."

"That is up to you," Pietro said. "The men of my brigade are aware of the dawn attack you launched against one of our smaller units yesterday. They thirst for revenge. I'm sure they would prefer to repay you in kind. Shall I order the attack to begin, or would you rather think about it?"

The captain stared at Pietro sullenly, then stood up. "Will you allow me to discuss the matter with my junior officers?"

"Take all the time you need," Pietro said. "So long as it does not exceed five minutes. I grow impatient."

The captain stepped from the room and Kavanaugh whispered, "Take it easy, Pietro. Big talk can make people mad. What if he decides to get tough?"

Pietro clasped his hands behind his back. "When one is holding an empty hand, my friend, one does not offer a small wager. We must bet it all. Keep a confident face when he returns. Swagger, if you can."

But it wasn't necessary. The German officer came back moments later and it was obvious from the sloping set of his shoulders that the decision had been made. He unsnapped his holster and removed his Walther. As he handed the pistol to Pietro, he said, "We have no choice but to accept your terms. How soon will we be allowed to leave for the border?"

"Soon," Pietro said. "First, you will stack your weapons and assemble your men outside in the street. You will then march to the town hall, where you will be met by a complement of my officers. Your men will be locked in the hall until we are certain you have followed my instructions. If we find one single weapon in your possession, I will order the mortar attack to commence. Do you understand?"

"I understand," the captain said.

"Then begin," Pietro said. "We will wait for you at the town hall." He gestured to Kavanaugh and stalked out of the room.

As soon as they were away from the barracks, Kavanaugh groaned. "You've got balls of brass, Pietro. When that guy reached for his pistol, I thought we'd had it."

"I was a bit concerned myself," Pietro admitted.

Kavanaugh sighed. "We aren't out of the woods yet. What happens when they get to the town hall and see us with only a dozen men?"

"They will see a dozen of my highest-ranking officers," Pietro answered. "They will not see the bulk of our force. I've decided to keep our mortar units on high ground until the Germans are safely locked away. I may have to send several couriers back and forth to my unit commanders until it's done."

Then, as they approached the town square, they saw Salvo and Veterano standing in front of the ice-cream store, pounding backs and hugging new figures. Veterano broke away from the group and hurried toward them through the rain, his stubbled face split in a wide grin. "Luisa," he called. "She's safe. She just came in by the south road with Dante and three others."

Pietro's face blossomed into a smile of its own. "There, you see?" he told Kavanaugh. "Everything is working for us. Now we have sixteen men. Once the Germans are locked away and some of the townspeople armed, we'll have even more."

"Then what?" Kavanaugh asked.

"Then you and Dante will take half a dozen men to Musso and set up that roadblock David asked for. Take axes. If you must, drop a forest on the road so that nothing can pass. Did not our forefathers harass Caesar's legions in just such ways? We'll stop Mussolini's Valtellina drive yet."

6

It had been a fruitless watch at the hotel above Grandola. The cars stayed parked in a semicircle in the courtyard, and every two hours new guards replaced the old at the front entrance. From time to time civilians came out of the hotel and fetched items from the backs of the cars, extra clothing, tins of food. But there had been no signs of moving on, no further glimpses of Mussolini.

As he crouched in the low-growing branches of the fir tree with the Britisher, Landry's lack of sleep and state of wet, bone-chilled weariness began to tell. Twice, he felt his eyes go gently out of focus; only the gray chauffeur's cap sliding down to rest on his nose jerked him back from the edge of sleep. He tried to keep awake by worrying—was Stefanini having any luck with the radio? Would they be able to get through to OSS headquarters in Bern before the enemy brigades showed up? They were on the thin edge of time, when everything could be lost or won, and this waiting was madly frustrating.

But worry didn't help. Sleep came anyway. The chauffeur's cap glided down and covered his face. Landry didn't know it until Willoughby shook him in the darkness. His cheek came off his shoulder and he fumbled at the cap. "What?" he said.

Willoughby pointed to the trees behind them. There, coming up the slope, a figure moved from bush to bush. It was Lucertola, the Lizard. Willoughby rose from the sheltering branches of the fir and beckoned. The Lizard crossed over to them, bent almost double, and flopped to the ground beside them.

"The Blackshirts?" Landry asked.

The Lizard shook his head. His lungs heaved for air, as though he had climbed the whole two kilometers on the run. He took several deep breaths, then said in a halting splutter, "Not yet, David. But a German convoy came. Many trucks. Maybe twenty-five or so."

"What kind?" Willoughby asked.

The Lizard gulped and stuttered again. "Blue uniforms. Luftwaffe, we think. The trucks are full of some kind of equipment. The Waffen-SS guards at the school made them stop and wait."

"What for?" Landry asked.

"We don't know. Perhaps to form an escort for Mussolini."

"Damn," Landry said. "What about transportation for us? Have you found any?"

"Don Ottorino has borrowed the baker's truck. It burns wood for fuel. There is a box in back for billets. They are cleaning it out now. Don Ottorino says it will hide two or three men. It is waiting on the north side of town. I can take you there."

"What about the radio?" Landry asked. "Has Stefanini got it working yet?"

"No, too many parts are missing. He says it is useless without the parts."

Landry looked down at the hotel, at the caravan of treasure-laden cars. "Then we might as well take off," he said. "We'll never stop them here without help from headquarters. We'll have to find Pietro and warn him."

As Landry spoke, an unmuffled engine putted up the snaky road and a single headlight cut through the trees, casting mottled shadows. Landry pushed his two companions into the bushes. A German military motorcycle swerved into sight, kicking up gouts of mud, and came to a stop in the hotel courtyard. A messenger hurried inside.

The Lizard grinned. "From the truck convoy," he said. "I beat him. On foot I beat him. Going downhill, it will take us even less time to get back. But wait, I almost forgot. Franca sent you this." He plunged his hands in his pockets and pulled out two big chunks of bread. They were fresh baked, but the Lizard's pockets hadn't been rainproof, and tobacco crumbs also clung to them. Landry didn't care. He bit into his share after scarcely brushing it off, and swallowed blissfully as the Lizard led them down the mountainside toward Menággio.

It was a strange war, and getting stranger, Landry decided, when a wood-burning truck, a stolen cap and a piece of bread could seem a hundred times more valuable than all the wealth they were leaving behind.

7

Mussolini stared without hunger at the tray of food his secretary had brought him. Truffled eggs in aspic. Half a guinea fowl served with applesauce. Crème caramel. The hotel had obviously done its wartime best. Mussolini felt touched, but on such a night as tonight, he couldn't find a single morsel tempting.

The day had passed in rain and gloom, with nothing but bad news to show for it. Pavolini and his army of Blackshirts still had not appeared. No word at all from Como. Radio reports, coming in on the hotel manager's big walnut console, had hammered at them steadily all afternoon, both from Milan and Locarno, one dismal bulletin after another. Three of Mussolini's friends, Buffarini-Guidi, Angelo Tarchi and Paolo Zerbino, had set out much earlier in the day to test the possibility of crossing the border into Switzerland, but only Zerbino had returned. They had been stopped, Zerbino reported gloomily, by border guards. When Buffarini and Tarchi dismounted to argue, the guards arrested them. Only Zerbino, who had stayed in the car, managed to escape.

Now, with the night full on them and the rain still drumming down outside the hotel, Lieutenant Häger had come to Mussolini with a motorcycle messenger from Menággio, bearing news that a German truck convoy was waiting there, and that the commander of the convoy, a Luftwaffe officer named Fallmeyer, had consented to join forces with Mussolini's small caravan in an effort to reach the Austrian border. Mussolini considered the possibility, but made no decision. He was still hopeful that Pavolini would show up with the Blackshirt volunteers.

Unable to eat, Mussolini sent the food away and spent the fading hours of the evening alone in the office with his Valtellina battle plans, making marginal notations, organizing them. He began to wish someone of stamina and military precision, like Marshal Graziani, had accompanied him on this frustrating journey. But Graziani, damn him and his white-haired soldier's honor, had opted to join an Army unit at Mandello, instead of standing by his Duce in his hour of need.

Then, just before midnight, an hour after Landry and Willoughby had withdrawn from the trees outside, Mussolini heard another vehicle pull up in front of the hotel, followed by a stir from the lobby. Someone cheered and several people applauded, a spontaneous ripple of clapping hands. Almost immediately, a knock sounded at the office door. Mussolini folded his Valtellina outline and said, "Enter."

The door opened and Lieutenant Häger leaned in. "Duce, Pavolini is here. He just arrived in an armored car."

"Pavolini?" Mussolini's mouth went dry and he stood up, shaking with excitement. "Where? Take me to him."

They hurried into the candlelit lobby. Several people were crowded near the windows, trying to see into the rainy darkness. When Mussolini appeared, they broke from the windows and surged around him. The hopelessness that had gathered in their eyes during the long day of waiting now waned, replaced by flickers of optimism. Hands reached out, fluttering to touch him, and he grasped them all without breaking stride, smiling beneficently.

Alessandro Pavolini came through the door, shaking raindrops from his black military greatcoat. Beadlets dripped from his eyebrows and ran down his cheeks. Mussolini rushed to him and gripped his hand. "You've come," he said.

"Yes, Duce."

"You have brought the Blackshirts?"

Pavolini hesitated. "Yes, Duce, but . . ."

"The full three thousand?"

Pavolini's eyes were apprehensive. He looked at the ring of expectant faces behind Mussolini. "No, Duce. Not exactly."

"How many, then? Fewer? Don't keep us in suspense. How many did you bring? A thousand? Five hundred?"

Pavolini's face filled with despair, and he could no longer meet Mussolini's gaze. He dropped his chin and stared at the floor. "I tried," he said. "I brought all I could find."

"How many?" Mussolini repeated. His voice was touched with panic.

Pavolini sighed. "Twelve, Duce."

Color drained from Mussolini's face, and he turned away. He tottered for a moment, then pushed through the circle of ministers and wives and hangers-on, and stalked across the lobby toward the office. As he reached the door, he seemed to recover himself. He paused and gestured for the German, Lieutenant Häger, to join him.

Häger hurried over. "Yes, Duce?"

Ashen-faced, but standing fully erect, Mussolini said, "This perfidy requires that I change my plans. The Valtellina is no longer a viable option. Please inform the commander of the Luftwaffe convoy that we will join him in two hours."

Day Seven

Zitti, zitti moviamo a vendetta,
Ne sia colto or che men l' aspetta.

Quietly, quietly we plan our revenge,
Let him be taken when he least expects.
                            —Verdi, *Rigoletto*

1

In strange silence, Landry and his companions covered the final miles of lake road from Menàggio north to Musso. The foul-smelling, wood-burning truck was far from silent. It rattled and clanged and poured out great fumes of thick black smoke into the premorning darkness. But the road seemed unaccountably stripped of the enemy. The Lizard was at the wheel, Piccione riding beside him, with instructions to talk their way through any Fascist or German checkpoints if possible, otherwise to drive like hell and let the men in the rear offer covering fire. But towns and villages that only two days earlier had been crawling with Germans and Blackshirts now offered only merrymaking civilians and openly displayed red scarves and small red flags. Even in Rezzonico, Viviana's village, there was no sign of Fascist authority. Windows in the Fascist Federation building had been smashed and bullet holes pocked the walls. Posters bearing Fascist slogans had been slashed and splattered with excrement. Landry could only shake his head in wonder.

When the truck curved up the road and dipped down toward Musso, they encountered their first roadblock, but it was manned by a handful of townspeople, not Germans. The Lizard braked the truck and a man in a worn black suit approached them through the early darkness, holding a rusty old rifle out in front as though he were afraid of smudging his clothing. "Who are you?" the man demanded. "What do you want?"

"We might ask you the same," the Lizard stammered back at him. "We're partisans. Members of the Veroli detachment."

The man smiled suddenly, exposing stained teeth. "Veroli partisans? We have some of your compatriots here, commanding us." He waved at a figure on the far side of the barricade.

A man came toward the truck, shading his eyes against the glow of the headlights, and both Piccione and the Lizard whooped with delight, then bounded to the pavement. It was Dante. They grabbed him by the arms and danced him in a circle in front of the truck cab. Another figure emerged from behind the roadblock. X. B. Kavanaugh.

Landry, who had crouched down in the truck bed with the others at first sight of the roadblock, stood tentatively and called out, "X.B.?"

Kavanaugh caught sight of him and grinned, teeth shining in the yellow glow of the headlights. "Hey, David," he shouted back. "Look at us. We've got a roadblock."

Dante also saw Landry and came to the side of the truck. "David," he said. "We control the lake. From here to the Ponte del Passo. It's a great day for Italy."

Landry took off his chauffeur's cap and slapped it against his knee, shaking off raindrops. "What news of Pietro?" he asked anxiously.

"Safe," Dante answered. "He's just up the road, in Dongo."

"We have to see him," Landry said. "Mussolini and his party are on the lake. They may come this way at any moment."

Dante's smile vanished instantly. "His army as well? The Blackshirt Brigades?"

"Not when we last saw him," Landry said. "But there was a

large German truck convoy standing by in Menággio. Maybe as many as two hundred men. How well are you dug in?"

"Not well," Dante said. He glanced over his shoulder at the darkness. "There are less than a dozen of us here at the road-block. How much time do we have?"

"It's hard to say," Landry admitted. "It could be hours before they show up. Or they might be right behind us."

"I'll need reinforcements," Dante said. "You must carry the word to Pietro." He gestured Piccione and the Lizard back into the cab of the truck. "Tell Pietro we can hold out for a while, if we must. If Mussolini and the Germans appear before he locates the extra men, I will send word."

"There's something else," Landry said. "We sneaked a look in one of Mussolini's cars. The Valtellina funds, they're here too. Cartons of currency and gold. Even if you can't hold the Germans, you've got to find a way to stop the funds."

Dante groaned wordlessly at the added responsibility. He gestured again, and men grabbed one of the trees blocking the road and quickly eased it aside. The truck rolled on in a billow of its own smoke.

Stefanini, beside Landry in the bed of the truck, craned his neck to watch the roadblock fall behind. "This is unreal," he said. "All those months hiding in the mountains, and now there's not a damned German in sight. I think I'm going to like this."

Landry started to remind him of the German convoy, then clamped his mouth shut. Let Stefanini enjoy himself while he could. At any moment the curtain could go up for the act they had been instructed to stage. It was nothing much, and nothing that Freddy couldn't sympathize with. Bluff a tyrant and steal a massive fortune. Act One.

2

Rain-soaked carnations lay in tangled ruins in a small garden in front of a cottage passed by Pavolini's armored car. Mussolini loved flowers, and the sight disheartened him. He leaned back silently and stared straight ahead. The stubble on his jutting chin was dark and thick, accentuating sickly white skin. His eyes were empty and extremely weary. He was like a man already dead as he rode uncomfortably in the jouncing jump seat of the armored car, hands in his lap, watching the slow progress of the German lorries that preceded them.

The interior of the armored car, shielded by slabs of steel plating, had grown lighter with the coming of dawn. It was large and roomy inside, yet the six men who occupied it with Mussolini and Pavolini were crowded together in the rear by an overflow of valises and cartons and sacks that jingled whenever Nicola Bombacci or Francesco Barracu or Fernando Mezzasoma shifted to try to find a more comfortable position.

They had been traveling for four hours, making torturously slow progress. At times, when they passed through some of the smaller fishing villages, the trucks and the armored car had been reduced to a crawl, inching through streets that seemed too narrow even for the smaller civilian automobiles that trailed behind. Now the rain had stopped and the clouds broke open. A weak sun rose above the peaks on the far side of the lake and cast an orange pall through moisture-laden air, tinting mud puddles on the road. Spears of early sunlight began to jab through gun slits of the armored car.

Except for the droning engines of the convoy, the lakeside road was quiet. Swallows flew. Fish popped from the water. There were no people. Mussolini sighed and closed his eyes, thinking of the beaten-down stalks of the carnations. He let his chin droop to his chest. He considered sleep, taking deep, even breaths, trying to induce it. But before sleep could come, a far-off stutter of noise, like firecrackers in a deep valley, brought his chin off his chest and his eyes to the forward gun port. The sound continued for several seconds. It seemed to come from a point several hundred meters up the road. The trucks and cars braked, closing up the gaps, and Pavolini wrenched the steering wheel to one side to avoid hitting the German truck ahead.

"What is it?" Mussolini asked. "What's happening?"

"I'm not sure. Guns, I think." Pavolini bobbed his head, trying to peer up the road, but his view was blocked by the large truck ahead. Several blue-clad Luftwaffe troopers leaned through the canvas covers at the rear of the truck, also seeking the source of the commotion. One of the soldiers looked down uneasily at the Italian armored car, as though convinced it contained the focal point for this newest of perils.

Another ripple of sound erupted, this time definitely gunfire, and this time overlaid with the heavier sound of German guns. It rattled sporadically, then subsided. Silence swept in again.

The eight men in the Italian armored car waited apprehensively. There were shouts from the front of the column, then the sound of boots as someone came running toward them. Pavolini opened his door and leaned out. Colonel Vito Casalinovo, Mussolini's adjutant, appeared on the side of the road, carrying a German submachine gun.

"What is it?" Pavolini called. "Who fired on us?"

The colonel slowed and came toward the armored car. "Partisans," he said breathlessly. "On the outskirts of Musso, ahead of the convoy."

"How many partisans?"

"It's hard to say. They're hidden in the trees. We got at least two of them, I think."

Mussolini leaned over so Casalinovo could see him. "Why have we stopped?" he asked. "Why don't we force our way through?"

"We can't, Excellency," the colonel said. "They've pulled trees across the road. When the Germans tried to move them, the partisans opened fire from high ground."

Pavolini snorted. "The Germans could wipe them out in minutes, if they wanted to. I've never seen a partisan yet who wouldn't turn tail at a show of force."

Bombacci, kneeling behind Mussolini, wet his lips and said, "Maybe not. These mountains are full of partisans. There could be hundreds of them. The German officers know best."

Colonel Casalinovo fidgeted nervously below the open door and said, "Excellency, with your permission, I must continue to the rear of the column. Lieutenant Fallmeyer plans to parley with the partisan leader. He asked me to fetch Lieutenant Häger as translator."

"Yes, go ahead," Mussolini said.

"Parley!" Pavolini snapped when Casalinovo had moved on. "Have we come to this? Duce, say the word and I'll break through. We'll let the Germans parley all they want and go on without them."

Mussolini seemed not to have heard. He stared at the tailgate of the German truck ahead.

"Very well," Pavolini said. "Give me leave and I'll turn around and go back to Menággio. We can force our way across the frontier into Switzerland. With your permission, Duce?" His hand touched the ignition.

Mussolini turned and peered into the face of Fernando Mezzasoma. "Give me your fountain pen," he said. "If it is necessary that we wait, then I must use the time to good advantage."

Pavolini withdrew his hand from the key. Mezzasoma nervously passed his fountain pen forward and Mussolini slipped his spectacles on and opened his briefcase. He pulled himself into a tight shell, ignoring the others, and began to sort and ponder documents, scribbling occasional notes in margins already filled with handwritten observations.

The road to Musso climbed steeply for almost a kilometer, then leveled off for a few hundred meters before dipping into the outlying houses of the village. The roadblock, set between a huge wall of rock on one side and the lake on the other, lay across the narrowest point and was covered by three gun emplacements in the hills and two more on the low side, one along a jetty and the other on the balcony of the first house at the edge of the village.

X. B. Kavanaugh and Dante, who had only a handful of men to back them, had no way of knowing whether or not Mussolini was a part of this convoy, but they had nevertheless sent a runner to fetch Pietro and Landry from Dongo as soon as they saw the trucks looming over the rise, and were now busily stalling the Germans until Pietro could arrive. Dante told the German leader that there were forty partisans overlooking the road and another two hundred in Musso's twin village, Dongo, just up the road. He warned the German officer that he had orders to stop all traffic until it was cleared by his brigade leader, and the officer warned Dante in turn that the Germans had orders to drive through and intended to do so. Now they were stalemated and waiting to see who would back down first.

Under a white flag, they stared at each other with silent hostility, Dante and Kavanaugh on one side of the barricade, the German Luftwaffe lieutenant and a Waffen-SS lieutenant on the other, while the sun climbed higher above the lake. Finally, in a voice loud enough for the Germans to hear, Dante told Kavanaugh that he was going up to check the fortified positions and make sure none of the partisans, particularly those manning machine guns and mortars, broke the truce. Kavanaugh understood. There had been one casualty already, an unfortunate farmer who had crossed the road on his way to Musso during those first moments of confusion and had been shot by the Germans, and Dante was determined to have no more shooting if he could help it. So Kavanaugh stood alone at the barricade and waited.

It was a few minutes past eight o'clock when Pietro, accompanied by Landry, Piccione and Veterano, drove up in a big Bugatti touring car that Pietro's partisans had liberated from a Fascist villa in Gravedona.

Landry leaped out with Pietro, eyes on the German convoy beyond the barricade. Landry could see only a few of the trucks, since the road curved beyond the roadblock, but he could tell already that the partisans were badly outnumbered and outgunned. He whispered to Veterano and Piccione to climb above the road and see just how extensive the convoy might be, then, hanging discreetly to the rear, followed Pietro to the roadblock. Landry felt his muscles tighten involuntarily when his eyes fell on the Waffen-SS lieutenant waiting there. It was surely the same officer he and Creedmore had seen in the room with Mussolini.

"We have orders to take this convoy to Merano," the Waffen-SS officer told Pietro upon being introduced to him by Kavanaugh. "And we intend to do so. From there we will go on to Germany and continue the battle against the Allies. We have no quarrel with Italian partisans, and we will not fight you unless you continue to obstruct us."

Pietro folded his arms. "I understand," he said. "I, on the other hand, have orders to stop all enemy columns and let no one through. That applies in particular to Italians. Have you any Italians in your company?"

The Waffen-SS lieutenant hesitated. "There is an armored car with us," he said, "and a few Italian civilians in private cars who have joined us for protection. But they are unimportant people and would be of no interest to you."

Italian civilians—this had to be it. Landry shook his head slightly at Pietro, who acknowledged the signal with a curt nod.

"We must decide whether or not your Italian passengers are important," Pietro said. "As you can see, we are in a position to keep you here as long as we wish. We have a heavy force here and an even stronger one waiting in Dongo, less than one kilometer to the north. If you are willing to surrender your arms to us, we will guarantee safe conduct to the border. But under no circumstances will we allow Italians to accompany you."

The two German officers deliberated briefly in their own language, then the Waffen-SS man said, "We cannot agree to that. The Italians have placed themselves in our care and are therefore our responsibility. They must be allowed to continue with us."

"Then we cannot let you pass," Pietro said. The rest of his lines came easily. He and Landry had worked out a quick scenario, and some of the ploys were those he had used successfully against the Gravedona garrison. "Not without permission from our High Command. If you would care to withdraw for a few moments to discuss it?"

"We have nothing to discuss," the Waffen-SS man said.

"Nevertheless, take a few minutes," Pietro said. "One should not rush to die."

The two Germans exchanged looks, then stepped away from the barricade. Junior staff officers joined them and they began a whispered debate.

"You recognize them?" Pietro murmured.

"One of them," Landry said in a low voice. "The Waffen-SS man. He was in Grandola with Mussolini."

Kavanaugh moved in closer. "What was all that stuff about needing permission from a 'High Command'?" he whispered. "Hell, Pietro, you *are* the High Command."

"The Germans needn't know that," Pietro said. "They are trained to understand military procedure and the chain of command. They might not be so understanding if they thought we were working without orders. Tell me, what did they say to each other when they spoke briefly in German?"

Kavanaugh glanced at the Germans on the far side of the barricade and swallowed. "Well, the Luftwaffe guy isn't too keen on a fight. He suggested they abandon the Italians and move on. The other guy, the Waffen-SS officer, seems a little more determined. I'm not sure he's going to give up as easily as that garrison commander yesterday."

While they waited for the Germans to conclude their deliberations, Veterano and Piccione hurried back from the heights. "That's a big damned convoy," Piccione reported quietly. "There must be thirty trucks, jammed with troops and guns, and an armored car. They could blow us to hell, if they wanted."

"What about Mussolini?" Landry asked.

Piccione shook his head. "We didn't see him. But there are about ten civilian cars at the rear of the column. I'll swear they're the same ones we saw outside the hotel."

The feeling of urgency shared by Landry and Pietro mounted. Landry could see it in Pietro's eyes and feel it in his own. "Then we've got to figure some way to split them off from the Germans," he said. He thought a moment, then said to Pietro, "Why don't you invite one or both of the officers to accompany you back to your headquarters? We can send someone ahead to pass out the rest of the confiscated guns from the Gravedona garrison, and have everyone line up on both sides of the street. If we put on a good show, maybe we can convince the Germans they have no choice."

"We have already pressed into service everyone who knows how to use a gun," Pietro whispered. "The rest are amateurs."

"It doesn't matter whether they can use them or not," Landry said. "Just put them out where the Germans can see them. We can get the rest of the townspeople to help, too. Those who don't have guns can tie red kerchiefs around their necks and pretend to patrol the hills. Have them stand in plain sight. If they're far enough from the road, have them carry sticks. Anything that might look like more guns."

"Yes, yes, I see," Pietro said eagerly. "We will make the Germans believe we have hundreds of people waiting for them. Oh Christ the Savior, why do we not have more men capable of using the captured German mortars? Then we could really show the bastards we have teeth." Improving on the plan, he went on. "We will also place a group of men on the Vallorba bridge. Veterano, you have heard. You will take the word. Tell them to dig holes in the approaches to the bridge, then cover them over. When David and I bring the Germans, I will stop and ask if the mines are ready. They are to tell me the fuses will be lit as soon as I order it. Quickly, go now. There may not be much time to prepare."

Veterano nodded solemnly and left the roadblock, jogging down through Musso and toward nearby Dongo. "Send me, too," Piccione urged. "Veterano will never get all the details straight."

"Veterano will handle it," Pietro said. "Your duty is equally important, Piccione. You know which cars carry the Fascist treasury. They must be pointed out carefully to Dante. If this ruse works and we succeed in sending the Germans on alone, Dante must see that none of the cars get through the roadblock, nor turn back to join any Blackshirts who may yet follow. David, quickly, any special strategy for the cars?"

The Germans interrupted. Apparently made nervous by Veterano's hurried departure, they broke up their discussion and the Waffen-SS lieutenant came to Pietro. "Where is that man going?" the lieutenant demanded.

"I sent him ahead to warn the roadblocks that we might be coming," Pietro said. "I have decided that I cannot take responsibility for what happens to your convoy. If you are to pass, it must be with the permission of my superiors. As soon as my messenger has time to prepare the way, we will drive you to our headquarters. It is only a few kilometers from here."

"We have no intention of going with you," the lieutenant said.

Pietro raised dark eyebrows. "It would be advisable for you to do as I suggest. Direct contact with my superiors is the only way you can hope to gain clearance."

The young German frowned. "How long would it take?"

"We'll be quick about it," Pietro said. "An hour, perhaps."

"That's too long. Make up your mind now."

"Impossible," Pietro said. "I can't let you pass. Unless my superior officer gives me the order, I must hold you here."

The lieutenant looked indecisive, then said, "Very well. I will go with you. But you must guarantee that I will return."

"You have my word," Pietro said.

The sun soared higher over the lake, burning the clouds away, and early morning became midmorning, with still no movement by the convoy. Partisans crouched behind stone walls, fingering their rifles and pistols restlessly. Villagers from Musso wandered out on the road to watch the impasse, though only a few of them were brave enough to approach the German trucks or the Italian cars. One who did was an enterprising old man who rolled a barrel of dark-red lake wine out to the convoy on a wheelbarrow and made a remarkably brisk business of filling German canteen cups in trade for German cigarettes. Some of the Fascist families at the rear of the convoy, fearful that they would never be allowed to pass, sneaked away from their cars and sought refuge in farmhouses. A pair of them even approached a village priest and asked for sanctuary.

As minutes oozed into hours, Mussolini continued to read through his documents, coming out of his self-constructed shell from time to time to listen to intermittent news broadcasts on the wireless, even smiling at one point when he heard a report that he had been captured by partisans in a town far away from Lake Como. There was a new occupant in the armored car now. Claretta Petacci, dressed in coveralls, had slipped in through the rear panel just past nine that morning and had settled wordlessly beside him.

Shortly after noon, after hours of waiting, Lieutenant Häger returned to the convoy and strode back to the armored car. Pavolini saw him coming and nudged Mussolini, who took off his glasses and waited for word of what was happening. Häger looked embarrassed. He came to a stop beside the armored vehicle and said, "I'm sorry."

"Sorry?" Pavolini said. "Sorry for what?"

"We've been unable to negotiate passage for you," Häger said. "Only for the German troops. We were lucky to arrange that."

"But . . . but you can't," Bombacci complained from the rear. "Your duty to the Duce . . . to the rest of us . . ."

"There are hundreds of them," Häger said. "They outnumber us three to one. I've seen them with my own eyes. I even visited their command post, but their leaders refused to see me. They know they have us outnumbered."

"You are sworn to protect the Duce," Pavolini barked. "Do you refuse to honor your commitment?"

Häger said, "No, we have a plan. The Duce will disguise himself in a German greatcoat and helmet. We will hide him in one of our trucks. The partisans say there is another roadblock in Dongo, where they intend to search our vehicles, but I'm sure we can sneak him through."

"That isn't fair," Bombacci wailed. "We're all in this together. It isn't right that he should be the only one to get away."

"Nicola is right," Mussolini said. "I'm afraid you must get other coats, Lieutenant. Enough for all of us."

"That isn't possible, Duce. The partisans would detect it."

Mussolini looked at Claretta, who was listening with wide, luminous eyes. "At least for my friend," he said. "You must bring a coat for my friend."

"It can't be done, Duce."

"Then I shall not go."

Häger sighed. "I will fetch a coat and helmet for you, Duce. Please be ready when I return. We are on the verge of departing, and we must not delay."

As the German lieutenant stalked away, Claretta crawled out of the armored car and stood on the side of the road. Her eyes clouded with thick, wet tears. Mussolini remained in his seat for several minutes, staring stiffly ahead, then stepped down beside her. "Don't weep, signora," he said. "I won't leave you."

Häger came back with a Luftwaffe greatcoat and a German helmet. "Please, Duce," he said to Mussolini. "Put these on."

Mussolini stared at the coat with its corporal's insignia, then blinked at the armored car and his companions. "No, Lieutenant," he said. "If my ministers and my friends cannot have the same protection as myself, I refuse to move."

Häger's face tightened. "Duce, this is your last chance."

Mussolini shook his head and stared off toward the lake. Then, abruptly, almost convulsively, he stepped forward and took the coat. Häger helped him slip into it, and handed him the helmet. They walked quickly to the rearmost lorry. Two German enlisted men helped Mussolini climb over the tailgate. Häger stepped to the side of the road and signaled for the convoy to get under way. The trucks ground into gear.

"No, wait!" Claretta cried. She ran to the truck and tried to pull herself up. "Please," she begged. "Take me with you. Please!"

Mussolini looked down at her, then raised his chin to the armored car and gestured for help. Pavolini dismounted and hurried to her. He had to use all his strength to pull her away from the tailboard.

3

After the Luftwaffe trucks were allowed to drive on toward Dongo, Piccione looked earnestly for Dante. There had been opportunities to speak to him earlier, but with German officers standing about on the other side of the barricade, listening to everything the partisans said, Piccione had decided it would be best to wait. Now with the Germans gone, he wanted nothing so much as to point out the cars full of gold to Dante and be done with it. Dante could do the worrying from now on.

Many of the partisans had advanced beyond the barricade as the trucks pulled away, and surged up the hill to confront the Italians in the armored car. They appeared to be engaged in a shouting match, and Piccione thought he spotted Dante and X. B. Kavanaugh among the disputants. It struck Piccione as a highly incongruous game. Here on this narrow road beside the lake, where the full flood of the Italian war was draining to the last significant trickle, life should have been forever changed. After all, had he not beheld only yesterday the monster who had tried to ruin his country, the black beast himself, Mussolini? And was not the beast still on the lake somewhere, perhaps there among the Italians in the armored car, possibly only moments from capture? But life was stupidly the same, filled with errands, filled with waits, filled with inconsequential people who could find nothing better to do than argue. Yet the information Pietro had delegated him to pass along to Dante, already too long delayed, was important. He hurried up the hill to join them.

Two of the occupants of the armored car, an elderly civilian with a gold medal pinned to his lapel and a dark-haired man in a

Fascist black shirt, had stepped down to the side of the road to face the partisans. The older man looked quizzically at Piccione when he nudged into the circle. "Who are you?" the older man demanded. "Are you also a partisan?"

"I am," said Piccione.

"I am Francesco Barracu," the civilian said, as though that should mean something. He indicated the younger man in the black shirt. "And this is Alessandro Pavolini. Will you please persuade your comrades to step aside? We mean to follow the German column and we have no desire to fire on our own countrymen, even if they are partisans."

Piccione didn't know why the man had chosen to speak to him. His cursed face, perhaps, which made him look like a young prince instead of a stalwart son of the people. He turned away and refused to respond. One of the other partisans said, "No, no, no. We have told you and told you, you will not be allowed to follow the Germans. You must surrender, for that is your only choice."

The man in the black shirt, face already red with anger, actually shook his fist. He shouted, "What kind of Italians are you? You let the Germans pass without a murmur, and hold your own people?"

Dante spoke. All partisans fell into a respectful silence. "We don't need lessons in patriotism from the likes of you," Dante told the red-faced man stiffly. "It was you and your kind who welcomed the Germans to our soil in the first place. It was you who allowed the deportation and murder of good Italian citizens, not us."

"Now, now," Barracu said soothingly. "I'm sure we all did our duty as we saw it. The point is, you are soldiers, and you appear to act like soldiers. Surely you can understand an old soldier like me. We have sworn to defend Trieste from the military encroachment of Tito and his mob of Bolsheviks. If we can get through, I am sure we can rally a force and save at least that part of our homeland for which so many Italians have lost their lives."

Piccione, who, like Dante, had always regarded himself as a Communist, though not strictly a Party-line man, was offended by Barracu's disparaging reference to Tito's Bolsheviks. Piccione made a face and tried to catch Dante's eye, but Dante was too wrapped up in the argument.

"The fate of Trieste will be decided by the Allies," Dante said coldly. "As for letting you pass, even if we were so disposed, you would only be stopped again by other partisan roadblocks."

Another momentary silence fell, and Pavolini turned angrily and leaned into the armored car, whispering something to one of the men who had remained inside. Dante seemed instantly suspicious. He pushed past the two Fascists and leaned into the armored car himself.

"Well?" demanded Pavolini. "Did you get an eyeful? Who did you expect to see?"

"We will tell you when we find him," Dante said.

Piccione tried again to catch Dante's attention and this time he succeeded. Dante turned to X. B. Kavanaugh and said, "If they try to move, open fire on them." Then he stepped to Piccione's side. Preoccupied with his own problems, he made an open-palmed, empty gesture with one hand. "As far as we can tell, Mussolini is nowhere among these cowards," he told Piccione. "We can check the other cars, but it's possible they found shelter for him somewhere along the lake south of here."

"It's about the cars that I wanted to speak," Piccione said. "What was inside that armored car when you looked in?"

"Only frightened faces and piles of luggage."

"The luggage should be examined," Piccione said. "If it's like the Fascist cars we followed to Grandola, it will contain money. Gold. Riches you wouldn't believe. Pietro said I must point out to you the cars that I recognized. They are not to pass, on any account."

Dante looked dubious. "Show me," he said.

Piccione led him back along the sweeping curve where the other Italian cars were parked, doors hanging open, stretching down and around the large rocks for several hundred meters. Most of the cars were unoccupied by now. A few of the Fascist families still stood on the roadside, but they wouldn't look at either Dante or Piccione, even when the two partisans detoured to the cars and began to probe through them.

In the first car, Dante found the back seat filled with sacks of gold coins and two cases of banknotes, covered with only the barest of camouflage, two folded sheets here, a layer of clothing there. His face turned stony.

In the second car, the same. Cases of banknotes and a small chest of unset diamonds beneath a green blanket. Color appeared in Dante's cheeks. Even Piccione was surprised by the diamonds.

The third car offered gold bars, a layer that came level with the seat, two cartons of banknotes and some rolled paintings. Now Dante's breath began to come harder. Piccione tried not to show his own excitement.

As they moved to the fourth car, neither man speaking, they swung around large roadside boulders that had blocked their view from the top of the hill, and for the first time they could see the tail end of the caravan. Piccione jerked to a halt. There below them, almost at lake level, he could see a swarm of Musso villagers, grown bolder since the departure of the German trucks. The villagers had crowded around the last two cars in the column and were cheerfully looting them. Three men leaned through open doors, passing jewelry and banknotes to grasping hands. Two women shrugged into furs that had been brought along by Fascist wives and compared notes, running their hands lovingly, almost with awe, over the soft, smooth textures. A limping peasant in his sixties staggered away bearing two heavy gold candelabra. A small group of giggling children, none of them more than six years old, dragged a Florentine painting in a massive gilt frame across the road, trying to get it out of sight.

"Stop!" Dante shouted. He started running, and Piccione followed. The villagers, startled by Dante's approach, scattered almost instantly and fled into a field, carrying their booty with them. Dante slowed and watched them disappear into the trees beyond the field. "We must call for help," he told Piccione. "These riches are the property of the state. We must get them back."

"They didn't get that much," Piccione said. "Just a little from two cars. Don't worry. We can put some guards back here to keep them away from the others."

"There's so much of it," Dante said. He was still watching the trees, as though worried about the looters. "Perhaps we should unload it all and send it to the top of the hill where we can watch it. We'll need more men. We . . ."

A sudden rattle of gunfire broke out from the direction of the roadblock, followed by the distinct *crump* of an exploding hand grenade.

"Oh my God!" Piccione said. "The armored car! Hurry!"

They raced back up the hill, panting, but the brief firefight had already ended. When they reached the top, they saw that the armored car had moved, but not far. It now leaned at a drunken angle over the edge of the road, one wheel blown off and its frightened occupants huddled together on the pavement with their hands over their heads. The driver, the Blackshirt officer Barracu had called Pavolini, had apparently bounded off the side of the road and jumped down into the water, but Kavanaugh and two of the partisans had caught him and were already dragging him back up the hill. He was bleeding from the foot.

"What happened?" Dante demanded.

A middle-aged townsman with a rifle said, "They tried to drive past us. We opened up like you told us to, and one of your boys blew off their wheel with a bomb. What do you want us to do now?"

"Hold them here for the moment," Dante said. "Something more important awaits us at the tail of the column. I want half a dozen men to come with me. We have some cargo to unload."

The townsman spat on the roadside. "Begging your pardon, commendatore, but I didn't take up arms and join you to become a common stevedore. I want to fight."

Piccione thought of cuffing him for spitting in the presence of his chief, but he decided to be kind. "You won't mind this unloading job," he said. "You won't mind it at all."

4

As the German trucks braked to a stop in the city square of Dongo, twin city to Musso, David Landry thought he would never again endure such an awesome moment or see such an awesome sight. Dongo's great old medieval buildings crowded down to the square on three sides, with the fourth side open to the lake, mirror blue in the partial sunlight. The clouds, which had burned away during the long morning's wait, seemed to be gathering again, lending an ominous air to the scene of strung-out trucks and swarms of townspeople that now edged slowly toward them. Everywhere were red kerchiefs, so numerous that the Germans must surely be convinced that they faced an army of hostile partisans rather than the twenty-odd men Pietro had been able to muster. But was anything in war absolutely sure?

Pietro came out of the town hall with his Puecher partisans and strode down to stand on the steps beside Landry and the ALOTs. He placed his fists on his hips, looking very cocky, but his voice was uncertain as he said, "Well, David. Now we must prepare for the greatest bluff of our lives."

Landry primed his Thompson and tried to hide his own doubt. "How do you want to do it?" he asked.

Pietro looked out across the square a moment, then said, "With élan, my friend. The more brazen, the better. I suggest you and your ALOTs separate, one to each search party. I don't expect trouble, but we must be prepared for it. Your presence will give my men confidence."

Creedmore touched tongue to dry lips. "You don't think Mussolini is dumb enough to be on one of those trucks, do you? I mean, damn, if he is, they're not likely to let him go without a fuss."

"I doubt we'll find him," Pietro admitted. "But be on your guard, anyway. If we find Mussolini or any other Italian, they must not be allowed to pass."

Stefanini said, "Listen, let me go with the search team that takes the lead trucks. From the markings, this is a communications outfit. I think I saw an equipment locker in the back of one of those trucks up there. Maybe I can find the missing radio parts I've been hunting."

"Very well," Pietro said. "But remember, they are *German* trucks. You must be careful. As long as they think they will be allowed to continue after the search, our bluff should work. Don't threaten them, don't make them feel cornered, or they may choose to fight. We wouldn't want that." He looked anxiously at the waiting vehicles. "We'd best begin without further delay. We mustn't let them think we are indecisive. Salvo will accompany Lieutenant Stefanini to the head of the convoy. Lieutenant Creedmore and Veterano can take the middle with some of the new recruits. David, you take the trucks to the rear. I will remain here on the steps with enough men to make it seem we have manpower to spare. Send word to us quickly if you note anything suspicious."

They broke apart and joined the three search teams waiting in the square. Landry set off toward the rear of the convoy with his own team. None of the faces were familiar to him. Recruits from among the Dongo townspeople, he assumed.

At the rear of the convoy, he sorted his search group into twos and threes and assigned them trucks. "Be firm, but not aggressive," he warned them. "If you see anything, back away and come to me. If it's important, we'll send for Pietro. We don't want to start anything unless we have people to back us up."

The new recruits looked at each other nervously, and Landry could almost hear the thunk of Adam's apples in dry throats. He picked out the most nervous-looking, a whiskery man with a patch over one eye, and told him to come along. The other recruits seemed instantly to forget which trucks they had been assigned, and there was a general movement toward trucks up the line. It was as though they found comfort in being as close as possible to the team searching the middle of the convoy. Landry sighed and swung toward the last two trucks, the one-eyed man at his heels.

The next-to-last truck already had its tailgate down, and German troopers had pulled the canvas cover aside to make it easier for them. One German reached down and offered Landry a hand up, but he curtly declined it and scrambled up on his own. There were ten men in the truck, most of them without weapons, sharing their space with rolls of cable and boxes of gear. Landry looked them over carefully. He was surprised to see that most of them were in their late thirties and early forties, with tired, lined faces. They seemed not at all impatient with the search, but rather appeared to accept its inevitability, even to the point of producing their military paybooks without being asked, as though they only wanted to get it over with and get moving again.

Landry rejoined the nervous one-eyed man on the pavement and they circled to the last truck. But this truck was different. The tailgate was still in place and the canvas flaps hung closed. When Landry pulled the canvas back, he saw close to twenty soldiers sitting stiffly on their benches, staring straight ahead. The one-eyed man tried to climb over the tailboard, but it was latched in the up position, and he couldn't quite manage it with his rifle in one hand. For some reason, sweat broke out on the man's face, and he turned such a wild look on Landry that Landry quickly put a cautioning hand on the man's arm. "Never mind," Landry said. "You can stay here and hold my gun." He handed his Thompson to the man and used both hands to pull himself up.

Once Landry was inside, no one spoke. He walked along the benches, staring at the faces, looking into eyes that refused to meet his own. Something was wrong. He didn't know exactly why, but these men seemed extremely anxious. Landry began to wish he hadn't left his Thompson outside, and especially that he hadn't left it with a stranger who at any moment might lose the rest of his nerve and try to kill the whole twenty Germans, not to mention Landry, with one enthusiastic burst.

When Landry reached the front of the truckbed, he saw a man squatting by two petrol tins, bundled in a German greatcoat, helmeted head down in his arms.

"Who is this?" Landry asked.

At first, it seemed no one would answer; then one of the soldiers, a watchful sergeant with red-rimmed eyes, said in quick Italian, "Don't worry about him. He's one of us. He's just had a little too much to drink." The sergeant made a tipple gesture with his hand. "Vino. Lots of vino. You understand?"

"Oh," Landry said. He looked once more at the man in the greatcoat, wondering if he should speak to him directly, but the sergeant with the bloodshot eyes was still staring at him. Landry backed away. He turned and made his way quickly to the back of the truck, stepping through the tangle of legs. No one reached out for him, though he could see the hands in laps and somehow had the unreasoned fear that they wanted to. Then he reached the tailgate and was allowed to climb over. He dropped to the ground and looked back. "Thank you," he said, then wondered why he'd said it.

Landry told himself to get his wits about him. He took his Thompson from the one-eyed recruit and murmured quietly, "Go get Pietro."

The man's good eye widened. "Is something wrong?"

"I don't know," Landry said. "Tell him there is a man in this truck. A German said he was drunk, but he didn't smell it. And his coat is too small for him."

"You think he's an impostor?"

"Perhaps," Landry said. "If he's who I think he is, the honor of taking him should go to Pietro."

The man swallowed hard, then nodded. He slipped around the side of the truck, moving cautiously until he was beyond the German line of sight, then he clutched his rifle and took off, an awkward, gangly run that carried him quickly across the square to the town hall steps. Landry watched him approach Pietro. They spoke briefly, with the one-eyed man waggling his arms and pointing, then Pietro gestured to the partisans around him and they headed toward Landry.

Pietro marched up and said, "You have something? One of the hierarchy?"

"It's possible," Landry said. Canvas rustled behind them, and Landry looked around. Two of the Germans, peering through a four-inch gap where someone had pulled the flap aside, saw Pietro and the armed partisans, and their faces fell. The canvas dropped back into place.

Pietro motioned for his partisan bodyguard to unlimber their guns and wait, then climbed into the truck with Landry. This time Landry kept his Thompson. He nodded toward the huddled figure in front. Together, they picked their way through the legs to the man in the greatcoat, and while Landry covered the Germans, Pietro leaned over the man and prodded him with a pistol. "You," Pietro said sternly. "Are you an Italian?"

The man was still for a moment, then his head came up slowly to face Pietro. With a defeated sigh, he said, "Yes. I am an Italian."

Pietro gasped. Landry looked over his shoulder and immediately saw why. Even in the canvas-covered gloom, the face was unmistakable. A flush of heat spread across Landry's temples like a sheet of fire. Pietro jerked his head toward the rear of the truck. "It's the Duce!" he cried in a stunned voice. "We've caught the Duce himself!"

Pietro's partisans heard his startled proclamation, and one of them pulled away from the tailgate to repeat it to the other partisans and to townspeople who had crowded closer to the truck to see what was going on. There was a shocked silence that lasted several seconds, then an old man's voice rose in a gleeful curse, followed by an outburst of cheers that grew and expanded all up and down the line of trucks until it seemed one's eardrums might burst from the sound. . . .

5

They pulled Mussolini down from the truck, a frightened old man in a German greatcoat, and crowded around him. For a moment, no one seemed to know what to do. German officers had apparently instructed their men to remain in the trucks, but there were enough sullen faces peering down at the partisans through canvas flaps to make Pietro uneasy. So he turned Mussolini over to his Puecher bodyguard and told them to take him to the Dongo town hall, an aging structure that had once been the Palazzo Mangi. The Puecher partisans set off immediately, and the mass of spectators followed, swirling across the piazza like an army of ants.

Pietro and Landry didn't accompany them. They stayed in the square with some of the new recruits, waiting to see if the Germans would gather their nerve for a fight. But the Germans had no stomach for more fighting. With the Austrian border barely two hundred kilometers farther north, they seemed ready to wash their hands of Mussolini and head for home.

Finally, when it became obvious that the convoy would move on without incident, Pietro left to seek a telephone. There were no provisions for direct communication between partisan units on the lake, but he hoped to contact Federation members in Como and through them to secure reinforcements from other units to the south, or at least to petition for official guidance on what should be done next.

Landry, in the meantime, headed for the front of the convoy to see if he could help the search teams led by Creedmore and Stefanini.

Ashen-faced, Mussolini stood in the center of a long room on the first floor of the Dongo town hall. The room was full of partisans and townspeople, with more coming all the time, and the press of swaying bodies made him feel ill. He asked humbly for permission to remove the German greatcoat and one of the Puecher partisans nodded. Mussolini unbuttoned the coat with trembling fingers and began to strip it off. A hand reached out to help him and Mussolini acknowledged the assistance gratefully. He dropped the coat on the floor, then took off the German helmet and let it fall on top of the coat. Another partisan pointed toward a bench and told him to sit. He obeyed meekly. Bareheaded, wearing only a black shirt, militia cavalry officer's trousers and riding boots, he sat stiffly on the bench and folded his hands in his lap. He was careful not to look directly at anyone.

Several minutes passed, and at long last the sound of truck motors drifted from the square and the German trucks began to pull away, one by one, continuing up the lake road on their way north. Mussolini squeezed his eyes shut and frowned.

One of the partisans noticed Mussolini's expression and said, "Don't worry about the Germans, Duce. They'll get what's coming to them. We understand there are three hundred Garibaldini massed at the Ponte del Passo, waiting for them."

"I don't care what happens to the Germans," Mussolini said.

"What then?" the partisan asked. "Are you concerned for yourself? You needn't be. We won't harm you."

Mussolini looked at the man, then sighed. "I know you won't. The people of Lake Como have always been kindhearted."

The polite exchange seemed to rankle one of the people crowding close to Mussolini. He was a stranger to the partisans, though he carried a gun and wore a red kerchief tied to his sleeve. He glared at the Puecher partisan and said, "Don't coddle the bastard. He betrayed Socialism years ago, when he was only a piss-ant newspaper editor. We owe him nothing."

"I didn't betray Socialism," Mussolini said. "Socialism betrayed itself."

"And what of Matteotti?" the man demanded. "The whole world knows you had him murdered."

"That wasn't my doing. It was the work of Fascist zealots."

Another villager, emboldened by the stranger's attack, called out, "What about your son-in-law? You had your own son-in-law put to death for treason. What kind of a monster would do such a thing?"

The Puecher partisan waved for quiet. "Leave him alone," he insisted loudly. Then, to Mussolini, "Duce, you need not answer their questions."

"I must," Mussolini said. "It's important that they understand. Count Ciano was convicted by a legally appointed court. He wasn't executed at my bidding. There are records to prove it."

Voices rose in derision. More people shouted at Mussolini. "What about our own comrades?" a man yelled. "You have allowed good Italians to be arrested and tortured by Germans. Do you deny it?"

"That was unavoidable," Mussolini said nervously. "It was the German SS under General Wolff. My hands were tied."

"You brought the Germans here. That makes you responsible."

"I had no control over the Germans. Complex forces were at work."

Questions and accusations continued to fly at him, and nothing the Puecher partisans said or did seemed to diminish them. Mussolini tried for a time to answer them all, as though by responding freely to their questions he felt he could placate his captors, turn aside their anger. Finally, the gravity of his predicament, coupled with all the talking he had been forced to do, made him complain of a dry throat. One of the Puecher partisans brought him a glass of water.

While Mussolini sipped slowly, perhaps trying to stretch out the brief respite, the hall door opened and Pietro came in, accompanied by Dante and Piccione, just back from Musso. Pietro's face hardened when he saw so many people in the room, and he raised his voice instantly. "Everyone out," he shouted. "Clear the room. I will have no one here save myself and those I indicate may stay."

"Who the hell do you think you are?" demanded the man with the kerchief on his arm whom the partisans had never seen before today.

Pietro didn't answer the man, but rather gestured to the Puecher partisans, and they quickly organized a party and swept the room clean, pushing people toward the door with raised rifles.

The man with the red kerchief on his arm, seeing the guns come up, was among the first to leave.

As the crowd thinned, Pietro bowed to Mussolini and said, "My apologies, Excellency. I will see that it doesn't happen again."

"It doesn't matter," Mussolini said in a low voice.

When Pietro's Puecher men started to close the door, there was more commotion, someone fighting the tide of bodies in the corridor, and Landry pushed his way inside with the Britisher, followed closely by Creedmore and Stefanini. The four men were carrying cartons filled with copper wire, coiled insulation, alligator clips, vacuum tubes and a soldering iron. From the way they were grinning, one might have thought they were carrying some fabulous treasure.

"What have you there?" Pietro asked.

Landry and the others put their cartons on the floor and Landry said, "Radio parts. Freddy found a stockpile in one of those Luftwaffe trucks. Maybe now we can get that damned transmitter working."

Stefanini nodded cheerfully. "No sweat. Tubes, coils, resistors. We've got it all."

Landry noticed Dante for the first time. Landry's face broke into an eager smile and he gripped Dante's hand. "How did it go in Musso?" he asked.

"It went well," Dante told him just as eagerly. "We took several prisoners. There may be more of them hiding in the countryside. We left Captain Kavanaugh to look for them."

Creedmore joined them. "What about the Fascist war funds?" he asked. "Was everything in the cars like we said it would be?"

Dante looked from Landry and Creedmore to Pietro. "Mother of God," he said. "You should have been there. Enough money and gold and diamonds to buy the whole of Corsica."

"Diamonds?" Landry said.

Piccione said enthusiastically, "It's true, David. The car we opened yesterday was only a trifle. Wait until you see what Dante and I found in all the others. Our people are stacking it on the roadside now. A pirate's plunder. Unbelievable. They'll fetch it here to Dongo when they bring the rest of the prisoners."

Landry turned and studied Mussolini's sagging figure for a moment, then asked Pietro, "What about him? You can't keep him here, can you?"

"Probably not," Pietro admitted. "The Germans might still gather their nerve and come back. I've been trying to get through to the Federation for instructions, but the lines seem to be down."

"The lines? Where?" This from Piccione.

"Below Menàggio, I assume," Pietro said. "That was as far as I could make a connection."

Piccione slapped a palm to his forehead. "That's my fault," he said. "I cut the wire yesterday. I didn't know we'd be needing it."

"That's unfortunate," Pietro said. "A capture such as this is too important for us to handle alone. I'll send a car with some men. Perhaps they can repair the break, or drive farther south to make the call. I must have guidance."

Dante looked at Mussolini. "What can we do with him in the meantime?"

Landry said, "Why not send him to Germasino? There used to be barracks up there for frontier guards. He should be safe there for a time. At least until you think of a better place."

"The barracks at Germasino," Pietro repeated thoughtfully. "Yes, they're empty now. That's a good idea. We'll do it." He raised his voice and told the Puecher partisans, "Prepare the prisoner. We'll move him immediately."

As the partisans approached, Mussolini looked up in confusion. "What's wrong?" he asked. "Where are you taking me?"

"A few kilometers up the mountainside," Pietro told him. "Don't worry. It's only a temporary measure until we can arrange better accommodations. You'll be quite comfortable."

One of the partisans helped Mussolini from the bench and pointed at the German greatcoat lying on the floor. "Would you like to put that on, Duce? The clouds are gathering again. I imagine it's chilly outside."

Mussolini glanced at the coat and shook his head. His answer, when it came, was so low that the others could barely hear it. He said, "Thank you, no. I don't care if I never see another German uniform."

6

Trembling and chuffing like a locomotive eager to be gone, the wood-burning truck waited in the darkness with clouds of steam rising from its engine. Lucertola, the Lizard, sat patiently behind the wheel. Freddy Stefanini arranged himself among cartons beside the Lizard. Pale yellow light gleamed wetly from the porticoed windows of the Dongo town hall as Landry hurried to the truck to bid them both farewell. Leaden lake clouds had ripped open once more with the coming of night, and rain spatters blew and swirled across the empty piazza in fresh, heavy gales, racketing down on the cab of the truck.

Stefanini leaned through the window on the passenger side and called to Landry, "We'll start testing this stuff just as soon as we get to Menàggio, but I'll probably have to make some modifications. With luck, maybe we can be back on the air sometime tonight. Tomorrow morning, for sure."

"Okay," Landry told him. "We're counting on you, Freddy. Now more than ever. God, I can't wait to hear what the brass have to say about Mussolini's capture." To the Lizard, he said, "Listen, paesano, I want you to tell Viviana that Rezzonico is clear now, and she can come home if she wants to. Ask her if Freddy can use her house to set up our radio watch."

"What about you and the others?" the Lizard asked.

"We'll stay here, at least for tonight. Pietro may need us."

The Lizard struggled with a stuck word for a moment, then said all in a rush, "You want me to come back after I tell her? Or should I stay and help Lieutenant Stefanini with the radio?"

Landry grinned. Franca's witchery rather than Stefanini's radio was more likely the Lizard's lure. "You can stay," he said. "At least until Freddy gets the radio working. If we need transportation, Pietro can assign us one of the Fascist cars." He looked across the steaming hood at the empty plaza. "Maybe you should wait a couple of minutes while I run back inside and have Pietro write a pass for you," he said. "Dante tells me there are roadblocks springing up all along the road."

The Lizard waved his hand contemptuously. "Summer partisans," he muttered. "I'll write my own pass. They won't know the difference."

"You're the boss," Landry said. "Oh, while you're down there, ask Viviana if she's willing to come to Dongo tomorrow. Pietro wants a full inventory of the Fascist treasure, and Luisa may need some help."

"I will bring her myself," the Lizard said.

Landry waited until the Lizard shifted into low, then hurried back to the town hall. He ducked through the nearest door. Partisans, some familiar, most new, crouched in dark, plaster-peeling corners, or sprawled on the floors, sleeping. Slapping rain off his cap in a now habitual gesture, Landry headed for the stairs and climbed to the large, candlelit room that Pietro had set aside as the repository for the treasure. He found Pietro inside, poking through the boxes and valises with Creedmore, Kavanaugh and Willoughby.

Apparently they had given in to curiosity and decided not to wait for the full inventory. Stacks of paper money lay on a table near the center of the room, separated by types and denominations, and Kavanaugh was marking down the totals on a pad of legal-sized note paper. He looked up when Landry came in and wordlessly handed him the list.

It read:

Partial Account of Items Taken from Fascist Cars

Paper money, crated		Value in dollars
Pounds sterling . . .	2,722	$13,610
Gold sovereigns . . .	2,150	$17,737
Swiss francs . . .	278,421	$65,088
American dollars . .	149,723	$149,723
French francs . .	18,500,000	$4,625,000
Italian lire . .	780,000,000	$7,800,000
	Subtotal —	$12,671,158

"You're kidding," Landry said.

Kavanaugh shook his head and said something that sounded like, "Mmmmmf." He tried again, and with effort found his voice. "That's only the beginning," he croaked. "Over twelve million

bucks, and we've barely started. We haven't touched the hard stuff
yet. There's still the . . . the . . ." His voice failed and he gestured haphazardly at the knee-high rows of gleaming gold bars
stacked beneath the windows, shiny yellow ingots that played
tricks in the flickering candlelight, glowing, winking, as though
some inner fire radiated from the core. Apart from the gold, scattered in piles around the room, rested personal plunder from the
Fascist cars, gold and silver art objects, religious relics and museum salvage, half-open valises and suitcases from which dangled
strands of pearls, precious stones, thumb-sized diamonds.

Even Willoughby seemed stunned by the dazzling heaps. He
said slowly, "We've been trying to assess the total value. Pietro
and Kavanaugh did a quick approximation of the hardware before
we counted out the currency. Kavanaugh figures between eighty
and ninety million American dollars, but we won't know for sure
until Luisa undertakes an official inventory sometime tomorrow. I
frankly don't envy her the job."

Pietro said, "We don't have it all. There's more. You heard
about the looting by villagers? Once we have settled the problem
of what to do with our prisoners, we will institute a house-to-
house search. I won't have it thought my people withheld a single
item."

"Don't worry," Creedmore said. "It's probably all minor stuff.
Let's forget it for now. We should be celebrating. Look what we
accomplished today."

Pietro brightened. "Yes, we do have much to celebrate," he
said. He threw open his arms, encompassing the treasure. "This.
And prisoners. Dante took forty-eight prisoners at the roadblock
in Musso. He's with them now, preparing a list. Ministers, military
men, families. We have almost the entire Salò government, locked
up here in Dongo. What do you think? Shall I send for a bottle of
wine, since we have so much to drink to?"

Willoughby said, "Send for two. It might help us work faster."

While Pietro called out to a partisan guard in the hallway,
Creedmore explained the process to Landry. "We're sorting things
out for Luisa," he said. He gestured at the piles. "Pick a suitcase,
see. Any suitcase. Pile the jewelry and stuff on that table by the
door. If you find any money, put it here with the rest. All these

candlesticks and crucifixes and things, we stick by the wall, depending on whether they're gold or silver or just plain old. Anything else, ask Pietro. He'll decide where to put them."

Pietro smiled. "A task that I find most enjoyable."

Landry discovered he had been staring steadily at the massed riches. With difficulty, he tore his eyes away and said, "Okay, I'll learn by example."

Gingerly, they moved back into the rows of collected booty. The partisan guard returned with two bottles of white wine and a corkscrew, and Pietro began to uncork one. "Isn't it amazing how quickly fortunes can change?" he said. "Two days ago we were all in the mountains, not knowing whether we were to live or die. Now we are in total command. I doubt there is a Fascist or German on the whole of Lake Como who is not under guard." The cork popped loose, and Pietro passed the bottle to Creedmore, the nearest man, for the first drink.

"That sounds fine to me," Creedmore said.

"Yes," Pietro went on, "but do you know what I like most? Spread your feet. Feel the floor. It's flat. You can walk the streets and it's that way everywhere. Flat. I don't care if the Germans counterattack with six divisions, you will never get me back into the mountains. I'll stay here, on flat ground, if I have to die for it."

Landry grinned. He accepted the bottle from Creedmore and let a stream of cool white wine rush down his throat. He closed his eyes for a moment to enjoy it, but Kavanaugh startled him by whooping in delight.

"Look what I found!" Kavanaugh called out.

Landry turned and saw him standing over a brown leather bag. A padded brassiere dangled from two outstretched fingers. Landry muttered, "You oversized pervert. Get serious."

Kavanaugh flushed red. "No, no, you got me wrong. Here, feel these lumps in the lining." Then, without giving Landry a chance to feel anything, he unsheathed his trench knife and slit the lining open. Two multifaceted rubies, as large as plover's eggs, fell into his palm. He held them over a candle flame. Darts of red light jetted to the walls and ceiling.

Creedmore stared at the rubies and the slit brassiere. "My Lord," he said reverently. "I'd sure like to know the woman who wore that contraption. Talk about some old gal having a treasure chest."

It wasn't that funny, but Kavanaugh laughed. It was catching. Pietro and Creedmore giggled, then guffawed, and Landry and Willoughby joined in. The laughter was a celebration, a regeneration, also a belittlement of the great treasure in which each man knew he would never share.

When the laughter died, they could hear footsteps approaching, and they all sobered like naughty children. The door opened to admit Dante and Piccione. Dante let his eyes touch the glittering sprawl of wealth, then peeled his weapon from his shoulder. "We may have something for you," he told Pietro. "You know the woman who was riding in the car with the consul from Spain?"

Pietro made a sound of disgust. "The man is no Spaniard, no matter what he claims. I talked with him earlier. He doesn't even speak the language."

Dante shrugged. "Well, whoever he is, the woman from his car is Claretta Petacci. Piccione is sure of it."

Pietro turned alertly to Piccione. "Is this true?"

"I'd almost swear to it," Piccione said. "She asked some peculiar questions while I was in there with her. She even wanted to know what I thought would happen to Clara Petacci if the partisans caught her." His face became thoughtful. "She said something else, come to think of it, something about the Spanish consul. She slipped once and referred to him as her brother. Do you suppose he's a Petacci, too?"

"I will question her myself," Pietro said. "David, you will come with me?"

Landry agreed promptly and gladly. After having hooked the big shark for whom they had angled so long, he found he was more than eager to meet the shark's remora.

Pietro put a hand on Dante's arm. "Piccione will take us to her. I have another mission for you, my friend. Someone must take full and complete charge of the treasure. It must be guarded night and day. Are you willing to accept the responsibility?"

Dante looked reluctantly at the piles around the room. "That is a large undertaking. Are you sure you want me to do it?"

Pietro said solemnly, "I can think of no man in whom I could place more trust." Then he turned briskly to Piccione and said,

"Very well, take us to this woman whom you think is Clara Petacci."

Piccione led them down a long corridor to a closed room at the far end of the building. He glanced nervously at Pietro and Landry, then unlocked the door. "If you don't mind, I'll wait in the hall," he told them. "I don't want to talk to her again."

The woman was sitting on a cot when Pietro and Landry entered. She had discarded a pair of wrinkled coveralls in the corner, and was now dressed in a soft brown corduroy suit from an open piece of luggage on the cot. A white blouse, slightly soiled, was buttoned at her throat. She stared at them, wide-eyed.

"Mussolini is our prisoner," Pietro told her.

Her expression didn't change. "Is he?" she said innocently. After a moment's pause, she said, "They tell me he is a great man."

Pietro sighed. "We know who you are, signora."

"I am a Spanish citizen," she said. "You have no right to hold me."

"You are Claretta Petacci," he said. "Both you and your brother have been recognized."

"You are mistaken," she insisted.

Pietro shook his head. "You are Clara Petacci. We have it from one who is close to you. Cavaliere Mussolini himself. The last thing he asked before we placed him under guard was that I come to you and tell you all is well. He seemed quite concerned for your welfare."

She regarded him suspiciously, then stared at her hands. In a small voice, she said, "Did he truly send you to me?"

"He did, signora. He seemed quite worried about you."

She tried not to show any emotion, but she was too frightened. She trembled suddenly and said, "The partisans all hate me. They think I sold my love to the Duce for money and power."

"Didn't you?"

"No, of course not! My motives have always been unselfish. I thought only of his happiness, not my own." She looked up at Pietro and firmed her chin. "Will you help me, signore?"

"In what way?"

"I must prove myself to the world. Take me to him. I wish to share his fate, no matter what happens. If he is to be killed, then I want to be killed also."

Pietro gave her an incredulous look. "Are you serious, signora?"

"Of course," she said. "Did you think the partisans were right about me? If he is to be executed, then you must promise that I will be at his side, and that I will be executed also."

"You needn't concern yourself, madam. We have no intention of executing Mussolini."

She searched his face, then said solemnly, "I believe you."

Pietro flicked a look at Landry, then gestured and they left the room together. Piccione closed the door behind them.

"Now you see why I didn't want to talk to her again," Piccione whispered. "She's crazy. Can you imagine, begging for a bullet like that?"

"Do you think she means it?" Landry asked.

"Perhaps we will find out," Pietro said. He sighed again, sounding weary. "David, there are matters about which I must ask your advice. I've still had no word from the Como Federation, nor from Milan. I fear our success may turn sour unless we take further steps with Mussolini. Too many people know we've sent him to the barracks in Germasino. If the Germans should counterattack, we haven't nearly enough people there to hold them off."

"Why don't you move him again?" Landry said. "Pick men you can trust and have them take him to a new hiding place known only to you."

"Yes, I've considered that," Pietro said. "The problem is absurd, in a way. What is the proper hiding place, a prison, for a tyrant? Surely one needs a pigsty or a palace. Dare I imprison him in a mere villa? The world will soon know of our actions here, and I would not have it thought that the whole partisan movement is absurd."

Landry sympathized. Mussolini's actions had been so far from heroic that his capture, courtesy of a determined bluff, didn't exactly ring of victorious trumpets and the surrendering of swords. War, he was learning, might start with pomp, but it seemed to end far differently. "Maybe you should let Clara Petacci's request decide the matter," he told Pietro. "Are you going to send her to

Mussolini? If so, a woman like that wouldn't be very comfortable in a pigsty. Let it be the villa."

Pietro looked relieved. "You are right," he said. "At least the world will know we can behave like gentlemen. There's a villa in Blevio that I know. It's quite far south, but it should be comfortable. Piccione, you will take the woman. You and Salvo. You can leave with her as soon as I arrange transportation for Mussolini."

"To Blevio?" Piccione said. "That's a long way off. What if we need to get to him quickly?"

"The important thing is to keep anyone else from getting to him quickly," Landry said. "Use the villa, if Pietro thinks it's secure. Frankly, I think it's an unnecessary precaution. There's no harm in playing things safe, but everything has run very smoothly, so far. What could go wrong now?"

Pietro chuckled. "I suppose you are right, David. Things *have* run very smoothly for us. Isn't it marvelous? Perhaps we'll send him to the villa as a final safeguard, then we'll relax for a while. It's time we enjoyed our triumph."

7

The stunning news of Mussolini's capture reached Milan shortly before ten o'clock that evening. Ugo arrived at the public garden near the Piazza Cavour less than two hours later, fresh from an emergency meeting of the National Committee of Liberation. He saw that Valerio was already there, talking quietly to a group of twelve men, some of them in suits, some in work clothing. They were all armed, and each wore a tricolored armband bearing the initials "PCI." One of them, the cell commander who called himself Sandrino, had also stitched a red-felt star to his sleeve.

Valerio smiled at Ugo's approach. "We are ready, comrade."

Ugo glanced at the body of men, then turned his squashed, round face to Valerio. "They told you of Mussolini? That he is under partisan guard on Lake Como?"

Valerio swallowed. "Yes, comrade. They also told me that you recommended me to lead the expedition."

"Yes, the lake area falls in my region of responsibility," said Ugo, "and I insisted on a man of action. I believe you to be such a man."

Valerio's face lit up. "Thank you, comrade. I am grateful."

"How soon do we leave?" Ugo asked.

"The cars are being prepared now," Valerio said. "Comrade Ugo, I wish you to know how much I appreciate your faith in me. It is a signal honor you have bestowed on me."

"Perhaps more than that," Ugo said. He smiled to himself. He had handled himself well following the Committee session. With only fellow Communists remaining in the meeting room, the subject of the treasure had come up. Reports from the lake were sketchy, but apparently the partisans had discovered the vast wealth in the cars of the fleeing gerarchia. Ugo had pointed out to the comrades that all monies and personal belongings would revert to the state if there were no Fascist survivors on the lake. Further, with the help of loyal Party members among the Lake Como partisans, an even more profitable accommodation could perhaps be arranged.

"Do you think the Lake Como partisans will object when we demand the person of Mussolini?" Valerio asked.

"We will give them no choice," Ugo said. He stared at the small body of volunteers busily checking their weapons.

"Here come the cars now," Valerio said. Dim headlights snaked through the darkness. Two sedans and a cumbersome furniture van turned from the street and pulled into the park.

Ugo folded his hands behind his back. Everything flowed like clockwork. Just as he had promised his nervous comrades at the rump session. They had worried about the approaching Allied troops. He had reminded them that Palmiro Togliatti, chief of the Communist movement in Italy, had already issued orders that Mussolini was not to fall into Allied hands. Further, a message would go out this very evening warning the Allies not to interfere in the happenings on Lake Como. Otherwise partisans would open fire on them. The Americans wouldn't want that. They would cause no trouble.

The three vehicles pulled to a stop and a soft, misting rain began to fall. Valerio's men loaded up quickly. Ugo and Valerio climbed into the lead car and Sandrino took over as driver.

"What will become of Mussolini once we have returned him to Milan?" Valerio asked.

"Nothing," said Ugo. "He'll be dead."

"Dead! But I thought . . ."

The cars and the furniture van pulled out of the garden and headed north, toward the city limits, windshield wipers clacking. Ugo settled himself comfortably and thought of things to come. With Valerio as leader of the Mussolini volunteers, Ugo would be free to work more quietly in the background. First he would ask questions, seek out the most trustworthy partisans. Then there would be the arrangements about the treasure. Perhaps even . . .

"Comrade Ugo?"

"What?" Ugo said irritably.

Valerio hesitated. "About Mussolini. I thought the Committee wanted him brought back alive. Do we dare disobey their orders?"

"We have orders that supersede all Committee decisions," Ugo said. "The tyrant is to be executed. All members of his gerarchia, as well."

"But if the Committee wishes . . ."

"Our orders come from the Party," Ugo said. "We will carry them out ruthlessly and efficiently. Do you understand?"

Valerio shifted, and a momentary uneasiness crossed his face. Then, as though realizing his political future depended on his answer, he said firmly, "I understand, Comrade Ugo. The tyrant must die."

Day Eight

Saturday—April 28, 1945

È traditor. È traditor. Morrà.

He's a traitor. He's a traitor. He must die.
                                        —Verdi, *Aïda*

1

Claretta Petacci smelled good to Piccione, like flowers crushed underfoot. In the back seat of a small Topolino, she sat so close that her knee touched his. Piccione would have liked thinking about her, but there were too many distractions. It was two o'clock in the morning and the rain drummed steadily on the tinny top of the Topolino. Salvo, not much of a driver, hunched awkwardly behind the steering wheel and guided as best he could around the curves, blowing breath through loose lips every time the tires skidded on the wet pavement. There was another car behind the Topolino, following them south through the slanting rain, with a very special prisoner in the back seat. Mussolini. Partisans at Germasino, apparently worried about what might happen if the Duce were recognized by anyone, had given him a blanket for his shoulders and wound white gauze around his head, covering all but the eyes and nose. He looked like a wounded civilian, on his way to a hospital. Only the bandy legs and thick upper torso gave him away. It was just as well. Piccione had heard talk before leaving about vengeful villagers and even the possibility of a rescue attempt by Fascist sympathizers, and now both he and Salvo were seeing ghosts in every flicker of movement along the roadside, every swaying tree branch, every shift of wind.

The going was slow and tedious. They had encountered numerous official and unofficial roadblocks, many of which had already been abandoned, probably by neopartisans who found the rain not to their liking and had retired to the warmth of their homes. Piccione and the partisans in the other car had to get out time and again to move rocks and tree trunks aside.

At Moltrasio, far down the lake, they came to yet another roadblock, but this one was still manned. The cars pulled up in front of it and an armed villager plodded toward them, holding a lantern over his head.

"Clear the road," Piccione called. "We are partisans, on official business."

"My regrets," the man answered. "I wish only to point out something that you may not have noticed because of the rain."

"What is that?" Piccione asked suspiciously.

The man lowered his lantern and gestured to the south. "Those flashes in the distance. They appear to be lightning, but they aren't."

Piccione stepped out of the car and peered southward. The sky flickered with the quick light of exploding shells. A faint rumble of artillery groaned across the miles. "Americans?"

"We assume so," the man said. "Probably mopping up the Fascists at Cantù. If so, they should reach the lake soon. It's wonderful, eh?"

"Yes, wonderful," Piccione said. He leaned through Salvo's window and said, "We'll have to turn back. We can't allow our prisoners to fall into American hands unless Pietro orders it."

"But the villa at Blevio is to the south of us," Salvo said. "If we can't take him there, where will we go?"

Piccione thought for a moment, then said, "I know a farmhouse above Azzano that might be safe. The farmer and his wife have helped partisans many times. They won't ask questions." He waved his arm at the other car, then climbed in beside Claretta. Both vehicles swung around in the middle of the road and headed north once more.

It was almost four in the morning when Piccione directed Salvo to turn off the lake road and drive up through Azzano to a narrow wagon track that climbed to the farmhouse. It was a steep track and they were forced to leave the cars and walk. The rain had slacked off again, but the ground was muddy and treacherous, and Piccione instructed the Germasino partisans to help Mussolini and Claretta up the slope. They reached the edge of the farmyard and paused. Piccione whistled three times and waited until a sleep-lidded farmer and his wife appeared in an open doorway and held a kerosene lamp to guide them across the muddy ground. The small party hurried to the farmhouse.

"Buona sera, little bird," the farmer said to Piccione. "What brings you this way?"

"We have two prisoners," Piccione said. "They're tired. Will you give them shelter for the night?"

"Of course," the farmer said. He stood aside, staring with mild curiosity as the bandaged man and the woman were led inside. Piccione came last, carrying a piece of Claretta's luggage.

The farmhouse was poorly furnished, almost bare. It may have reminded Mussolini of the bleak building near Predappio where he had been born over sixty years earlier. If so, he gave no indication. He stood quietly until Piccione gestured him to a rough bench. Claretta sat down as well. Claretta's eyes were red, Piccione noticed, as though she had been crying. He hadn't seen any tears in the car. Perhaps it was only fatigue.

The farmer put his kerosene lamp on a bare table and built a fire to warm the room. His wife, wearing a tattered black dress that apparently served her as a sleeping garment, plucked timidly at Piccione's sleeve and said, "Are they perhaps hungry? May I get them something?"

Claretta redraped the blanket around Mussolini's shoulders and repeated the woman's offer of food. Mussolini shook his head listlessly. Claretta said, "He doesn't want anything, but I'd appreciate a cup of coffee."

The farm woman clasped her hands in apology and said, "We have no real coffee. Only barley coffee. Perhaps some potato broth?"

"That's fine," Claretta said. "Anything to take away the chill."

While the woman turned to the wood stove, Mussolini began to unwind the bandage. The farmer, sitting across the room near Piccione, watched curiously until enough of the well-known, jowly profile became visible to fill him with shock. He stumbled quickly to his feet and stood at a kind of bewildered attention, not certain what he should do.

Mussolini waggled a hand. "Sit down, sit down," he said.

"Excellency . . ."

"That was yesterday. Today I am dust. Sit."

The farmer sank timorously back to his stool. His wife, busily fanning the wood to flames, had missed the brief exchange, but she couldn't miss the look on her husband's face. She swung to see the shaved head and massive jaw that had put it there and turned pale with alarm.

Claretta said, "Is there a room where I can freshen up?"

The wife shook her head. "We . . . we are poor mountain folk, signora. You will have to go outside to wash." She lit another kerosene lamp with trembling hands and offered it to Claretta. Claretta thanked her and picked up the small suitcase.

Piccione said, "Just a moment, signora. One of us must go also."

"I intend to bathe my body," Claretta objected.

"Nevertheless," Piccione said, "one of us must accompany you." He regarded the partisans from Germasino. Their leader, a man who called himself il Gallo, the Cock, stared back at him with a malicious grin. "I will do it," Piccione said. "The rest of you stay here with our prisoner."

He followed Claretta into the yard and across to a shed where she hung the lamp from a peg on the wall, then he watched as she poured water from a crockery pitcher into a flat pan. She paused and looked at him, as though waiting, so he backed out of the shed and closed the door. Splinters of kerosene lamplight streamed through cracks in the wall planks. He fought briefly against the impulse to peek, then gave in to it and pressed his face to an opening. Claretta was in the process of slipping off her corduroy suit. She folded it neatly, then unbuttoned her blouse. Piccione held his breath and watched as the blouse came off and she stepped out of her underwear.

His eyes widened at the excellence of her white, healthy body in the flickering light of the lamp. Though she was surely in her thirties, she had a flat stomach and good, firm breasts. Piccione swallowed. It was easy to see why an old man like the Duce would be attracted to her.

While Piccione stared and tried to quiet the sudden flush of heat in his loins, she glanced up and caught sight of his face at the opening. He stiffened, expecting her to cry out or curse at him, but she didn't. She only sighed and sat down on a wooden milking stool, either too weary to care or perhaps hopeful that she might gain some slight advantage for herself and her lover by exposing her body to him.

She dampened a rag. With a last look in Piccione's direction, her face went blank and she began to wash. Despite the rain-chilled night, despite the cold water and the watching stranger, she prepared herself, ritually, to offer what comfort she could to Mussolini, to come to him cleanly and softly in the night should he indicate such comfort was desired.

Piccione stared at her white shoulders and her gently bobbing breasts. In his mind's eye, he saw himself jerk the door open and hurl himself into the shed. What was to stop him? He could take her by force, if necessary. Or perhaps he could lie to her, promise he would help her to escape. In her gratitude, she might give herself freely. But if she cried out, or if he lied to her and she later accused him, if it became known in any way that he had mistreated such an important prisoner, he might well face a firing squad. No adventure was worth that. He finally tore his face from the opening and stumbled away to stand in the darkness, several feet from the hut.

She finished washing and dressed herself in a fresh skirt and blouse, then opened the door and moved past him toward the house, carrying the lamp and her suitcase. She didn't look back. Piccione followed her. Once inside, he moved off into a corner and leaned against the wall, waiting anxiously to see if she would say anything to the others about his having watched. But she didn't. She sipped her broth, then spoke a few quiet, cheerful words to Mussolini and took him by the arm to help him up the stairs to the bedroom they were to share.

Embarrassed, Piccione cleared his throat and instructed il Gallo and his two Germasino men to stay at the farmhouse until morning, at which time he or Pietro would send relief from Dongo,

Then, with Salvo, Piccione went back down the hillside to the Topolino.

2

Allen Dulles was awakened before dawn by a ringing telephone. He pushed covers aside and groped for his glasses, then sat up and peered at a bedside clock. He allowed the phone to ring twice more before he picked it up and said a hoarse hello.

It was Cornfield, calling from the operations complex.

"Sorry to disturb you so early," Cornfield said briskly, "but I've just been checking night traffic in the message center. I've got some good news and some excellent news."

Dulles slipped fingers under the frame of his glasses and rubbed sleep from his eyes. "Give me the excellent news first," he said.

"Wolff has responded to our signal," Cornfield said. "He's accepted our cover explanation for missing contact in Lucerne, and he's prepared to follow through on Sunrise. He'll come to Caserta on Monday, two days from now, to meet with a surrender delegation."

Now Dulles was fully awake. "Oh lovely," he said. "Absolutely lovely. What's the *good* news?"

"The Lake Como team is about to come back on the air. A preliminary test signal came in about an hour ago. Static and shifting frequency kept us from getting the whole thing, but the radio guard thinks that can be cleared up in time for a full transmission contact later this morning."

"The Lake Como team?" Dulles said. Then he remembered. "Oh yes, Rossiter's group. Was there any explanation of their radio absence over the past few days?"

"No, sir. Not yet. But there was something about Mussolini and the partisans. They've taken him captive at a roadblock, we think. The signal faded during transmission, so we may have it garbled. We'll ask for confirmation when Lake Como's transmitter problems are worked out and we go for full contact."

Dulles breathed heavily into the phone. "Good Lord," he said. "Mussolini a prisoner? Is that possible?"

"It doesn't seem likely," Cornfield admitted. "But if it is, the Lake Como team may be in trouble. There's a new noninterference directive on the boards from Allied HQ in Siena. All Allied personnel have been ordered to stand aside if Mussolini or any of his Cabinet come in contact with Italian resistance units."

Dulles felt around for his bedroom slippers and found them just under the edge of the bed. "What brought that on?" he asked.

Cornfield hesitated, then said, "Apparently it's this Ugo, sir. We definitely should have warned the team about him. He's talked partisan officials in Milan into issuing an ultimatum. They threaten to open fire on anyone who interferes with Italian activities, particularly those activities that pertain to Mussolini."

"I see," Dulles said. "Well, we wouldn't want that. You'd better speed up this radio contact of yours and tell the Lake Como team to back off."

"It may be too late," Cornfield said. "Considering the orders we sent in by Rossiter, they may already be deeply involved."

"Then reverse their orders," Dulles said. "Sunrise is the only issue now. I won't have it disrupted."

"Sir?" Cornfield said. There was a note of confusion in his voice. "I recognize the danger this ultimatum might afford our Lake Como team, but how can it affect Sunrise? If the business about Mussolini and the partisans is correct, that's the end of our problems. The Valtellina situation is solved. Sunrise is a shoo-in."

"It won't be if we provoke a shooting incident with the partisans," Dulles said. "Wolff is an influential man, but he's still only an SS general. For Sunrise to succeed, we have to persuade General Vietinghoff and the German Army to go along with anything Wolff might sign. An outbreak of fighting between partisans and Americans might convince Vietinghoff that it isn't necessary."

"I see," Cornfield said. "Then you want us to knuckle under to the ultimatum. A full retreat."

"I don't think we have much choice," Dulles said.

3

An orderly retreat, to be handled in the proper manner, could be quite time-consuming, SD Lieutenant Gunther Stenzel decided. So many things to do before they could withdraw from the lake, papers to be destroyed, records burned, final radio contact. And now this unreasonable request from General Vietinghoff's Army headquarters.

Stenzel stepped into the dark hallway of the Cernobbio SD villa and summoned Sergeant Knaust. Knaust, outfitted in a shabby civilian jacket that was too narrow in the shoulders and a pair of brown trousers that sagged at the knees, hurriedly dismissed three SD troopers who were also in civilian clothing and sent them bustling toward the kitchen with their arms full of files and ledgers.

"Yes, Herr Untersturmführer?" Knaust said. The sergeant looked haggard and harried, yet he braced to attention and clicked the soft heels of his wing-tipped brogans with military precision. There was something laughable about the sergeant's stiff posture in the ill-fitting civilian clothing, and Stenzel might have smiled if he hadn't been so tired.

"Where is Major Richter?" Stenzel asked the sergeant.

"I believe he's in the library, sir."

Stenzel nodded wearily. "See to the destruction of the map room, and ready the men. We may have business." He left the sergeant and strode down the corridor alone. Stenzel was still in uniform, unlike the others, though the order to change into civilian clothing had been issued by Richter before dawn. It wasn't a matter of insubordination on Stenzel's part. Just so much to accomplish in so short a time. Stenzel's close-cropped blond hair was moist with sweat, and his heavy-lidded eyes were rimmed with red.

He could smell the smoky sharpness of Major Richter's own private bonfire, coming from the library. Not only paper, but leather as well. The major was apparently burning some of his favorite interrogation implements. Stenzel knocked. There was soft movement inside, then Richter's voice. "Come!"

Richter was poised above a metal wastebasket when Stenzel entered, feeding photographs from his personal files into a small, greedy fire. The glow of the flames bronzed the major's eyebrows and cast eerie shadows above the lips and nose, making him look like one of Macbeth's witches standing over a cauldron.

Stenzel stared beyond Richter at the tall library window. Outside, visible through half-drawn drapes, a cluster of dim figures had gathered near the front gate. Peasants and townspeople from Cernobbio, mainly, though a few of them seemed to be armed. "I see they're still there," Stenzel said.

Major Richter raised his chin slightly. Smoke curled up from the wastebasket into his face, bringing tears to his eyes. At least Stenzel assumed the tears came from the smoke. "There's nothing to worry about," the major murmured. "They won't dare attack."

"I'm not worried," Stenzel said. He watched Richter feeding the flames and felt mild loathing for him. Lieutenant Stenzel had never been comfortable serving under Richter. Stenzel, who came of good German stock, whose formative years had been spent in an environment of genuine refinement, knew the major for what he was. A crude policeman, nothing more.

Richter lifted an eye and caught Stenzel staring at him. The major's face changed, a quick hardening of the jaw, a flash of teeth behind a curling lip. Something about the fleeting change of expression told Stenzel that the mild loathing was mutual. Richter said, "I presume you sought me out for a reason?"

"Yes, sir," Stenzel said. "We've received an emergency communiqué from Army headquarters. A pity. Another ten minutes and I would have had the radio dismantled."

Richter didn't stop feeding the flames, though he did slow down, taking time to study each photograph before sliding it into the wastebasket. "What do they want this time?"

"There is a report that the Duce has been captured near Dongo," Stenzel said. "Apparently a convoy of German troops tried to get him through, but partisans discovered him and took him prisoner."

"So?" Another photograph slipped into the fire.

"Well, they've been unable to contact the Gravedona garrison, and the Como garrison has already pulled out, so they thought we might investigate, and if the report is true, undertake a rescue operation. I explained to them that there are only fourteen of us left, and that we are preparing to withdraw as well, but . . ."

"But they asked us to make the attempt anyway," Richter finished for him. His lip curled again, this time in a half smile.

Stenzel hesitated. "It was issued not as a request, but as an order," he said. "They referred to the Führer's long-established, personal interest in the welfare of the Duce. They insist he be rescued."

"Ridiculous," Richter muttered. "They don't know what's happening on the lake." He dropped another photograph into the flames. "The Führer is no longer concerned with the doings of that buffoon," he said. "Neither am I. Let the Duce look after himself."

Stenzel shifted uncomfortably. "Yes, sir. Shall I, then, signal General Vietinghoff and report our inability to intervene?"

"Report nothing," Richter said. "We have finished talking to the Army. Dismantle the radio and gather the men. We leave within the hour."

That, at least, was welcome news. Stenzel risked a smile. "Yes, sir. Home, sir? Or to Switzerland?"

"Neither," Richter said. "I've prepared a hiding place for us near Cadenabbia. It's an old villa, crumbling with age, but it's well supplied with food and arms. We will be safe there until our informant contacts us and clarifies this matter of the treasure."

Stenzel's chin jerked. "Cadenabbia? Wouldn't it be more prudent for us to . . ."

"I will not leave the lake in defeat," Richter snapped. "There are affairs to be concluded."

"But Major, Cadenabbia is twenty kilometers to the north, right in the heart of guerrilla country. The lake is no longer ours. With partisans and partisan sympathizers everywhere, how can we get from here to there?"

"Through the mountains," Richter said shortly. "The partisans did it to us for a year and a half with impunity. Surely our small band can manage it once."

Stenzel tried to remain calm. "Sir, what about the men? They're expecting to go home. Shouldn't we . . . ?"

Richter dumped the rest of his private file of photographs into the flames. "Our time for retreat will come, Lieutenant. But first we will give the partisans a taste of their own lawless medicine. There are issues to be settled. I will not leave until they have been tended. You may so inform the others."

The glossy photographs curled and burned, but not before Stenzel caught a glimpse of a naked feminine thigh. Then the picture blackened and shriveled and smoke rolled across the room.

4

When gunfire rattled in the town square, Landry bolted to his feet, caught completely off guard. "What the hell was that?" he gasped. Pietro threw aside a list of the Fascist prisoners he had been going over with Landry and Willoughby, and rushed to the window of the lower-floor office he had chosen in the Dongo town hall. On the far side of the square, near the roadblock, two cars and a yellow furniture van pulled to a hasty stop, and a tall man with a mustache leaped from the lead car, waving his arms angrily at the partisans manning the roadblock.

"Cristo, more fools shooting off guns," Pietro said. "There had better be a good explanation for that disorder, or I shall have to make an example of those dolts."

They hustled into the lobby. From a corner near the recorder's office, Pietro summoned a group of partisans who had been trying to sleep before their rest was shattered by the gunfire. Among them were Salvo and Piccione, back from their night of driving up and down the lake. Rifles in hand, they spilled out of the town hall, a growing number of armed men, but Pietro gestured for a halt when he saw Dante on the steps. Dante looked up at Pietro and Landry anxiously. Dante said, "We have visitors. They just drove in from the south."

"Who are they?" Landry asked.

"We don't know yet," Dante said. "But they act like big shots."

Pietro snorted. "We'll soon set them straight," he said. He signaled to the bulk of the partisans to spread out, then beckoned Landry, Willoughby and Dante to accompany him across the square.

At the roadblock, three Dongo partisans and several men from the cars had squared off in direct confrontation. Landry scanned the faces of the strangers. They all wore armbands indicating they were part of the resistance movement, but from the looks of their clothing and the arrogant way they carried themselves, he was fairly certain they weren't lake people. There were only ten or twelve of them, but they were well armed. At least four of the men, including a tall man with a mustache and an air of authority, carried Beretta 9mm submachine guns.

"What's going on here?" Pietro called out to his own men.

One of the partisans at the roadblock, an older man who had joined Dante's group the day before in Musso, pushed out his chin and said, "These jackasses tried to shove their way through the barricade, commendatore. We waved them down, but they wouldn't stop."

The man with the mustache reacted quickly to Pietro's own air of authority. He lowered his Beretta and said, "You are in charge of these clowns?"

"I am Captain Pietro, commander of the 52nd Garibaldi Brigade," Pietro said. "Who are you, and why have you ignored our checkpoint?"

"My name is Valerio," the man responded coldly. "*Colonel* Valerio, from Milan. These men are volunteers, and we represent the General Command. We are here on urgent business. Here is our authority." He produced a folded document and displayed it contemptuously between two fingers. "As for your ridiculous roadblock, we have been delayed over and over again along the lake, and we are tired of being stopped by ignorant peasants."

Pietro flushed angrily. He reached for the document and unfolded it, then looked up uncertainly. "This appears to be in order," he said. "But it tells us nothing of your purpose in coming here."

"I am here to take charge of Mussolini and members of his ruling gerarchia," Valerio said.

Landry saw uncertainty change to quick dismay on Pietro's face. "We have had no such orders," Pietro said.

"You have them now," Valerio told him haughtily. "You will deliver the tyrant and his hierarchy into our possession without delay. Refusal will be considered an act of hostility toward the General Command, and will be dealt with accordingly."

Pietro held the document so Landry and Dante could see it. It contained a simple typewritten message, stating that Colonel Valerio was acting on behalf of the National Committee of Liberation for the good of the country, and that he must be given co-operation by all levels of the resistance movement. It was an ordinary document, but it bore the official seal of the CLN and several important signatures had been attached. If it was genuine, and it certainly seemed to be, these men were armed with absolute authority, and authority, Landry knew, was a weapon with which Pietro had seldom been forced to deal.

Pietro seemed at sea. He said firmly enough, "I trust you also have identification to assure me that you are truly the Colonel Valerio mentioned here?" But Landry could see apprehension in his eyes.

A short, balding man with a squashed face pushed his way forward from the rear of the pack. Landry had assumed the man with the mustache was the leader of the group, but he noticed that all of the Milanese volunteers moved aside respectfully, even the one who called himself Valerio.

The short man smiled calmly. "There is a simple way to accomplish verification of our identities, comandante," he said in a quiet, chairman-of-the-board voice. "Ask your own companion who we are. Ask Dante."

Dante looked startled to hear his name from the mouth of a stranger. He peered at the man and recognition flickered in his eyes. "Yes," Dante said. "I know you. You came from Milan once to lecture at a cell meeting in Brunate. You are Comrade . . ."

"Names do not matter," the man said, cutting Dante off. "Be good enough to tell your people that we are legitimate."

Dante wavered, then turned aside to huddle with Pietro and Landry. "It's true," Dante whispered. "That one is an important man from Milan. They say he sits on the Committee itself. We will have to do as they wish."

Pietro looked at the short man, at his smiling, patient face. "But they wish Mussolini," he whispered back. "There is no mention of Mussolini in their document. How can we give him to them without direct, written orders from the CLN? What do you think, David?"

Landry knew Pietro was at a disadvantage. Although orders from the CLN or from Milan had been rare, wonderful things throughout the war for the hill partisans, now that the partisans had no wish or need for orders, they nevertheless could not be disregarded. "Perhaps there's been a misunderstanding," he told Pietro. "We ought to check carefully with Milan, to make sure these demands are authentic."

"We've been trying to reach Milan all morning," Dante pointed out. "Without success. The lines are still not functioning properly."

Pietro fell back on the ploy that had worked successfully before. "Perhaps we can stall them, at least long enough to try again. I'll ask them to come to my office for discussion. While we're busy there, Dante can try once more to get through to the Committee."

"I'll go with him," Willoughby volunteered. "If it's a washout, perhaps we can send someone down the lake to find a clear line."

"Yes, do that," Pietro said. "We must have word, and quickly."

The man with the squashed face was losing his patience. "Well?" he called. "Are you satisfied?"

Pietro hesitated. "I am now assured that you are, as you say, from Milan," he said. "Naturally, we will do what we can to help you. But there are complications. If you would care to come with us, we can confer in my office. Your men can wait here."

"Colonel Valerio will accompany you," the man said. "He is leader of this expedition. I am only here to advise."

Pietro shrugged. "Very well, then. Colonel Valerio?"

Valerio handed his submachine gun to one of his companions. "We can confer about anything you wish," he told Pietro. "But my demands will not be altered. I am here to collect Mussolini and the traitors who served under him, and I will not be put off."

It was only minutes before Dante and Willoughby returned. Valerio glanced at them without interest, because by then he was already engrossed in the list of Fascist prisoners he had spotted on Pietro's desk. He continued studying it with cold concentration. "This is a complete accounting?" he asked Pietro.

"We've listed everyone," Pietro said, "including the wives and children." He raised an eyebrow at Dante, but Dante shook his head. Landry heard Pietro sigh.

"We will take fifteen of them," Valerio said. "One for each of the patriots who died in the Piazzale Loreto last August. We will begin with this one, the secretary of the infamous Neo-Fascist Party." He made a check mark beside the name of Alessandro Pavolini.

Seeing Valerio shuffling paper, Landry felt an odd sense of danger, but he didn't know why. He asked, "What do you intend to do with them?"

Valerio made another check mark, this one beside the name of Fernando Mezzasoma, then regarded Landry. "You are not an Italian," he said. "Who are you?"

"He is a friend," Pietro said quickly. "A captain of the United States Army."

"An American?" Valerio checked two more names: Nicola Bombacci and Francesco Barracu. "I thought as much. Send him away. Americans have no part in this."

"He is not here as an American," Pietro said. "He is here as a companion-at-arms of long standing and a man whose advice has meant much to me."

"His presence will change nothing," Valerio said. "The fifteen innocents who were martyred by the Germans in the Piazzale Loreto were Italians, not Americans." He marked three more names: Paolo Zerbino, Augusto Liverani and Ruggero Romano. "These Fascist traitors will atone for their blood before a firing squad of loyal Italians."

Pietro's mouth dropped open in disbelief. "You intend to shoot them?"

"Those are my orders," Valerio said. He put a check by the name of Idreno Utimpergher, a Black Brigades commander, then added Paolo Porta, the Lombardy military inspector.

Dante was also shocked. "You can't shoot them," he stammered. "There was no talk of that. Neither in our discussion in the square, nor in the document you bear. These men have had no trial."

"Nor did the martyrs of the Piazzale Loreto," Valerio said. He studied the shortening list and added two lesser politicians, Mario Nudi and Alfredo Coppola.

Pietro shook his head violently. "I cannot accept that," he said. "All these months we have been fighting for the return of justice, and now you tell us we are to act the same as the Germans or the Fascisti?"

"Justice resides in the hearts of just men," Valerio responded dryly. "Not in courtrooms." He checked the names of Luigi Gatti, Mussolini's longtime secretary, and Colonel Vito Casalinovo, Mussolini's adjutant.

"I won't allow it," Pietro said. "Nor will my men."

Valerio studied the list carefully, running out of important names. He checked off Ernesto Daquanno, a journalist who had accompanied the caravan. "This is a political matter," he told Pietro, "authorized by the National Committee of Liberation, and therefore outside your jurisdiction."

"I cannot believe the Committee has authorized anything so grossly unjust," Pietro snapped.

Valerio didn't reply. He looked at Dante and said, "I am told that you are a loyal Party member. I must ask your assistance with these names." He held out the list and gestured toward the bottom. "This one. Who is he? Calistri? Pietro Calistri?"

Dante said shakily, "An Air Force captain. He isn't important. He just happened to be along."

"Nevertheless, he is a Fascist," Valerio said. He added the final check mark by Calistri's name. "There. That is fifteen. You will bring them to the lakefront. We will assemble the firing squad there. You will also produce the tyrant, Mussolini."

Pietro stared at him. "You intend to shoot Mussolini as well?"

"I intend to follow my orders," Valerio said. He stood. "I will wait in the square with my men. You will bring Mussolini and the hierarchy to us there. You have one hour to produce them."

Landry cleared his throat and said to Pietro, "It may take longer, comandante. We haven't that many cars available."

Pietro seized gratefully on Landry's hinted suggestion. "Yes, yes, that's true. We have scattered our prisoners in a number of hiding places, to forestall rescue attempts by the Germans. Some are in Germasino, some in Domaso. It will take time to assemble them. Perhaps several hours."

"One hour," Valerio repeated. He scowled at Landry and stalked through the door.

"Porca miseria!" Pietro swore. He spread his palms helplessly. "What happened with the phone call to Milan?" he asked Dante.

"The lines have been improperly repaired," Dante said. "We sent Piccione and Salvo to try a call from lower on the lake, but that will take time."

"Then we must buy the time," Pietro said.

"Perhaps you should disappear for a while," Landry told Pietro. "Find urgent business elsewhere. Partisan business. They'll have to wait if they can't find you. You're the only one who can tell them where Mussolini is being held."

"What about the men who stood guard over him? They're due back at any moment."

"We'll find them and warn them," Landry said.

Pietro shook his head. "I can't stay out of sight forever. Eventually, we must still give them what they want."

"At least we can keep them distracted," Dante said. "You disappear, as David has suggested. We will go ahead and assemble the fifteen members of the gerarchia for them, but we will do it slowly. Perhaps that will satisfy them. You can stay out of touch until we hear from Salvo and Piccione."

Someone approached from the hallway outside and was challenged by the partisan guard at Pietro's door. The response to the challenge must have been correct, for the door swung open. Freddy Stefanini came into the room with Viviana, followed by the Lizard and Tuono. Happy to see his friends again, the dog bounded forward with his ears back, greeting each of them with paws to the stomach. He allotted Willoughby a special wag of the tail, hitting the papers on Pietro's desk in the process and sweeping them to the floor. The moment's confusion gave Landry a chance only to offer an automatic welcoming smile to Viviana, but she didn't return it. Her face seemed troubled. Still dressed in the baggy worsted pants and boots Luisa had loaned her in the mountains, she looked the picture of a solemn partisan.

Stefanini had news. While the others picked up the papers, he said, "I finally got the damn radio going. I made a preliminary contact before dawn, but the signal wasn't good enough. Damn tuning coil kept slipping. I got it fixed, though, and tried again about an hour ago. They were waiting for us. We've got new instructions."

Landry felt buoyant with relief. "Thank God," he said. "You see, Pietro? Now everything will be fine. How soon can they get troops to us?"

Stefanini exchanged looks with Viviana. "Don't get too excited," he told Landry. "You aren't going to like what they sent. We've been ordered to stand aside. No matter what happens, we're to avoid any interference in partisan affairs. It was coded in as a one-one-oh. That means it comes straight from the top."

Pietro's face turned grim. "This is nonsense," he complained. "It isn't interference if I ask for your help. Don't they know that?"

"I don't think it matters," Stefanini said. "The problem is in Milan. It's a political snafu of some kind."

"To hell with them," Landry said. "There are strangers out there in the square who intend to shoot our prisoners in cold blood, unless we stop them. You get back to that damned radio and tell them Mussolini could end up in front of a firing squad. You tell them if we don't intervene now, the whole world will soon hear about it. How's it going to look, the American Government standing back and doing nothing while a head of state is executed without trial?"

Willoughby pursed his lips thoughtfully. "That smacks a bit of blackmail," he said. "But it might work."

"We'll make it easy for them," Landry said. "They don't have to stick their necks out all that far. Tell them all we want is permission to control outside meddling with Pietro's prerogatives as commander of the lakeside partisan forces. That isn't interference. That's sticking strictly to the book. If they're willing to go that far, Pietro can hold Mussolini on his own authority until military assistance arrives, and he can do it without disobeying a direct order from Milan."

Pietro nodded slowly. "Yes, I can accept that. Tell them it comes as a personal request from me." His eyebrows met in a frown. "Damn it all, David, life was far less complicated when we had to deal only with the Germans. I can contend with a good fight. But this political business, both from Milan and from your superiors, is beyond me."

"It's still a fight," Landry said. "Just a different kind. Things will be less complex when peace arrives."

"I doubt it," Pietro said. "If this is any indication, peace may be the most brutal time of all."

Three hours later, il Gallo, the partisan from Germasino, came into the Dongo square and saw the strangers from Milan milling around their cars. He had no idea who they were nor why they were there. He could see only that most of them wore the shiny medallion of the Volunteer Freedom Corps as well as tricolored armbands bearing the monogram of the Italian Communist Party. One, the driver of the lead car, had stitched a red-felt, five-pointed star to his coat sleeve. They looked very neat, very official. They also looked very angry.

Il Gallo knew nothing about them because he hadn't returned from the farmhouse to Dongo with the other two Germasino men. He had ridden only as far as Musso, then had climbed from the relief car to visit a cousin, a fisherman who had supplied partisans with occasional lake trout to supplement their poor mountain diets. The brief reunion with his cousin had put him out of contact just long enough to miss the warning about the Milanese volunteers and what they were after.

He stood in the square, wondering about them, and heard them cursing impatiently among themselves, especially a tall man with a mustache. Their anger seemed to be directed at the fact that Pietro had left on a mission and hadn't returned. There was something about members of the gerarchia, who had apparently been arriving from their various detention cells, but that hadn't satisfied them. They were more interested in someone else, someone who hadn't arrived yet.

Il Gallo decided it was none of his business and almost left the square, but then he saw a couple of civilians from Dongo, secret Party members like himself, hurry to the cars and whisper to a little runt of a man with a squashed face. They seemed to be pointing in his direction and il Gallo stood his ground, puzzled. The runt looked at him, then came toward him.

"You are il Gallo, a loyal Party member?" the runt asked.

"Who wants to know?" il Gallo said.

"Answer the question. Are you a loyal Party member, or not?"

The runt's eyes were deep and hot and filled with the kind of fanaticism one might expect to see in the eyes of politicians, clerics and madmen.

"I've joined the Party," il Gallo said uneasily. "Many of us in the resistance have. As for loyalty, I am loyal to my fellow partisans. In many cases that makes me loyal to the Party as well."

"Don't play word games with me," the runt said. "You've seen the armbands we wear. Does that tell you who we are?"

"I assume you are Party members," il Gallo said. He looked at the men near the cars. "City folk, most likely."

"Your assumption is correct," the runt said. "We are Party members from Milan. We now call upon you, as a Party member yourself, to help us."

"I don't know," il Gallo said. "I'm pretty tired."

The runt gestured curtly and the man with the felt star on his sleeve came toward them. The runt stared at il Gallo and said, "We are told you guarded the tyrant last night. Does that mean you know where he is being held?"

"It does," il Gallo admitted. "Why do you ask?"

The runt gestured again, and the man with the star on his sleeve suddenly reached under his coat and pulled out a pistol. Il Gallo twitched with surprise. Before he could speak, the runt said, "We have need of you. Please come with us."

5

The bedroom was small, like the other rooms in the farmhouse, and poorly furnished. Two small chests leaned against the wall, one with a framed wedding photograph on top of it, the other holding a catechism book and a small hand mirror. A pair of straight-backed chairs flanked the single window. The only other piece of furniture in the room was a sagging double bed, above which hung a faded religious print.

Shortly after three o'clock that afternoon, Mussolini and Claretta Petacci were in the bedroom resting when they heard footsteps in the farmyard. Claretta, brushing her hair by the window, looked out and said, "There are men coming toward the house."

"I heard them," Mussolini said. He didn't move.

The front door banged open. Blurred voices rose from the kitchen, then sounds of a scuffle, followed by rapid footsteps on the stairs. A man with a mustache burst into the room. He had a Beretta submachine gun in his hands and he glanced rapidly from Claretta to Mussolini. "Quickly," he said. "I've come to save your lives."

Mussolini blinked at him. "To save us?" he murmured. He had never seen the man before, nor any of the others who crowded the hallway behind him.

"Hurry," the man said. "We must take you to safety. Before the partisans send help."

"To safety?" Claretta chirped excitedly. "Can it be true?"

"Who are you?" Mussolini asked.

"My name is Valerio," the man said. "I have a car waiting down by the road. You must hurry. We haven't much time." Claretta squealed happily and began to rummage through the bed-clothes. The man swung his gun to cover her. "What are you doing?" he asked nervously.

"Looking for my petticoat," she said.

"There isn't time for that," Valerio said. "Come as you are."

"I must put on my boots," Mussolini said. He bent over and slid his feet into his riding boots. As he tugged them on, he asked, "Have you any news of my friends? Barracu? Bombacci?"

"Safe," Valerio said. "We are looking after them."

Mussolini sighed gratefully. "Good. Poor old Nicola was so frightened when we were stopped at the roadblock."

Valerio gestured with the gun and ushered them down the stairs where they found the farmer and his wife and the second shift of partisan guards huddled in a group, surrounded by men wearing armbands. Another partisan, older, stood awkwardly to one side, looking embarrassed. Il Gallo. Claretta recognized him and gasped.

"What is it?" Mussolini asked her. "What's wrong?" His spirits had begun to soar.

"That man," she whispered, pointing at il Gallo. "He was here last night. He's one of the partisans."

Mussolini stared at il Gallo, whom he did not remember, and his cheeks turned gray.

Valerio motioned them toward the front door. Mussolini took Claretta's arm and they all went outside and started down the hillside, leaving the farmer and his wife and the disarmed Lake Como partisans behind. The farm woman came to the window. She crossed herself and began to cry, but her husband pulled her back out of sight.

When Valerio reached the lead car, he pushed Mussolini and Claretta into the back seat and climbed in the front, holding his Beretta on them. The other Milanese volunteers dispersed among the cars and the big yellow van. With a splutter of engines, all three vehicles pulled onto the road and drove down through a village called Mezzegra, moving slowly. Chickens scattered. Faces peeped from behind curtains. The vehicles drove on.

About a hundred meters beyond the far side of Mezzegra, Valerio ordered his car to stop. It pulled up beside an ornate wrought-iron gate. A low stone wall stretched along the roadside, and beyond the gate a driveway led up to a large villa. Valerio stepped out and leaned through the rear window. "Get out," he commanded.

Mussolini looked confused. "Why?" he asked.

"Get out!" Valerio repeated.

Mussolini and Claretta climbed timidly from the car and Valerio pushed them up the road. They began to walk, Claretta weeping silently, clinging to Mussolini's arm. Valerio and the others followed them. They walked several meters, then Valerio told them to stop. Mussolini turned to face the men from Milan, his jaw trembling. Claretta leaned her cheek against his shoulder. She whispered, "Aren't you glad I came with you?" There was a pleading note in her voice, as though she sought some assurance that her sacrifice was at least appreciated, but Mussolini didn't answer her. He didn't even look at her.

Valerio produced a paper from his coat pocket and read from it rapidly and in a very low voice. When he finished, he put the paper back in his pocket and cranked the priming bolt of his Beretta. Claretta had held herself in check to this point, but when she heard the metallic rachet of the lever, she broke. She threw herself forward, shouting, "You can't kill us like this! You can't!"

She grabbed the perforated gun barrel of Valerio's Beretta with both hands.

"Let go!" Valerio ordered. She was hysterical, and sobbing too loudly to hear him or even to comprehend what he was saying, so he pulled the trigger. A burst of rapid fire tore through her neck and she thudded to the ground without another sound.

Valerio swung the Beretta toward Mussolini. Mussolini, a dazed expression on his face, looked from Claretta's body to the gun. Then, with shaky bravado, he tugged his shirt open and held the lapels aside. "Shoot me in the chest," he said.

Valerio obliged. The second burst ripped into Mussolini and slammed him against the stone wall. He slipped to the ground, breathing raggedly. Valerio walked to him and put the gun barrel to his heart, then pulled the trigger again. The body jerked spastically.

Ugo joined Valerio by the two bodies, and stared down at Mussolini for a long time. Then Ugo said, "The end of Caesar. Look at his slimy face. Doesn't that expression suit him?"

6

Luisa picked up a diamond clip and laboriously noted the description on a scratch pad. *One large, square-cut diamond, surrounded by*—she stopped and counted—*eight sapphires, arranged on a filigree of white gold*. She sneaked a look at Viviana, who was helping her with the inventory. Viviana was cataloguing paintings near the window. Luisa stopped writing and ran her fingers over the smooth, glittering stones set in the white gold clip.

Luisa was a country girl, and she had never seen such stones before. Until Viviana had tutored her, she could hardly tell a ruby from an emerald. Now, to handle them, to have them so close, hour after hour, so many of them, each so bright and pretty, so cold to the touch . . .

She let her eyes wander. Such riches. So many of them personal, like pages plucked from someone's life. Rolled paintings and golden statues, hurriedly taken from bedrooms and salons.

Knives and spoons and forks of silver and gold, some as much as
four or five hundred years old, according to Viviana. And the
boxes of personal jewelry, stacked on every surface, heaped
around the room. Here on the desk in front of Luisa, a little red
chest that had belonged to Claretta Petacci, lying open with its
flashing clutter, diamonds, rings, brooches—gifts from Mussolini,
most likely.

Luisa looked at the diamond-and-sapphire clip again, turning it
in her hands to catch the sparkles of light. It was too much, she
thought. Dante should have given the job of counting to someone
else, someone stronger. The terrible temptations. It would be so
easy for her to take something for herself. To pick up a handful of
the paper money, enough to make her rich for the rest of her life.
Or this beautiful little clip of white and blue fire from the little red
case. She glanced guiltily at Viviana and thrust the clip away.

Luisa picked up a bracelet, determined to do her job properly,
with no further thought of temptation or personal wealth. It was a
linked bracelet with several small diamonds. As she groped for the
proper terms to describe it, she heard a car approaching from the
distance, horn blaring noisily. The sound came closer, and she realized it was more than one vehicle, perhaps two or three. They
honked their way up the lake road and squealed to a stop below,
in the cobbled square. Viviana set a painting aside and moved to
the window, as if curious about the commotion. Luisa thought of
joining her at the vaulted window, but she was fairly certain what
she would see. It had been the same all afternoon—clusters of
townspeople standing about in tense, nervous huddles and fresh
carloads of partisans sweeping into town, bristling with guns.
Word of Mussolini's capture and the treasure-laden caravan had
spread quickly. Already Dongo was jammed with new faces, some
looking for more Fascists, some hoping to get in on the plunder.
When would it end?

"Two cars and a yellow truck," Viviana said. "The same ones
that were in the square earlier, I think."

Luisa listened to the commotion from the square, then decided
to ignore it. She began to write. *Small yellow diamonds, set in
links of* . . . A sudden surge of cheering voices rose from below,
a sound so intense that Luisa looked up. The cheer spread, thun-
dering against the medieval buildings ringing the plaza. The Amer-

icans? Could they have arrived already? She laid the bracelet aside and started for the window, but footsteps raced up the hallway outside the treasure room. Someone pounded on the door. Luisa wavered, then reached for a Brixia pistol on the desk.

"Luisa? Luisa, open the door." It was Dante. She put the pistol back in its place and hurried to unlock the heavy wooden door. Dante rushed into the room, his body trembling. He looked from Viviana to Luisa. "It has happened," he said.

"What?" Luisa asked.

"Mussolini. He's dead." Dante motioned them to the window and pointed down at the people crowding around the vehicles. "Colonel Valerio shot him to death not a half hour ago. The body is in the furniture van." He hesitated, as though something was sticking in his throat, then said, "Mussolini's woman, too. Petacci."

"Oh my God," Luisa said. "Does Pietro know?"

"Not yet. I sent some men to fetch him."

"But why the woman?" Luisa asked. "Why did she have to die?"

Dante shook his head. His face was pale and confused. "Valerio said it was ordered by the Committee. We mustn't question him. He . . . he must know what he's doing. I just spoke with his superior, a man named Ugo. He says there are important reasons of state security. He is to meet with some of us at midnight to explain it."

"How can anyone explain the murder of a miserable, frightened woman?" Viviana objected. "I hope Pietro makes him eat his reasons, one by one, then takes him out and shoots him."

"Pietro won't be there," Dante said. "The meeting is a special one, for ranking Party members only. Piccione, Salvo, me. Perhaps some others."

Viviana was silent for a moment, then said, "I see."

Luisa touched her arm. "Please, Viviana. Don't blame Dante. He had no part in this."

"Viviana may think as she wishes," Dante said stiffly. "The Party works for the good of Italy, and I believe in the Party. I must accept my share of responsibility." He hesitated again. "I must go. Valerio has ordered the gerarchia brought to the lakefront. Except for the guards, everyone has been instructed to gather at the jetty to watch."

"More executions?" Luisa said. She shivered. "I had hoped the killing was over."

"Isn't there some way you can stop them?" Viviana asked.

Dante stared at her for a moment, then his face softened. "I would stop them if I could, Viviana. I think these executions are a grave mistake. But there is nothing I can do. There is nothing any of us can do."

7

Landry leaned against the stone wall above the jetty, on the open side of the square, and gazed helplessly at the gathering crowd. Blue water lapped against three fishing boats tied off below the jetty, and sunshine, sparkling on all polished surfaces, lent an incongruous touch of gaiety to a pair of eyeglasses here, a pistol butt there. Landry had waited in the square through most of the afternoon with a small, anxious party of Pietro's partisans, hoping to step in and take charge as soon as Stefanini brought authorization from OSS headquarters in Switzerland, but word had reached them only moments before that it was too late. The men from Milan had found Mussolini. It was over.

Now townspeople and farmers from outlying areas, not to mention the hundreds of lakeside inhabitants from neighboring villages who had come streaming to Dongo to witness the excitement, began to pack the square in an almost solid phalanx of bodies, waiting for the Fascist ministers to be brought down to the water's edge. The partisans who had waited with Landry, stunned by the news of Mussolini and disappointed that they would be unable to intercede on Pietro's behalf, drifted away in frustration, some to sit on the stone wall, others to stand among the gathering spectators.

Willoughby, with Tuono on a short leash to keep him safe from shuffling feet, came to stand by Landry. The dog was subdued, greeting Landry only with a wet nose on the hand. It was almost as though he understood the misery underlying the crowd's titillation.

Landry bent to scratch Tuono's ears. "It shouldn't have happened that way," he said.

"I don't know," Willoughby responded thoughtfully. "Perhaps it's better, over and done with. Italy has suffered enough in this war without some great postwar tribunal sitting in judgment. This way, the country can go on to other things."

The crowd sounds died and a sudden, expectant hush settled over the square. The doors of the town hall opened, but instead of the Fascist prisoners whom they were expecting, the crowd saw only a tall partisan with two women. Dante, accompanied by Luisa and Viviana. Veterano, waiting on the front steps for them, shouldered his shotgun and broke a path, and they came toward the lakefront where Landry and Willoughby stood.

"You shouldn't be here," Landry told Viviana. Then, including Luisa in his gaze, "Neither of you should. This is apt not to be pretty."

"I tried to dissuade them," Dante said. "They insisted."

Viviana said, "Why shouldn't we be witness to it? The shame will belong to us all." She spoke loudly, and several people standing nearby turned in surprise to stare at her.

The crowd was still growing. Tuono's nose went up and he began to snuffle excitedly. He curled around Willoughby's legs and wriggled, and his tail thumped back and forth. He pulled loose from Willoughby and bounded a few yards to Landry's left. With a yip of pure joy, he thrust his forepaws into a stranger's stomach, tongue lapping the air uncontrollably. The man, a dark-skinned civilian in a shabby gray suit, stood beside a portly partisan, one of the recent recruits from a nearby village. Both the man and the partisan looked startled and tried to backpedal, but the crush of spectators was too dense.

Willoughby ran after the dog, but it was Landry and Veterano who reached him first. They pulled Tuono away from the man, and Willoughby hurried to join them. "Sorry," he told the man apologetically. "I don't know what got into him."

"That is all right," the man said. His voice was hoarse and uncultivated. He looked over his shoulder, as if still seeking a path through the packed bodies.

Willoughby took the leash from Landry. "Bad dog," he scolded firmly. "Never jump on strangers." Despite the firm tone, Tuono wriggled happily.

"I'm not sure Tuono considers him a stranger," Landry said. He studied the man's face. Dark brown eyes, more nervous than they needed to be. A wide, dry mouth, half open. He seemed terribly eager to be on his way. Stepping closer, Landry said, "Excuse me, friend. The dog acts like he knows you. Have you ever seen him before?"

"Never," the man said. "I must go." He tried once more to find a path through the crowd, and Landry suddenly saw a small gold square glinting at his watch pocket, a fragile sheath the size of a fingernail, with small engraved letters.

"Hold it," Landry said. He grabbed the man's arm and reached for the square of gold. Three tiny engraved stars were visible in the upper left-hand corner, a pointing hand at the bottom right, and three letters: ΦBK. Landry pulled it from the man's vest, and a slim, gold pocket watch came with it. He rolled it over in his hand, and his heart began to race. "Where did you get this?" he demanded.

"It belonged to my father," the man said.

"You're lying. I know this watch."

The man shrugged. "If you must know the truth, I found it. On a dead German."

"When?"

"A day or two ago. I don't remember."

Willoughby, puzzled by Landry's interest, said, "What is it?"

"Holloman's pocket watch," Landry said.

"The chap who disappeared?" Now Willoughby's interest was up as well. He tugged Tuono closer.

The man began to sweat. "I must go. Please return my property."

"Not until you answer some questions," Landry said.

The man reached for the watch, but Landry held it away. For a moment, the man stood quite still, then he whirled and plunged into the crowd, swinging his elbows to break a path. Curses and choleric mutters rose after him as he plowed through packed bodies. An older villager swore painfully as the man hit him in the jaw. Landry tried to follow, but the angry crowd closed quickly.

"You want me to clear the way?" Veterano asked.

Landry scanned the line of resolute faces, men and boys determined to hold their places. Some linked their arms, daring him to try. Landry shook his head.

Willoughby refused to accept defeat. "Perhaps we can intercept him," he said. He handed Tuono's leash to Landry and stood on tiptoe, checking to see which direction the man had gone, then said, "Veterano, you go by the sea wall. I'll go around the other way."

Landry held Tuono tightly while Veterano hurried to the stone wall and climbed up on it. The old partisan walked the wall precariously, like a carnival performer, shotgun held overhead as a balance pole, squirming mass of bodies to one side, ten-foot drop to the lake surface on the other. When he reached the rear, he jumped down and disappeared. Willoughby, taller than most of the Lake Como Italians, stayed in sight a bit longer, but he too soon vanished. When Landry looked for the portly partisan to whom the stranger had been talking, the partisan was also gone. Landry led Tuono back to Dante and the two women. Creedmore and Kavanaugh had joined them.

"What was that about?" Creedmore asked.

"I'm not sure," Landry said. He glanced at Holloman's watch, then showed it to Viviana. "Do you recognize this?"

Viviana looked at the watch briefly, then said, "Yes."

She didn't say anything more, for the doors of the town hall opened again and the prisoners were finally brought out. The crowd quieted. In the sudden silence, Landry could clearly hear the disturbed chitter of birds from surrounding rooftops and the scrape of shoe leather as the fifteen Fascists were led down the steps.

"Act Two of getting things over and done with," Landry muttered.

The prisoners came across the plaza in three groups, five men to each, and the men from Milan had to push the crowd aside to get them through. Colonel Valerio followed several paces behind. Once a small semicircle had been cleared near the jetty, Valerio produced a list of prisoners' names and began to read them in a loud, ringing voice, beginning with the important ministers and working down to lesser individuals.

By the time he reached the end of the list, a new commotion erupted beyond the sea of spectators and another path slowly opened. Pietro appeared, with three of his Puecher partisans. He came solemnly to the stone wall and confronted Landry. "How did they find him?" he asked.

"We can't be certain," Landry said. "They were in the square, waiting. Someone said they were talking to one of the Germasino partisans. Then they climbed into their cars and drove away."

"It was il Gallo," Dante said.

Pietro sighed and looked at the prisoners. He watched as Valerio put the list of names away and ordered them drawn into position. The fifteen men were shoved into a ragged line facing the town, with their backs to the water. "And now he intends to kill these men as well?" Pietro murmured.

"Unless you give us the word to stop him," Landry said.

Pietro's jaw clenched momentarily, and he seemed to consider it, but there were too many packed bodies pressing in around the Fascist prisoners. Pietro's jaw went lax and he said heavily, "We can't. He's capable of ordering his cutthroats to fire directly into the crowd. If we try to intervene now, many innocents might die."

Valerio drew his men into firing position. Quickly and officiously, he lectured them on the proper procedure for a firing squad, explaining the military proprieties and the commands. To make sure they understood, he put them through three hasty dry runs, calling them to order, charging them to aim, then giving a sonorous signal to fire. Each time hammers fell on empty chambers, with the fifteen trembling prisoners looking on.

Finally, when Valerio seemed satisfied with the dress rehearsals, he raised his hand for silence. The crowd noises tailed off and all eyes turned to the prisoners. Valerio began to pronounce the death sentence. The words carried across the square in a clear, loud voice. He was almost finished when he was interrupted by a shaky, "No, please!" Valerio clamped his mouth shut and looked around to see who had spoken.

Nicola Bombacci, standing in the second group of five with Pavolini, Mezzasoma, Barracu and Colonel Casalinovo, stepped forward timidly with his hands extended in front of him. He appealed to the silent crowd. "You mustn't kill us," he said. "We've done nothing." Pavolini, whose lower leg was covered with dried blood, tried to pull him back in line, but Bombacci wriggled free. "We have only tried to serve Italy," Bombacci cried. "Any of you would have done the same."

One of the Milanese volunteers shoved Bombacci back among the members of his group, then looked to Valerio for instructions. Valerio called loudly, "To order!" The volunteers dropped to their knees in front of the prisoners and loaded their weapons, bolts and magazines sliding home. It was a chilling sound. Even Pavolini's face turned white. Bombacci closed his eyes and hugged himself, murmuring under his breath.

"Aim!" Valerio called.

Francesco Barracu, cheeks splotchy, his lapel no longer sporting the military medal, firmed his chin and shouted, "Viva Italia!"

Fernando Mezzasoma crossed himself, and in a low voice began, "Hail Mary, full of grace . . ."

"Fire!" Valerio commanded.

It took more time than one might have expected. The bodies tumbled not all at once, but in domino sequence as the Beretta submachine guns raked the line from one end to the other. Half the bullets gouged chunks of clothing and flesh from the toppling prisoners. The remainder sprayed past them and between them and churned up geysers of clean, clear lake water far beyond the shore. Even after the bodies lay prone on the cobblestones, bullets continued to rake them. Pietro turned away, his eyes dead.

When it was done and the firing stopped, a shocked silence fell over them and the smell of cordite hung heavy in the air. Valerio walked up and down the line of bodies, prodding each in turn. Only Idreno Utimpergher needed a coup de grâce.

Several moments later, two of the Milanese volunteers brought another prisoner down to the jetty to confront Valerio. It was Marcello Petacci, Claretta's brother. Valerio said, "Signore, we know you to be an Italian, and you must now face justice."

"I am a representative of the Spanish Government," Marcello Petacci insisted. "You have no right to hold me."

"You are an Italian!" Valerio rumbled. "You are Mussolini's son, Vittorio Mussolini, and you were trying to escape with your father."

Marcello Petacci blinked. "I'm who?"

"The tyrant's son. You will now share your father's fate."

Petacci half laughed, then seemed to realize he was in worse trouble than ever. "I'm not Vittorio Mussolini," he said. "My God, I don't even look like Vittorio. I'm the Spanish . . . No, no, I'm a nobody. I'm Marcello Petacci. I . . ."

As Petacci babbled, the Milanese volunteers moved aside, and Petacci got his first look at the bodies strewn across the cobblestones by the jetty. His knees buckled. "Oh my God! What have you done?" He looked wildly from side to side, then wrenched free and tried to run. One of Valerio's men jumped in his path, but Petacci veered away and bounded over the crumpled bodies. He dove headfirst off the jetty into the water, and swam several powerful strokes before three of the volunteers reached the stone wall and cut loose with submachine guns, chopping the water to a red-stained frenzy. Then he floated, face down.

The milling spectators, treated to more than they had expected, began to edge back from the lakefront. Some turned and walked away rapidly. Others shuffled off in silence. Landry, sickened by it all, stood with Pietro at the edge of the landing and gazed down at Marcello Petacci's floating body. Two men with grappling irons hurried out to the end of the jetty and made several tries for it, then finally hooked an arm and dragged it in. Landry heard someone approach. It was Valerio, come to see the grappling process for himself. Pietro turned on him in futile anger and said, "He wasn't Vittorio Mussolini, you know. He really was Marcello Petacci."

"It doesn't matter," Valerio said. "Fascists are all alike."

"And now so are we," Pietro said. "What you have done this day will forever muddy the garment of our history. Italy may prosper in time to come, but the world will only remember our savagery. Nothing can wash away the blood you have spilled here. The true heroes of Italy will be forgotten because of fanatics like you."

Valerio made a sound of disgust. "You're an ass," he muttered. He walked away and called for his men to bring the yellow van.

The bitter taste of defeat seemed to linger on Pietro's lips as he and Landry rejoined Kavanaugh and Creedmore. By now the square was almost empty, except for Dante and the two women and a few of the lakeside partisans. They all drew together, as if seeking some dim comfort in a physical closeness. The late-afternoon sky was darkening.

Pietro turned his back on the bodies. "Yesterday, I was so proud of everyone," he said. "I thought we had accomplished something really tremendous. Now look at the result. If I had known this was to happen, I think I would have allowed the Fascists to drive through."

The yellow van backed up to the wall, and Valerio's men picked up the bloody, muddy corpses and began to sling them over the tailgate. It was grisly work. Landry saw a look of revulsion on Viviana's face and he urged that they all leave, but Pietro shook his head. He was determined to stay to the end. "You needn't be here," he told Landry. "Nor should Viviana or Luisa stay. A woman should not see the blood of these victims running so freely from their murderers' hands."

Viviana said, "Pietro is right. I have seen more than enough." With a quick, nervous gesture, she rubbed her palms across the stomach of the overly large flannel shirt she wore, as if to cleanse them, then looked dully at the baggy worsted pants and boots that completed her attire. There was no light in her vivid blue eyes. "I want a bath," she said, "and a change of clothes. I feel such shame. It's strange. This borrowed clothing was my badge of open partisanship, like Salvo's Luftwaffe cap, or Pietro's beard. After all, no last-minute recruit could have looked so improperly dressed or so dirty, could she? Dirty, indeed. Filthy, I should say. I feel filthy all over."

Landry was surprised that he had any emotion left after the afternoon's horrors, yet he felt deep and instant concern. He said, "I'll take you home. Pietro will lend us one of the partisan cars. Come on, we'll go right now."

Viviana drew herself up to her full height, and she was a tall woman. "No," she told him. The look she gave him was dull and indifferent. "I can find my own way, David. Perhaps your duty is here, but mine is done." She nodded briefly to them all and left the square. She didn't even bother to avert her eyes, Landry saw with distress, as she passed the yellow van and its mounting cargo of bodies.

Halfway through the loading process, Veterano reappeared, walking disconsolately across the deserted square. Landry roused himself and asked an unspoken question with his eyes. Veterano shook his head.

"What about Willoughby?" Landry asked.

"I don't know," Veterano said. "I lost sight of him, too."

As the last two bodies went thudding into the furniture van, the Lizard's wood-burning truck chugged smokily into the plaza and squeaked to a stop near the town hall. Freddy Stefanini jumped out. He spoke to one of Pietro's partisans on the town hall steps and was directed down to the lakefront. He came trotting toward Landry. He passed the van and stared in confusion at the bustle of Milanese volunteers tying off the doors. His eye fell on the welter of dark red smears on the plaza stones. "What's going on?" he asked.

"A massacre," Pietro answered dully.

Stefanini took a folded sheet of paper from his shirt pocket. "This just came in," he said. He handed it to Landry.

Landry unfolded it. It was a brief message from OSS/Bern. It said: "SIGNAL ACKNOWLEDGED. FOR THE SAFETY OF LAKE INHABITANTS, PLACE MUSSOLINI AND HIS PARTY UNDER PROTECTIVE CUSTODY. HOLD FOR FURTHER INSTRUCTIONS."

"Any reply?" Stefanini asked.

Landry shook his head. He crumpled the sheet and let it fall to the paving stones. "It no longer matters," he said.

Day Nine

Dividiamo il bottin!

Let's divide the loot!
  —Puccini, *La Bohème*

1

Dante took another mouthful of the sparkling Lambrusco wine presented him and Luisa as a special favor by the owner of the Dongo pensione, then snapped the barrel and recoil spring back into his Glisenti automatic. The old pistol glistened blackly. Freshly cleaned and oiled, it looked almost new, in spite of the deeply pitted slide assembly. He turned it over in his hands, staring at the minute blemishes in the dark steel. They'd always been there. At least for as long as Dante had carried the gun. Where had they come from? Who put them there? How many owners had the gun had down through the years? He sighed a little, then looked at a round-faced alarm clock sitting on the table beside his elbow.

Almost one in the morning. It was past time to go to the meeting, but Dante wasn't ready yet. He'd slept briefly, enjoying the luxury of a real bed in the shabby pensione whose doors the owner had thrown open to the partisans, but after midnight his thoughts and the impending meeting between lakeside Communists and the man from Milan, Comrade Ugo, had kept awakening him. He didn't know why he'd decided to get up and clean the automatic. Something about the merely mechanical, orderly task seemed to draw him.

Glance at Luisa, making small puffing sounds in her sleep. Take another swallow of the Lambrusco. Slap the loaded clip into the Glisenti and pull back the slide assembly to bring a shell into the chamber. The pitting had to be due to the touch of a human hand. Odd, that the insignificant film of oil on the fingertips could erode cold steel. There was something incompatible between a living organism and a gun. Dante smiled wearily and drank more wine. Most incompatible, especially if, like the poor, silly, frightened men who died today—no, now yesterday—the organisms were on the receiving end of the bullets.

He didn't know why it bothered him so. Reports were that other lakeside towns had staged public executions in their squares of minor Fascist bureaucrats. It was probably happening all over Italy. Dante didn't know if it were true, but a grapevine report from Cernobbio held that partisans there had even executed wounded Fascist soldiers trying to flee from a convalescent hospital. It had been a long, hard war. People lost their heads and did ugly things.

Dante quietly put the automatic in its holster, but, pouring more wine, he clinked the bottle against the glass, and Luisa's eyes blinked open in alarm. She raised herself on one elbow, bedsprings squeaking. "What is it?" she asked. "What's wrong?"

"Nothing," he said. "I have to go."

She sat up, clutching the bed covers. For the first time in months, it had not been necessary to sleep in their clothes. "No, please, not now," she said. "Please, Dante. I don't want to be alone."

"I must," he said. "Comrade Ugo called the meeting for midnight and I'm already late."

"Can't they meet without you?"

"No. I am an officer and the ranking Party member on the lake. Comrade Ugo asked specifically that I attend."

"I don't like him," Luisa said. "I wish you wouldn't be nice to him. Are you drinking wine? At this hour? Give me a sip."

He took the glass to the bedside. "Comrade Ugo is a very important man," he said, "and this meeting must also be important.

Otherwise he would not have stayed on the lake. He would have
gone back to Milan with Colonel Valerio and the others."

"I wish he had," she said. "They're cruel, all of them. No better
than the Fascists. Please, whatever this Comrade Ugo wants, don't
give it to him. Let Pietro deal with it."

"Pietro has nothing to do with it," Dante said patiently. "It is a
Party matter, and we must deal with it on our own. We have a
duty to our beliefs."

"The Party," Luisa said. She sipped from the wine glass, and
perhaps that was why she made a sour face. "Always the Party. I
know the Party has done much for Italy. You have told me.
But . . ."

"Now that we have achieved victory, the Party must do more,"
Dante said. He took back the wine glass and drained it. Useless to
preach to this sweet daughter of hard-working peasant stock.
Peasants were born with a capacity to endure.

He leaned to kiss her, and she slid her arms around his neck.
"Dante, I don't care about the Party," she said. "All I care about
in this whole world is you. When this is all over, I've hoped there
might be some little place for me near you. You would come and
visit. Just whenever you could get away, once or twice a week. I'd
work, of course, unless, well, even if a girl isn't married, sometimes babies come. I wouldn't be ashamed of that, but I'd want to
be able to look at my children, your children, and not feel shame
for other things we've done."

He was silent for a moment. The image of his mother's fine, in-
telligent eyes came promptly into his mind. His mother, also a
member of the Party, also unmarried, shaping the dreams of his
youth. As always since he'd come to the mountains he could remember only the eyes, glowing, burning with dedication. He
couldn't remember his mother's face. He said, "Yes, it makes a
pretty picture, doesn't it." But he wouldn't look at her.

Ugo and the others were deep in discussion when Dante arrived. They were clustered about an oaken table in the dining
room of another pensione near the Dongo town hall, faces rapt
and half lit by a single kerosene lamp hanging above the table.
They reminded Dante of some old painting. Piccione propped on
his elbows, hanging earnestly on Ugo's every word. Salvo sitting

back with his Luftwaffe cap at his elbow, puffing contentedly on his pipe, eyes narrowed to slits. Il Gallo, the partisan from Germasino, who had apparently been invited because of his assistance to Valerio's team. If so, il Gallo seemed uncomfortable with the honor. He looked thoroughly embarrassed. There were two other partisans, men whom Dante recognized vaguely as members of the Cravero detachment, on the opposite side of the table, mouths agape. And an outsider, sitting beside Ugo, listening intently, a man Dante had seen driving one of the cars from Milan, a hard-faced man with a star sewn to his sleeve. His presence was surprising. Dante had thought Ugo the only one who hadn't returned to Milan.

"Ah, Comrade Dante," Ugo said. "Please, come in. Sit down. I believe you know everyone?"

"Most everyone," Dante said. He sat and glanced pointedly at the man with the red star on his sleeve.

"Ah, this is Comrade Sandrino," Ugo said. "I've asked him to remain here with me to act as my driver and liaison with Milan."

Dante acknowledged the introduction and said, "I'm sorry I'm late."

"It doesn't matter," Ugo told him. "We were just talking about the treasure. Comrade Piccione smuggled me in to look at it. Remarkable. Really remarkable."

"Dante is in charge of the treasure," Piccione said proudly.

"So I understand," Ugo said. "It was good of your Captain Pietro to place the treasure in the keeping of a Party member. It should make things a great deal easier."

"What things?" Dante asked.

"That's what I wanted to know," said the Germasino man, il Gallo.

Ugo looked harshly at the Germasino partisan and said, "It might be better for you to wait until your opinions are requested. You are only here on sufferance. Had you not helped us . . ."

The Germasino man flushed. "I'm not proud of what I did."

"Be that as it may," Ugo said. He returned his gaze to Dante. "Our comrades in Milan have asked me to dispose of the treasure. I could, of course, send for a team of trusted men to help me disseminate it, but I prefer to work with the loyal people of the lake. It will make things neater."

"You're to disseminate the treasure?" Dante said. "What about Pietro? He's the ranking officer of the district. Won't he object?"

"Not if we handle it properly," Ugo said. "I'm told a woman, a friend of yours, is handling the inventory. A Comrade Luisa. Is that true?"

"She isn't a Party member," Dante said. "Just a good partisan."

"That doesn't matter," Ugo said. "As long as she is willing to do as we tell her. How many copies of the inventory will she prepare?"

"Four," Dante said. "One for me, one for Pietro, one for the Committee in Milan. The other is for the American, David Landry."

Ugo's face turned stony. "The American will not be here long enough to collect his copy," he said. "I am demanding that he and the other foreigners be withdrawn from the lake. Valerio is carrying the message to Milan at this moment."

"Pietro won't like that," Dante said. "He considers Landry a close friend. Many of us do as well."

Salvo blew a cloud of pipe smoke over the table. He seemed troubled. "Comrade Ugo believes the American troops may try to steal the treasure when they come," he said. "He thinks David might help them."

Dante blinked, suddenly wishing he hadn't drunk so much wine. "Why should David do that?"

"He's an American," Ugo said. "He'll have to follow American orders. That's why I want to be rid of him. Frankly, it might be convenient if the two copies of the inventory for Captain Pietro and Milan were also to disappear. Do you think you could arrange that?"

"I don't know," Dante said. "It depends on the reason."

"I have reasons," Ugo said. "Milan will take care of these American agents on the lake, but American soldiers will eventually arrive to take their place. We must dispose of the treasure before the troops arrive. That will be easier if there is no record of the amounts."

"What do you mean, dispose of the treasure? Are you talking about sending it to banks in Milan?"

Ugo permitted himself to smile. "Something like that," he said. "Since the former owners are now dead, it is within our rights to claim it as our own. It is your right in particular, since it was you and your brave men who captured it. The Party can use such funds."

"I don't think that will work," Dante said. "Too many non-Party members were involved in its capture." He drummed his fingers on the table. "Perhaps if we press the matter, we could insist on a policy of fair division. Half to the Party and half to the state. There would be opposition, of course, but maybe we could make a case for it. After all, we've fought as hard as anyone, and we deserve some compensation."

Ugo cleared his throat delicately. "I quite agree, Comrade Dante. As far as you go. But I believe we can end up with everything, if we play our hand carefully."

"Everything?" Dante said. "You're dreaming. Pietro and the others wouldn't sit still for it."

Ugo smiled solicitously. "On the contrary, comrade. Pietro and the others won't know. I have a plan. One that has already been approved by Party leaders in Milan. It will call for precise timing and a body of trusted partisans, but if we work together and carry it out properly, no one will ever suspect that we are behind it."

"What kind of a plan?"

Ugo spread his palms on the table and lowered his voice. "A very simple plan, my friend. Since Pietro has seen fit to give you temporary control of the treasure, you will assign three or four of your most voluble Party members to guard it. All loyal, incorruptible Communists. The cream, one might say, of the lakeside crop. Then, during their tenure on guard duty, an armed force of men will assault the treasure room, preferably during the dead of night. The guards will be killed. The treasure will disappear. Since the Communist Party of Italy will be the organization that has suffered, with our own men dead, no one can possibly suspect us."

Dante stared at him. "Are you serious?"

"Of course I am. Don't you see? What could be simpler? It would be virtually impossible to detect. After all, with our own men shot down in the attack, who could blame us?"

Dante looked at the others. Salvo and Piccione seemed stunned. Il Gallo, reputed to be more loyal to the mountain men of Lake Como than to his politics, had turned red in the face. But none of them spoke. Dante said, "That's your plan? Kill our own men?"

The smile flickered. "May I remind you, Comrade Dante, that the good of the Party must come first? We must do what is expedient."

"To kill our own people isn't expedient. It's crazy!"

Salvo took the pipe from his mouth and said breathlessly, "Calm down, Dante. It's only a suggestion. Let's hear him out."

But Dante was too incensed. "No. I won't listen. He's talking about murder. He's talking about taking brave men, men who have risked their lives, men only days away from peace and freedom, and shooting them."

"Brave men have died before," Ugo said.

"Fighting the enemy, yes," Dante said. He shoved his chair back and stood. "But not shot down by men whom they trust. Throw away your own lives, if you wish. Commit suicide for the Party. That's your privilege. But you aren't going to kill men who fought like heroes for you. Not while I'm alive. I won't permit it."

"I agree with Dante," il Gallo said. "This is madness."

"You're both out of order," Ugo said sharply.

"And out of patience," Dante said. He looked from il Gallo to Piccione and Salvo. "Are you coming?"

Il Gallo stood. But Piccione glanced nervously at Ugo and said, "We should hear him out, Dante. His orders come from Party headquarters."

"Stay, then," Dante snapped. "Listen to anything you wish. But for me, I will hear no more!" He stalked from the room. Il Gallo hesitated, then followed him.

Ugo gripped the edge of the table and watched the door slam behind the two partisans. His neck and ears burned with anger and he would have liked nothing more than to send Sandrino after the fools, to shoot them down immediately, perhaps to shoot all of them, hillside simpletons, get them all out of the way so professionals could be brought in to do the job properly. But because he still hoped for lakeside co-operation, he forced himself to smile at Dante's two friends, the ones who called themselves Piccione and Salvo. "Your Comrade Dante is rather sensitive," he said, passing it off lightly.

The older one, Salvo, sucked on his pipe and said, "He's something of a purist. Maybe he's right. Killing our own people does seem drastic."

"Drastic measures are often called for," Ugo said stiffly.

"Not this time," the older partisan said. "Dante can be difficult if you get him mad. You try something like that now, he might go crazy."

"If he stands in our path, we'll walk over him," Ugo said.

The pipe came out of Salvo's mouth. "What do you mean by that?"

Ugo debated whether to say more, then decided these simple-tons might as well know where they stood. "I mean that your Comrade Dante just came very close to getting himself killed. It could still happen."

The man with the pretty face, Piccione, said, "No, wait. You can't kill Dante. He's our friend."

"He cannot be a friend if he opposes us," Ugo said. "Our first duty is to the Party. That should be quite clear. You must ask yourselves the simple question: Will you do as the Party requires, or not? If your Comrade Dante stands in our way, will you be willing to face the consequences?"

Salvo hesitated. "If you mean will we kill him for you, no." He glanced at Piccione, then at the two men from the Cravero detach-ment. Each answered with a negative shake of the head. "I'm sorry, Comrade Ugo. You see how we feel. We'll do anything else. We'll steal the treasure if you want us to. We'll break a few heads and risk our necks. But Dante has been a good leader. We've been through a lot with him. If you want him dead, you're going to wind up with enemies instead of helpers." The others murmured agreement.

Ugo flicked a look at Sandrino. "Very well," he said. "It was only a suggestion to be thought upon. The idea is dismissed. We will fall back on Comrade Dante's original plan. A fair division— half to the Party and half to the state. Agreed?"

"Is it all right if we tell Dante?" Salvo asked.

Ugo nodded sullenly. "Tell him anything you wish. But tell him it was our unanimous decision, freely arrived at. Not the result of any pressure he may think he has placed on us."

"I'm sure he'll appreciate that," Salvo said.

"I don't care whether he appreciates it or not," Ugo said. "And now you may go. This meeting is closed."

He waited angrily while the partisans stood. The older partisan, Salvo, hesitated as though he wanted to say something more, but Ugo waved him away. Finally they drifted toward the door.

When they were gone, Sandrino plucked lint from the felt star on his sleeve and said, "Are you really going to knuckle under to that backhill bastard?"

"No," Ugo said. "As of now, the lakeside partisans are out of it. We will handle this ourselves."

"You'll want help, then? From Milan?"

Ugo nodded. "Send for a support team immediately. I want them here by this afternoon. Tell them to come in pairs and threes."

"Are we going to do it the way you said? Storm the city hall?"

Ugo stuffed a cigarette in a black holder and leaned back to light it. "That wouldn't be prudent. Not anymore. We'll have to think of another way."

Sandrino smiled coldly. "And this Dante? What of him?"

"He has signed his own death warrant," Ugo said. "The others as well. Every man in this room heard what was said tonight. It would be a mistake to let them live."

2

Gray dawn brought an unusual sight to the apartment dwellers surrounding the Piazzale Loreto in Milan. Early Sunday risers were startled to see two muddy sedans and a yellow furniture van pull through the great square and come to a stop near a gas station on the far side. They were even more startled when a dozen men piled out of the two cars and proceeded to dump bodies from the van, eighteen in all, on the pavement in front of the gasoline pumps. A tall man with a mustache, wearing an armband of the underground resistance, ordered six of the unloaders to stay behind as guards, and the three vehicles drove away.

By eight o'clock that morning, word of the grisly trove of

corpses in the piazza had spread, and the great square began to fill
with people, come to see the Fascists in their final public appearance. The guards unpiled the bodies and arranged them in a line,
Mussolini with his head resting on Claretta's breast, Pavolini to
his left, Mezzasoma to his right, and so on, stretching across the
concrete pod of the gasoline station. The growing crowd, quiet at
first, soon turned restive. Someone spat on the bodies and muttered an obscenity, and another someone kicked Mussolini. The
six guards tried to discourage them, but the crowd quickly became
a mob, picking up rocks, bricks, sticks, anything that came to
hand. They jabbed and pounded. They kicked and cursed. The favorite target seemed to be Mussolini, and heel after heel crunched
into flesh and bone until the Duce's face caved in, leaving only a
hideous mask, rubbery, obscene, a distorted travesty of the once-
famous visage. Two of Valerio's men fired shots in the air, but it
did no good. Nothing could stem the spontaneous tide of emotion.
Helplessly, hopelessly, the six guards retired and watched the gory
spectacle from a distance.

The mob continued to swirl about the bodies, kicking and spitting, until a lone man appeared above the heads and shoulders
and climbed to the top of a gas pump. The man perched on the
pump and threw a rope across an overhead beam. With the crowd
exhorting him, he tugged at the rope, hauling until feet appeared,
and a body swung into view, hanging upside down, arms dangling.
The crowd roared approval. Though the face was by now unrec-
ognizable, the bald, battered head, the militia pants, the single
militia boot satisfied the onlookers. Voices began to chant, "Mussolini! Mussolini! Mussolini!"

The man atop the gas pump yelled, "Who next?"

"Petacci! Petacci! Petacci!" thundered the voices.

Another rope flew up and snaked across the beam, and legs appeared, followed by a small, slender figure. She swayed back and
forth and her skirt fell across her face. The mob hooted joyously
until a frail woman in black climbed up beside the man on the gas
pump and tucked Claretta's skirt between her knees and tied it
with a black mourning band.

Valerio's guards stood motionless in the distance, caught up by
the hypnotic chanting of the crowd. They watched while two more
battered bodies were strung up. Then one of the guards broke

away and hurried to find a telephone, to report what was happening. By the time reinforcements arrived, the worst of the crowd's anger would be spent.

3

The house-to-house search in Musso had already turned up a number of bizarre items looted from the Fascist caravan, so bizarre that Landry scarcely raised an eyebrow when one of the partisans brought him a bedpan stuffed with Italian lire and claimed he had found it under the bed of the former Musso mayor. After all, there had been six pairs of Mussolini's personal silk underwear, found that morning on the person of an unemployed tanner, worn one on top of the other. And a woman trying to pay her pharmacy bill with a check made out to Mussolini's longtime secretary, Luigi Gatti. And four truant schoolboys playing an improvised game of marbles with stolen gold sovereigns. But the most awkward item to reclaim was the looted paper money. Most of the fields and vineyards around Musso were littered with empty banknote wrappers, fluttering like leaves in fall, gusting against stone fences, blowing across plowed furrows. Once the wrappers were removed, it was almost impossible to prove which money had come from the caravan and which had not.

With the former mayor, it wasn't so difficult. A silkworm entrepreneur whom the villagers claimed to be bankrupt, the onetime mayor had only this morning called in a team of stonemasons and ordered them to begin construction of a new villa. When Pietro confronted the man with the bedpan full of bills, the man protested loud and long that the money was his, had always been his, and that he had hidden it only to keep the Fascist tax collectors from his door. He might have convinced Pietro had his aproned wife not blundered in from the kitchen with flour on her hands, wearing a diamond tiara and a fur coat two sizes too big. After that, the former mayor grew noticeably subdued and Pietro chewed him out soundly.

Each new discovery was delivered for cataloguing to the living room of a Musso piano teacher, where Luisa and Pietro, assisted by Wesley Creedmore and Freddy Stefanini, had set up shop to handle the new inventory chores. Luisa moved quite slowly, eyes clouded for such a sunny morning, and it occurred to Landry that he should send to Viviana in Rezzonico and ask her to help Luisa once more. At minimum, it would give him an excuse to see Viviana and perhaps find out why she had left the Dongo square so abruptly the day before. But when he approached Luisa with the suggestion, she shook her head. "I can work, David," she told him. "I'd rather work. I'm just worried about Dante."

"What's wrong with Dante?"

"I don't know. He went to some kind of meeting in the middle of the night, and he seemed so restless and irritable this morning at breakfast. We argued. Well, not really an argument, but words. You know how he can be, quiet and distant. Then he said he had duties elsewhere and went out. I haven't seen him since."

"He'll show up later," Landry reassured her.

"Yes, I'm certain he will."

Although Salvo and Piccione came to the Musso piano teacher's house with X. B. Kavanaugh's search team, looking red-eyed from lack of sleep and apparently worried over some problem of their own that they refused to share, the first news of Dante was brought late that morning by Lucertola, the Lizard. By then, the pile of recovered treasure items filled a space almost equal in size to the upright piano beside which it rested. The bulkiest find of the morning, just hauled in by Kavanaugh's group, was a wooden chest filled with a gold-plated table service. At Luisa's request, Pietro and Landry were unloading it, separating plates from excelsior, when the Lizard returned from an earlier errand to Dongo.

The Lizard leaned his rifle against the piano and stammered his report. "I had to summon the Dongo bank manager from Sunday Mass to open the bank," he said. "But it's all done now. Everything is deposited in Luisa's name, as you suggested." His eyes touched the bedpan with its cargo of tightly rolled bills. "Oh no, is that more money? Do I have to go back?"

Pietro said, "Eat something first." The piano teacher, a slender widow in her sixties with tufts of wild gray hair that stood out from her temples like exclamation points, had spent the morning cooking, and from her kitchen came a steamy fragrance of beans and pork rind.

The Lizard sniffed approvingly, then sat on the floor beside Salvo and Piccione to wait. The Lizard's mouth worked and he said, "Things aren't so good on the lake. The boys in Domaso found another body this morning."

"Who this time?" Pietro asked.

"The town druggist, old Russo. He had a note pinned to his chest. *Spia Tedesca*. German spy. He makes the third since yesterday."

Pietro set aside a vast golden platter in disgust. "German spy. That's nonsense. I knew old Russo. Sharp-tongued and cranky, but he was no spy."

"That's what the boys in Domaso figured," the Lizard said. "They think it's just another revenge killing. Someone with a grudge."

They were silent for a moment. Landry considered the inhumane chaos of peace that seemed the aftermath of the chaos of war. Then the Lizard said, "I saw Dante while I was in Dongo."

Luisa looked around eagerly. Salvo and Piccione looked up as well, but uneasily. Piccione said, "Where?"

"Coming out of the telephone office," the Lizard murmured. "He intends to move the treasure to Como. He wants to use me and the wood-burning truck."

"Why move the treasure?" Landry asked.

The Lizard shrugged eloquently. "He says it isn't safe in Dongo. He wants me to drive the first shipment tonight. Something about a bank in Como with a big vault."

"Dante is right," Piccione said too quickly from his resting place on the floor. "Anything is better than that old cracker box of a town hall in Dongo."

Landry peered at the handsome young partisan. There was a puzzling note of urgency in his voice, as though he knew the real reasons for Dante's sudden change of plans. Even Salvo, usually so serene, fiddled nervously with his pipe. Were they keeping something back?

"I told Dante I'd do it," the Lizard stammered. "I'll probably take part of it tonight. Then if Dante can get us a bigger truck, maybe I can take the rest tomorrow."

"Yes, all right," Pietro said. "Dante is in charge of the treasure. Do whatever he thinks best."

Landry and Pietro returned to the chest of gold plate, stacking its contents where Luisa could reach them more easily for a count. Kavanaugh loitered near the kitchen door, as if hoping to hurry the food, and Salvo, Piccione and the rest of Kavanaugh's search party found chores to keep themselves occupied. Though there were still several houses in Musso as yet unprobed, the fragrant smells from the kitchen were strong magnets and none of them wanted to miss lunch. They were still waiting when someone knocked at the front door and the piano teacher came through the living room to admit two more fresh arrivals, Veterano and Willoughby this time.

Landry waved a golden butter dish at the Britisher. "Where have you been?" he asked. "No one has seen you since yesterday afternoon."

"I took a bit of a walk," Willoughby said. "And now I have some news. That man in the square. The one who had Major Holloman's watch. I think I may have found him."

Creedmore and X. B. Kavanaugh drifted closer. Even Pietro looked up with interest. Landry said, "Where?"

"A little mountain village above Germasino," the Britisher said. "A place called Garzeno. I had help tracking him down. You remember that partisan who was talking to him in the square? The fat one? I caught him trying to waddle away during all the commotion. It turns out they're related. Fourth cousins, or some such."

"What fat partisan?" Pietro said. "Do we know him?"

"He's one of your new recruits," Willoughby said. "Told me his name was Tardini, but I wouldn't swear to it. He seemed awfully frightened. I suppose he could have lied."

"I know a Tardini," Salvo offered. "He joined us three days ago in Gravedona. If it's the same Tardini I think it is, you're smart not to trust him. He has a poor reputation. A loafer. Never works. Some say he is a thief. Dante could tell you more about the man. It was Tardini who brought us word after Gualfiero died."

"One thing is certain: This Tardini was absolutely petrified when I cornered him," Willoughby said. "I had to put on my best menacing act to open him up. Once he admitted the relationship, it was easier. I made him take me up the mountain to look for his cousin. This morning I saw him opening a grocery store. The cousin's name is Lusso. Angelo Lusso."

Piccione said sharply, "Angelo Lusso in Garzeno? That's Gualfiero's older brother. I met him once, about three months ago. Gualfiero was grieving for that damned dog of his. We sneaked into Garzeno on a scouting trip to pick up Tuono and buy some food."

Landry said, "That explains how Tuono recognized him in the square yesterday. Did you ask how he got Holloman's watch?"

"I didn't have a chance to ask him anything," Willoughby said. "One look at me and he slammed the door in my face. I tried to talk to him through the panels, but he wouldn't answer."

"He doesn't like partisans, either," Piccione said. "He charged us double for the food. His own brother, too. He probably likes us even less now that Gualfiero is dead."

Willoughby hesitated. "I don't think your friend is dead. I talked to a few people in Garzeno, and there were hints that this Angelo Lusso is hiding someone in the countryside, to keep him safe. I tried to find out who, but the people up there have an almost morbid suspicion of strangers, particularly foreigners. I thought I'd send Veterano up to poke about a bit more, if Pietro will give his permission."

"Of course, of course," Pietro said. "This could be very important to us. Do you really think Gualfiero might still be alive?"

"He couldn't be," Kavanaugh objected. "The poor bastard was shot all to pieces. You remember, Salvo. It was the day after Holloman disappeared. We found him on the trail above Acquaséria."

Salvo shrugged. "He was in bad shape, but he was still breathing. Fat Tardini brought word to Dante's camp a week later that he was dead. We never had reason to doubt it."

"There, you see?" Kavanaugh said. "Why tell us he was dead, unless he was really dead?"

"Where is this Tardini now?" Landry asked Willoughby.

"Ah, that's a problem," Willoughby said. "I couldn't keep an eye on him and his cousin simultaneously. Tardini slipped away while I was reconnoitering the grocery store. I'd like very much to find him again. I have a hunch he knows far more than he told me."

"We'll find him for you," Landry said.

"You might try the pensione in Dongo," Salvo suggested. "The manager gave us some rooms for the night and a lot of the boys stayed there. Or maybe he's with relatives. I think he has a sister living in Dongo or Musso. I'm not sure which."

"We will all look for him," Pietro said. "We will separate and comb both towns. The first to find him will send word here, to this house."

"Shall I help, or go back to Viviana's house?" Stefanini asked. "I'm due to make another radio contact in a little over an hour."

"We can do without you," Landry said. "Kavanaugh and Creedmore will help us look for Tardini."

X. B. Kavanaugh sniffed wistfully at the rich odors coming from the kitchen, then said, "Okay. But it seems like a waste of time to me."

Landry grinned at him. "Don't worry," he said. "Lunch will keep. Tardini might not."

4

Emilio Tardini, Gravedona's most infamous loafer, hadn't held a steady job in twelve years, yet he always seemed to have money for a morning cup of wine, for a lunch of white fish in a restaurant overlooking the pier, for a leisurely afternoon shave by the town barber. There were those who said he sponged off his friends, though it was difficult to find anyone who really claimed to be his friend, and almost impossible to find anyone who admitted lending him money. Others slandered him by claiming he was a thief, a second-story man who prowled by night, lifting anything that wasn't nailed down, but he was too portly, too soft and flabby to scamper up drainpipes or skitter across roof ledges in black night shadows. A few even complained that he had been too intimate with Fascist authorities, always skulking after Blackshirt officers, whispering in their ears, no doubt selling information to them about his poor neighbors who had been forced to turn to smuggling or the black market just to make ends meet, and yet when Pietro and his small band had come down from the mountains to Gravedona three days ago, it was Tardini, fat Tardini, with lather on his face and the barber's towel still around his chubby neck, who had greeted them at the very first and begged for a gun so he could join them and help wrest the town from Fascist and German control.

Lying on his back in his sister's Dongo bedroom, staring at the ceiling, feeling sorry for himself, Tardini asked the world at large what good it had done him to gather his courage and play the role of patriot. No one in Gravedona would ever hear about it. Not now. Once the Britisher returned from Garzeno and told everyone that he, Tardini, had lied to Dante and the partisans, they would surely take his gun away and cast him out, back to the streets. And the people of Gravedona would keep on wondering, as they always had, where he picked up his occasional pocket change. A sponger? Not unless one counted the pittance his sister paid him to stay in Gravedona, away from Dongo. A thief? Only the infrequent wad of lire taken from his sister's purse or the rare bit of silver from the dining room, the odd bit of unused furniture. Once he had taken a valuable rosary, one that had belonged to his dear departed mother, but his sister had accused him point-blank of stealing it, her own brother, and he'd been forced to sneak it back into the house on his next trip down.

As for that other thing people called Tardini, an informer, that was plain nonsense. Tardini had never informed on anyone, unless maybe it was that fisherman, that Scalzi, who always cheated at bocce, and Tardini only mentioned once that Scalzi was hoarding food. Of course Tardini talked to the Fascisti from time to time. Who else had money to pay for the few odds and ends he had liberated from his sister's house?

A door opened downstairs and Tardini sat up. His sister back already? She'd be furious if she caught him lying on her bed with his boots on. He quickly kicked off the boots and put them on the floor. He worried again, not for the first time, about what he would do if she forced him to leave her house. The partisans would surely be looking for him by now. What did they do to people who told lies? Was there a punishment beyond banishment? A beating, perhaps? Or . . . or even the firing squad? Damn it, why had he done anything so foolish? His cousin Angelo had taken advantage of him, that's why. Talked him into it against his better judgment. And all Tardini had gotten in payment were a few cans of tinned fruit. It wasn't fair.

Yes, that was his sister on the stairs. He could hear her sharp voice, floating up from below. Who could she be talking to? She knew better than to bring anyone home while he was here. He'd told her quite firmly that he didn't want anyone to know where he was hiding. At least not until he was sure where he stood with the partisans. And yet there she was, coming up the stairs with someone, chattering away like . . . no, not chattering. Arguing. What could they be arguing about? His sister's voice, shrill as always, rising, saying . . . Madonna, what was that? Gurgling sounds, like someone drowning or choking. Was she sick? Is that why she wasn't alone? She'd taken ill while shopping and someone had helped her home? He held his breath. Footsteps moved closer to the bedroom door. He listened for the voices, but there were only the soft footfalls. Perhaps his sister had fainted.

The doorknob turned, ever so slowly. "Who's there?" Tardini called out.

The door opened and a figure stood back in the shadows of the hallway. "Signore Tardini?" Almost a whisper.

"Yes," Tardini said. He squinted, trying to see who it was. "What do you want? Where is my sister?"

"The partisans are looking for you."

Tardini tried to smile. "Looking for me? I wasn't hiding. Only resting. Did my sister tell you I was hiding? She lied."

"You have something we want. Information."

"I don't know what you're talking about," Tardini said.

"Gualfiero Lusso. Where is he?"

Tardini's eyes blinked involuntarily. "Gualfiero? Gualfiero is dead. He was killed two months ago. Everyone knows that."

The figure stepped carefully into the room, sliding from shadow to shadow. "You took the Englishman to Garzeno. Is that where Gualfiero is hiding?"

"My cousin Angelo lives in Garzeno," Tardini said. "That's the only reason I took the Englishman there." He squinted again and said, "Let me light a lamp."

He started to rise from the bed, but the figure stepped closer and blocked his way. "Never mind," the voice whispered. "I prefer the darkness. What did you tell the Englishman about me?"

Tardini was genuinely surprised. "About you? Nothing. I don't even know you."

Closer yet. So close that Tardini could feel warm breath on his forehead. "If you're lying, I'll kill you," the voice said.

"Why should I lie?" Tardini said frantically. Sweat trickled down his collar and he wanted to look up, but he studiously kept his eyes on the belt buckle inches from his face.

"There are people everywhere, searching for you," the voice whispered. "They may be here soon. Tell me what I want to know, and I'll help you to a place of safety."

Tardini forced a shallow laugh. "Why should I need a place of safety? I've done nothing. I have only repeated what Angelo saw fit to tell me. He's the one you should be talking to."

Breath hot on his ear. "You're sure you know nothing of Gualfiero Lusso?"

"Nothing at all," Tardini protested. "You can take me to the others and let them question me. I have nothing to hide. I insist you take me to the others. I'll swear it before them all. If anyone lied, it was Angelo. Not me."

"Get up," the voice murmured.

"Yes, of course," Tardini said. "I'll go anywhere you want me to. You'll see. I'll tell everyone else just what I've told you. Angelo, he's the one."

"Get up," the voice repeated.

Tardini stood quickly and mopped his forehead with a wrinkled handkerchief, careful not to look directly at the face before him. "Where are we going?"

"Why don't you ask your sister? She's waiting in the hall."

"Is she going as well?" Tardini asked. He padded toward the bedroom door in his stocking feet. "You have to understand," he said. "My sister sometimes says strange things. If it turns out that Gualfiero is alive, that's not my fault. I only told people what . . ."

His feet thumped into something in the hallway and he felt wetness through his stockings. He looked down to see what it was and his throat closed convulsively. There was a thing on the hallway floor, just outside the bedroom door. The thing was the size of his sister, and dressed in his sister's clothing. But the throat of the thing gaped open like a second mouth, a wide lipless slash that drooled strings of blood across the worn carpet.

Tardini choked and tried to turn away, but a hand came quickly across his shoulder and grabbed his hair, jerking his head back. Before he could object, something hot and stinging raked across his throat. A flood of warm liquid belched over his shirt front, drenching him. He tried to turn his gaze downward to see what it was, tried to protest, tried to say again that he was no liar. If the words came, he never heard them.

5

"But I understood that the OSS was to be disbanded after the war," said a lightly sweating American general. A waiter passed with a drink tray and the general stared into his nearly empty martini glass but didn't reach for a fresh one.

"Perhaps," Allen Dulles said. "If it *is* disbanded, we'll have to start it up again within two years. You mark my words. The war has changed things. Our new world will be too complex for governments to survive without access to secret intelligence. The Russians have learned that lesson, I guarantee you."

"I don't like it," the general said. He sipped delicately at the dregs of his martini, as if trying to make it last. "Give me a wide-open battle any day. Russians, Germans, I don't care who it is. Man against man. Gun against gun. None of this skulking around and hiding behind lamp posts."

Dulles smiled and swirled the ice in his own drink. He enjoyed the give-and-take of cocktail-party conversation. "Those days are behind us," he told the general. "There are new weapons on the horizon that will render your kind of world untenable. I'm afraid we'll have to settle for my kind of war, just as dangerous perhaps, but far more efficient."

"Efficient?" the general said. "Baloney. A bunch of college kids and broken-down baseball players. Name me one thing the OSS has accomplished that's worth talking about. A couple of piddling trains derailed, a few Germans with their throats cut, maybe an official document or two swiped out of a dresser drawer. The rest of the time, likely as not, we get nothing but misinformation out of your boys."

Someone signaled to Dulles from across the room and started through the party guests. It was Hobart, frowning and looking tiresomely serious. Dulles decided to ignore him. "Ah," he said to the general, "but more important things can happen, if one has the vision to conceive them. For example, tomorrow, in a small room in Caserta, a few gentlemen will meet to sign a document. A small, simple document. The signing of that document, General, will be the culmination of months of hard work, done entirely in secret. I can't say more about it at the moment, because it's still classified, but you'll soon be hearing about it. It will be the single most important intelligence accomplishment of the entire war."

Dulles smiled expectantly, waiting for the general's reaction. The general stared at him for a moment, then said, "Where's that waiter? I need another drink." He walked away, leaving Dulles with the smile frozen on his face.

"Ass," Dulles murmured. He regarded his own glass, wondering if he should fight his way to the bar for a refill, but Hobart reached him before he could make up his mind. "Well, well," Dulles said. "I didn't expect to see you here."

"Cornfield told me where to find you," Hobart said. "Something's come up. I think you should come with me."

"Not today," Dulles said. "There are important people here. I really must circulate." He caught the eye of the British ambassador and waved.

"It's important," Hobart said. "It's about the Lake Como team."

Dulles groaned. "Not them again. What is it this time, another veiled threat? I won't have another display of insubordination like that business about Mussolini yesterday. You tell them to follow orders from now on, and keep their disruptive suggestions to themselves."

"No, this isn't from them," Hobart said. "This is *about* them. We've had another complaint from Milan. The Communists have demanded that they be withdrawn from the lake immediately."

Dulles was puzzled. "Why? We've ordered them to stay clear of partisan affairs. That should be the end of it."

Hobart gestured futilely. "They must have meddled anyway. All I know for certain is that the Communists are upset. Apparently this Landry is too cozy with the lakeside partisans, and he's offended someone beyond endurance. The Communists threaten unilateral action unless we comply immediately with their demand that the team be withdrawn."

"Can they back that up?" Dulles asked.

Hobart nodded. "As long as the occupied territories remain on a war footing, they can do almost anything. They could have the team seized, even executed."

"Oh my God," Dulles said. "That's all we need, with Sunrise coming to a head. By all means, get our people out of there. Send the word tonight."

"Shouldn't we hear their side of it first?"

"They don't have a side," Dulles said. "Sunrise is all that matters. Tell them to conclude their affairs immediately and report to Milan. As far as I'm concerned, the Lake Como team no longer exists."

6

Lucertola, the Lizard, stared into the darkness from the cab of the wood-burning truck, watching the fan of headlights sweep past jutting embankments, but his thoughts kept sliding back to the bed of the truck. There, tied securely under an oil-stained tarp, rested the first shipment of plunder from the Fascist cars, six leather bags containing several million Italian lire, a tweed suitcase stuffed with foreign currencies, five valises of jewelry and Claretta Petacci's little red chest and twenty of the gold bars, stacked neatly in a dented blue footlocker. It was only a small portion of the overall treasure, but it was still more wealth than most ordinary men could imagine.

The Lizard suddenly laughed to himself. If he were to make a wrong turn somewhere, and end up in Switzerland, he'd be one of the richest men in the world. The road to Switzerland was well marked, but he could blink. It was dark. Mistakes could happen.

He knew he wouldn't do it, but the thought was incredibly tempting. The richest man he'd ever known was a Don Ubaldo, back in his home village, a man who owned two vineyards and an olive-oil factory. Don Ubaldo had a house three stories high. With the riches riding behind the truck cab, the Lizard could build a house tall enough to reach halfway to the moon. He could climb stairs the rest of his life and never reach the top.

Still, he wasn't completely without his share of the treasure. There was the money, the French money, that he had taken from the car outside the inn in Grandola. Not much. He'd been nervous about taking any at all, but Piccione and the American, Stefanini, had filled their pockets, and it wasn't as though the money belonged to anyone back then, before the roadblock.

Having the money made him nervous. If Dante or any of the others were to see him flashing it, they might think he had stolen it later, from one of the suitcases in the bed of the truck. He wouldn't want that. Maybe he should throw it away. What was the point of having money if he couldn't enjoy it?

And then, suddenly, he remembered a movie he had once seen. An American movie about a man who was rich, rich enough to light his cigars with paper money. Maybe that's what he could do with it. Once he got to Como and unloaded the treasure shipment at the bank, he would buy some cigars and go to one of the cafes down on the lakefront, and then, while everyone was watching, maybe even some girls, he would whip out a cigar and light it with French money. He tried to picture himself elbowing girls away with a burning French banknote in his hand. Maybe even . . .

The reverie dissipated abruptly as a roadblock loomed up ahead. The Lizard pumped the brakes and fumbled for his pass, signed by both Pietro and Dante. He pumped the brakes again and the truck rolled to a stop in front of a sawhorse barricade. Several men moved into the headlight beams, cradling submachine guns. They were better dressed than most of the lake partisans, and they looked serious. The Lizard stuck his head through the window and said, "Clear the road. I'm on official partisan business."

A stout man came toward the truck, ignoring him. "Get out," the man said.

"I have a pass," the Lizard told him.

"I'm sure you have," the stout man said. "Now get out."

The Lizard sighed and opened his door. He stepped down and stammered impatiently, "I'm under the orders of Captain Pietro, leader of all the lake forces. I have a valid pass. Read it quickly, then make way." He handed the pass to the man, only to see him tear it in half without looking at it. "Hey, what are you doing?" he demanded. "Captain Pietro isn't going to like that."

"Your Captain Pietro can suck eggs," the man said. "We take our orders from other quarters." He beckoned someone from the shadows, and a man with a felt star stitched to his coat sleeve came into the fan of light, carrying a long-barreled pistol.

"Who are you?" the Lizard asked.

The man with the star on his sleeve stared at him coldly, then gestured with the gun. "On your knees," he ordered.

"What for?" the Lizard asked.

The man raised the pistol and cocked it. "On your knees!"

The Lizard knelt slowly, looking bewildered. "You can't stop me like this," he stammered. "I'm on urgent partisan business."

The man walked around behind him and lowered the pistol to his ear. The Lizard heard the hammer click back. He opened his mouth to object, but all conscious effort congealed in a blinding flash of light. The front of his face erupted in a fine pink mist, a split-second kaleidoscope of spraying color that propelled him instantly into bottomless darkness, and he flopped to the pavement.

Book Three

THE TREASURE

Day Ten

Monday—April 30, 1945

In questo suol s'ammanta la sventura
Di gemme, d'oro e di leggiadri fior.

In this land misfortune is cloaked
In jewels, gold and lovely flowers.
          —Donizetti, *La Favorita*

1

Spring's counterattack after the rains left flowers in victorious possession of every clay pot and tiny terraced bed visible from the windows of Pietro's temporary office in the Dongo town hall. There were red roses and white roses, purple irises and yellow tulips, white arum lilies and blue salvia, all in glorious blossom, but their battle was not yet won. They fought, perhaps with dim awareness, against an encroachment of pansies and wallflowers, pinks and wisteria, all struggling stubbornly for existence.

Landry turned away from the riot of flowers and found himself looking into the faces of disheartened men, Willoughby and Pietro at the desk, Salvo and Piccione on the floor. For them, the struggle seemed to have ended. The morning had come fresh and sunny and filled with bad news. Salvo and Piccione had found fat Tardini, but too late. Someone had killed him, and his sister as well, butchered them both in the sister's small Dongo home. If that wasn't enough to darken the day, Freddy Stefanini had sent word from Viviana's house that OSS/Bern had just issued a final radio directive. Landry and the ALOTs were to conclude their affairs within twenty-four hours and leave the lake.

Salvo had succumbed either to the early hour or chronic weariness and had fallen asleep on the office carpet, head resting on his haversack and feet propped in the lower shelf of a bookcase. Piccione, slumped dejectedly against the wall beside Salvo, also appeared to be near sleep, chin nodding. Pietro took pity on the two partisans. He tried to keep his voice low. "How can they take you from the lake?" he demanded through gritted teeth. "We need your help now more than ever." His face reflected no morning sunshine at all, but more a dreary October fog.

"There's nothing we can do about it," Landry said.

"Do you think it would help if I talked to your superiors?" Pietro asked. "Perhaps if I explained . . ."

"Don't waste your time," Landry said. "We're just little parts in a well-oiled machine, as far as they're concerned. The big switches go click, click, and we do what we're told."

"What about the traitor?" Pietro objected. "Someone is now killing people right in our midst. Tardini and his sister. And what about this watch, the one that belonged to Major Holloman? We must have your assistance if we are to pursue these matters."

"I know," Landry said. He glanced at the window, outside which flowers battled gamely. "None of us are happy about this, Pietro. Damn it all, we were all better off when we were strictly on our own, wishing we had orders. Now every order we get means a disaster."

Willoughby matched Pietro's look of gloom with one of his own. "Landry is right," he said. "Frankly, I'd like to see this through, but they've left us no choice."

Pietro slumped back in his chair. "How will you go? And where?"

"There are American troops in Milan, according to the dispatch," Landry said. "We've been directed to an Army G-2 office that is setting up near the Parco Sempione. I'd hoped you could lend us a car."

"Of course," Pietro said. "I'll arrange one for you this morning. What about Viviana? Does she know?"

"Probably," Landry said. "I imagine Freddy told her as soon as

the message came in. But I want to tell her myself, as well. The
last time they pulled me off the lake, I left without saying good-by.
I won't make that mistake again. I thought we'd finish our business here, then drive down to Rezzonico this evening. The other
ALOTs can join us there, and we'll leave for Milan in the
morning."

"I don't envy you the task," Pietro said. "I doubt Viviana will
be happy to hear it, no matter who does the telling."

The door swung open abruptly, and Dante burst into the room
with Luisa. His face was livid, and his hands clutched his jacket to
his chest as though he were protecting a wound. Luisa watched
fearfully as he glared at them, then, without warning and with
great force, he threw his jacket against the wall. The two sleepy
partisans, Piccione and Salvo, sat up instantly, bewildered expres-
sions on their faces.

Pietro pushed out of his chair. "For the love of God, Dante.
What's wrong with you?"

Dante scowled. "The Lizard. He's dead."

Landry felt his stomach sink. "Lucertola? Dead? How?"

"Shot in the back of the head," Dante hissed. "Partisans from
the Tomasic detachment found him at daybreak on the roadside
below Lenne, wearing the *Spia Tedesca* label." He spat angrily.
"What filth with which to befoul a loyal man."

Salvo and Piccione were on their feet, speechless, casting mur-
derous glances that could find no target but the eruption of spring
flowers outside in the sunlight. Landry wondered if his own face
reflected the same bafflement. Even Pietro and the Britisher
looked helpless, stunned, like men suddenly feeling the ground
shift beneath their feet. This must be what defeat felt like, Landry
decided, to feel victory sift away like shifting sand.

"There's more," Dante said. He clenched his fists and lowered
his head. "I have failed you, Pietro. You trusted me to protect the
treasure. Both the truck and the shipment I placed in the Lizard's
hands are missing."

"Who did it?" Landry asked.

Dante's eyes hooded briefly, as though the question had
touched a sensitive nerve. He said hesitantly, "We can't be sure.
Maybe that man from Milan. That Comrade Ugo."

Pietro's cheeks reddened. "Bring him here," he demanded. "Arrest him and bring him to me."

"We can't," Dante said. "We have no proof."

Salvo clamped his teeth together. "Maybe not," he growled, "but we all know he did it."

"Then bring him," Pietro insisted.

Piccione spoke up timidly. "We can't arrest him without proof, Pietro. He's a pezzonovante. He sits on the Committee. If we try to push him around, all hell could break loose. We could get in trouble."

"I'm not afraid of any pezzonovante from Milan," Pietro said.

"Perhaps you should be," Piccione cautioned. "We all should be. We stick our necks out, and he might chop them off."

Dante said, "Pietro's neck need not be involved. Comrade Ugo is *our* problem. We will see to him ourselves." He looked searchingly at Salvo and Piccione, especially Piccione. "Are you with me, or against me?"

"With you," Salvo said. "The bastard has gone too far."

More hesitantly, Piccione said, "Yes. Yes, I suppose so. We are both with you."

"Good," Dante said. "We will go to him now. The three of us. I want to look at him, look into his eyes, and then I'll know for certain. If he and his men did it, we will take care of them. That way, no one from Milan can ever blame Pietro or the others for what happens."

"I'm going with you," Landry said. "Lucertola was my friend."

Dante's jaw tightened. "No. No one will come with us. It is our fault, Salvo's and Piccione's and especially mine, that this has happened. And the Lizard was under my command. This becomes a matter of vendetta for members of the Veroli detachment. The bastards owe us, not you." He glanced at Luisa and said, "Stay with Pietro." Then he gestured to Salvo and Piccione and led them out the door.

Willoughby cleared his throat in the silence that followed, and said, "I know we've been ordered to keep hands off partisan affairs, but don't you think we ought to follow them anyway?"

"You can't," Pietro said. "None of us can. Dante has claimed the right of vendetta. We can only wait until he calls for assistance."

Landry let his breath ooze out. "Jesus. First a traitor. Then handcuffed by orders from Switzerland. Now vendetta. God help us all."

2

As if he were expecting them, Ugo was in the pensione near the Dongo town hall, the same dining room, seated behind the same oaken table. Sunlight streamed through a dirty window, creating patchwork on the worn wooden floor. Paperweights, pencils, an inkwell and a legal-sized pad of yellow foolscap had been added to the tabletop, making it look impressively official. On the wall behind Ugo, tacked up with broad-headed nails, hung a red banner, hand-lettered with the ubiquitous "P.C.I." This time Ugo was surrounded not by lakeside partisans, but rather by his own men, Sandrino sitting to his left, and six tough-looking strangers in ill-fitting coats and ties standing around him like a palace guard.

Dante said to Ugo, "I see you've made yourself at home."

Ugo clasped his hands on the tabletop and smiled. "A temporary measure," he purred. "We've been assigned to act as a provisional office of justice. A mere formality, of course. A more permanent judicial commission will be appointed as soon as things settle down and outside contact is resumed."

"Very clever," Dante said. "But it won't work."

"I can't imagine what you are talking about," Ugo said. "Justice always works. And our appointment is authentic. You may check with Milan, if you wish."

"You know what I mean. You killed one of my men last night."

Now it would begin. Both Salvo and Piccione tensed, waiting for Ugo or one of the six strangers to make the slightest move, but Ugo only looked surprised. "One of your men is dead?"

Salvo was intimidated by the banner and the official look of the table, but he was also angry. "And the first shipment of treasure is missing," he put in.

"No!" Ugo said with a mock gasp. "But who could have done such a thing?"

"You know damned well who did it," Dante said.

Ugo spread his hands and let his face register hurt. "You are accusing me? Comrade Dante, how could you? I've been right here, under the eyes of all manner of witnesses, working to provide a foundation of sanity for a lakeside in chaos. I've already composed a number of proclamations, though I suppose I shall have to have your Captain Pietro's support before I can issue them."

Dante switched hostile eyes to the strangers standing behind the table. "You or your men did it. You admitted to us that you intended to steal the treasure. And now you've done so with a portion of it. But you won't steal any more. We'll see to that."

Ugo's round face became bland. "Comrade Dante, I will try to explain this once, and only once. It's true that I dreamed briefly of expropriating the Fascist funds. I had hoped to see it put to good use, turned, one might say, to stamp out the very principles that permitted it to grow in the first place. Even if I were responsible for the death of your man and the disappearance of a share of the treasure—and I do not admit that I am—I would think a man of your known loyalty to the Party would understand." Dante started to speak, but Ugo cut him off with a curt gesture. "No, let me finish. We now find ourselves emerging from a prolonged and bloody conflict, one in which good Communists have died by the tens of thousands at the hands of the Germans and the Fascists. Go to any city in Italy and you will find bereaved families whose sons have fallen in battle, or who have been arrested and tortured, or shot in cold blood by Fascist execution squads. And what is our reward? Party members have carried the brunt of partisan activities, and yet we have been tricked and cheated by the Allies at every turn. Our men left unsupplied, our political adversaries financed secretly with enormous British and American funds while we are forced to come, hat in hand, begging for a pittance. If we are to survive this war, then we must use extraordinary means. What is the life of one man, balanced against the deaths of tens of thousands? What is the life of one man against the survival of our political beliefs?"

Dante replied, "It is a pity Lucertola is no longer here to answer you. His life was no doubt very important to him."

"One man?" Ugo said. He seemed exasperated. "You mourn

for one man when so many have already died at the hands of the Germans?"

"I mourn for any man who risked his life against the enemy, only to be struck down by those he considered his friends."

"Mourn for whomever you like," Ugo said. "Mourn for yourself, while you're at it. Do you think I care, one way or the other, whether you approve of what I'm doing? The disbursement of the Fascist plunder has been determined by far more important Party functionaries than you or I. My likes and dislikes will not affect the outcome, nor will yours. It is not my place, nor is it yours, to question their methods. Any man who does may find himself justifiably considered an enemy to our cause, and his life considered forfeit. Do you understand what I am saying?"

"I am not afraid of death," Dante said.

"Perhaps not for yourself," Ugo said. He smiled icily. "But I am told you have a certain affection for the woman, Luisa. Make sure you understand. If we are forced to deal with the treasure without your co-operation, then we will also be forced to wipe away all concrete traces of the treasure. That includes the two women who inventoried it."

Dante's cheeks turned red, as though they had been slapped. He planted his fists on the table and leaned toward Ugo. "You will not touch Luisa. You will not touch another of my partisans, any of them. You already must answer to me. You, personally. Not your men. You. Do *you* understand?"

Ugo's smile remained tightly in place. "This meeting is ended," he said. "Get out."

Salvo and Piccione seemed shaken by Ugo's icy threat, and by Dante's hotheaded rejoinder. Piccione said, "Come, Dante. Let's go." He put a hand on Dante's arm, but Dante pulled loose.

"I mean it," Dante said. "Touch Luisa, and you'll die slowly, in ways the Germans taught us. By inches."

It took Salvo and Piccione both to turn Dante toward the door. Dante allowed himself to be hauled outside. As soon as they hit the morning air, Salvo murmured, "You shouldn't have threatened him, Dante. That was a mistake."

Dante's cheeks were still flaming. "You heard him. He all but admitted it."

Piccione was worried. "What can we do to stop him? He'll

surely try again. Shouldn't we tell Pietro about this and ask for help?"

Salvo agreed. "Yes. Maybe he'll give us more guards for the treasure."

Dante shook his head. "If more men must die defending the treasure, they must not be outsiders. The problem is ours alone to grapple with, and I say we must move the remainder of the treasure away from here, far from Ugo's reach."

"They'll just be waiting for us to try that," Piccione objected.

"Let them wait," Dante said. "Perhaps we will give them more than they reckon for."

Dante looked back toward Ugo's pensione and then drew Salvo and Piccione down a cobbled street. They stopped in front of a baker's shop, perhaps drawn by a rich fragrance of baking bread that wafted from it. "Here is what we will do," Dante said, squatting near the open doorway. "We will set a trap. We will load another shipment, to go out tonight. Enough gold and currency to . . ."

"Wouldn't it be better to use empty cartons?" Piccione ventured.

"No, Ugo might have us watched. Or someone might let it slip. It needn't be a large shipment, but we must make it tempting. We will load it openly into a car and leave, as if we're merely attempting another transfer to the vaults at Como. But this time, two escort cars will follow, with our best comrades, our best guns, even mortars from the German garrison in Gravedona. God, I hope they try to stop us. We'll blow them off the lake."

Salvo cleared his throat. "Permit me to ride in the treasure car, comandante. It will be the main target, and so . . ."

Dante shook his head. "No, I must be in the car, as part of the bait. Ugo would expect it, and he has made it clear that he wants to kill me. We must live up to his expectations, so that he may die by ours. Of you and Piccione, I ask the hardest job of all: to stay behind. Someone must remain to deal with any possible survivors from Ugo's squad. And I also ask this favor of you, my friends: Make certain that Luisa is safe."

"You know we'd never let anything happen to Luisa," Salvo said.

"I know. But to make sure, help her arrange it so no one can get the remaining currency from the Dongo bank without her signature. That way, at least, anyone will think twice before they try to touch her."

"You make it sound as though you expect to die," Piccione objected.

"One must be prepared for any eventuality," Dante said. "This is a battle, just as was our war with the Germans, and we all know anything can happen when bullets fly. It might even be worth it, to take a man like Ugo down with one."

Piccione argued, insisting that Dante should not endanger himself by going in the treasure car, but Salvo sat quietly, smelling the wonderful fragrance of the bread. Wonderful indeed, that flour, so long in short supply, suddenly seemed to be reappearing in such abundance. Salvo didn't argue because the good subordinate never argued with his superior. He never once admitted to himself that in this battle, between partisan and Party, he would find it difficult to stick a gun barrel into Comrade Ugo's fatherly face.

3

At two o'clock that Monday afternoon, far behind Allied lines, SS General Karl Wolff, dressed in a gray civilian jacket and accompanied by two German SS officers, stepped from an American bomber and was driven to an office in Caserta where he was met by an Allied surrender delegation.

A document was placed before Wolff, calling for the surrender of all German troops in Italy. The surrender was to take place in two days, on Wednesday, May 2, at 12 noon Greenwich time, 2 P.M. in Italy. Wolff read it over carefully, then reluctantly attached his signature. Lieutenant General William Morgan signed for the Allies, with a Russian representative, Major General A. P. Kislenko, looking on. Allen Dulles was not there, having decided his continued presence in Bern would help shield the highly secret surrender process.

When the document was complete, General Morgan asked Wolff, "And do you guarantee that all hostilities will cease on schedule, according to the particulars you have just signed?"

Wolff said stiffly, "I can guarantee only the actions of my subordinates and of the SS in Italy. Whether or not the Army will honor the surrender is up to General Vietinghoff."

"We understand," Morgan said. "But you have at least discussed the terms with General Vietinghoff?"

"General Vietinghoff has not yet made up his mind," Wolff said. "For that we must wait until Wednesday. I am sorry, gentlemen. I have done all I can. The rest is in the hands of the German Army."

To Wolff, the disturbed look on the American general's face was soothing. Each word Wolff had spoken was true, but he felt no obligation to these conquerors to provide them with his private opinion. The dusty, weary American soldiers who had met his German plane near the front and transferred him to an American bomber for the trip to Caserta had looked discouraged and dirty. But Wolff was a fighting man. He knew from first glance that each of the young Americans still had a hundred battles in him, as must every other American and British fighting man on the Italian front. Wolff could not say the same for the battered remnants of the German Army.

4

SD Major Ernst Richter, wearing well-tailored civilian tweeds, ventured out of the ramshackle abandoned villa above Cadenabbia, but only to creep through weeds and yellowed grass to a walled-off lower garden, where a stand of magnolia trees struggled to survive. He could see the township below through a break in the garden wall, see the afternoon sun beat down on bell spires and rooftops and a curving stretch of beach, see figures as small as ants, dressed mostly in black, working among the fishing boats, scurrying along the streets to market. Black was the peasant color, the color of poverty, and many of the lakeside peasants wore it out of custom, but it was also a funereal color and Richter found it appropriate that the villagers of Cadenabbia below his dilapidated mountainside retreat were so dismally outfitted on this grim Monday, as though already in mourning for the lost and dying Third Reich and its decaying junior partner, the Fascist regime of Italy.

He clamped his teeth and strolled deeper into the magnolias, shutting off the view below, trying not to think of the terrible defeat in store for his homeland. Even now, with the end only hours or days away, Richter knew there was still time to exact his own form of retribution. Some of the more dedicated members of the SS and the SD had seen the war coming to an unsatisfactory end and had already organized a method for rescuing valuable Nazis, an underground apparatus that would whisk key men out of Europe and see them to safety in a variety of holding stations where the Allies couldn't get at them. Called the Kameradenwerk, the escape organization would need funds, not only to facilitate the rescue of important Nazis, but also to finance them while they planned for the future. The Fascist treasure, taken from Mussolini's caravan by the partisans in Dongo, would buy a very large share in that future. And the man who brought it to the Kameradenwerk would be a hero.

As he reached the outer edge of the trees, toward the center of the ruined garden, a voice spoke softly behind him. "You're late. I've been waiting for almost twenty minutes. I can't stay much longer. I might be missed."

Richter didn't turn around. He stared at leathery green leaves and said stiffly, "I have other duties. I can't drop everything and come running on the say-so of a traitor and a turncoat." He kept his voice level. No need to admit his own personal excitement about the treasure.

"You've always seemed eager to talk to me before."

"And I am eager again," Richter said. "But in my own good time. There are many things to be done if I am to prepare the way for our withdrawal."

Silence, then the voice said, "If you have so little regard for me and the information I bring, perhaps we should end our association. I don't care much for lost causes, anyway."

"But you do care for riches," Richter said. "And our agreement stands. Twenty per cent to you of anything that comes to us. How goes it with this fabulous Fascist treasure of yours?"

"There are problems," the voice said. "I tried to contact you, but no one was monitoring the proper frequency."

"All radio contact is out," Richter said. "I don't want anyone homing in on our new location. What problems?"

"A shipment went out last night."

Richter felt a tingle of concern, but he kept it from his voice. "Why so premature?"

"Difficulties with a political commissar from Milan. It didn't help. The shipment was intercepted and disappeared."

"How much was involved?" Richter asked.

"Several millions."

Richter scowled. "You should have come to us sooner. Perhaps we could have diverted it."

"I was busy," the voice said. "Besides, it doesn't matter. The bulk of the treasure is still in Dongo. You'll have to move on it soon. I suspect the commissar will try for it all, unless we do something."

"Have you any suggestions?"

Hesitation, then, "I'm not sure. A second shipment, a smaller one, is scheduled to leave tonight, but there's something peculiar about it. Too much activity around the town hall. I believe a trap is being set for the Communists. I've tried to find out what's going on, but security is tight."

"Keep trying," Richter said. "I'll have a man in Dongo by midafternoon. If you discover anything, tell him."

"Send someone I know. Send Lieutenant Stenzel."

Richter inspected his fingernails. "No, not Stenzel. He might be seen. You know what that could mean."

"Who, then?"

"Sergeant Knaust. He'll wait for you in the church. He'll be dressed as a laborer. Get to him as quickly as you can."

"I'll try." Another pause. "There's something you should know. All American personnel have been ordered off the lake. The deadline is noon tomorrow."

"I see," Richter said. "And you wouldn't want that, would you?"

"There is common ground between what I want and what you

want," the voice said. "If I'm right about the shipment tonight, about the possibility of a trap, I may be able to disrupt everything. Perhaps even cause the orders to be changed. But there is a favor you must do for me in return."

Richter frowned. He didn't like dealing with quislings and renegades, particularly when they made demands, but this time it was necessary. "And it is?"

"There's a man. A man who may know too much. The partisan, Gualfiero. I thought he was dead. It now appears that his brother may be hiding him. One of the older partisans is out now, trying to find him. If he's truly alive, then something must be done about him."

Richter almost smiled. "You want him killed? Again?"

"If necessary. If he tells the others about me, I won't be able to help you anymore. Do you think you can handle it?"

"Easily."

A doubtful pause, then, "That's what you said about Landry. You haven't done so well with him."

Richter's smile faded, and he looked directly into the leafy branches at the shadowy face of his informant. "There is time enough yet for your Captain Landry. Perhaps we can dispatch them both at the same time. As always, we will help in any way that we can."

5

As the day wore on, and sparkling sunlight mellowed to golden afternoon, then slipped softly to blue evening, word magically filtered through the lake villages that the Germans had signed a surrender document and that the long-awaited peace would become a reality the day after tomorrow. A corporal from a tank battalion of the U. S. 1st Armored Division, holding ground north of Milan, first mentioned the news to a trio of timid little girls selling roses to American soldiers. The corporal hadn't the vaguest notion of the rumor's source, but it had already swept through his own tank unit, as it had almost every combat outfit in northern

Italy. After one of the girls told her mother, and the mother passed it along to an itinerant tinker, and the tinker mentioned it to a cousin who farmed near the town of Como, the news soared quickly up the lake. It was generally believed and preparations for celebration began. Busy lakeside citizens near Dongo, Musso and Crémia had little time or attention to spare for five apparently disconnected actions:

. . . In the courtyard of the Dongo town hall, open to the view of anyone who cared to look, two sacks filled with gold sovereigns were relayed from the upstairs treasure room to a waiting car. After the sacks came twenty gold bars, then several armloads of furs and personal art objects. Soon the car was so heavily laden that the fenders almost touched the tires. The men acting as loaders were then dismissed, and the courtyard gates closed. Two more cars, waiting on the far side of the courtyard, pulled into place and a band of carefully selected partisans came out of the building, carrying submachine guns, grenades, and two 10cm "Nebelwerfer" mortars confiscated from the arsenal of the German garrison at Gravedona.

. . . Several blocks away, a big man with protruding ears and deep-set eyes, dressed in brown trousers that sagged at the knees, entered the central Dongo church and made his way through the dimness to a pew toward the back. He crossed himself and knelt to pray. Though he was here on the orders of Major Richter, and the purpose of his visit was strictly business, the prayer was real. He prayed for home, he prayed for survival, he prayed for a quick and lasting peace.

. . . In Musso, Salvo approached a sidewalk cafe and sat down behind a hedge to light up his pipe. He had been busy all day, first following Dante's instructions in Dongo, then arranging through the Musso undertaker for the preparation and burial of the bodies of the Lizard, Tardini and Tardini's sister. There had been some argument over payment. The undertaker, unwilling to take a chit to be paid later by the government, had to be paid from a portion of the treasure funds that Pietro had set aside to pay his partisans, but Pietro had okayed the expenditure without hesitation. Now Salvo was weary with tension and ready for a bottle of wine and supper. Maybe even a good night's sleep, if he could keep his mind off Dante and the danger that awaited the second shipment of treasure.

. . . In Crémia, farther down the lake, the two Cravero partisans who had attended Comrade Ugo's postmidnight meeting with Dante and the others only the day before, completely unaware that Ugo had begun to follow through on his planned deflection of the treasure, had spent the afternoon visiting relatives in lakeside villages, the first time they had been able to do so openly since joining the resistance movement. Now with evening approaching, they intended to hitch a ride back to the South so they could rejoin their detachment.

. . . Piccione, made nervous by the angry follow-up meeting with Ugo this morning and the man's obvious threats toward Dante and anyone else connected with the treasure, had stayed out of sight most of the day. He would have continued keeping to himself, except that Salvo had proposed sharing dinner, and he didn't want Salvo to think he was afraid. So shortly before sundown, he hiked from Dongo to Musso and wandered through the streets, heading toward the sidewalk cafe. . . .

Sergeant Knaust peeled back the frayed sleeve of his shabby civilian jacket and peered at a wristwatch incongruously fine for a man so poorly dressed. It wasn't the only incongruous thing, as far as Knaust was concerned. He felt himself too big, too well fed, too light in complexion to pass for an Italian farmer, even in the dim light of the church auditorium. Not only that, he'd also been in the church far too long. Italian women, yes, they often communed with God and the Blessed Virgin and the hundreds of saints from whom they sought favors, pressing knees to prayer boards for hours on end. Men were more likely to make a quick pass at prayer, just for appearance's sake, then head back into the daylight and beeline it for the nearest bar. But Knaust had alternated between deep thought on the bench and deep prayer on his knees for almost two hours, without a sign of Richter's pet informer. The priest, a portly man with five-o'clock shadow, had passed him several times, at first smiling beneficently at Knaust's obvious piety, then beginning to look a bit suspicious. No one stayed this long unless he had the devil's own number of sins to expiate, yet

Knaust hadn't made a single move toward the confessional. He couldn't. His Italian was too heavily accented.

He was on the verge of giving up, regardless of what Richter might say, when someone slipped into the pew behind him and whispered, "Don't look back. It's me."

"You took your time," Knaust muttered in relief.

"I couldn't help it. Tell Major Richter it's too late to intercept the second shipment. It leaves within the hour, with two escort cars to protect it. But tell him the third shipment, the largest, will say here. And the ALOTs. I've made certain of that."

"What have you done?"

"Never mind. Just tell Richter the partisans will not be happy when this night is over, and there will be no more shipments for a time."

"You've told the Communists about the escort cars?"

"I've done what was necessary."

"Major Richter won't like that. You should have done nothing at all. It would be better for the money to find its way to the Italian Government, rather than into the hands of the Italian Communist Party. Can you stop what you've done?"

There was no answer.

Knaust wrapped his hands in a prayerful attitude. "I assure you, the major will be upset if the Communists profit further from the treasure. Is it too late to stop them?"

Again there was only silence.

"Are you there?" Knaust asked. He waited a moment, then risked a cautious look over his shoulder. But the informant was gone.

Salvo brushed his mustache back and sipped from a glass of red wine. He rolled the wine on his tongue, then slowly and with great delight allowed it to trickle down his throat. He leaned back and looked across the hedge, watching for Piccione, wishing the youngster would hurry. Salvo was growing hungrier by the minute, and had already demolished six bread sticks in the waiting. But the wine was cool and the evening was cool, and the promise of a leisurely meal stalled his impatience, so he turned his eyes to regard the other patrons.

The sidewalk cafe was an airy, candlelit assortment of tables and chairs grouped behind a two-foot-high hedge, low enough to afford an excellent view of passing people. An elderly waiter with curly gray hair stood near the break in the hedge with a round metal tray tucked under his arm, and two families with children were seated near the plate-glass front of the cafe. Closer to the hedge, like Salvo, were a pair of solitary men sipping wine in the dusk, basking in the peace and quiet that came with the end of the day. The lake people were so changeable, so chameleonlike in their willingness to turn adversity to advantage. Gone now were the red kerchiefs, the quick symbols of encouragement to the partisans. Now red, white and blue bunting began to appear, laced through the wrought-iron bars of balconies to honor the Americans who would soon course up the lake. Street lights back on again, after so long in the darkness. It was as though the war had already ended, and the citizenry of the lake villages could hardly wait to begin their new peaceful existence.

Salvo sighed contentedly. He thought he saw Piccione approaching along the sidewalk on the far side of the street, but when he raised his chin to check, a car came sputtering around the corner from the opposite direction. It was an ancient American DeSoto, but so highly polished, so trim, that it looked dear to someone's heart. Indeed it was. Salvo picked up his Luftwaffe cap and waved it eagerly, and had the pleasure of seeing David Landry and the Britisher wave back. The DeSoto was the prewar pride of a vineyard owner, who, as Salvo knew, had bricked it up in a storage shed and had risked bringing it out only that morning. He'd been premature. The few cars on the lake had mostly been pressed into service by partisans, and the DeSoto was no exception. Pietro had presented this particular DeSoto to David, an American car for his American friend, and Salvo had a strong hunch where David and the Britisher were going—straight to Viviana's house, now that their day's work in Dongo was done. Peace offered time not only for wine, but also for lovers' meetings. Salvo raised his glass in a silent salute and drank.

Salvo looked once more for Piccione, failed to see him and gave thought to calling the waiter over anyway. It wouldn't hurt to order. He could always dally through the soup, perhaps have an extra bowl if Piccione were slow to show up. Salvo even went so far as to gesture to the waiter, but as the gray-haired man approached his table, Salvo changed his mind about ordering and pointed at the wine carafe instead. "Pour it for me," he said.

The waiter smiled. He recognized Salvo as one of the partisans down from the hills, and he surely knew how bereft of luxury the partisans had been these many months. He set his tray on the table and made a great show of wiping the lip of the carafe and pouring delicately, ever so delicately, into Salvo's wine glass.

Another car slid around the corner. Automobile traffic was still fairly unusual. The thought occurred to Salvo that this time it might be Dante, setting off on his deceptive journey to the South. Salvo felt a pang of guilt that he wasn't with Dante, that he was here, enjoying the evening, while Dante took all the possible danger on himself. Salvo strained his eyes in the gathering dusk, trying to see if he could recognize anyone in the car. It was a black Fiat, and it came slowly, swinging out of its lane to approach the sidewalk cafe and the low hedge. Someone in the back seat rolled a window down, apparently to hail him. Salvo smiled and got ready to wave again.

But as the car drew closer, an object appeared in the open window, and Salvo's blood froze. He had time to see the gun barrel, perforated and black, then flame burst from the muzzle and the car sped up. Bullets zizzed helter-skelter all about Salvo, striking sparks where random slugs caromed off the tiles. There were shrieks from terrified patrons and the sound of breaking glass. The wine carafe blew up in the waiter's hands, and the waiter pitched across Salvo's table, knocking the remaining breadsticks to the floor.

Salvo tried to backpedal, tried to reach his weapon, leaning against the low hedge, but the bullets continued to spray, even as the car squealed its tires, and he felt something heavy, something hot, tear through his chest, his stomach, his thighs. He flopped through the hedge, a tangle of arms and legs, and his head hit the sidewalk. The bullets kept coming, churning all around him. The last thing he saw was red wine and his own blood mingling on the concrete and running in red rivulets toward the curbing and the gutter.

The two Cravero men, a little tipsy from cognac, had already indulged several whims before heading for the highway and the hoped-for ride down the lake. They had been to a real barber and sat in real barber chairs for shaves and tingling facial massages. They had gone into a market and bought real lettuces and broad beans and french beans to take back to their comrades. They had visited a small newsstand and purchased a handful of magazines, though only one of them could read. Now they were looking for a cathouse that a citizen of Crémia told them had once serviced the local Fascist policemen. They had found the building, but it was closed and dark. They would have given up and gone back to the highway, but instead, feeling gay, feeling tanked to the gills, they went from door to door, knocking loudly, sing-songing in unison, "Girls, girls, come out wherever you are." They covered a block of houses that way, some dark, some faintly lit behind closed curtains. Faces peeped out at them occasionally, but mostly they were ignored. No one opened a door or window to speak to them.

They were near the alleyway of the second block before they saw any signs of life. Three men, with hats mashed down over their ears and sunglasses veiling their eyes, stepped from the alley and gestured to them. The men were wearing raincoats, and they looked friendly, as though they might help find the girls the two partisans were seeking. The two Cravero men exchanged looks and leered happily. They swaggered toward the alleyway, only to see the waiting strangers fumble open their raincoats and disengage slim, tubular automatic rifles, which dangled from their belts. With rapid, practiced moves, the waiting strangers brought the guns speedily to their cheeks, leveled at the two partisans. The gunfire was swift and accurate. Just as before, when the partisans had pounded and yelled their way up the block, no one opened either window or door to see what the shooting was about.

Piccione leaned against a wall two blocks from the outdoor cafe and lowered his head to vomit for the third time. He had seen the waiter kicking his heels on the tiles, like a teen-ager in the prime of life instead of an old man in his death throes, had seen a family of diners near the window dive for cover, only to be showered by a spray of broken glass, had seen Salvo ripped up by bullets, spurting blood like some rag-doll fountain, bright red arcs that splashed into the air in four different directions, then tamed until they were only minor burbles, soaking his clothing, soaking the cobblestones.

Piccione had seen it all from the sidewalk across the street. He wanted to go to Salvo, would have gone had there been any chance that Salvo was still alive. But Salvo was so obviously, irretrievably dead. Just the quick, passing car, the splatter of gunshots, and bodies sprawling everywhere. So Piccione had turned instead to flee. Around one corner, away from the cafe, then stopping to catch his breath. The retching, horrible taste of bile heaving out of his stomach. Another block. Throwing up a second time. A few stumbling steps and heaving once more. Now the dry heaves, nothing else in his stomach to come up, yet it kept trying.

He knew he should get to Dante. Tell him. Or Pietro. David. Anyone. But he didn't dare. The men in the car would surely be seeking him as well. What then? Where could he go? Where could he hide? He had no money, save the few French banknotes he had taken from the Fascist car in Grandola, some days before. He had no friends, save the members of his own partisan group, two of them dead already. He had nothing worth saving but his life.

He leaned against a wall, tasting the sour residue in his mouth, and looked to the dark mountains above Musso. There, beyond the peaks and ridges where he had hidden and fought the Germans, lay Switzerland. If he went now, said nothing to anyone, he might be able to cross over and disappear. He would never be able to come back. Ugo and his kind had long memories. He would never see his family again, never enjoy the fruits of victory, never be able to look over his shoulder without expecting someone with a gun. But he would be alive.

And so Piccione, a brave man many times over in the face of the enemy, a coward in the shadow of his friends, began to run.

6

Three kilometers from Rezzonico, Landry was astonished to see Viviana driving smartly along the road in a trap drawn by a little chestnut mare. He braked the DeSoto, which promptly died, and, since Viviana's pony trap was still ahead of him, he jumped out and ran through waves of fragrance to catch up with her.

Willoughby was discreet enough to stay with the car, but Tuono leaped out after Landry and galloped with him beside a hedge of pittosporum. Landry hadn't seen Viviana since the afternoon of the executions, and he was hesitant to approach her, but when he called her name, she turned and reined in the mare with a calm smile. "You?" she said. "My spies didn't warn me you were coming. Climb in. No, not you, Tuono. See what I've found? Fresh butter. Chickens. And a beautiful leg of mutton. Don't dare let Tuono close to it. If you can stay with me tonight, I shall finally be able to give you a proper dinner."

The mare showed her resentment at being stopped by stamping and jerking her head. Landry found he had a thousand things to say to Viviana, but he asked the most important thing first: "You aren't angry with me for not coming sooner?"

Viviana's fine eyebrows rose. "What nonsense," she said. "Do you forget that gathering information was my wartime specialty?" She counted on her fingers. "First, I know you have been busy, just as I have been. Second, you have slept in some dusty corner of the town hall for the past two nights. Third"—she smiled—"you slept alone. But fourth, I've been off to one of my father's farms, so I had no warning you were en route this evening. Don't just stand there, David. Climb in. See what else I have? I've been after it for years."

The mare began to chew on the hedge while Viviana tore at the brown-paper wrapping of a large parcel next to a string shopping bag on the seat. The pony trap was jammed, and two chickens stirred, then squawked, from the floorboard. She succeeded in peeling back part of the paper, revealing a silk coverlet embroidered in what looked like gold thread, and, for some reason, Landry felt his spirits sink.

"You left so abruptly that afternoon in the Dongo square," he said. "I was afraid you might be angry with me."

Behind them, Willoughby stopped banging on the carburetor of the DeSoto and approached the pony trap, calling Tuono by name. But Tuono had smelled the mutton and kept trying to scramble in, rather than returning to his new idol. Viviana grabbed him by the collar and held him tight. "I had to leave," she told Landry. "I was worried about my cats. Poor little things, they were missing, you know. We'd been searching everywhere for them. You should have heard me, trying to mew like a mother cat. Do you know where they were? They moved in next door. They spent the days we were away lounging on the lap of my neighbor, a woman whose husband owns a factory in Turin. Oh good evening, Captain Willoughby. Come take this dog of yours, and take a peek at my prize."

Willoughby peered at both prizes, the leg of mutton and the silk coverlet. "Very nice," he said. "Especially the mutton."

"You shall have it for dinner tonight, à la Bretonne," she said. "Do you mind if David rides on with me for a while?"

"Not at all," Willoughby said. "I'd trade him for a share of mutton Bretonne any day. I hope you won't mind if I'm tardy following you. That carburetor is pretty badly gummed up. I'd like to spend some time on it before Landry beats me to it. We'll want the car in good shape if we're to leave tomorrow."

Willoughby led Tuono back to the DeSoto without waiting for a response, and Viviana cocked her head at Landry. "Leave tomorrow? What does he mean?"

"It's true," Landry said reluctantly. "I thought Freddy would have explained it all by now."

"I told you, I've been to my father's farm. I haven't seen Freddy since yesterday. Where are you going?"

Landry sighed. "We've been ordered off the lake. We leave for Milan in the morning. After that, who knows?"

Her good cheer vanished and she turned away. "Oh David. Is it to happen again? Will they never leave us alone?"

"As long as there's a war on, they're calling the shots."

She was silent for a moment, then she lifted her chin. "I refuse to let it spoil our evening," she said. "We won't talk of it until later." She clucked at the chestnut mare and Landry found himself bowling down the road. Green saliva flew back at them from the mare's still-munching mouth, but Viviana only wiped her cheek with a quick, absent gesture. "If Franca puts the joint in the oven the moment we get home, we can dine before it gets too terribly late. Do ask all your friends. It's a lovely big leg of mutton. The house is still a wreck, but perhaps they can put up with that. Franca can manage beds for them somehow."

Landry managed a smile. "I'm sure the others would love it," he said. "But frankly, I don't want to waste the time driving back to Dongo to tell them. It's been days since you and I had any spare moments together. It may be even longer after tonight."

"Shhh," she said. She took a bent whip from its holder and gave the mare a tap. The little mare gave her a surprised look, but it trotted on more swiftly. In a light tone, she chattered on, "You don't have to drive back to Dongo, David. Don't you know the telephones are working again? How do you think I got my daily reports on you? I telephoned Pietro and asked."

He decided to match her mood. "That simple, huh? I guess I thought it was more cloak-and-dagger stuff. You know, watchful eyes. Message drops. The mysterious lady spy, doing her part for the war effort."

It was the wrong thing to say. Her face sobered. "I'm through with all that," she said. "As far as I'm concerned, the war is over. I'm done with spying, done with partisans, done with it all."

"Is it that easy?"

"Why not?" she said. "If you can give up the war, why can't I?" They entered the village and she slowed the mare. "Besides, my work here is finished. What more reasonable act than to put what is past behind one? I have declared my own peace, a little early, perhaps, but oh what a lovely peace it is."

Landry dropped his eyes to a large yellow cheese in Viviana's string shopping bag. He felt as if he had been long absent in a far country, and this country in which he found himself—even the steep street down to Viviana's house, freshly swept by someone, even the cheese from some farmer's secret stash, even the pony trap and mare that Viviana had conjured up—seemed only alien to him. The welcome sight of Viviana's house made him feel somewhat more at home, but not much.

Though Franca's young stonemason friend had obviously already been at work repairing the damage, most of the rooms through which he wandered while Viviana conferred about dinner were still a shambles. A delicate inlaid desk, wrecked. A vast armoire overturned. Walls chewed up by gunfire. Smoke-blackened entryway. Had it all happened during that brief German attack? Or had the Germans systematically added to the havoc out of frustration at missing their own prey?

Landry picked up two shattered lamps. The base of one seemed intact, but its socket was broken. He could cannibalize a socket from the other, and together they would make one whole lamp. He pulled his trench knife from his boot, sat down on the floor and started. It was a simple job. He'd almost finished by the time he heard the DeSoto sputter to a stop in front of the house. Viviana hurried through the ruined rooms to answer Willoughby's knock at the door, and Landry set the lamp on a table and made himself comfortable on a gilt-trimmed chair.

Viviana, laughing effortlessly, led Willoughby into the room. "Indeed you won't go," she assured the Britisher, in answer to a murmured excuse he had made. "Lieutenant Stefanini will be down to join us shortly. Pietro has found bicycles for the others, and they'll be here soon as well. I've already telephoned, you see."

Willoughby took another of the gilt-trimmed chairs turned upright for him by Viviana. He seemed prepared to make sherry-party conversation. "Grand to be able to pick up a telephone instead of having to foot it all over the lake, isn't it?" he said.

She found another chair for herself. "Yes, but thank heavens the long-distance lines to Switzerland aren't too efficient, or I would be getting one call after another from my father. It makes him nervous when I'm out from under his thumb. Wasn't it exhilarating, up in Dante's camp in the mountains? I've never been so off the map before. No one knew where we were. No one knew where to find us. No one could bother us for any reason—except the Germans, of course. I think I might have enjoyed that kind of life."

Landry became alert, perplexed but deeply interested. "But you have to admit that being completely out of touch that way is a little scary," he said, probing.

"Of course. That was part of it."

Franca entered, bearing a tray of wine. "This is the Trebbiano, from your father's warehouse," she told Viviana. "It's the best I could find."

"It would serve him right if we drank it all," Viviana said. She must have seen Landry's curious stare, for when Franca left she said, "My father hid all sorts of things when the war began. Cases of the best wines, concealed at one of his properties in Velzo, above Menággio. Don't you think it's a good joke on him? He's also hoarded a whole warehouse full of olive oil in Velzo, waiting for a price to his liking, and now prices will surely start to tumble. That will teach him to be such a wretched capitalist."

"Dante would be surprised to hear that from you," Landry said.

"Naturally, but Dante has never understood that excesses, whether Communist or capitalistic, are dangerous pastimes. I loathe all excess—except my own."

Willoughby smiled, apparently at Landry's expression. "I fear Landry finds you mystifying, Viviana. That's all very appropriate, since you're a woman, but shall I give him the simple key?"

"If you know it," Viviana said.

"I do. Yours is a happy temperament. You take the best of any situation you encounter, and you let the rest go hang. Isn't that more or less right?"

"Heavens," she sighed. "To think that I'm so transparent."

Landry didn't notice that he had drunk his wine. He groped toward understanding and toward a great ray of light he thought he perceived over the horizon of his future. His and Viviana's future. "Well, but you were hopping up and down over some silk coverlet you managed to buy," he said to Viviana. "What if you had to settle for a plain blanket?"

Now she looked surprised. "Like in the mountains?" she said. "They were lovely blankets. They were warm when we needed warmth."

Landry gestured toward the black slacks and shirt and fragile sandals she wore. He had seen the shirt before. It was still missing a button. "And silk blouses? What if you had to make do with a flannel shirt, like the one Luisa loaned you? I noticed you couldn't wait to change out of it."

"I'd make do, that's all. Changing my clothing was a different matter, David. After what they did in the square, I didn't feel clean any longer. Do you understand?"

"Yes," he said slowly. Outside, street lights blinked on, lighting Rezzonico as other villages had been lit for the first time since the Germans had imposed a blackout rule, but Landry didn't notice. He was thinking busily about a construction shack in Siam. "Yes, I think I do."

Viviana smiled back, so Landry realized he must be smiling. From the kitchen came a faint tinkle of pots and a wonderful fra-

grance of mutton à la Bretonne, and Landry's far country receded
so far away that it scarcely existed. He had come home, and home
was where Viviana was, even if only for one last night. Later, after
dinner, he would discover for sure if Viviana felt the same way.
"Look," he said, pointing at the window, "the sky is a perfect
shade of purple, just like the lake. It's going to be a beautiful evening."

7

Shortly after darkness gently wiped the last trace of color from the
skies, Dante nodded at the eight men and two drivers standing by
the escort sedans, then climbed into the treasure-laden car with his
own driver, the Germasino partisan who called himself il Gallo.
Dante nestled a rifle between his legs, barrel leaning against the
dashboard, and laid his loaded Glisenti automatic on his lap.
"Let's go," he told il Gallo. "Drive normally, but stop for nothing
until I tell you."

The treasure car pulled slowly through the courtyard gate,
fenders scraping as the load of bullion and stacked cartons
jounced in the back seat, and wound around the Dongo plaza with
the two escort cars following at a discreet distance.

"Do you think this will work?" il Gallo asked.

Dante, watching the headlights of the escort cars through the
rear window, said, "There's no reason it shouldn't. If they are as
greedy as I believe them to be, they'll try to stop us before we're
halfway down the lake."

"I hope the boys in the escort cars stay awake," il Gallo said.

Dante glanced at the man. He had a reputation among the fol-
lowers in his small band of being quite daring and brave, but his
tongue kept touching his lips as he hunched over the steering
wheel. Nervous, no doubt. Dante didn't blame him. In spite of the
two escort cars, the first blows by any attackers would be directed
at this car, the lead car. Any delay in springing the trap and both
Dante and il Gallo would have to face the danger alone.

They drove cautiously through the streets of Dongo, the treasure car leading the way, the two escort cars hanging behind, drawing no more than casual stares from pedestrians and balcony sitters. Weak electric street lights, glowing for the first time in years, led them to the edge of the township and around the gentle curves that separated Dongo from its nearby twin, Musso.

"So far, so good," il Gallo said.

"It won't happen here," Dante said. "If they fall for the ruse at all, they'll be waiting farther down the lake."

They were halfway through Musso when they noticed some kind of a disturbance at a small sidewalk cafe near the center of town. A large crowd, standing half in the street, ringing the sidewalk and a low hedge, gawking at something. Beyond the tops of heads, Dante thought he saw broken glass in the cafe windows.

"You want to take a look?" il Gallo asked.

"Keep going," Dante said. "It has nothing to do with us."

They passed the hill where Dante's original roadblock had stopped the Fascist caravan, then wound down into open countryside, swinging along the edge of the lake. Il Gallo, sighing regularly, tried to speed up, but the heavily loaded treasure car labored at each incline. Darkness surrounded them until they reached Pianello, gave way briefly through town, then took over again.

At Crémia, there were more disturbing signs. Windows shuttered, doors closed, lights out. It was as though the village had been frightened off the streets and had closed in on itself. Il Gallo, shaken by the silence, by the absence of people, drove through town as fast as he could. The escort cars stayed right behind.

"Where will it happen?" il Gallo asked.

"In the countryside, most likely," Dante said. "They won't dare make a try for us in the towns. Too many witnesses."

Rezzonico came next, and Dante considered breaking his own rules. One stop wouldn't hurt. Here, in Rezzonico, David Landry and the American intelligence men might all be at Viviana's house by now, perhaps sitting down to dinner. Maybe if he stopped and explained the situation to David, the Americans would all pile into the old DeSoto sedan Pietro had given them and come along, providing extra firepower. And yet he knew he wouldn't stop. Ugo and his minions were Dante's problem, not a problem for the

Americans. Besides, David had been so long separated from Viviana. Let them stay together.

The dark stretch of road that sprawled between Rezzonico and Acquaséria was the most promising of all. Moonlight, which had given them at least some visual aid beyond the headlights, disappeared, swallowed by a black-and-silver cloud that drifted across the lake. Except for the cone of lights fanning out from the treasure car and similar cones from the escort cars, they could see nothing. Not the towering mountaintops, not the glint of moon or stars on the lake surface. Nothing. Il Gallo strained at the wheel. Dante repositioned his two weapons. They drove on, waiting for Ugo's men to appear.

Then, like dawn breaking through storm clouds, the weak, glittering lights of Acquaséria appeared around a curve and they drove out of the darkness once more and into civilization. Il Gallo relaxed visibly and said, "I may wet my pants if this goes on much longer."

Dante laughed. He, too, was feeling the nervousness of anticipation. "Don't worry," he said. "They're bound to try soon. Perhaps between Acquaséria and Menággio."

They passed through the center of Acquaséria, smiling foolishly at the people on the streets, allowing tense muscles a momentary rest, feeling warm and grateful toward perfect strangers. They even waved at a small knot of schoolgirls standing on the church steps.

As they neared the southern edge of town and began to tense, thinking of the stretch of darkness that awaited them beyond the town limits, an unexpected thing happened. A truck, a dilapidated, wood-burning truck, pulled out of a cross street just after il Gallo drove past and jerked to a halt, blocking the road behind them. The two escort cars, with no room to swerve around, screeched to a halt.

"Stop!" Dante shouted. Then, with horror, he recognized the truck through the rear window. It was the Lizard's borrowed bakery truck, the one that had disappeared with the first shipment of treasure the night before. "No, get going," Dante yelled. "Get going! Fast!"

Il Gallo, confused by the contradictory orders, nevertheless jammed his foot on the accelerator. The bottomed-out car, hanging low under its heavy load of treasure, groaned and crept forward, straining to pick up speed. The truck and the two stalled escort cars fell behind.

And another car, a black Fiat, nosed into the street after them. Dante watched it close the distance, coming fast. "God damn them!" he shouted. "Not like this!"

And the car drew closer. . . .

Day Eleven

Delle monete
il suon già sento!
L'oro gia viene,
viene l'argento;
in tasca scende:
eccolo qua.

I can already hear
the jingle of coins!
Gold is coming,
and silver too;
in pockets it falls:
here it is now.

—Rossini, *Il Barbiere*
  di Siviglia

1

The return of chaos left Landry feeling as helpless as a dust mote
tossed frantically near the center of a storm. Chaos was complete
when Pietro shouted at Luisa, "I'm sick of this treasure. It's cost-
ing me good people, and I want it off my hands."

Luisa had been weeping only moments before. Now she bowed
her neck like an animal at bay, and she and Pietro glowered at
each other. Viviana stepped to Luisa's side. Freddy Stefanini
stepped to Pietro's. Only X. B. Kavanaugh showed good sense.

The big man shambled in between and said quietly, "No. If they can start us arguing among ourselves, they've won. Let's all cool down and try to think."

It was a grim-faced Pietro who quickly apologized to Luisa and put a brotherly arm around her shoulders. There was a lot to cry about. Salvo shot down at a sidewalk cafe. Piccione missing. Dante's escort cars returned without him, and Luisa convinced that he was dead, too. Landry feared she might be right about Dante, but, like Pietro, he found it hard not to be appalled as well at the disappearance of a second shipment of treasure.

Viviana belted a blue robe tighter around her waist and nudged Pietro's arm from Luisa's slumped shoulders, replacing it with her own. "You will stay here with Franca and me," she told Luisa. "We will take care of you."

Luisa sobbed and shook her head vehemently. "No, Dante has died to protect the treasure. I must do what I can, as well."

Pietro turned exasperated eyes to the ceiling of Viviana's living room. "Luisa, you can't do anything. Your own life is in danger. Can't you understand that? You're the only one who can sign for the deposited currencies."

"I'll call the bank manager," Viviana said. "He's a friend of my father. I will tell him what has happened and warn him that the money is to be given to no one, no matter what the circumstances."

"You can't call anyone," Landry said. "That's Pietro's whole point. No one must know that he's brought Luisa here. A telephone call from you would be like putting an ad in a newspaper."

"But if I stay here," Luisa sobbed, "who will avenge Dante?"

"We will all avenge him," Pietro said. "I promise you that."

Luisa's red-rimmed eyes reddened afresh. "It was that man from Milan, that Comrade Ugo. He's the one. Salvo told me about their argument before he . . . before . . ." Her shoulders began to shake, sounds sticking in her throat.

Landry signaled to Viviana, and she was instantly joined by Franca, and the two women led Luisa up the stairs toward Viviana's bedroom, clucking and sympathizing. Women's lot, thought Landry. A woman always got the hardest job. He asked Pietro, "Did anyone see her at the roadblocks?"

Pietro waved toward the street. The shutters were closed and the drapes drawn, so Landry had to guess that the gesture was directed toward the big Bugatti touring car in which he had driven Luisa down from Dongo. "I hid her on the floorboards, under some potato sacks," Pietro said. "I assure you, no one save the people in this room know her whereabouts."

Kavanaugh and Creedmore both looked dubious. "Maybe not," Creedmore said, "but they know which way you were going. Those damned roadblocks are a pain in the ass. All someone has to do is ask whether or not you passed, and keep asking until they find one where you didn't, and they can pinpoint you easy."

Pietro looked startled. "Then I shall have the roadblocks removed."

Freddy Stefanini cleared his throat and said, "What about this Ugo guy? If he's responsible for these killings, he doesn't deserve to live."

"*If,*" Pietro said. "On such little words are tyrannies launched. We must be certain. I shall post men to watch the pensione where he has set up his butcher shop. I shall send others up and down the lake to seek information about the two missing shipments of treasure. But short of shooting him down without trial, and thus offering our own heads to Milan, I can do no more."

"What about the rest of the treasure?" Stefanini said. "While you waste time looking for proof, what's to keep this guy from charging in with his hoods and grabbing what's left?"

"That worries me as well," Pietro admitted. "I have been thinking of ways to protect it since the escort cars returned to report the ambush." He turned a look of grim determination on Landry. "David, I must ask you a great favor. I must ask you and your friends to remain on the lake for a time and take charge of the rest of the treasure."

"We can't guard that stuff," Kavanaugh said. "There aren't enough of us."

"There would be if you moved it," Pietro said. "If you could smuggle the rest of the treasure from the town hall and hide it, put it in some safe location known only to you, then Ugo would have to reconsider his position. As Americans, you would present an obstacle that even he would find difficult to surmount. He knows the American Army will be here soon. He wouldn't dare attack you."

Willoughby interrupted, "I hate to be the one who brings it up, but we're under orders. We're due to leave the lake this morning."

Landry looked at him dismally. "Captain Willoughby is right," he told Pietro. "We can't stay. Not without a change of orders. And that isn't likely. Not again."

"Sure it is," Stefanini said. "The honchos at headquarters just don't know what's going on out here. All we have to do is fill them in on what's happening and they're bound to give us a green light. I'll bet Viviana could find a hiding place for us. Her old man has property all over the lake. Across the border in Switzerland, too. If she can tell us where to stash the goodies, we wouldn't need more than a couple of guys at a time to keep an eye on it."

Pietro came as close to pleading as perhaps he ever would. "I know the treasure would be dangerous for you, David. And I am reluctant to ask any man to place himself in peril. But I must. Already my men and I have allowed so much of Mussolini's millions to sift through our fingers. We can't leave the rest in Dongo. It's too inviting, and the town hall too vulnerable. Nor can we take it down the lake, as Dante twice attempted. There is only the one road, so the route is too predictable. No matter what precautions we take, it is conceivable that we would be outwitted. Unless the treasure is moved, placed in your hands and hidden, more of us might die."

Stefanini said, "Come on, David, let's hit the radio. I can code up a message in minutes, explaining the situation. Even if they say no, we haven't lost anything."

Landry nodded. "Okay, we'll ask."

By the time Viviana came back downstairs, they were all in the library, where Stefanini kept the ancient radio. Stefanini had prepared a coded summary of the changing lakeside situation, and now the radio was warming up. The speaker crackled at them and Stefanini adjusted dials. He picked up the clumsy microphone and said, "Cue-tee-pee, cue-tee-pee."

"What's a cue-tee-pee?" Landry asked.

Stefanini fine-tuned the frequency setting and said, "It's part of the emergency Q-code. We borrowed it from the British. Cue-tee-pee is a shorthand way of asking them to accept a priority message." He pressed the transmitter button and repeated the three-letter combination twice more.

Viviana came to stand by Landry. He asked, "How's Luisa?"

"She's terribly upset, as I would be in her place," Viviana murmured. "This war you've fought and won just won't stay ended."

"What about your own war?" Landry asked. "I thought you'd done with fighting. If you hide Luisa here, you're right back in it."

"This time it is a war of my own choosing," Viviana said.

Stefanini tried again. "Cue-tee-pee, cue-tee-pee. Come on, you guys, give us an answer."

The radio was silent for a moment, then the speaker squawked and a voice responded, "Cue-are-vee."

Stefanini grinned. "Got 'em," he said happily. He gestured for the message sheet containing the prearranged cipher blocks and Willoughby handed it to him. Stefanini read them quickly into the microphone, breaking them into groups of five. When he finished, he turned and said, "Now we wait. It'll take them a minute or two to decode, then they'll give us a cue-pee-eff. That means message received. Pretty soon after that, we'll get our answer."

They hovered about the radio, but when the response came, it was two sets of letters, not one. The voice said dryly, "Cue-pee-eff. Cue-are-yew."

Stefanini's face sagged. "Aw hell," he said. "That does it. We're finished."

For a moment, Landry didn't understand. He said, "What do you mean? What did he say?"

"He gave us a cue-are-yew. That means they have nothing for us. They're gonna ignore our whole damned transmission."

Landry felt something inside his psyche creak and groan. He took the microphone from Stefanini. Stefanini started to object, but Landry punched the transmitting button and said, "This is David Landry. What the hell do you mean, you've got nothing for us? Don't you understand our request?"

The voice came back quickly. "Cue-pee-are, Lake Como. Do you read me?"

"He's telling you to stick to procedure," Stefanini whispered. "We're not supposed to talk in the clear."

"We haven't got time for your damned procedures," Landry told the microphone. "Listen, we need a change of orders. We can't leave the lake now."

"You are breeching radio security," the voice said. "Go to code immediately, Lake Como. Do you read me?"

"Yeah, I read you," Landry said. "Now you read me. The partisans are in trouble. Unless you want to explain a lot of dead friendlies, you'd better countermand our departure orders, and fast."

The voice said wearily, "I'm only the radio guard, Lake Como. If you want a change of orders, you'll have to appeal to a higher source."

"Then get someone," Landry said. He hesitated and pressed the microphone to his chest. "What were the names of those guys in Switzerland?" he asked Willoughby. "The two you said sent us here?"

Willoughby seemed amused. "Cornfield and Dulles," he said. "Cornfield would be better."

"Yeah, Cornfield," Landry said. He spoke into the microphone again. "Get Cornfield in there. I want to talk to him."

There was a shocked silence, then the voice spluttered, "You said his name. In the clear. Are you crazy?"

"Just get off your duff and get him," Landry said. "We'll wait."

There was another silence, a lengthy one. Then the speaker crackled again. This time it was a different voice, a more authoritative one. "This is Cornfield," the voice said. "Landry, what the hell's going on out there? My man says you've broken radio security."

"I had to," Landry said. "If you'll take the time to read the communication we just sent, you'll see why."

There was another pause, then Cornfield said, "Very well, I've read it. Please tell Captain Pietro that I sympathize, but your orders are unchanged. You'll have to leave the lake."

Landry stabbed the button again. "Listen, we've got close to forty million dollars in Fascist loot floating around here. Maybe more. Another forty million is already down the tubes. The partisans can't handle it by themselves. People are dying. You want that on your conscience?"

"I understand," Cornfield said softly. "And I'm sorry. I wish I could do something about it." He sounded as though he meant it.

Landry hesitated only a moment before he said, "Your signal is fading. Please say again." Then he leaned over Stefanini and askcd quickly, "Is there anything in that Q-code of yours that means an enemy is closing in and we have to break off?"

Stefanini swallowed. "That's a cue-yew-oh," he said. "But we don't use it unless there's imminent danger."

"What do you call this?" Landry took a deep breath and pressed the transmitting button. "Listen, Cornfield, we've got a cue-yew-oh here. We'll try to get back to you."

Cornfield came on again rapidly. "Hold it," he said. "Don't you pull that on me, Landry. Your orders are unchanged, do you hear? You've got two hours to . . ."

Landry flicked the power switch and the speaker went silent.

Willoughby smiled wryly. "Your radio etiquette leaves something to be desired," he observed. "But the end result is quite effective."

"What if they try to call us back?" Stefanini asked.

"You fixed the radio," Landry said. "So unfix it. Blame it on the German parts." He looked at the others. "Anybody doesn't want to go along with this, say so. Creedmore? Willoughby? Kavanaugh?"

Willoughby nodded.

Creedmore said, "Count me in. The way things stand, I'd just as soon give headquarters a little time to cool off. Like about five years."

Kavanaugh hesitated, then said, "Oh hell. Me too, I guess."

"Does this mean you will help us?" Pietro asked anxiously.

"We'll try," Landry said. "How much treasure remains to be moved? In bulk, I mean."

Pietro thought it over. "I would guess between six and seven hundred kilos, counting the rest of the gold bars."

Stefanini said, "My aching back. That's more than a thousand pounds."

"Perhaps less," Pietro said, as if worried that they might still back out. "I can give you some men to help, if you wish."

Landry shook his head. "No, if we go ahead with it, it's better that we move the treasure ourselves. That way, none of your partisans can be tempted or threatened to tell where we've hidden it. Viviana, can you help us find a place to stash everything?" She thought about it, then nodded affirmatively. "Good," Landry said. "That does it, then. We may as well get started."

Pietro beamed. "You won't be sorry, David. I promise you."

"I hope you won't be either," Landry said.

2

Veterano was exhausted by the time he reached Dongo, having walked down from the villages above Germasino, but he tried not to show it. He went straight to the Dongo town hall, intending to ask Pietro where he could find Landry and the Britisher, and was surprised when two of Pietro's partisans stopped him at the portals.

One of the partisans, a lanky ex-gardener named Menefrego, said, "You can't go in. No one can. Pietro is conducting confidential business with the Americans."

"Are David Landry and the Englishman with them?" Veterano asked. "I must see them. I have news."

"Pietro left orders that no one is to be admitted until they finish," the partisan said. He seemed puzzled by his own instructions.

"It's important," Veterano insisted. "David and the Englishman sent me to Garzeno themselves. They will want to hear what I have found."

The partisan looked at the closed doors, and his eyes lit up slyly. "Well, if it's important," he said. "Perhaps we shouldn't wait. Perhaps I will escort you inside myself."

They left the other man on guard and entered through the empty reception hall. The partisan obviously had no idea where Pietro and the Americans were sequestered, nor what they were doing, and he led Veterano back and forth through the building for several minutes, footsteps echoing oddly through the barren corridors, before they finally encountered two of the Americans, Freddy Stefanini and X. B. Kavanaugh, coming around a corner. Each of the Americans carried two gold bars, hunched over as though the small ingots were unbelievably heavy. Stefanini saw them and said, "Oops."

The partisan's face registered shock. "What are you doing with our gold?" he asked.

Pietro came to the head of the stairs and leaned across the bannister. "Menefrego?" he called. "Is that you?"

"Yes, Chief."

"You were supposed to stay outside," Pietro reminded him.

"I brought Veterano, from Dante's detachment," the partisan called back. "He has information for David and the Englishman."

Pietro sighed. "Very well. You might as well come up."

Stefanini and Kavanaugh grunted toward the inner courtyard with the gold ingots. The partisan watched them go, then gestured for Veterano to precede him up the stairs. When the partisan reached Pietro, he whispered, "Chief. The Americans. They're taking our gold."

"I know," Pietro said. "It's only for a short time. I will explain it later. I want you and some of the others to make sure everyone hears about it, once we are done here." He took them into the treasure room. Landry and the Britisher were busily transferring the last of the treasure to the doorway, readying it to go down. Tuono ranged back and forth, looking excited. He sniffed the partisan's trousers, wagged his tail at Veterano, then toenail-clicked his way into the corridor and down the stairs.

"They're taking it all," the partisan whispered in confusion.

"Shhh," Pietro told him. Then, "David, Veterano has asked to speak with you and Captain Willoughby. Have you a moment?"

Landry wrestled a gilt-framed triptych to the floor. "Sure," he said. "What's up, paesano?"

"I've just come back from Garzeno," Veterano said. "You remember what you sent me to find out? Well, I have found out. I bring news."

"Good news, I hope," Willoughby said. "We could use some."

Creedmore came into the room, followed shortly by Stefanini and Kavanaugh, puffing from the climb. Veterano watched them pick up the triptych. "Yes, the news is good," he said. "The partisan called Gualfiero. He is alive."

Kavanaugh looked up. "I'll be damned. Where? Did you bring him?"

Veterano shook his head. "He wouldn't come with me. He was

afraid. I had to promise I would say nothing to anyone of his hiding place. But he says he will meet with David. Alone. Tonight."

Creedmore frowned. "Alone? What the hell is that all about?"

"Yes," Landry said. "Why should he be afraid to come to us?"

"I don't know," Veterano admitted. "He wouldn't tell me. He wouldn't even talk to me at first. Not until I told him I was sent by David."

"How did you find him?" Stefanini asked.

"It was not easy," Veterano said. "No one in Garzeno would help me. So I hid above the village and waited. Early this morning, the brother left the grocery store with food. I followed. He went to a small cave. When I approached, he grew very angry. But the young one, Gualfiero, was only frightened. He thought I had been sent to kill him. I told him no, but he wouldn't believe. I had to let him hold my gun."

Pietro said disapprovingly, "I don't think I like this. It's bad enough that he pretended to be dead, but for him to suggest that a partisan, one of us, would come looking to kill him? Did he offer nothing in explanation?"

"Only indirectly," Veterano said. "He spoke briefly of an enemy, someone he saw on the trail, the day he was shot. He seems to think the man will try again to silence him."

"The traitor!" Kavanaugh said. "He saw him? Who? Did he say who it was?"

"Not to me," Veterano said. "He will speak of it only to David." The old man looked at Landry with a glint of new respect. "He says he remembers you well. From the old days, before Major Holloman came. He says you are a fair man. He trusts you. He says he has many things to tell you. But only you. He will meet you tonight, if you come alone."

"Where?" Landry asked.

"The cove north of Dongo, where the lake dips in toward the road," Veterano said. "The brother will meet you there. You are to show him something from me, a sign we have agreed upon, to prove your identity. Then he will take you to Gualfiero."

"What do I show him?"

Veterano glanced in embarrassment at the others. "I am sorry," he said. "The brother made me promise that no one but

David would see it." He dug an object from his pocket and kept it covered with a large calloused hand. "It bears the brother's mark, made by his own hand."

Landry took it. It was one of Veterano's shotgun shells. He transferred it to his own pocket. "What time do I meet them?"

"An hour after sunset," Veterano said. "You will walk alone across the top of the cliff. Once you show the sign to the brother, he will take you to a place where Gualfiero can see you, to make certain you are truly the right man."

Kavanaugh looked incredulously at Landry. "You aren't going?"

"I have to," Landry said. "If Gualfiero knows something about our informer, I've got to talk to him."

"We can't even be sure it's Gualfiero," Kavanaugh objected. "Veterano has never seen him. That ambush in the hills happened weeks before Veterano joined us. What if it's someone else? What if it's the informer himself? You could walk out there and get yourself shot."

Creedmore said, "Kavanaugh could be right, David. They get you out there in the darkness alone. They're the only ones who get a good look. It's too pat."

"Why should anyone set a trap for me?" Landry said.

Kavanaugh grimaced. "Why should Gualfiero pretend all this time that he's dead?" he countered. "If he knows who the informer is, why didn't he come tell us? And how did his brother get Holloman's watch? I don't like it one damned bit."

Willoughby said casually, "We might like it even less if this is on the up-and-up and Landry misses connections. Once we go into hiding with the treasure, the last thing we need is an informer running loose to spread the word."

"Are you saying the informer is one of us?" Kavanaugh asked angrily.

"Take it easy," Landry said. "That's not what he meant. But if there's a chance we can catch our traitor, we've got to follow it up. In the meantime, we've got the treasure to worry about. Let's get the rest of this stuff down to the DeSoto. I'd like to get set up in our new location and arrange a watch schedule before anyone figures out what we're up to. Veterano, will you help us with the loading?"

Veterano groaned inwardly, feeling the ache of fatigue in every bone, but he pitched in on the paintings and gold bars and some heavy sacks that he assumed, from their weight and the way they jingled, contained coins, perhaps even gold coins. Menefrego helped also, and they set up a constant stream, from treasure room to shiny car in the inner courtyard, like ants carrying pebbles along a preordained path. By the time they finished packing the car, Landry had worked out a guard schedule. He called them aside when they returned to the treasure room, all but Willoughby, who was still down in the courtyard with the last armful, and gave them their instructions. Veterano and the Britisher were to take the treasure to Velzo, a small mountain community above Menággio. There they would find a locked warehouse, an olive-oil storage facility that belonged to Viviana's father. As soon as Willoughby and Veterano were safely away, Pietro and his partisans would begin to spread the word that the remainder of the treasure had been placed in American hands. That, Landry predicted hopefully, would keep Ugo and his men off Pietro's back. Wesley Creedmore and X. B. Kavanaugh were to hole up for the afternoon and sleep, for they were to relieve Veterano and Willoughby at midnight, and keep guard until noon tomorrow, at which time Landry and Freddy Stefanini would take over. With luck, American troops would roll in from the south in the next day or two, and the treasure could be handed over to them for safekeeping. In the meantime, none of the ALOTs were to walk the streets if they could help it, nor were they to speak to strangers, nor even friends for that matter, and they were to exercise extreme care coming and going up the mountain to Velzo, to make sure they weren't followed. The same instructions applied to Veterano.

When he finished, Landry asked uneasily, "What's keeping Willoughby? He should be here by now."

"He was stuffing things in the back seat of the car, last I saw," Creedmore said.

They went to seek the Britisher, but he appeared before they reached the stairwell. He was at the far end of the second-floor corridor, checking doors, rattling knobs on some, opening others and looking inside. He saw them and his face twisted in mild vexation. "Has anyone seen Tuono?" he asked. "I can't find him anywhere."

"Jesus," Kavanaugh said. "We worry about him getting his throat cut, and he's only worried about that damned dog."

3

Word of the treasure transfer reached Ugo that afternoon, less than an hour after Veterano and Willoughby, minus the missing dog, drove away from the town hall in the heavily laden DeSoto. Ugo knew already that something unusual was taking place. Two of his men had reported Pietro's sudden closed-door policy at the town hall entrances, and had later reported the departure of the car and the scattering of the remaining American intelligence men. But it wasn't until Pietro and Menefrego hit the streets and began to inform the other members of their partisan band that the Americans now held the treasure that Ugo finally understood. When he heard, he exploded with fury.

"I won't have it," he stormed at Sandrino. "This is gross interference in Italian affairs."

Sandrino shrugged. "Captain Pietro requested the Americans' assistance, the way I understand it."

"He has exceeded his authority," Ugo snapped. "I want that treasure found and returned to Italian hands."

"Why not let them keep it?" Sandrino suggested. "We have enough. To try for the remainder would surely mean more deaths."

"I won't give it up," Ugo said. "We must have it all. Send men down the lake to ask questions. Americans will not be able to move about unnoticed. Once we've narrowed down their route, we can enlist the aid of Party members in the lakeside villages."

Sandrino flushed. "If we ask questions openly, Comrade Ugo, a number of people will know we have been looking for them. Remember, the Americans are technically our allies, no matter how far they carry their interference. Even if we find where they are hiding the rest of the treasure, we may have to kill one or two of them to get it. How do we explain their deaths if there is an official investigation?"

"Why this sudden reluctance?" Ugo asked him. "You've not questioned my methods before."

"We were dealing with partisans before," Sandrino said. "You could kill a battalion of them, and no one would even miss them. Americans are different. They keep records. If I'm going to kill any Americans, I want some kind of authority to back me up."

"Pin them with the *Spia Tedesca*," Ugo suggested.

"That's not good enough," Sandrino said. "No one would believe it. Even if they did, there would still be questions."

"Then we will cloak it with legality," Ugo said. "I'll summon members of the Como Federation and convene an Extraordinary Court of Assize this very evening. The lake partisans have proven themselves incapable of controlling the treasure. They've allowed two shipments to disappear already, and now they have placed the entire remainder in American hands, where it is certain to be confiscated by American troops. It is our patriotic duty, and the duty of the Court of Assize, to see that such criminal negligence is punished. By the time you and your men locate the treasure and remove it, I will have death warrants issued on every American and Italian traitor who has taken part in this seizure of state property."

Sandrino hesitated. "I'm not sure that will work. The Court of Assize is meant to deal with collaborators. The Fascists are all gone. With whom can you accuse the Americans of having collaborated?"

"Don't worry," Ugo assured him. "I can prove they've collaborated with enemies of the state from the beginning. The partisan leader Dante, for one. By the time the Federation members take their seats on the court, I'll have witnesses ready to swear that Dante assisted Fascists in making away with both earlier shipments of treasure, with the full knowledge and consent of the Americans. Dante, if he wishes, may speak in rebuttal."

Sandrino smiled coldly. "I don't think Dante can make it," he said. "Dante is currently visiting the fishes at the bottom of the lake and they may not be willing to let him go."

"That," Ugo said, "is a problem which concerns only Dante. We will leave a space for him on the court agenda. If he fails to appear before the court, it might even help convince the Federation members of his culpability."

Sandrino, who seemed to feel better now that Ugo had promised him a quasilegal assumption of authority, said, "He will fail to appear, comrade. I guarantee that."

4

Shortly before sunset, Viviana walked Freddy Stefanini out to the pony trap. She waited until he climbed up behind the little mare, then handed him a parcel of food for the men standing guard at the warehouse. "When will you return?" she asked.

"I'm not sure," he told her. "I may stay there for a while. One of the guys asked me to trade shifts." He took the bent whip from its holder. "You sure you'll be okay?"

"We'll be fine," Viviana said. But as the pony trap rolled up the street and she went back into the house, a feeling of utter gloom descended over her. From the kitchen, she could hear Franca and her stonemason friend laughing softly over some crude exchange. Though Viviana couldn't hear Luisa, she knew exactly what the girl was doing—sitting in the front room weeping. Landry wouldn't be coming this evening, off instead playing chief guardian dragon over the Fascist treasure, and Viviana was both glad and sorry. The darling fool was obviously on the verge of discovering that he wanted to marry her, and while Viviana had no intention whatever of marrying anyone, she found the prospect of a night without his warm presence like a portent of a long loneliness to come.

This, on an evening when the rest of the lakeside was celebrating the prospect of peace. Viviana would have liked to celebrate, too, but with Luisa sobbing before the front-room fire, any show of happiness on Viviana's part would have been inappropriate.

Viviana sighed so deeply that her shoulders seemed to collapse. She steeled herself to confront Luisa's listlessness once more and slipped into the front room. Viviana reached for the pull chain on the lamp Landry had repaired for her, but Luisa said, "No, please. No light."

Viviana clucked patiently. "Darling Luisa, you mustn't sit in the dark and cry so," she said. "You'll make yourself sick. And you really must eat something. How do you expect to keep your strength up, fasting this way?"

"What's the point?" Luisa said.

"The point is, life goes on," Viviana said. In the gloom, she made a face at the triteness of her words. Mere words would never help Luisa anyway. Street lights began to blink on outside, and a ray shining through the drapes caught Luisa's tragic expression and highlighted two fresh tears rolling slowly down her marred cheeks. Almost as if in answer to Viviana's needs, someone rapped at the front door. Viviana turned gladly. A caller, someone who might provide comfort for Luisa?

Franca bustled from the kitchen. Viviana listened to the sound of her voice at the door, low and questioning. A man's voice, heavily accented, responded. There was a moment of confusion, a thump as though the door had been pushed open against Franca's will, then Franca's voice rose in alarm, calling to Viviana. A jumble of booted feet scraped across the threshold. Franca screamed, one sharp, piercing note, then her cry was cut off, as though muffled by someone's hand. Heavy footsteps pounded through the foyer, rushing into the house.

Viviana's first thought was of Ugo and the danger to Luisa. Viviana bolted to the living-room door and tried to close it, but she was too late. Two men burst into the room, shoving her back, and swung automatic weapons from corner to corner as they checked to make sure the women were alone. Beyond them, visible in the hallway, came at least four more, dragging a wriggling Franca. The young stonemason rushed out of the kitchen, and one of the men smashed him with the butt of a Schmeisser. He toppled headlong across the hallway tiles that he had earlier been mending. He struggled to rise and the man hit him again.

"Don't!" Viviana cried. "You'll kill him!" She pushed her way to the door to help, but another of the men elbowed her roughly and sent her reeling to the floor. Someone spoke in guttural undertones, a command of some sort. Viviana, dazed, looked up. German? How could it be German? The Germans were all gone. And what could they want here?

The men crowded into the living room. Luisa, sitting stiffly on the edge of her chair with bloodless hands gripping the armrests, stared at them in complete surprise. "You?" she said.

Viviana tried to see to whom Luisa was speaking, but the leader of the men, a young blond with short-cropped hair and heavy-lidded eyes, stepped forward and gestured at Luisa. Two men jerked her to her feet and dragged her squirming toward the door.

"No, damn you! Leave her alone!" Viviana cried.

But the young blond leader only pointed at Viviana and said, "Take that one as well. We'll need her at the bank."

5

Landry approached the darkened cove north of Dongo as though he were treading eggshells, with frequent looks over his shoulder and his hand resting on the butt of his government-issue .45 automatic. Not that he suspected a trap, as Kavanaugh and Creedmore had earlier suggested. But if Ugo's people were truly on the prowl, as Pietro seemed to think, then Landry himself might make a tempting target for Ugo, walking alone on the dark lakeside. All Ugo needed was to grab one of them, any one, and he might well tear the information he needed out of his captive by force.

By the time Landry reached the cliff above the cove, he knew he was alone. No one could have followed him across the open expanses of rocky beach, nor up and down the spills of scree, without being noticed. It should have made him feel better, but the night was dark and full of strange sounds and Landry's nerve ends continued to tingle with every whisper of the wind, every lap of wave against the shore, every stir in the underbrush beyond the narrow highway.

He stood in the darkness for several minutes before walking the last fifty yards, trying to make out the irregular shapes at the top of the bluff. The cove wasn't really a cove. More like a dent in the long shoreline that hauled up among rocks at the foot of a small but fairly steep cliff. He saw one shape near a boulder, a dark blob that looked something like a man, and he stared at it intently, but even with a moon that kept dipping in and out of clouds, he couldn't be sure. Finally he gave up wondering and crunched across the open ground.

Sure enough, the blob moved. A figure stood and waited as he drew nearer, and a dark right arm lifted a bulky object. It turned out to be a fisherman's lamp with a metal face plate covering the light. Hinges creaked as the plate was raised, and a strong yellow light flared across the ground. Landry shielded his eyes with his hand.

A voice said, "You are the American who calls himself Landry?" Landry nodded and the light came closer. "I know you," the voice said. "You are the man who stole from me in the Dongo square."

At close range, light bounced from Landry's clothing and reflected softly across the man's face. Landry said, "And you are the man who had Major Holloman's watch."

"My brother gave it to me," the man said. "You had no right to steal it."

"I only want to ask you some questions," Landry said.

"Any questions you may have, you must ask of my brother. Have you something to show me?"

Landry produced the shotgun shell. The man took it and rolled it over in front of the lantern, staring at it. Then he handed it back.

"There is another test," the man said. He took Landry by the elbow and guided him to the edge of the bluff. They stood for a moment, listening. The soft, rhythmical plop-plop of oars drifted up from the water below and a small rowboat nosed into the cove. The man held the lantern by Landry's face. "Is this the one?" he called down to the rowboat.

After a brief silence, a voice, heavy with relief, called up, "Yes, yes, he's the one. Bring him down."

The man lowered the lantern and shook his head. "He will have to come down on his own. I will not stay. I want no part of this."

"Don't worry, Angelo," called the voice from the boat. "This is the American I told you about. We can trust him."

But the man clamped the face plate across the lantern and said, "Trust whom you wish, but do so without me." He turned and walked away, leaving Landry alone in the darkness on the edge of the bluff.

"At least he might have left us the light," murmured the voice from below. "It's good to see you, David. Come down. Be careful of the rocks. Some are loose."

Landry hesitated, uncertain, then began to lower himself over the edge. The face of the wall was steep, but filled with rock outcroppings that gave adequate hand and foot purchase. By the time Landry reached the pebbled bottom, the rowboat had nudged against the shore and the man held onto a jutting crag to keep it steady.

"Get in," he told Landry.

Landry hesitated again, just long enough to make out the slim, nervous face of Gualfiero Lusso in the dim moonlight, then stepped into the boat and said, "This is a welcome surprise. We thought you were dead."

"I know," the young man said. He picked up the oars and pushed away from shore. "I wanted everyone to think that."

"Why?"

"In a moment," Gualfiero said. He glanced nervously at the top of the bluff and began to stroke them out of the cove, into the lake proper. When they were fifty meters offshore, Gualfiero laid the oars in the bottom of the boat and sat back. "I feel safer out here," he said. "Are you sure you came alone?"

"I came alone," Landry told him. "Why, Gualfiero? What's going on? What are you afraid of?"

Gualfiero looked back at the dark shoreline. He was quiet for a moment, and Landry could hear a steady lap-lap and feel the slow, lazy bobbing of the rowboat. "Things changed after you left," Gualfiero said. His voice was tight, barely more than a whisper.

"So I hear," Landry said. "There is suspicion that we harbor an informer. Veterano says you saw him."

Gualfiero made a face. "I saw two. One of them was an American."

Landry said, "American? Are you sure of that?"

"I'm sure. Enough to know my life would have been worthless had they not thought me dead. How much do you know about the disappearance of the American leader, Major Holloman?"

"Only that he left Viviana's house with you and someone else."

"Luchino," Gualfiero said. "You remember Luchino? Long

nose, slumped shoulders? Never did anyone any harm in his life, except for a few Germans. They killed him. He was dead before he hit the ground. I would have died, too, but I saw it coming and ate sand. I got a bullet across the scalp, two in the leg, and this." He tugged his collar from his neck and showed Landry a deep, irregular scar.

"Who did it?"

"The Germans. They were waiting for us. They knew we were coming. It was a trap."

"Do you know who set you up?"

"I know one of them. We were supposed to stay at Viviana's house, but one of your people told Major Holloman to sneak out and meet him in the hills above Acquaséria. He said he had important information for us, but when we got there, Richter, The Drowner, was waiting. When we were at point-blank range, his people jumped out and started shooting."

"Who betrayed you?"

Gualfiero ducked his head. "The quiet one. Lieutenant Tucker."

"Tucker is dead," Landry said. "A week ago. Someone killed him in Dante's camp."

Gualfiero nodded. "I am not surprised. The other one probably did it. He would have killed me, too, had my brother not helped by telling everyone I was already dead."

"What makes you so sure there is another?"

"I saw him. He was with the Germans when they fired on us. Afterward, when they came into the open, I heard them talking. I think they were arguing about Major Holloman's money."

"Who was it?"

Gualfiero shrugged. "I can't be sure, David. I was dazed and bleeding badly. There was much, much blood on my face and in my eyes. Also, I was afraid to move. I thought it would be better if I pretended even then to be dead."

"What happened to Holloman?"

"They killed him. Not right away. He was wounded in the shooting, but he was still alive. I could hear him weeping. He had his arms around the satchel with the money, and he wouldn't let go when they tried to take it from him. That's when Lieutenant Tucker and the other one began to argue. I could see their legs as they wrenched it from him. Then they shot him. After that, I closed my eyes and held very still. I may have passed out."

Even though he'd already accepted the notion of Holloman's death, Landry found himself breathing hard at Gualfiero's brief confirmation of facts only surmised. "Holloman's body wasn't there when Dante's men found you," Landry said. "What happened to it?"

"The Germans hid it, I think. I remember Lieutenant Tucker's voice, very frightened. He begged the Germans to make it look as though Major Holloman had shot Luchino and me himself, as though he killed us and ran away with the money. The strange thing is that the major really intended to . . ." He stopped and cocked his ear. "What was that? Did you hear that?"

"Hear what?"

Gualfiero stared hard at the cove. "I thought I heard something, David. Are you sure no one followed you?"

"No, I wasn't followed. I was very careful."

Uneasily, Gualfiero returned his gaze to Landry and said, "Salvo and Captain Kavanaugh found us the next day. I guess they'd been sent to search for us when Major Holloman didn't come back. Luchino was dead. I almost was. I'd lost much blood. They buried Luchino and sent for Dante, then some people from Acquaséria carried me across the mountains to my brother. As soon as I was strong enough to think about it, I knew what would happen to me when Lieutenant Tucker and the other one found out I was still alive, so I convinced my brother that he should send word back to Dante's camp that I had died."

"Why didn't you tell the truth?"

"Accuse an American of treason? Come, David. Who would have believed such a thing? The word of an ordinary partisan against that of an American officer?"

"You should have warned the others," Landry said. "You owed them that."

Gualfiero dipped his chin guiltily. "I couldn't, David. I was afraid. Even if they had been willing to listen, I could only have identified Lieutenant Tucker. His friend would still be loose, and would still consider me a danger."

The wind shifted slightly and a sound, a kind of whimper, carried across the surface of the lake to them. Gualfiero's eyes grew wide and he said, "There it is again. You heard it, surely?"

"It's only a dog," Landry said.

But the sound made Gualfiero edgy. He picked up the oars. "I will take you back now," he said.

"Will you come to Dongo with me and talk to Pietro?"

"What good would it do?" Gualfiero said. He hauled on the oars and the rowboat began to move. "Il signore Tucker is dead, and I still don't know who the second man was."

"You needn't worry about your safety," Landry said. "Once you openly tell everything you know, there will be no reason for anyone to consider you dangerous. You can begin to live again."

"It would be joyous," Gualfiero admitted. He continued to stroke, grunting with the effort, and seemed to think it over. "Perhaps you are right. I will talk it over with my brother."

Landry frowned. "Listen, about your brother. There are still questions. He had Holloman's watch. Some of us were wondering how he got it."

"I gave it to him," Gualfiero said. "In partial payment for his help in hiding me. My brother is a practical man. He likes to keep things on a practical plane."

"How did you get the watch?" Landry asked. "You couldn't have taken it from Holloman's body. The body was gone. You said so yourself."

Gualfiero rested on the oars for a moment and the boat continued to glide toward the cove. "You suspect me, David? You think I have not told the truth?"

"Hell, I believe you, Gualfiero. I'd just like an answer."

"Major Holloman gave it to me before we left Viviana's house to meet Lieutenant Tucker. It was a present. Do you believe that?"

"If you say so. But why? It was an expensive watch."

"Not so valuable as the money he carried. That is the strange thing of which I spoke earlier. I told you Lieutenant Tucker wanted the Germans to make it look as though Major Holloman had run away. The truth is, Major Holloman actually intended to run. He asked me before we left if I could show him how to cross the mountains into Switzerland. I think he was frightened because the Germans had captured Luisa and the others. I think he worried even then that someone was betraying us. We were to meet the lieutenant on the trail above Acquaséria, as though nothing was wrong, but as soon as we completed our business with him, the major wanted me to send Luchino back to camp and help him across the border with the money. I think he intended to put it in a bank and hide until after the war."

"How do you know that?"

"Well, I don't really. But he seemed very nervous, and toward the end, those last few days, the money became an obsession with him. He wouldn't put it down, not even to eat. When Lieutenant Stefanini left Viviana's house to try to help Luisa and Lieutenant Creedmore escape from the prison in Tremozzo, the major refused to go with him. The major didn't want to let the money out of his sight, not even long enough to help his own comrades. I think he would have let us all die, rather than lose the money."

The boat had drifted into the cove, and Gualfiero dipped his oars to guide them to the narrow, pebbled landing. Landry hunched forward, his mind busy assimilating this new information. A question formed and he opened his mouth to ask it, but before he could speak, someone or something moved at the top of the bluff, dislodging a chip of stone. It rattled down the face of the bluff and plunked into the water. Gualfiero froze the oars in mid-stroke. Landry hesitated, then ripped the .45 out of his shoulder holster.

They sat very still for a moment, staring at the dark rim above them. At first there was nothing, then a shaggy, long-eared shape nosed into sight and they could hear a dog snuffling. It seemed to catch their scent. Instantly the ears pricked up and the dog let out a happy yelp.

"That's Tuono!" Gualfiero gasped. "What is he doing here?" He cupped his hands to his mouth. "Tuono! Here, boy! We're here."

"Quiet!" Landry hissed. "Someone might hear you!"

"But that's Tuono," Gualfiero said. "I'd recognize his bark anywhere. Here, boy! Down here!" A frenzied yapping answered him.

Alarm drilled through Landry's brain. He knew it was possible that Tuono, off on a carouse, had followed their scent to the cove, or even happened across them by accident. But it was more likely that he had not.

"Pick up the oars," Landry whispered. "Get us out of here."

"Why?" Gualfiero said. He reached hesitantly for the oar handles, but kept the blades out of the water. "What is bothering you, David? It's only . . ."

Then, out of the shadows above them, something dark and heavy tumbled through the air and clattered to the bottom of the rowboat. Landry twitched in surprise and stared at it. A gray metal object with a wooden handle rolled toward the center of the boat. It was hissing.

For a horrified moment, Landry was frozen to his seat, unable to speak. Then he yelled, "Grenade! Jump!" He launched himself backward, arms and legs flailing, expecting Gualfiero to do the same. But Gualfiero seemed too stunned to move. Even as Landry plunged into the water, he could see Gualfiero's hands still gripping the oars.

The water closed over Landry. It was as though it burst around him. There was a jolting roar and the lake water bear-hugged him, belted his eardrums, crushed the air from his lungs. His body was dashed down, flipping head over heels. He almost lost consciousness, but the first gulping swallow sent him into a panic and he began to struggle and kick frantically, clawing for the surface.

He broke clear moments later, groggy from concussion, lungs screaming for breath. He splashed and choked, hurting, and saw what was left of the rowboat, a half-disintegrated shell and scattered bits of smoking debris, bobbing in water that had been churned white by the explosion. There was no sign of Gualfiero.

Dazed, Landry struck out for the shore, arms chopping the water almost automatically. He thought he could hear voices calling, but it could have been the ringing in his ears. Something in his numbed frontal lobes kept telling him he should be swimming in the other direction, away from shore, but he couldn't remember why. All logical thought seemed shut off.

After what seemed forever, his arms and knees touched solid ground and he pulled himself onto the pebbled beach, struggling for air. He rolled onto his back, water squelching from his clothing, and sucked several deep breaths into his lungs.

As he lay below the cliff, trying to remember where he was and why, footsteps approached along the edge of the cove, as though someone had come down to the beach to help. Moments later,

something warm and wet touched his cheek. He opened his eyes
and saw Tuono crouched above him, tongue lapping the air.
There was a rope leading from Tuono's neck to a hand. A man's
hand. The hand was connected to a muscular body, topped by a
hazy face with a cloth cap pulled low over the eyes. Another
hand, barely visible beyond Tuono's straining head, held a Mauser
automatic pistol.

The hazy face spoke to Landry, guttural words that ended with
rising inflection. Landry listened, not understanding, and only
after a second of confusion did he realize that the man had spoken
in German. Landry tried to sit up, but his arm slipped from beneath him and he felt his head dropping back among the pebbles
and rocks in harmless slow motion.

On the bluff overlooking the inlet, Scharführer Fritz Knaust
waited. He could hear the three enlisted men as they scraped
along the shoreline, searching for survivors. Knaust didn't really
expect them to find any, not after that explosion, and he was eager
for them to finish and climb back up before the sound drew anyone from the direction of Dongo. But when Corporal Puhler led
the dog toward the outer edge of the cove, it began to whine and
tug at the rope, and Knaust reluctantly began a descent to see
what, if anything, the dog might have divined.

As he lowered himself down the rocky face of the bluff, Knaust
heard Puhler speak to someone, a soft, low question, answered by
a groan and the sounds of slippage in the rocks, a figure struggling
to get up, but failing, obviously falling. Then Puhler's voice rose.
"Sergeant? This one is alive. Shall I finish him?"

Knaust dropped down to the waterline and cocked his weapon,
then hurried toward Puhler and the dog. Knaust could see another
shape at Puhler's feet, a man stretched out on his back. The dog
pulled against the rope, trying to reach the prone man.

"He's still alive," Puhler told Knaust again. "He must have
jumped clear at the last moment."

Knaust bent over the motionless figure and found himself looking into the face of the American, Landry. He knew what his answer should be. Richter had long since promised this American's
death, and now would be an easy time to deliver it, with the
American barely conscious, and Puhler to pull the trigger. But the

American groaned again and his eyes fluttered open and tried to focus, and Knaust saw only a lonely railroad trestle a century ago, and hands wrapped around an American Thompson submachine gun. He remembered the moment of indecision, followed by a sudden, unexpected moment of compassion.

"Shall I finish him?" Puhler asked once more.

Knaust spent his own moment of indecision, with logic and conscience debating silently, unevenly. Then he frowned and said, "No, let this one live. We'll take him back to Major Richter."

6

The decaying villa squatted in moonlit darkness among lemon trees and dry, untended camellia bushes, high on a hill overlooking the sleeping town of Cadenabbia. Landry, his arms gripped by two of Knaust's enlisted men, stumbled up the driveway and wondered why he had been brought here. Plaster and paint had flaked off the front wall in great measled patches, and windows, many boarded up, others agape with broken glass, stared like blind eyes at the dark sky above the lake. Along the rim of the driveway and in the ruined garden where flowers were meant to thrive, weeds grew thick and tangled. The abandoned villa had a name among the townspeople below, though neither Landry nor the villa's current German inhabitants were aware of it. People in Cadenabbia, mindful that the villa had been empty since its last owner died by his own hand in a Milanese insane asylum, called it the Villa Triste, or Sad Villa. Most of them refused to go near it. Some even thought it might be haunted.

Landry paused to catch his breath, but one of the mufti-clad Germans yanked him on toward the building. An orange moon faded behind clouds as they walked, and they picked their way through darkness to a set of rubble-strewn steps. At a word from Knaust, one of the Germans tied Tuono to a weathered pillar, then shoved Landry up to the front door. Planks, once nailed across the doorway to keep the curious at a distance, had recently been ripped from the jamb and left in a heap on the veranda.

Sergeant Knaust spoke hurriedly to his men before they went in. Landry was able to make out two names, Richter and Stenzel. Richter, of course, was a name Landry knew, the SD major who had once commanded the security detachment in Cernobbio, the man responsible for so many partisans dumped into the Cernobbio vortex. Stenzel, it seemed, was also an officer, an Untersturmführer who acted as Richter's No. 2. From the hushed way Knaust spoke of them, it sounded as though he feared he might have made a mistake in allowing Landry to live, and now was worried about facing the consequences.

The conversation ended. Two of the enlisted men pushed Landry into a dark hallway. A soft glow of candlelight came from a room down the hall, and voices, murmuring in German, wafted through open double doors. Knaust whispered to the enlisted men and they turned Landry loose and retreated toward a stairway. Knaust nudged Landry on down the hall.

"What was that all about?" Landry asked in Italian.

Knaust didn't answer for a moment. There was trouble in his deep-set eyes, and his protruding ears seemed attuned to the murmurs from the candlelit room. Finally he said, "I've done all I can for you, my friend. From now on it's up to Major Richter and Lieutenant Stenzel. We will wait for them in the detention room." He prodded Landry toward a closed door on the left. "Open it," Knaust whispered. "You will have a moment to gather your thoughts before Corporal Puhler fetches the major."

The room was pitch-black, with no hint of light, not even from the windows. Landry groped his way inside.

"There should be a candle," Knaust said. He pressed a box of matches into Landry's hand. "Find it. Don't try anything. I will be here with my weapon on you."

Landry lit one of the matches and held it head high. The room was sizable, sparsely furnished, perhaps a sitting room at one time, though there were no longer any chairs or sofas. The carpets had long since been taken up and the windows boarded and he could see faded squares on the walls where paintings had once hung. A broken table lamp leaned on its side near an empty fireplace, and at the far end of the room, curtain rods stretched forlornly above the boarded windows, naked and useless without their curtains. On the floor beneath one of the windows rested a dead pot plant, dirt so packed and dry that the surface had cracked. Farther to the left, a bare, grimy mattress lay on the floor, and beside it, sitting atop a wooden box, an unlit candle stub.

Landry started toward the candle and heard someone moan. It was only then that he realized he and Knaust were not alone in the room. Landry lit another match, and in the sudden flare he saw a small, blindfolded figure huddled on the far side of the mattress. Landry hurriedly lit the candle, then rolled the figure toward the light and removed the blindfold. It was Luisa. Her face was badly battered. Trickles of blood seeped from her mouth and both nostrils.

"Luisa?" he said. "Luisa, can you hear me?" She winced when he lifted her, and he quickly laid her back, worrying that he might have hurt her by moving her. Rage welled up in his chest, and he hissed at Knaust, "You bastards! What the hell have you done to her?"

Knaust looked as surprised and shocked as Landry. "I didn't know about this," he said. He leaned closer. "I didn't even know she was here. They must have brought her after I left for the cove."

Luisa coughed, a soft, tearing whisper. Landry looked across the room at the fractured lamp. "Bring light," he demanded.

Knaust actually started toward the lamp, then caught himself. "It will do no good," he said. "There is no electricity." He sounded apologetic.

Landry picked up the candle and held it close. Both of Luisa's eyes were swollen nearly shut. Someone had beat her unmercifully, not only about the face, but on the body as well. Landry touched a finger to her throat, but the pulse was faint and irregular. She seemed to be hanging to life by the merest of chances.

"She needs medical attention," Landry said. "Urgently."

"We have no doctor," Knaust told him. "And I doubt seriously that Major Richter would allow us to summon one."

"She'll die if she doesn't get help," Landry said. "She may die anyway." He huddled over her, feeling impotent. "Haven't you at least got some morphine? Something to cut the pain?"

"I could try to find something," Knaust offered. "Perhaps in the dormitory."

But before Knaust could move, Corporal Puhler brought two

men to the door. One was a tall, older man, splendidly dressed in tweeds with leather patches at the elbows. He looked like a Scotch laird, come to welcome guests to his estate. Landry guessed him to be Richter. That meant the other, a younger man with short blond hair and drowsy-looking eyes, was probably the Lieutenant Stenzel about whom Knaust had warned him.

Knaust jumped to attention and started to stammer, but the older man cut him off with a gesture. The older man came across the room toward Landry, the younger man following at his heels. The older man spoke briefly to Knaust in German, apparently a quick reprimand, for Knaust's face colored and his eyes dropped. Then the man turned a solemn expression on Landry. In fluent Italian, he said, "My apologies, Captain Landry. This is most lamentable. But the sergeant should have known better."

"You know my name?" Landry said.

"A close companion of yours has identified you," the man told Landry. "I fear your fate has been sealed for some time."

"What companion?"

Major Richter, for that was undoubtedly who the man was, smiled and said, "That isn't important at the moment. The important thing is that this is a very busy night for us, and I have no time for you. I must leave shortly, but I will leave Sergeant Knaust and Lieutenant Stenzel to rectify this unfortunate mistake."

"And I'm the mistake?"

"Just so," Richter said.

"How are they to rectify it?"

"I fear they will have to take you outside and shoot you," Richter said. "I wish there were some other way. You've given us quite a run. But I have made a promise."

"I certainly wouldn't want you to break a promise," Landry said.

Richter tilted his head. "Sarcasm, Captain Landry?"

"Only facing facts," Landry said. He looked down at Luisa and his jaw tightened. "I've seen how you bastards keep your promises."

Richter sighed. "I am not responsible for that, Captain Landry. I had her brought here, but I had no idea this would happen. None of us did. We don't brutalize women, no matter what you might think."

"That's a crock. You've had your hands on her before."

"Ah yes, but that was different. That was war. To elicit information, we have been known to apply pressure. But this woman was savagely beaten, even after she gave us what we wanted. She will die, no doubt, and for that you must thank one of your own people. We had nothing to do with it."

"You're lying," Landry said.

"Why should I? I admit that I detest partisans. I consider them the dregs of humanity, the coffee grounds at the bottom of our bubbling wartime pot. And I have little regard for their women, either. But this happened after we withdrew from the room. The same traitor who has delivered so many of your comrades into our hands, the traitor who has informed us of your every movement—that same person is alone responsible for what happened to this unfortunate girl."

A motor sound crept up the hill and pulled into the ruined garden outside. Richter listened to it, then spoke briefly to Corporal Puhler. Puhler clicked his heels and disappeared.

"We will be leaving shortly," Richter said to Landry. "I'm sorry you and I couldn't have met under better circumstances."

"You're going to kill me now," Landry said. It was a statement, not a question, and oddly, he felt resigned to it.

Richter smiled in wry amusement, then shook his head. "As a matter of fact, that will have to wait until we are gone," he said. "Another friend of yours is being held in the car that just returned. A rather close friend, I am told. I've asked Corporal Puhler to bring her inside. I want her to see you, to know that we have you, but I'd rather she not realize what is to happen to you later. I would appreciate your silence on the matter. For her safety, as well as your own."

Dread boiled up inside Landry. "What are you talking about? Who have you got?"

"You'll soon see," Richter said. "We have further need of her, once our work on the lake is done. I'm hoping her concern for your well-being will persuade her to co-operate. She might not be willing if she knew you were to die anyway."

Landry started to speak, but Puhler came back to the door with two Germans and a woman. It was Viviana. Her eyes stared blankly ahead, face empty, as though she was in shock over what she had already seen this night.

"Viviana!" Landry said.

Her eyes flickered. For a moment there was only confusion in them, then her chin came up and she peered into the room, seeking him. "David?" she said. "David, are you here?"

"Damn you!" Landry bellowed at Richter. "She has nothing to do with any of this. If you hurt her . . ."

"At the moment, she is quite valuable to us," Richter said. "As soon as we've kept our last rendezvous, she will lead us to a place of safety. After that, who knows? Perhaps we'll even turn her loose."

Viviana squirmed at the doorway. "David, they have Luisa. And the bank. They made me . . ."

Richter gestured curtly, and Puhler clamped his hand over Viviana's mouth. She struggled for a moment, then closed her eyes and stopped fighting. Richter said, "Good-by, Captain Landry. I leave you in the capable hands of the sergeant and Lieutenant Stenzel." He nodded to Knaust and the young man with heavy-lidded eyes, then headed for the door, signaling the others to follow him outside with Viviana.

Knaust leaned close to Landry and said, "I'm sorry. I tried."

The young lieutenant waited until he heard the car engine start up again, turned to look at Landry. "I'm sorry," the lieutenant said in Italian. "The major insists that the, ah, adjustment be made before Sergeant Knaust and I join him in the mountains. Perhaps it would be better if we finished it at once. Sergeant, will you take him outside and . . ."

Knaust opened his mouth, closed it, opened it again. "Sir, he once had a chance to kill me, and didn't."

"I know," the lieutenant said. "Nevertheless, you are still a soldier. You must obey Major Richter's orders."

As the lieutenant spoke, Luisa became restless. It was as though his German-tinged Italian had touched an exposed nerve. Her head moved from side to side and her hands clutched at Landry's sleeve. A low, hollow moan, like a small animal in desperate pain, bubbled through puffy lips. "Help me," she said.

"Easy," Landry told her, trying to reassure her. "Hold on."

She didn't seem to hear. The restlessness increased. "It's a lie," she mumbled. "All a lie." Then, with frightening suddenness, her backbone arched in a spasm and she screamed.

Knaust's cheeks turned white. "My God, what's wrong with her?"

"I don't know," Landry said helplessly.

Landry gripped her shoulders, trying to hold her still. Knaust quickly laid his weapon aside and knelt on the opposite side of the mattress. It took both of them to quiet her. After a moment, her eyelids parted and dilated pupils cast about from face to face. "All a lie," she panted. "He's alive. I saw him."

"Who's alive?" Landry asked her.

Her shoulders stiffened and she went into convulsions again. "No, please," she wailed. "No more! I've given you everything!"

"Luisa," Landry said urgently. "It's me. David. Try to be calm."

Her pupils darted to and fro feverishly, then came to rest on his face. She seemed to recognize him. "The bank," she said. Her hand clawed at his wrist. "They made me sign the papers. They want the rest of the treasure. You must stop them."

Landry took her hand. "Yes, I'll stop them."

The young lieutenant said in a shamed voice, "I regret this, Captain Landry. I know it doesn't help, but I regret it all, particularly my part in it."

"Be quiet," Landry said. "When she hears you, she starts that thrashing." But Luisa seemed to have lost consciousness again. Landry looked up at the lieutenant. "Who did this to her? Tell me his name."

"To what purpose?" Stenzel said. "You will be unable to do anything about it. You must die, as this poor girl is bound to do."

Knaust raised troubled eyes. "Lieutenant, what about the peace directive from Bolzano? The war is over, as of tomorrow. At least for us. Can't we let him go?"

Stenzel shook his head. "We are still in a state of war until two o'clock tomorrow afternoon, Sergeant." He hesitated. "Nevertheless, I can understand that it might be difficult to kill a man who has shown you compassion. If the task is too much, perhaps I will do it for you."

Knaust seemed almost relieved. "Thank you, sir."

Luisa moaned again and her hand reached out feebly. Landry took it in his own. "What about the girl?" he asked the two Germans. "Can't you do anything for her?"

"What remains to be done?" the lieutenant said. "You know what the end will be." He stared at Luisa's hand, held tightly by Landry. "I suppose we need not carry out the major's orders instantly. She won't last long. And I do feel a moral culpability for what has happened to her. It was I who fetched her here. Perhaps we can give you a few minutes. Then at least she will die with a friend at her side."

Knaust said, "She's in such pain, Lieutenant. I was about to go look for something when you and the major came in. I may at least have some codeine tablets in my kit. A prescription for a toothache."

"Get them," Stenzel said. To Landry, "As for you, if you are a religious person, speak to your Maker. Pray that the girl dies within fifteen minutes. I can give you no longer. Say a word for me as well, for having to do as I must. Don't waste your time trying to escape. It's quite impossible. The windows are boarded; the door will be locked. Just do what you can for the girl and prepare yourself for my return."

Landry heard the key turn as the door closed behind Stenzel and the sergeant. He sat back on his haunches and listened to their footsteps, then gently released Luisa's hand and tried the door. Locked, as Stenzel had said it would be. Landry looked back at Luisa, considering what, if anything, he could do to comfort her. But he also considered alternatives. If he could find a way out, perhaps he could carry Luisa down to Cadenabbia, maybe even find a doctor in time. He surveyed the room quickly, seeking something, anything, that might offer some hope of escape. Heavily boarded windows. Lamp on its side by the fireplace. Pot plant. Mattress, with its small bundle of broken humanity. No, don't look at Luisa. Postpone grief. Keep a clear mind. Fifteen minutes. Perhaps less. He would need every second.

He emptied his pockets, looking for something that might work to his advantage. Handkerchief. Comb. Key to Viviana's house. The shotgun shell with Angelo Lusso's mark on it. A few Italian coins. He paused and stared at the shotgun shell. Slightly damp to the touch, from his dousing in the lake. The glimmer of an idea began to form. Would it work? Would the powder be dry enough?

He knelt on the floor near the candle and spread his handkerchief. He worked quickly, using Viviana's house key to pry the cardboard plug out of the shotgun shell. Luisa moaned again, restlessly, but he forced himself not to listen. If he was to be of any use to her, he had to keep at it. He poured shot into his hand, then pried the air-cushion out of the shell casing and tapped powder onto the center of the handkerchief. A few grains stuck to his fingers, but the bulk of it seemed dry. He spread it across the handkerchief evenly and thinly, to allow air to get to it, at least for the few minutes he had left.

He put the loose shot into his shirt pocket, then fetched the lamp and, after some hesitation, the dead pot plant. He quickly dismantled the lamp, unscrewing the base from the hollow tube that bore the wiring, then removed the bulb and socket from the top and reeled the wire out of the tube. It was metal of some kind, perhaps brass. Straight. About a half-inch bore. A small aperture at one end, where the electric cord had emerged.

Footsteps moved back toward the door, and Landry stiffened, startled. Could his allotment of time already have passed? Quickly, he shoved the brass tube under the edge of the mattress and picked up the candle, carrying it to the far side of the room so no one would see the handkerchief with its layer of gunpowder. The key turned in the lock. Landry stood still, waiting.

It was Knaust. The sergeant leaned through the door and said, "I am sorry. I couldn't find the codeine. There was only this. Some aspirin. It isn't much, but . . ." He held out both hands. Six white tablets rested in the palm of one and a glass of water in the other.

"Anything might help," Landry said. He took the pills and water and waited for the sergeant to close the door. But Knaust continued to stand there, looking miserable. "Something else?" Landry said. His mind screamed for the sergeant to go away, to leave him so he could get on with it.

"I offer my regrets for this great misfortune," the sergeant said. "Major Richter intends to take prisoners. I heard him say so. We will need them to help with the . . ." He stopped and swallowed. "I'm sorry the major did not elect to make you one of them. The lieutenant has agreed that I need not watch. This is the last time we will see each other. Please, I beg your forgiveness for not having done more."

"You did what you could," Landry said.

Knaust withdrew. The door closed. The key turned once more. Landry looked at the aspirin tablets in his hand. How paltry, how pathetic. But he carried them to the mattress. He set the candle next to Luisa. Then he saw that her eyes were half open. The pupils, glazed and dull, stared back at him, unseeing. He felt quickly for a pulse, but found none.

For a moment, Landry couldn't move. A film of moisture leaped to his eyes, clouding his vision, and a feeling of self-reproach, just as uncontrollable, clouded his mind. Somehow, at some passing moment, while he worked hurriedly, unthinkingly at her side, she had died. Alone. As alone as if he'd never been in the room.

He may have wasted a full minute, kneeling beside her, trying to put a clamp on his feelings of guilt. He even gave brief consideration to giving up, to slumping against the wall and waiting for what was to happen. But then he thought of Viviana and of what the German major had told him about Luisa, that it was one of his own people, an American or a partisan, who had done to her what had been done. Shame became anger, and guilt shaded into resolution. A sudden hunger for vendetta, the ageless, cleansing vengeance of the Italians, formed calluses over his emotions. The time to mourn would have to come later.

He stood and studied the room again, finding it hard to see through the sheen of tears that, irrationally, would not go away. He wiped his eyes angrily and clamped his jaw, taking strength from flowering hatred. Something for wadding and something to use as a ramrod. The mattress would provide the wadding. He could use Viviana's key or perhaps his belt buckle to dig it out. Ramrod? He moved to the boarded windows and took down one of the slender curtain rods. With everything around him, he jammed one end of the lamp tube into the dry, packed earth of the flower pot, twisting until the tube was solidly in place and the small aperture rested a fraction of an inch above the dirt. Then he wound the loose electric cord around the tube for extra strength. Though he worked feverishly, it seemed to take forever to finish.

The door would open at any moment. Stenzel would come in, and it would be over.

But suddenly the crude weapon was done and the door was still closed. Slowly, carefully, he picked up his handkerchief by the corners, funneling the powder into the tube. He used a tuft from the mattress as wadding and rammed it down into the tube to pack the powder, holding his thumb over the side aperture so none would be forced out. How much time left? A minute? Less? Don't think about it. Don't think about anything. He took the shot from his pocket and cupped his hand to the tube to pour the shot in, then tamped it down with another wad of mattress stuffing.

When it was ready, he carried it to a point about five feet from the door. He sat on the floor and braced the pot plant between his legs, aiming the open end of the tube toward the door. He poised the candle flame above the thumbhole. And waited.

Now came the difficult part. With his hands no longer occupied, his mind began to work. It touched on Luisa and he shook it away. It touched next on Viviana, and he shook that away as well. He thought about the young German lieutenant, a decent-seeming man whom he was going to do his damndest to kill or incapacitate, but he knew he had to try or otherwise die himself. His mind moved then to the things that could go wrong, and he began to sweat. What if the powder wouldn't ignite? What if he missed? There would only be the one chance. What if . . .

Softly, ever so softly, he heard footfalls in the hallway outside the door. Stenzel's voice, somewhat sad, called out in Italian, "Captain? Are you ready?"

Landry looked at the candle in his hand. Could he bring himself, even to protect his own life, to strike at Stenzel without warning? Could he actually touch the candle to the powder, when it was no better than shooting a man in the back? He swallowed, uncertain of the answer, and said, "I'm ready."

Doubt, misgivings, indecision, all vanished the moment the door swung open. Stenzel, no fool, stood at a crouch with his pistol extended before him, as though expecting Landry to come leaping through the air at him. When he saw Landry on the floor with an odd tubular contraption in front of him, he flinched visibly and stabbed the pistol downward and pulled the trigger. Flame burst from the pistol barrel and a slug sizzled by Landry's ear. Instantly, without further hesitation, Landry touched the candle to the powder aperture. Everything seemed to happen at once. The powder caught and blew such a backwash that the candle went out, plunging the room into darkness. Burning powder flared out of the fusehole and seared Landry's wrist. At the same moment, the slender tube flashed and bucked in Landry's grasp. The German lieutenant, backlit by candlelight from one of the rooms across the hall, spun halfway around, crying in pain, and the pistol clattered to the floor.

Landry leaped for the pistol as Stenzel threw his arms over his face and staggered blindly into the corridor. Landry followed, and saw the German stumble to his knees. A vague half light from the double-doored room across the hall fell on Stenzel's face. It had the raw-meat look of hamburger, but without the massive damage a real shotgun might have done. There was still a face—nose, cheekbones, chin—but he would never look the same.

Someone rattled down the stairs at the front of the house. Landry whirled to see Sergeant Knaust appear, holding a Schmeisser. Landry aimed the pistol at him. "Don't try to stop me!" he warned.

Knaust looked from Landry to Stenzel writhing on the floor. "The girl?" he asked.

"She's dead," Landry told him.

Knaust sighed like an old man. "Then go," he said.

Landry put a hand against the wall and inched toward the doorway, step by step, pistol leveled at the sergeant. When he reached the door, he hesitated, then said, "I'm taking the dog."

"Of course," Knaust said. "From you I would have expected nothing else." Landry started to back through the door, but Knaust spoke up once more. He said, "This makes us even, Herr Rumpelstiltskin. Let us try never to cross paths again."

Day Twelve

*Ma prudenza! . . . Siete cinto
di nemici . . .*

Take care! . . . You are surrounded
by enemies . . .
                    —Cilea, *Adriana Lecouvreur*

1

A six-dog pack of local mongrels, out foraging in the night to
avoid interference from humans, sniffed at both doors of a dark,
graceless, concrete-block building on the upper edge of Velzo,
then noticed the five men standing in the shadows on the far side
of the narrow street and quickly trotted away.

The men ignored the dogs, watching the building instead.
Above a sliding, corrugated-iron door hung a paint-peeled sign
bearing the name "Armellini." Another door, smaller, opened into
a corner office, and it was this one at which Ugo squinted in the
darkness, finding himself peculiarly tense. "Are you sure this is
the place?" he asked Sandrino.

Sandrino wiped a trace of perspiration from his upper lip and
said, "Yes, comrade. They changed the guard at midnight. Renso
saw two Americans go in. Isn't that right, Renso?"

One of the men behind them edged closer. "Yes, sir. The car
passed through Menággio about an hour ago, and turned up the

mountain toward Velzo. I followed. They came here. I sent word
to you as quickly as I could." His breath was foul, like an animal's
in a zoo, or like a human's before breakfast, and Ugo turned his
face away.

"Are you sure they were Americans?" Ugo asked him.

"Yes, comrade. I think so. They were big men, with American
weapons. And they were driving one of the partisan cars. The
other two—one was the older man, Veterano—came out a few minutes later and drove the car away."

"Which of the Americans went inside?" Ugo asked him. "Kavanaugh, the one with the big nose? Landry, the leader?"

The man with the unfortunate breath looked uneasy. "I . . . I
don't know, comrade. Americans all look alike to me. Big. Well
fed. Does it matter?"

"It will matter eventually," Ugo said. "I want them all."

Sandrino murmured, "Let us tend to these first. Shall I send for
help?"

"Why should we need help?" Ugo said. "There are five of us
and only two of them."

Sandrino seemed quite as tense as Ugo felt. Sandrino said, "We
can't be certain there are only two. Renso had to leave the building to send word to us. What if others arrived while no one was
here to watch?"

"There are only the four Americans and the Britisher," Ugo
said patiently. "And they must surely have other duties as well.
We have no reason to think they would all gather here, under one
roof."

He squinted again at the warehouse. Quiet. Dark. Just as it
should be. The foraging dogs had apparently found it quite ordinary. Ugo could understand Sandrino's reluctance, since the man
had never been eager to deal with the Americans, but Ugo wasn't
sure why he, himself, should be so uneasy. Was it because he was
out of practice? His small physical stature had never prevented
him from committing the acts of violence required of the neophyte
ranks of Party musclemen, and yet he had long since risen to the
level at which personal participation was no longer expected of
him. No matter. This time he wanted to be there, to see the looks
on the foreigners' faces when they learned the bitter price of their
interference.

He drew his pistol and said, "Let us see to it, comrades." They moved silently across the street, Ugo and Sandrino in the lead, and crowded up beside the smaller office door. Ugo looked at Renso and whispered, "Are there other exits in back?"

"No, comrade. Just these two doors."

"Good," Ugo said. He nudged Sandrino. "You break the lock. We'll all rush in together."

But when Sandrino tested the door, it swung inward without effort. "It's open," Sandrino said. He sounded confused. "That shouldn't be."

Ugo shrugged it off. "Good fortune for us. They must have a great deal on their minds."

He leaned inside cautiously. The office was empty. He gestured and the others crowded in behind him. Sandrino moved quietly to an inner door and tried it. Also unlocked. Ugo eased it open and they slipped into the warehouse proper. Rows of wooden-staved barrels, stacked almost to the ceiling, gave them temporary concealment.

"Wait for my signal," Ugo whispered. He leaned past a barrel and stared toward the center of the warehouse floor. There, in the glow of a kerosene lamp, rested a heavily laden DeSoto, its back seat jammed with cartons and trinkets. Three Americans, not two, were gathered in the pool of light. One, the young Italian-American known as Freddy Stefanini, stood awkwardly near the DeSoto's front fender. The other two—one was the big man Kavanaugh and the other was Creedmore, the American with the maimed hand—sat like stiff mannequins on the running board. From the array of playing cards spread out between them, and the stacks of gold ingots at their feet, it was obvious to Ugo that they had been playing poker and betting the borrowed gold as stakes. But for some reason they seemed to have stopped.

"It's too easy," Sandrino whispered.

Ugo's eyes had gone to the gold. All his own vague misgivings vanished against its glitter. "Don't be so timid," he murmured back. He gestured for Sandrino and the others to fan out, then stepped from behind the olive-oil barrels. They tiptoed quickly across the floor, but none of the Americans appeared to notice. When the others were in position, Ugo cocked his pistol and walked calmly into the rim of light.

He said, "Bad tidings, gentlemen. It would appear someone has been extremely careless."

Inexplicably, none of the three Americans moved a muscle. Then, from the darker regions of the warehouse, from the rows of barrels stacked along the sides, a polished, German-accented voice said, "Not nearly so careless as you, Herr Ugo."

2

American flags had appeared from God knows where and hung limply from darkened upper windows in Cadenabbia. Arches of box, pine and intertwined ivy stretched from corner to corner across the streets. At one end of town, strung across the main lakeside road, a wide welcoming banner awaited the dawn of a day that would bring peace at last, and perhaps the arrival of friendly troops. The banner, oddly enough, had been decorated, in this land where flowers bloomed in every ditch, with red, white and blue tissue-paper roses.

But Landry had no time to think of peace or celebration as he hurried through the streets, tugging a whining Tuono on a rope. He had to find help. He had to warn the others about the Germans and try to figure out what they were up to. And he had to do it soon, if he was to be of any use to Viviana.

He hurried to the center of town, only to confront a closed, padlocked telephone office. Cadenabbia slept, except for an old man in a blue smock, sweeping the cobblestones, his own contribution to the celebration to come. Landry spoke to him, but the old man had no idea who staffed the telephone office, nor where they lived. Landry jogged on through town, heading north. With Tuono dragging on his rope like a big fish determined not to be landed, he ran, sometimes in panic, sometimes in desperation, the full four kilometers from Cadenabbia to Menàggio, stumbling through the darkness. As he ran, his fears for Viviana began to multiply. Viviana, with her temper and her exasperating ability to make him lose his own. Viviana, with her spoiled rich girl's ways, and her vanity, and the sly, warm smiles that suddenly made everything all right. If anything happened to her, he knew his life would become insipid. And yet, and yet, he'd never even asked her the simple question that would create commitment. He'd told her he adored her, cherished her, reveled in making love with her, often. But the words of commitment, never. Was it too late? Would he ever see her again?

Menággio had also prepared for a celebration. The main road lay waiting in the dark morning, strewn with fresh grass cuttings and flower petals. Faded bunting, this time in the red, white and green of the Italian flag, dangled from balconies on both sides of the street. Breathless, Landry slowed. It was time for a decision. Menággio was his crossroads. Pietro and partisan help lay to the north, at Dongo, five miles up the lake road. The ALOTs were at Velzo, a mile and a half above Menággio. It had to be one or the other.

Either way, he knew he would make better time without Tuono, so he sought out the house of the only person he knew, Don Ottorino Perfetti, the schoolmaster, intending to leave the dog and hurry on alone. Don Ottorino agreed quickly to take Tuono in, and in addition, after hearing Landry's babbled tale, seemed to have at least one necessary answer. Perhaps Pietro could be reached by telephone after all. The telephone office in Menággio was also closed, and would remain closed in honor of the coming peace, but a schoolmaster was a personage of respect, and the plump, dignified woman who managed the public exchange would open its doors briefly, even at this hour, for him.

But the puzzled partisan who answered Landry's call to the Dongo town hall, a man who seemed to think telephones worked properly only if one shouted into them at the top of one's lungs, said Pietro wasn't there. He had left in the night, the partisan bellowed loudly, something to do with a crisis in Rezzonico, and he hadn't come back. The crisis? The partisan knew only that some woman named Franca had sent word of a misfortune, and Pietro had driven south in his big Bugatti. In the meantime, the partisans in Dongo were looking for Pietro as well. There had been a shooting at the bank, a terrible shooting. Three men dead. No, he had no idea what it was all about. The Britisher and one of Dante's Veroli partisans, the old man they called Veterano, were at the bank now, trying to make sense of it. Or at least they had been earlier. They might be gone by now. They, too, had been seeking Pietro and might well have driven south to look for him.

Landry hung up with his ears ringing and his nerve ends tingling. He tried a call to the Dongo bank, and when there was no answer, he leaned against the wall of the wooden phone booth, with the manager plugging new routes at her switchboard outside, and listened with increasing desperation to the unanswered rings, repeating, repeating, at Viviana's house. If no one was at the bank, and no one in Rezzonico, that left only . . .

Velzo.

Two cars were there, outside the warehouse. Landry stopped in the shadows and tried to make out the outlines. With a surge of hope, he recognized the Bugatti. A man stood guard beside it, holding an ancient shotgun. Veterano. Landry hailed him and hobbled forward.

Veterano's whiskery face split in eager surprise when he saw Landry stumbling toward him through the darkness. He hurried to meet Landry. "Pietro said you would come," Veterano murmured.

Landry put a hand on Veterano's shoulder and asked, "Where is he?"

"Inside," Veterano said. "There has been trouble, David. Terrible trouble. Here and in Dongo." His eyes filled with misery. Hesitantly, he said, "In Rezzonico, too. Some men came to Viviana's house last night. Not Ugo's people. Germans. They took both Viviana and Luisa."

"I know," Landry said.

"You know? But how?"

Now it was Landry's turn to be hesitant. "I'm sorry, Veterano. I bring bad news. Luisa is dead."

Veterano looked as though he had been punched in the throat. His mouth worked and he seemed to grow shorter. "You are sure?"

"I was with her when she died," Landry said.

Veterano was very still for a moment. Questions welled up behind rheumy eyes, but he seemed unable to ask them. Finally, in a voice that was old and vulnerable, he said, "Come. Pietro will wish to hear."

The first thing Landry saw as they passed into the warehouse proper was a blood-soaked body sprawled on the floor, fingers stretching toward a fallen handgun. Veterano led him past the corpse, stepping carefully to avoid rivulets of clear, yellowish oil that had spilled across the floor. Some of the wooden storage barrels had taken hits. A sharp, overpowering tang of olive oil and a sweeter stench that was blood filled the warehouse, forcing Landry to wrinkle his nose.

Landry's wondering eyes took in Pietro and Willoughby, kneeling on the floor beyond toppled barrels, holding flashlights on yet another body. The DeSoto, doors hanging open, had been emptied, except for a few scattered gold bars lying on the floor. Someone, probably Pietro or the Britisher, had switched on the DeSoto headlights to help illuminate the dark building, and two more bodies lay in front of it. The dead men all looked Italian, though Landry didn't recognize any of them. Pietro looked up and said, "David! We wondered what had become of you."

"I was detained," Landry said. "What happened here?"

"An ambush, it would seem," Pietro said. "The rest of the treasure is gone, of course. Except for a few things overlooked in the rush. Captain Willoughby thinks it may have been Germans."

"I'm sure of it," Willoughby said. He opened his palm and played his flashlight across a handful of cartridge casings. "They're 9mm Parabellums. I found them on the floor behind the barrels. From the number they poured in, I'd say automatic weapons, probably MP40s."

Landry looked at the scattered bodies. "Any idea who they are?"

Pietro sighed. "As to that, yes. They're part of the contingent from Milan. The man at your feet is named Sandrino. The others are lesser lights. Unfortunately, their leader, Ugo, is missing. He was last seen driving away from Dongo in the company of these men. His people are quite disturbed that he has not returned. I fear there may be grave repercussions unless we can account for him."

Veterano leaned close to Pietro's ear. Pietro listened to his whispered words and swung a woeful face to Landry. "Luisa is dead?"

"Yes," Landry said.

"But how? Why?"

Landry glanced at Veterano. Landry was aware of the old man's affection for Luisa, and was reluctant to go into detail with him listening, so he said, "We'll discuss it later. What about Kavanaugh and Creedmore?"

Willoughby seemed to understand. With a quick look of his own at Veterano, he said, "They're missing as well. So is Freddy Stefanini. It's possible they've all been taken hostage, along with Ugo."

"Freddy?" Landry said. "What makes you think Freddy was here?"

Willoughby's mouth thinned in embarrassment. "Sorry, old man. I'm afraid he told Franca and Viviana that he was planning to trade shifts with one of the others. I know you've warned me about jumping to conclusions, but I imagine he either lied, or if he *did* trade shifts, the man whose place he took might well be our informer."

Landry's cheeks reddened. "You still think the informer is one of the ALOTs?"

"Everything points to it," Willoughby said. His voice was soft and apologetic. "Except for Pietro and Veterano, no one among the partisans knew we were using this warehouse to hide the treasure. None of them knew where we were hiding Luisa, either. And there's more. The Fascist currency was stolen from the Dongo bank late last night. It was an American who did it."

"You're sure?"

"We're sure," Willoughby said. "The bank manager tells us an American came to his home just before midnight with Viviana. He had release papers signed by Luisa. Since Pietro had spread the word that the treasure was in the hands of the Americans, and since Viviana was there to vouch for the American, the bank manager didn't suspect anything. They took the manager to their car, where some other men were waiting. Germans, the manager says. That's when he realized something was wrong."

"Maybe the Germans forced someone to do it," Landry said. "I saw the way they pushed Viviana around. Maybe they forced the American, too."

Pietro shook his head. "I'm sorry, David. He wasn't forced. There were three partisans on guard at the bank, with instructions to admit no one. The bank manager says they recognized the

American, greeted him with friendship, traded words. Then, when they turned their backs, he shot them. All three of them."

"Do you believe the bank manager?"

Willoughby said, "It would be hard not to. After he took the money from the vault, the American shot him as well. The man is quite seriously wounded. The doctor isn't sure he'll live. I'm sorry, Landry. It must be galling to learn that one of your countrymen, perhaps a friend, has turned traitor. But I tried to warn you, you know."

Landry looked away. "Yes, I know. I'd about come to that conclusion on my own. Too many coincidences. There were Germans waiting at the cove last night when I went to meet Gualfiero. Only a few of us knew about that meeting at the cove." Disgust, anger and great sadness thickened his throat.

"What happened to Gualfiero?" Pietro asked.

"He's almost surely dead," Landry said. "The Germans grenaded us. I didn't see him after that. Then they came down the bluff and took me."

"That's how you came to be with Luisa?" Pietro asked.

Landry nodded, not trusting himself to speak.

Willoughby looked thoughtfully at the older partisan and said, "Perhaps you'd better go outside and check the cars, Veterano. We may have to leave in a hurry."

But Veterano saw through Willoughby's sympathetic artifice and quickly shook his head. "No, I wish to hear it too. Tell it, David."

Landry was still reluctant, but he told it rapidly and he told it all. The meeting with Gualfiero at the cove. The sudden appearance of Knaust and the other Germans. The haunted villa and Viviana being dragged into the night. Luisa's last words. Veterano kept his eyes on a small pool of olive oil at Pietro's feet and seemed not to be listening at all, but his neck was bright red by the time Landry finished.

Pietro stood in aching silence and said, "Poor Luisa. That explains how they came by the bank papers."

"I'm sorry," Landry said miserably. "It's all my fault. Willoughby warned me that the traitor might be one of us, but I wouldn't listen. If you hadn't trusted us, perhaps none of this would have happened."

Pietro put a consoling hand on Landry's arm. "No, David. It was not your doing. Further, no matter what Captain Willoughby says, this horror may not be entirely the fault of an American. From what you have told us, Luisa recognized one of the men who broke into Viviana's house. Franca told us the same thing, but Franca swore they were all Germans."

"All Germans? Are you sure?"

"That's what she said. She was understandably upset, and I put little credence to it at the time. But your account of Luisa's last words give more weight to what Franca told us. Perhaps the informer is a stranger to us after all."

Landry frowned, trying to make sense of it. A suspicion was forming in his mind, but it didn't seem to jibe with the facts.

Pietro let his hand fall. "Poor Luisa." His bearded face looked sick. "The pity is that there is nothing we can do. To think that we have lost it all, and to think that the final victors are the filthy Germans."

"Like hell we've lost," Landry said. "They've got Viviana. We've got to go after them."

Pietro said, "How can we? We don't even know where to begin. They might be anywhere by now."

Landry shook his head. "There's only one place they could have gone. Your people are blocking the road to the north. I came from the south, and I sure didn't see them. With nothing but lake water to the east, that leaves just one direction: west. Across the mountains to Switzerland."

Pietro looked incredulous. "Across the mountains? With a heavy treasure weighing them down?"

"He could be right," Willoughby said. "Switzerland should look quite appealing to them, after all this. A night's march could put them there." He regarded the empty DeSoto and the few discarded gold bars. "How many do you think there are?" he asked Landry. "I calculate two gold bars per man, plus the other lighter items. That should put their strength at something between thirteen and sixteen men, wouldn't you say?"

Landry did some quick figuring of his own. "That's a fair guess," he said. "About sixty pounds per man. That should slow them down pretty good."

"But into the mountains?" Pietro said. "We could search for a year and never see them."

"Not necessarily," Landry said. "They won't use the Porlezza pass. Too close to the Swiss border garrison. I'd say straight across from here, and a little to the south. Probably toward Lake Lugano. Richter said something about Viviana leading them to a place of safety. Her father has a house on Lake Lugano."

Willoughby said, "As Landry suggests, they'll have to move slowly. I'll wager a small body of men could catch up to them by daybreak."

Like sunrise, a dim look of hope began to shine through the defeat on Pietro's face. He said, as if to himself, "A battle. A simple little battle, with the enemy finally known." Then the hope faltered. "But most of my veteran partisans are scattered, looking for Luisa. It might take hours to bring them back together."

"We haven't got time for that," Landry said. "They have Viviana. We have to go now. The four of us."

"But without more men . . ."

"Perhaps we won't need them," Willoughby said. "If we can catch up to the Germans, close enough to keep them in sight, perhaps we can summon the Swiss authorities. They'll do the rest."

Pietro thought about it, and hope seemed to return. "Very well," he said, with more than a hint of his old, commanding spirit. "We will leave immediately. But only the three of us. Veterano will return to the lakeside and gather what men he can find. With luck, perhaps they can catch up to us."

"No," Veterano said. He broke open the shotgun and checked the chambers, then popped it shut. "If you go for the Germans, I go also."

Landry hesitated only briefly, then said, "Let him come. I have a feeling we're going to need him."

3

They found their first trace of the retreating Germans at five in the morning. After hours of climbing from Velzo in the darkness, enduring cold and a touch of early-morning fog, they passed beyond the timberline and broke onto a clear, high plateau where the slope flattened and a belt of dying stars sprawled like a fading rash across a chilled sky. Ahead of them, on a broad plain strewn with rocks and white-budded bistort, no more than a hundred yards off their course, something gleamed in the starlight. Veterano saw it first. It was a single, shiny gold ingot, lying abandoned in a patch of rotting snow. Boot tracks, many of them, at least a dozen pairs, mushed across the narrow strip of snow and disappeared among the rocks. They took their first rest stop at the edge of the snow, huddled around the cast-off gold bar, spirits rising. When they started up the slope again, Pietro carried the gold bar with him.

They encountered no more tracks as they continued toward the summit, but they did find more ingots. Seven in all, dumped among the rocks by men grown weary, men who had chosen to lighten their loads, no doubt in secret, in the chill darkness. Veterano picked up the second gold bar, and the third as well. By the time they reached the fourth, they realized the folly of trying to salvage the gold. Pietro was already breathing raggedly, and Veterano, in spite of his strength, had fallen well behind. So they left the gold bars in a pile and continued on. When they passed the fifth, sixth and seventh, they did so with scarcely a second look.

Sunrise came on them abruptly, like a swirling column of flames. One moment they were in deep gray shadow, teeth chattering in the cold, surrounded by more patches of rotting snow, and then a pinprick of red appeared behind them and burst across peaks and crevices and moraines and slabs of shale and granite, spreading like Greek fire, turning the roseroot and saxifrage around them to molten bronze.

It took them another two hours to reach the summit, and they paused, letting the sun warm them, expecting to see some sign of the Germans on the downslope side. Instead, they saw only vast rocky terrain dropping toward a sea of dark, silent timber. Farther to the west, blanketed by morning haze, hung more mountains, the Lepontine Alps of southern Switzerland. Below, toward the base of their own mountains, cradled by lesser peaks, shimmered the dark, glassy surface of Lake Lugano, some fifteen miles long and a mile in width, straddling the border between Italy and Switzerland. Wearily, they started down toward the nearer end.

By ten o'clock that morning, they were well on their way down the slope and the sun had risen to follow them. Landry's calves had tightened to hard knots during the descent, and breath came harder with each step. He was tired, desperately tired, and his heels were rubbed almost raw from the pace Willoughby and Pietro had set. Willoughby, after a furtive look at Landry, said, "Perhaps it's time for another break. We'll need our strength when we catch up to them."

Landry was tempted. But Viviana was down there somewhere, and he didn't want to be the cause of any delay. He said, "No, not yet. We'll go on."

Pietro, face red with exertion, said, "Have mercy, David. There are others here who would welcome a moment of rest."

Landry was convinced that Willoughby had suggested the rest primarily on his account, but the bearded young partisan seemed sincere, and a moment's rest was profoundly tempting. Landry said, "All right. Five minutes. No more."

Pietro sank down on a pile of rocks. Landry sat next to him and nursed his blistered heels. Veterano, who looked just as tired and footsore as the rest of them, stayed on his feet and wandered in slowly increasing circles, scanning the rocky ground for tracks.

Willoughby came to squat in front of Pietro and Landry and leaned on his Thompson. "Do you think Don Ottorino will take good care of Tuono?" he asked.

"I don't see why not," Landry said. "Why?"

"Just wondering," Willoughby said. "If no one objects too much, I'm going to take him home with me when all this is done."

"If we ever get home," Landry said. "How much longer before we hit flat ground?"

Willoughby looked down the mountain. "That depends," he said. "We could reach the lake in a couple of hours, assuming that's where they're headed." He nodded vaguely to the low mountains beyond Lake Lugano. "That's the Porlezza pass over there. If they've headed that way, we may be off course."

"God, I hope not," Landry said. He turned his face to the sun, imagining that it made him feel warmer. Birds trilled a peaceful song from the timber below.

"I think we have cause for optimism," Willoughby said. "Think how the Germans must feel by now. Not only have they covered the same ground, but they're also carrying a great deal of weight."

Pietro sat up. "Not as much as when they started," he said. "And who can say how many gold bars we might have missed in the darkness?"

"My point, exactly," Willoughby said. "How exhausted would you have to be before throwing away something worth perhaps three or four thousand pounds sterling? I imagine even the paper money has started to feel heavy by now."

Landry flexed his muscles, testing the kinks, then pushed himself slowly from the rocks. "Let's get going."

Pietro rose and said, "What's wrong with Veterano?"

The older partisan was crouched behind a boulder some seventy yards below them, neck craning, head and body still, like a bird dog on point. Pietro called out to him, but he didn't answer. They gathered their weapons and slowly, curiously, made their way down to him. When they were closer, Pietro hailed him again. "What's wrong? Are you hurt? Didn't you hear us call?"

Veterano beckoned them to the boulder. "There," he said, pointing down the slope. "About a kilometer beyond the fold. Where the trees thin."

They all stared hard, following the direction of Veterano's extended hand, but it was Landry who saw them first, a string of gray-clad figures, barely discernible through the distant trees, walking in single file. "Yes, there," he said. "It looks like they're back in uniform."

Willoughby finally spotted them. His mouth turned up at the corners. "I see them," he said. "Heading straight toward the lake. By God, we've got them."

It took another two hours, as Willoughby had predicted, to close the distance, most of it through heavy stands of fir, pine and larch, and most of it without catching any further sight of the Germans. Then suddenly, as they approached the lake and emerged from the trees into an open meadow knee-deep in wildflowers, they walked almost into the middle of the German column.

Willoughby, first out of the trees, startled Landry and Pietro by dropping to his belly in the meadow grass. They instantly lurched down beside him. Pietro gestured discreetly but frantically for Veterano to keep low, but the old man seemed to have disappeared, perhaps taking cover in underbrush. There, scarcely fifty yards ahead, plodding through breeze-blown saffron and squill, chests and armpits sweaty under a golden sun, shoulders bent under heavily laden haversacks, marched a long line of uniformed men, heading down toward a wooded point jutting into the lake.

Landry raised his head just enough to peer over the grass. "There are more of them than we thought," he whispered. "Looks like seventeen or eighteen men, at least."

"They aren't all Germans," Willoughby whispered back. He gestured toward the middle of the pack. Landry raised his head another quarter of an inch and saw five figures in civilian clothing, flanked by guards with automatic weapons. Creedmore, Stefanini and Kavanaugh trudged along in the center, carrying heavy loads. A few feet behind them, straining under a bulky duffel, hobbled a grim-faced Ugo. And out to the side of the column, arm locked in the grip of one of the guards, limped Viviana.

"They're using them like pack animals," Pietro objected.

A shouted order came from the meadow. The German column ground slowly to a halt. Some of the soldiers dropped their burdens into the grass. Many of them, including the three ALOTs and Ugo, sank to their haunches to rest. Viviana stared for a moment down at the lake, then abruptly, without warning, whirled and kicked her guard in the kneecap. Her voice came across the grass, shouting, "Run! Run!" Both Creedmore and Kavanaugh stirred for a moment, but they seemed too dispirited to make the try. And then it was over. Viviana's guard, howling with pain, grabbed her by the hair and jerked her to the ground.

Landry groaned and started to rise, but Willoughby tugged him back. "Easy," the Britisher whispered. "Don't do anything rash."

They could see Richter, the German major, watching from the front of the column. Richter came back toward Viviana, smiling in amusement. He said something to her guard, then detoured to join two of his men. One of them was Lieutenant Stenzel, head wrapped in a bandage that covered the eyes and nose. He was leaning on Sergeant Knaust's arm. Knaust and the two German officers appeared to talk for a moment, with Major Richter gesturing and pointing, and then Knaust broke away from Richter and Stenzel and selected a pair of enlisted men from among those sitting in the grass. They set off alone, leaving the exhausted column behind, and strode purposefully down toward the water's edge.

Landry opened his mouth to speak, but a twig crackled in the brush behind them, and they jerked their heads around in unison. Veterano came toward them on his elbows and knees from the direction of a small hill at the edge of the meadow.

"Where have you been?" Landry whispered.

"To the top of the hill," Veterano said. "I wanted to see on the other side of the point. There is a boat."

Willoughby's face stiffened. "What kind of boat?"

"A power boat. I do not know what you call it. There is a cabin and a high bridge. They have pulled branches over it, but one can see the mast above the scrub."

At the point, sure enough, Landry could see the whip-thin tip of a mast protruding above the brush. Willoughby murmured, "Oh bloody hell. They've outfoxed us. We'll never be able to keep up if they take to the water."

"What can we do?" Pietro asked.

"I'm not letting Viviana out of my sight," Landry said. "We'll have to stop them here."

Pietro lifted his head briefly, then brought it back down. "Perhaps we could open fire from here. We have the advantage of slightly higher ground and the element of surprise."

"It's too risky," Willoughby said urgently. "If we start shooting, they might turn their guns on Viviana and Landry's ALOTs. I vote we deal with the boat. Perhaps we can scuttle it. At least we could keep them on foot and within reach that way." He glanced at Veterano. "You saw it. How is it situated? In open water?"

"No," Veterano said. "There is an inlet. Trees on both sides."

"Well, we shall just have to improvise," Willoughby said. He rolled over in the grass and stripped off his back pack, then handed his Thompson to Landry. "I'll take Veterano along to provide cover. Give us about fifteen minutes to get around to the far side of the point, then you and Pietro see if you can attract their attention. Thrash around in the underbrush or the like, then take off. If you can keep them busy looking for you, perhaps I can swim into the inlet without being seen."

"Don't be a fool," Landry whispered. "If someone spots you, you're a dead man. Viviana is my problem, not yours. Let me do it."

"Sorry," Willoughby said. "I have my own stake in this, you know. There's still a traitor down there somewhere."

He tapped Veterano on the shoulder and they crawled rapidly toward the ridge. Landry and Pietro watched their progress by the waving tops of squill and meadow grass. Landry caught one last glimpse of Willoughby's head, bobbing up for orientation, then they disappeared over the hillock and into the trees.

"He is either a brave man or a complete fool," Pietro whispered. "How do you wish to handle this, David? Shall we separate and attempt to draw the Germans off in two directions, or should we stay together and lead them into the pines?"

Landry studied the terrain. "We'll separate," he decided. "If I can lead enough of them away from the meadow, maybe you can come down from that piece of high ground and help Viviana and the others break loose. Do you think you can work your way over without being seen?"

Pietro squinted across the top of the grass. "Yes, I can do it."

"Good," Landry said. He gripped Pietro's wrist. "Viviana means a great deal to me, old friend, but don't try anything unless I can drain away most of the guns. If too many Germans stay behind, you keep your head down. We'll think up something else later, after . . ."

A figure appeared on the point, far below the men resting in the meadow, and shouted something in German. It was Knaust, apparently relaying an all-clear, for Major Richter waved in reply and ordered his squatting men onward. Grudgingly, the soldiers picked up their loads and began to wind on down through the wildflowers toward the water's edge.

Pietro froze. "David, they're going on to the inlet. What do we do now?"

Landry tried to control his own panic. "Quick," he told Pietro.

"See if you can catch up to Willoughby and Veterano. Warn them. Tell them the boat will be swarming with Germans in a matter of minutes."

"And you?" Pietro asked.

"I'll follow the Germans. If we don't get Viviana out of there, she's going to be in a hell of a lot of trouble."

4

Richter watched with pride as his men unloaded the treasure onto the deck. It was, perhaps, a small prize compared to the larger one his country was losing in the bricks and rubble of Berlin, but it would buy several shares in the future, regardless. Possibly even lay the foundation for a Fourth Reich, if the Kameradenwerk used it wisely.

Or if they used it at all. His feeling of personal pride gave way to a small quiver of guilt. He hadn't actually made up his mind yet. At first, yes, that had been his thought, to turn the treasure over to the underground operatives of the Kameradenwerk. But now, after seeing it, after touching the stacks of currency, after feeling the smooth weight of the gold bars, he was no longer so certain.

True, to deliver these riches into the hands of his vanquished comrades and thereby offer them a means to support the many men they hoped to rescue would no doubt secure him a high and honorable position in a continuing, though secret, aristocracy. But suppose he didn't hand it over? Such wealth, used discreetly, could assure him just as easily an open, public position in the new, postwar aristocracy. Could he not do as much for Germany as a man of recognized rank and wealth? Or was he really thinking only of himself?

He turned his attention to Sergeant Knaust and the two men stripping branches and pine boughs from the boat. Knaust was a good soldier, one whom Richter had been proud to have at his side these many years, but the man seemed to be working far too slowly, spending more time in whispered conversation than was necessary. "Hurry!" Richter urged him. "We must cross into Swiss waters quickly, before someone on this side sees us and alerts the Swiss border authority."

Knaust paused in his work. "What if the Swiss see us coming?"

"We will keep to the shoreline until we are safely beyond the border," Richter told him. "If they see us, we'll shoot our way free."

"Shoot at the Swiss?" Knaust stammered. He looked uneasily at the two men helping him. "But Herr Sturmbannführer, if we do that, we may never get home. They'll chase us down and kill us all."

"Any German soldier is more than a match for the Swiss," Richter said. "The important thing is to get this cargo to a proper hiding place. Once we have accomplished that and contacted the Kameradenwerk, you are free to do as you wish. Flee. Surrender. Continue on with me. Whatever you do, you can do it with your head held high."

There, he'd said it. The decision was made.

Or was it? Could he really bring himself to give it all away? It would be so glorious to return to Germany in triumph rather than in defeat. Not right away, of course. A few years in Switzerland, at least until the Allies grew slothful and careless in victory. Then to return, a fabulously wealthy and successful man, ready to pick up the pieces. He could have anything he wanted. Anything.

Of course, if he kept it and if Knaust or any of the others elected to stay with him, there would have to be an accommodation. Shares for all. That shouldn't be too difficult. Except for Lieutenant Stenzel, they were all working men from humble backgrounds. A million marks or so for each, and they would be satisfied. But what to do about Stenzel? The man was such a boastful ass. How to satisfy him?

Richter looked around sharply as a guard ushered Viviana and Ugo and the three Americans toward the boat. "Let the woman come on deck," he told the guard. "We'll need her to direct us to her father's property. Relieve the others of their loads and keep them on shore. They will not be going with us."

Ugo's mouth dropped open as the guard shoved him back. He raised apprehensive eyes to Richter and said, "What are you going to do with us?"

"That should be obvious," Richter told him. "You are still our enemies."

"What about me?" one of the Americans said.

Richter hesitated, then, "Yes, allow that one to come aboard."

The German guard moved aside and let the man pass. The man clambered on deck with Viviana and said gratefully, "Thanks. For a moment there, I thought you intended to leave me behind."

Richter said icily, "As to that, I have not yet decided."

The man frowned. "But you promised me . . ."

Richter cut him off with a gesture. He looked for Stenzel. "Lieutenant, come here," he called.

Stenzel, clinging to an enlisted man near the cabin, turned to Richter's voice and groped his way toward the stern. His hand touched Richter's chest, and Richter brushed it away. "Don't feel your way around like a cripple," Richter whispered to him. "Act like a man. You've an example to set."

"Yes, sir," Stenzel said. He pulled himself to attention.

"That's better," Richter said. "Take two enlisted men ashore and deal with the rest of the prisoners."

Stenzel's bandaged face tilted awkwardly. "But I can't see."

"What possible difference can that make?" Richter said impatiently. "You have only to give the order. Others will carry it out."

The lower half of Stenzel's face, all that was visible to Richter, seemed strained. "Couldn't we let them go? We'll be far away by the time they can walk out and find help."

The informer plucked at Richter's sleeve. "Hey no, you can't do that, Major. You can't let them go. You promised me there would be no witnesses."

Viviana, standing a few feet away, scowled at the American and said, "If anyone is to die, it should be you. You are disgusting."

"Keep quiet, both of you," Richter told them. "I am quite capable of making up my own mind." He turned again on Stenzel. "You make my stomach turn," he whispered. "Even the woman has more nerve than you. How do you think the men would react if they knew one of their officers had lost his spine? Go back to the cabin and stay out of my sight until this is done. You're useless to me."

"What about me?" the informer suggested. "Let me take care of the prisoners. It's an easy job. Give me a gun and let me do it."

"Keep still," Richter snapped at the man. Richter stepped away, seeking Knaust, and saw that he was now on the bank, talking quietly with some of the other enlisted men. "Sergeant, come here," Richter called.

Knaust pulled away from the men, looking almost guilty, and came toward the rail. "Sir?"

Richter leaned out. "I'm afraid Lieutenant Stenzel is not feeling well," he said. "I wish you to become my second-in-command. Take the prisoners beyond the knoll and dispense with them." He looked over his shoulder and lowered his voice. "The informer, as well. I can't abide his whining."

Knaust swallowed. "No, sir, I can't. We've been talking this over. We think things have gone far enough."

Richter sighed heavily. "You too, Sergeant? I expected better of you."

"What's the point?" Knaust said in a pleading tone. "The war is over, Major. No one expects anything of us anymore. Let's just go home."

Richter looked down at the sergeant with a feeling of disappointment, a wave of feeling so strong that it made him queasy. He opened the flap of his holster and drew out a Walther PPK. He leveled it at Knaust and said, "I have always liked you, Sergeant. I have always regarded you as one of my strongest assets, a capable soldier who wears duty and loyalty to the Fatherland like a badge of honor. But unless you do as I say, I will not hesitate to shoot you."

Several enlisted men looked at each other hesitantly, then gathered behind Knaust. One of them said, "You will have to shoot us all, Major."

The sergeant took a deep breath. "You don't need us anymore," he said. He thrust his chin at the mounds of treasure stacked along the deck. "You have what you want. Take it and be welcome. But let us go. We'll walk around the lake and cross into Switzerland on foot. Maybe the Swiss will let us pass, maybe we'll have to give ourselves up. But one way or another, we want to go home."

Richter felt his face redden. "Don't be a fool, Sergeant."

Others on deck had been listening, and now they drifted to shore to join Knaust. Even Lieutenant Stenzel, hanging onto the edge of the cabin, stretched his hands out. "Someone help me," he said. "I want to go, too." Two of the enlisted men detoured to help him, and Stenzel clutched at their hands gratefully.

Richter could feel himself losing control. "The treasure isn't for me," he said. "Don't you understand? This is for the future of the Fatherland. We can't turn back now."

Sergeant Knaust seemed to relent. "Come with us," he pleaded from shore. "There's still time, Major. Let's just leave all this here and go home together."

Richter said, "No. I will not betray my principles."

Knaust shrugged. "Then we wish you good fortune." He gestured to the others and they began to back away.

Richter wavered, then shouted, "Don't be fools! If you leave me now, you'll be branded traitors!"

No one paid any attention. One by one, they turned their backs on him, Knaust first, then a few others, then everyone. They headed up the bank toward the top of the hill. Richter watched until the last man reached the crown and started down on the other side, then called, "Sergeant, come back! Please! I need you." When they continued on, Richter lost his temper. "You are Judases," he shouted. "You'll be hunted to ground and executed."

"Let them go," the informer murmured. "All the more for us."

Richter had almost forgotten the man. "Shut up!" Richter snarled. "Get away from me. I want nothing more to do with you." He gazed down at the three confused prisoners standing on shore. He would need them after all, to help handle the boat. "You three," he called. "All of you. Come on deck."

"No, no, leave them," the informer said. "Shoot them and leave them. We can do it without them."

Richter pushed the man away, delicately, with the tip of his pistol. "I told you to get away from me," he said. "Go stand by the woman. I have no intention of dealing any further with you. Once we reach our destination and unload the treasure, you die."

"Now hold on," the informer said. "You can't kill me. Not after all the things I've done. You swore an oath . . ."

"Get away from me," Richter repeated. He looked again at the three men on shore, the Italian Communist and the other two American agents. "Do as I say!" he shouted down at them. "On the boat! Now!"

But the men on shore had heard enough to know they had nothing to gain by obeying. They looked at each other hesitantly, then split apart and raced for cover.

"Stop!" Richter shouted. He cupped the pistol in both hands and fired twice. One of the men dropped to the ground, bleeding from the back. Another managed three steps, then grabbed his thigh and spun behind a tree. The third man hurdled a bush at the top of the low hill and disappeared.

At the same moment, Richter heard the woman gasp and something bustled behind him. He started to whirl, but a coil of rope dropped over his head, tightening around his neck and chin. He struggled, but the informer had him off balance. The more he thrashed, the tighter the coils grew. His eyes began to bulge and the gun trickled from his fingers. He tugged at the rope, choking, gasping, and his vision turned red, then gray, then black. He felt himself sinking. . . .

The informer held the rope tightly against Richter's windpipe, wrenching, throttling, until Richter's tongue swelled in his mouth and the breath stopped. He held it tighter while Richter's toes danced against the hardwood planking of the deck and his bowels voided. The informer yanked even tighter until the body, foul-smelling, sagged in death and hung limp in his hands. Then, with Viviana screaming for him to stop, he held it some more, squeezing, squeezing, to be sure. When he finally released his grip, the body tumbled quietly across the deck rail and hung there for a moment, then tipped over of its own weight and fell into the water with a splash. It rolled over once, then floated, face down.

Viviana came at him with clenched fists, but he held her off and scooped up the major's pistol. He stood at the rail for a moment, breathing hard, watching the body float, then his eyes turned hungrily to the cartons and cases stacked on the deck. It was his now. All of it. He needed only to get it away from here, to hide it. Millions. Enough for a lifetime. Several extraordinary new lifetimes whose outlines he only now was beginning to imagine. Amazing how calm, how comfortable it made him feel to realize that the problems that beset most of mankind—bills, frustrated ambitions, a slavish existence laboring for a living—would no longer be his.

He took Viviana by the arm and was about to cast loose the

stern line when a sound from the trees stopped him. Someone coming. Footsteps crashing through the underbrush at the rear of the inlet. Quickly, without hesitation, he shoved Viviana to her knees and hissed, "Be very quiet." Then he vaulted across the rail to the shore and ducked behind a fold in the rocks.

Seconds later, a figure appeared through a break in the foliage and came slipping and sliding down the hill toward the boat. It was Landry, a Thompson submachine gun clutched lightly in his hands. As he burst from the trees and raced past the man's hiding place, Viviana screamed, "David! Look out!"

The informer stepped into the open behind Landry and said, "That's far enough, amigo. Put the gun down."

Landry skidded to a halt. He stood for a moment, staring up at Viviana, as though debating what to do. Then he laid the submachine gun cautiously on the ground. Without turning, he said, "Hello, Creedmore. I was afraid it would be you."

5

Wind rustled through the trees. Landry stood with his hands at his sides, feeling incredibly foolish. He had seen the bulk of the Germans walk away from the inlet, and it had puzzled him. Shortly after, he had heard the shots. Someone with a more cautious intelligence might have hung back, at least long enough to determine what had happened. But those two sudden, unexpected shots had filled Landry with alarm and brought him on the run, his mind blotted out by frenzied concern for Viviana. It was a reckless thing he had done. Now he waited, his back to Wesley Creedmore, wondering what price he would have to pay. Apparently Creedmore was uncertain as well, for there was a moment of indecision before Creedmore finally said, "Get on the boat."

"Why?" Landry asked.

"You're going to help us cast off," Creedmore said. "Then the three of us are going to take a little boat ride across the border into Switzerland."

Landry looked up at Viviana and considered alternatives, but decided against them. One foolish move was enough. He might not survive a second. Nor could he afford to jeopardize Viviana. He turned cautiously and swung onto the boat. As his feet touched the deck, he saw Richter's body floating face down next to the hull. "You've been busy," he said.

"He was going to do it to us," Creedmore said. He followed Landry to the deck and grabbed Viviana's elbow, pulling her in front of him as a shield. "Get back to the stern and cut us loose," he told Landry. He watched as Landry silently retreated to the stern line, then said, "How did you know it was me?" He sounded genuinely mystified.

"Luisa told me," Landry said.

Creedmore's eyes shifted suspiciously. "She couldn't have. She never saw me. Richter kept her blindfolded the whole time."

"Perhaps," Landry said. "But she had it figured out. The last thing she said was that it was all a lie. That she had seen someone. Someone she thought was dead."

"That could have been anyone," Creedmore said. "Dante. Tucker. Holloman. Anyone. She never had any reason to think I was dead."

"She didn't mean you," Landry said. "At least not directly."

"Who, then?"

"She was talking about one of the Germans," Landry said. "Someone she saw at Viviana's house. Someone you supposedly shot during that phony escape from the Fascists in Tremozzo. But you never shot anybody. Luisa and Piccione thought you did, but it was a setup. The Germans let you go and staged the whole thing. Luisa didn't realize it until she saw one of the 'dead' Germans still alive. Which one was it? Stenzel?"

Creedmore smiled with one corner of his mouth. "Okay, smart boy. So you worked it out. I told Richter he was a damned fool for sending Stenzel to Viviana's house." He touched the pistol to Viviana's ear. "Come on, get busy. Cast off."

Landry lifted the stern line, then turned questioning eyes to Creedmore. "Why did Richter let you escape? And why the phony theatrics at Tremozzo?"

"We made a deal," Creedmore said. "Richter figured it was the only way to put me back among the partisans and the rest of the ALOTs without making them suspicious. If I'd busted out of that

Fascist cell by myself, no one would ever have trusted me. So he let us all go and sent Stenzel and a couple of noncoms in at the last minute to make it look legitimate. They put on a good show. I thought I'd really killed someone when the first one flopped over."

"And you went along with it? Why?"

Creedmore's jaw firmed. "You'd have done the same," he said. He lifted his left hand, the mangled fingertips covered with gnarled, dead skin. "While the rest of you were screwing off in the mountains, enjoying yourselves, they did this to me. You don't know what it's like, day after day, beatings, hand screws, pain, getting punched out by a bunch of Germans. I couldn't take any more. I'd have sold my own daddy, if they'd wanted the worthless old soak."

"Luisa had it just as bad. She didn't break."

"Horse manure. She didn't have anything worth telling them, or she would have spilled her guts. Anyone would. You included. Now cast off that damned line and get forward. Otherwise, your girlfriend here is going to end up with an air-conditioned head."

Landry poised himself to throw the line, then froze. With a sudden prickle of awareness, he saw ripples and bubbles coming around the far point, moving slowly into the narrow inlet. It had to be Willoughby, swimming under water. Pietro hadn't reached him in time to warn him off.

"Quit stalling," Creedmore called.

Landry dropped the line into the water and stepped back. He groped for something to say, something to keep Creedmore occupied. "How did you talk Richter into turning you loose? He didn't seem the type to make deals with anyone from our side."

"Shoot, that was easy," Creedmore said. "I told him about Holloman and that pile of OSS loot he was carrying. I offered to make a trade. Holloman for me. It must have sounded good to him, a big shot like Holloman and all that money in exchange for a country boy with a busted hand. So we got Tucker to lure Holloman up to the trail, and we did the rest."

Water gurgled as the bubbles drew nearer, and Landry spoke quickly. "Why did you bring Tucker into it?"

"We had to. I didn't know where Holloman was hiding. I offered to go looking for him, but I guess Richter was afraid I'd run for the hills and never come back. So I told him how to find

Tucker instead, and they brought him in. The rest was easy. You know how chicken Tucker was, all nerves and scared half to death. They cuffed him around awhile, just enough to get him spooked, then they turned him over to me. He was half out of his wits by then. When I told him about the trade I'd worked out with Richter, he almost wet his pants in gratitude. Hell, man, they offered us a good deal. Twenty per cent of Holloman's money. A bounty for every partisan and ALOT we gave them. Even better, they guaranteed protection for as long as we continued to co-operate. Old Tucker's eyes lit up like fireflies at milking time. I guess the money interested him a little, but it was that guarantee of safety that really got to him. No more worrying about whether we'd live to see the end of the war. Money in a Swiss account when it was over. We had the best of it both ways. And all we had to do was dole them out a few bodies from time to time."

"Your own comrades?"

"Don't give me that comrade crap. No one did anything to help me when I was sitting in that stinking Fascist cell. I heard about that fight you had with Holloman. He wanted to ignore us, right? He wanted to let us rot. And you were only interested in your Italian buddies. You didn't give a damn about me."

"That isn't true," Landry said. "We wanted . . ."

The water beside the boat suddenly exploded as someone came bursting from it, gasping and choking in surprise. Willoughby's voice, half strangled, said sharply, "Bloody hell!"

Creedmore pushed Viviana away and leaped to the deck rail. There below him, eyes wide with astonishment, was the spluttering Britisher, treading water. Willoughby had apparently come up for air, only to bump into Richter's floating body, and the shock had startled him into giving himself away.

"Well, hello there," Creedmore said. He kept the gun low, out of sight, and grinned cheerfully. "We were hoping you'd show up, old chap."

Willoughby's astonishment turned to confusion. He could see Landry and Creedmore looking down at him from the deck of the boat, and no Germans save the one floating beside him. "What's going on?" Willoughby asked.

"Nothing," Creedmore answered. "The Krauts have all done a bunk. Viviana's up here, too. Come on out. The air's fine."

Landry shook his head minutely, and Willoughby saw it. He continued to tread water. "No, thanks," he said. "If you're who I think you are, I'm perfectly comfortable down here."

"Now that's downright rude," Creedmore said. He raised the gun so Willoughby could see it. "I guess I'll just have to insist."

Willoughby looked helplessly from Creedmore to Landry, then swam to the side of the boat. He reached for the deck stringer and pulled himself up. As he slipped over the rail and touched one foot to the deck, he glanced at Viviana, then made a sudden swooping lunge at Creedmore. A lesser athlete might have been taken by surprise, but Creedmore sidestepped Willoughby's move easily and slashed him across the top of the skull with Richter's pistol. Willoughby plummeted to the deck in a heap. Viviana made a startled sound as water cascaded across the planking.

"What the hell did you do that for?" Landry demanded.

"Don't worry," Creedmore said. "I didn't hit him that hard. We're going to need him later to help with the unloading. In the meantime, I'd just as soon deal with only one of you at a time. How many more are there?"

"How many more what?"

"People, you dumb asshole. You and Willoughby didn't come up here alone."

Landry let a heartbeat of silence intervene before he said, perhaps too slowly, "Pietro is out there with eight of his men. They should be ringing the inlet by now."

Whether Creedmore believed Landry or not, the possibility obviously bothered him. He waved his gun and said, "Let's get moving. You crawl around to that bow line while Viviana and I get up on the bridge. Don't try anything or I'll blow hell out of her and your English buddy. When I get the engine started, you cast us loose."

Landry glanced at Viviana, trying to gauge her state of nerves. As if in answer, she swept her arms around Creedmore's neck and shouted, "Jump, David! Jump!"

He couldn't, of course. Not with Viviana and Willoughby still on the boat. So he stood helplessly while Creedmore wriggled loose and shoved her away.

"You never give up, do you?" Creedmore railed at her. He looked around at Landry. "David, you better control this damned woman of yours. I'm getting fed up with her. She's been doing stuff like that all day. She gave the Germans fits coming across the mountains."

"Why don't you let her go?" Landry said.

"Are you kidding? We're going to need her most of all. Her old man has a summer house down at the Swiss end of the lake. That's why Richter brought her along in the first place." He waved the gun again. "Tend that bow line. I'm getting a little impatient, David."

So Landry climbed up on the gunwale and worked his way slowly around the cabin. Creedmore pushed Viviana to a ladder and started up after her. For a moment, they both disappeared from view, blocked off by a corner of the cabin and the lower planking of the flying bridge. Landry gave fleeting thought to reversing his field, to trying to come up behind Creedmore while the freckled ALOT was busy with Viviana, but Viviana's head and shoulders reappeared at the top of the bridge, high above Landry, and Creedmore and the gun reappeared also.

"Stand by," Creedmore called. The starter mechanism ground and whined, ground and whined again, and the inboard engines sputtered and caught. Creedmore moved his hand across the instrument panel, adjusting gadgets, regulating the fuel mixture, and the sputter smoothed into a throaty, powerful rumble. "Okay, cut us loose," he called to Landry.

Landry fumbled with the bow-line knots as slowly as he could, stalling for time. Creedmore watched testily from the bridge, allowing Landry to fritter away perhaps a minute and a half, then called, "What's the holdup?"

"It's stuck," Landry shouted back. "I could use some help."

But Creedmore wasn't having it. He leveled the pistol and yelled, "Get that line off, David, or I'll shoot it off. And you with it."

Landry hesitated, wondering if Creedmore meant it, and decided he did. He let the rope fall into the water.

"Now get back to the cabin and climb up here where I can watch you," Creedmore called. It was hard to make out what he was saying above the heavy-throated rumble of the engines, but Creedmore gestured menacingly with the gun to make sure Landry understood.

Landry worked his way back along the gunwale, conscious of Creedmore watching him from above, following his slow progress with the pistol. When Landry stepped from the gunwale to the ladder, he heard Creedmore shout, "One rung at a time, David. Both hands in plain sight."

Frustrated, Landry looked back at Willoughby, sprawled on his face on the wet deck. The Britisher lay as still as death itself. Landry started to pull himself up, then his eyes touched a second puddle of water on the opposite side of the deck. He stiffened. Willoughby hadn't made that one. A trail of wet spots, like footmarks, led toward the cabin. Landry let his eyes roam. The cabin door was ajar. That was changed too. It had been closed earlier. He was almost sure of it.

"Get on up here," Creedmore called impatiently.

Hand over hand, Landry pulled himself up, trying to piece together what he had seen. Someone else had come on deck while he and Creedmore were occupied with the bow line. But who? Veterano? Pietro? If so, why had they gone to the cabin? Why not up the ladder, to take Creedmore from behind?

On the bridge, Creedmore waved Landry over beside Viviana. "Put your hands on the rail," Creedmore told him. "Keep them where I can see them."

Landry stood meekly, his mind racing to absorb and understand the meaning of the fresh water spots. Creedmore throttled the engines from rumble to roar and began the ticklish process of guiding the launch out of the narrow slip. He moved his head back and forth, checking the clearance, and the boat moved slowly through the overhanging trees. Sunlight, touching them only in leafy dapples, came down in full force as they eased from the inlet into the lake. Creedmore waited until the stern was clear, then gunned the engines and spun the wheel, turning them toward the center of the lake. As the boat slapped against swells, picking up speed, Creedmore looked at Landry and Viviana and grinned. "Pretty good for an old country boy from the dust bowl, wouldn't you say?"

"Beautiful," Landry said without enthusiasm.

Creedmore adjusted the throttle and fuel mixture, fine-tuning the boat's progress. When it suited him, he grinned again. "You poker-faced sonofabitch," he said. "You were bluffing about Pietro and his eight men, weren't you?"

"I guess so," Landry said. He thought hard about the trail of splashes to the cabin. Could he have misread the signs? Why had no one yet made a move toward the bridge? He put his hand on Viviana's arm and patted it.

Creedmore must have noticed his deep concentration, for Landry suddenly felt Creedmore's elbow at his ribs, an almost playful gouge, and Creedmore said, "Why so thoughtful? You and Viviana trying to get up the nerve to jump me again?"

Landry shook his head. "No. I was just wondering why you bothered to bring me along too."

"Hell, David, I've got nothing against you," Creedmore said. "We don't have to go at this like a couple of hound dogs fighting over a bone. I've got mine now. Back there on deck. Plenty of it. I figure if you're willing to do me a couple of favors, maybe I'll let you have some quick slobbers, too. There's enough for both of us. It's going to be a funny new world out there, and I could use a friend."

"No, thanks," Landry said.

"Don't be so damned pious," Creedmore said. "I saw the way you looked at the treasure that day in the rain up at the hotel. You wanted to stick your paws in it as much as I did." He gave the wheel a sharp turn, heading them westward toward Swiss waters. "Look, the way I see it, I'm not going to have a whole lot of time to stash this stuff, once Viviana shows us where to put it. Hell, the Swiss could come swarming up on us at any minute. You give me a hand, hiding all the goodies, and I'll cut you in: twenty, maybe even thirty per cent. Think about it, David. You could be as rich as Viviana's old man. Maybe even richer. Doesn't that give you a whole new way of looking at things? You could have anything you want, old buddy. All for a couple of hours of easy work."

"And when we finish? A bullet in the back?"

"Aw come on," Creedmore said. "I don't want to kill you, David. Why should I?" He sounded completely sincere. Landry found it confounding.

"Yeah, I've seen some examples of your gratitude," he said. "Harry Tucker, Gualfiero, Luisa."

"Hey, now, wait a minute," Creedmore said. "I couldn't help any of that. Tucker was a nervous Nellie. He was about to crack wide open. And Gualfiero, well, he could have ruined everything. If he'd stayed dead like he was supposed to, nothing would have happened."

"Gualfiero didn't know about you," Landry said. "He never saw anything but your legs."

"Really?" Creedmore said. "I'll be damned. I figured he was about to blow everything." He gave the instrument panel a puzzled look. The boat seemed to be slowing, though Creedmore hadn't changed the throttle setting.

"What about Luisa?" Landry asked.

"That was an accident," Creedmore said. "She was just so stubborn. She wouldn't sign the bank papers. The Germans had to belt her around a little."

"The Germans didn't do it. You did. Richter told me about it."

"Who are you going to believe? Me, or some damned Nazi? Oh I might have punched her a few times, but I didn't beat her that bad on purpose. Hell, I'm no monster, David. It just happened. Besides, she saw Stenzel at Viviana's house and recognized him. You said so yourself."

"And you knew she recognized him," Landry said. "That's why you deliberately beat her to death."

Viviana, who had been listening to the rapid flow of English with fierce concentration, broke out, "Assassino!" She switched to English herself and, for good measure, spat, "Filth!"

Creedmore looked at her warily as he thumped the rpm indicator. It was holding steady, but the boat was definitely slowing. "Okay, okay," Creedmore said, his eyes scanning the instrument panel. "So maybe I overdid it a little with Luisa. Don't make such a big thing of it. I tell you, David, if you'd ever spent any time on a ten-yard line, you might have learned a little about what life's really like. People hitting you, trying to tear your arms off over some stupid ball game. Well, this game is real, it's worthwhile. I did what I had to. It isn't like I could let her go around telling everyone what she saw. How can a man make a fine, new start if he has to keep looking over his shoulder all the time?" He slapped the rpm indicator with his open palm. "What's wrong with this thing?"

"And Rossiter? Was that your doing?"

Creedmore nodded in distraction. "Yeah, but that wasn't my fault, either. He was out roaming when he should have been in Dante's camp. He caught me using a German radio, checking in with Richter. I had to put him down. Don't worry, no one will ever find him. I buried him about a quarter of a mile from camp."

"What about Viviana and me?" Landry said. "And Willoughby? You can't really afford to let us go, can you?"

Creedmore opened the throttle another jot, but the boat continued to act sluggish. "Shoot, is that what bothers you?" he said. "Don't worry about it, buddy. Once I get everything converted to cash and stashed away in a Swiss bank, I plan to do some expert disappearing. No one's ever going to find me. If you want to go back and tell everyone, that's up to you."

"Sure it is."

"No, I mean it. Frankly, if I were you, I'd a whole lot rather be rich than a hero. It'd be a lot easier for you to stick with me and disappear. Hell, bring Viviana, too. I don't care. Haven't you ever wanted to go to Egypt and see the pyramids? Pyramids. Isn't that crazy? It's hard to figure out just where I'd like to start. Everyone would think we're dead, especially after that shooting back there on shore. But if you've got the hots for playing big man, go ahead and do it. It's no skin off my nose. Just as long as I get my own pig trough filled."

He stared at the gauges again. In spite of the flickering needles and the churning engines, the boat was rapidly slowing to a standstill. It obviously baffled him. He tried to ram the throttle farther forward, but it was full out. Not only that, the boat now seemed to be settling. The prow drooped lower and water lapped only a couple of feet below the gunwales. Creedmore throttled back and shut off the engines, then gave Landry a hurt, unhappy look. "All right, you sonofabitch. What have you done to her?"

"Me?" Landry said. "I haven't done anything. You've been watching me the whole time."

In the silence, with the engines off, they could hear an odd gurgling, like water backing up through a clogged bathtub drain. Willoughby had also begun to stir, and they could hear his moans coming from the deck. Creedmore shot a quick look down at the Britisher, to make sure he was still on his face, then said accusingly, "One of you must have done something. Boats don't just stop with the engines running flat out." He wavered, then backed toward the ladder, holding his gun on Landry and Viviana. "Don't move, either of you," he told them. "You stay up here where I can keep an eye on you. You so much as wiggle, and I'll put holes in both your noses."

He groped with his left foot for the first rung, watching Landry and Viviana carefully. As his toe found purchase and he reached down to grip the riser, a dark, calloused hand appeared above the rim of the bridge flooring and wrapped olive-skinned fingers around his ankle. Creedmore's eyes ballooned with shock and he tried to jerk around, but the hand twisted at his leg and yanked him backward. He hurtled out of sight, arms flailing. Landry heard him hit the deck below.

Landry and Viviana both rushed to the ladder and saw Creedmore spread-eagled across the planks. Veterano, standing at the foot of the ladder with brawny arms outstretched, coiled his legs and leaped through the air at him. Creedmore shrieked in terror. He raised the gun and pulled the trigger three times, as fast as he could, and Veterano did an awkward half somersault in midair and landed heavily on his shoulder. Creedmore pushed hurriedly to his knees, clutching his ribs. Veterano rolled over in pain and looked wordlessly at two neat patches of blood high on his own shirt front. The two men stared at each other for a moment, then Veterano moved toward Creedmore again. Again the gun came up.

"Look out!" Landry yelled. He braced against the bridge rail and dived. Creedmore, startled by Landry's cry, faltered, trying to decide which of them to shoot. He made up his mind in a split second, but it was too late. By the time the gun started to swing around, Landry piled into him. The gun went spinning away.

Landry was first to right himself, and he sprawled across the deck for the gun, expecting Creedmore to fight him for it. But nothing happened. When he lurched around with the gun in his hand, he saw Creedmore hunched over on his elbows and knees, holding his side. "Damn it," Creedmore whined. His breath came in near-sobs. "I think that old fart broke a couple of my ribs."

"What a pity," Landry said. He tried to hold the gun steady, but his hand was shaking. Shaking so hard that he was afraid

Viviana might notice. He let the gun droop to his side and turned anxiously to Veterano. "Are you badly hurt?" he asked.

Veterano eased to his feet and stared at the two red-rimmed holes in his shirt, one high on the chest below the collarbone, the other in the side, below the armpit. "No, I am all right." He cast a stony look at Creedmore. "It is true what I heard, David? He killed Luisa?"

There was deadly hostility in Veterano's eyes. Creedmore said, "Hey now, don't try to pin that on me. I only roughed her up a little. It isn't my fault she died."

"See to the Britisher," Veterano said flatly. "I will watch over this one."

Landry hesitated. The emotionless sound of Veterano's voice spoke of dark hatred, and Landry worried that the old man might do something foolish. Veterano seemed to understand Landry's quandary, and dipped his chin, as if to promise no precipitate action. Landry looked to Viviana and gestured her down from the bridge.

She clambered down the ladder quickly and came to kneel by Willoughby, who had rolled to his side near the starboard gunwale. She touched matted hair where a king-sized lump had risen, and Landry was gratified to see the Englishman wince. Viviana cupped both hands and dipped lake water, now only inches from swamping the boat. She splashed it in Willoughby's face. The first double handful accomplished little, so she dipped and splashed again. This time Willoughby jerked, and his eyes fluttered open. Viviana reached for more water, but Willoughby raised his palm and murmured, "Enough. Quite enough, thank you."

Creedmore, seeing how easily Viviana had dipped water over the side, clutched a deck cleat and said, "Holy God, what's happening?"

"That should be obvious to anyone but a fool," Viviana told him in disgust. "We are sinking."

Creedmore struggled to his feet. He staggered past Landry to the rail and peered at the rising line of water. "Jesus, she's right," he said. "Come on, get busy. We've got to get this boat back to shore."

Veterano said, "It's too late. The boat will go no farther. I opened the sea cock."

"You did what?" Creedmore shrieked. "You damn old idiot! There's close to forty million dollars here! We'll lose it!" He pushed Landry aside and hurried back to where the treasure lay on the deck. Clawing madly with his fingers, he tore open one of the cartons and began to stuff paper money into his shirt. "Come on," he yelled at Landry and Willoughby. "Quick! Grab as much as you can!"

Even as Creedmore frantically transferred currency from the box to his shirt, water tipped over the forward gunwales and washed across the bow and the boat settled faster and faster, bow end first. Landry helped Willoughby to his feet and said, "It looks like we'll have to swim for it. Are you up to it?"

"I can make it," Willoughby assured him.

Landry stuffed the gun under his belt and gestured for Viviana to join him at the rail. He helped her over the side, then the deck shuddered and slipped a few more feet into the water. Willoughby staggered with the sudden slippage and almost fell. Landry lurched forward to brace him. "Come on, into the water," he said urgently. "There isn't much time." He helped Willoughby across the rail, then straddled the gunwale and beckoned to Veterano.

Veterano hesitated. His chest wounds were bleeding slowly and he swayed slightly on the tilting deck, but his eyes were bright and he seemed strong. "I'm all right," he told Landry. "I am in no pain. Go. See to Viviana and the Britisher. I will be right behind you."

The deck slipped again, a wrenching, gliding movement, and Landry felt a touch of panic. He plunged in between Viviana and the Britisher and gave them both a push, trying to get them to swim away from the boat. Viviana understood and stroked away, but Willoughby, still dazed, only moved a few feet and Landry had to give him another shove to get him started. The Britisher began to stroke weakly, and Landry followed, watching to make sure Willoughby was all right. Landry thought he heard Creedmore and Veterano splash in behind him, but it was only the sound of lake water slushing and burbling into air pockets inside the sinking boat. Landry wasn't aware that they were still on the deck until he'd covered about twenty yards and heard Creedmore scream.

It started as a cry of surprise, Creedmore's voice howling angrily, "What the hell do you think you're doing?" Then, with a touch of panic, "Let me go, you stupid old bastard!" It quickly turned into a frantic wail of anguish. Landry and Viviana both stopped swimming and wrenched around. Creedmore, his pockets and shirt front stuffed with colorful bills, stood perched by the settling stern rail, struggling to break loose. Veterano, whiskered face oddly composed, stood behind Creedmore, arms encircling him in a firm bear hug.

"Let me go!" Creedmore screamed, a high-pitched whine that rose and tore from his throat. But Veterano clung tightly and the boat sank lower and lower.

"Oh my God," Viviana murmured.

"Leave him!" Landry shouted. Water sloshed again and the cabin filled, adding its weight. The boat began to slide under in one long, continuous glide. "Jump, Veterano! For God's sake, jump!"

Creedmore's voice rose as the water touched his knees and crawled to his waist. He thrashed against Veterano's arms, using his athletic young muscles with a frenzy born of terror, but Veterano held on. Creedmore screamed in falsetto as the water covered his chest and reached his armpits, and screamed even louder as it rose to his chin. Then, suddenly, the boat was gone and both heads disappeared beneath the water and the screaming stopped.

Landry and Viviana bobbed in stunned silence, Willoughby a few feet beyond them, and waited, half expecting Veterano or Creedmore or both to reappear, but no one came. There was only roiling water and floating currency and a stream of gurgling bubbles. Then, after a long silence, the lake surface smoothed and a calm, unruffled quiet settled over the spot where the boat had gone down. Landry continued to tread water for a few moments, throat tight with shock, and finally, when it became obvious to him that it was over, he turned slowly with Viviana and stroked for shore.

6

On a grassy bank, Landry collapsed beside Viviana and Willoughby. Landry turned his face to the sun. A fly buzzed in the silence. He could hear Viviana and Willoughby breathing hard, but no one spoke. Finally, as breath came more evenly and the afternoon sun began to bake some warmth into them, Viviana roused herself. "I see someone coming toward us," she said.

Landry considered Viviana's words, but it was hard to think about anything but the heat of the sun on his eyelids. He didn't want to move. It was as though his body, troubled and sore, had been cut adrift from his mind, and his thoughts floated as shapelessly as water. Then, like water collected and forced through a funnel, reality flooded back and he opened his eyes. "Where?" he asked.

She gestured to the east, across a meadow, and Landry sat up. Topping a knob of treeless ground that crowded close to the shores of Lake Lugano, three men moved slowly through golden buttercups, supporting a fourth. Landry raised a hand to shade his eyes. It was Pietro and Stefanini, bringing the man they called Ugo, and Kavanaugh limping behind them. Kavanaugh leaned heavily on a crooked larch branch, favoring his right leg, but even so, he appeared to be in better shape than Ugo. Ugo's round, balding head lolled like some separate appendage, swaying to and fro above his chest, and his toes dragged helplessly through the flowers.

"The rest of the troop is accounted for," Willoughby said. He sounded suddenly schoolboyish. He rose and started across the meadow to meet them, but Viviana put a hand on Landry's arm, and they stayed on the grassy bank.

"They'll be here soon," Viviana said.

"Yes," Landry said.

"We may not get another chance to talk," she said. "Once we get back to Lake Como, I suppose you and the ALOTs will have to leave for Milan."

"Yes, we will." He looked at a bruise on her forehead. He hadn't had time to notice it before. "I'm sorry about all this, Viviana. I wish you hadn't been here to see it."

"It's my war, too," she said. "They forced it back on me when they dragged poor Luisa from under my roof. Oh David, they . . ."

"Hush," he said. "I know you tried to stop them." He sketched the bruise with gentle fingers, without actually touching it. "When I saw you at the villa and couldn't do anything to help you . . .

When I thought they might have hurt you, even killed you . . ."

"I know," she said. "When I thought *you* might be dead . . ." She sighed and leaned into his arms, butting her bruised forehead against his shoulder. "Damn it, I suppose I shall have to come with you when you leave the lake. I warn you, I shall even come with you if you insist on returning to America. I don't want to in the least, but I discover that I can't contemplate life without you."

"Nor I without you." He found a smile. "We'll probably make each other miserable, but there doesn't seem to be much else we can do."

Her answering smile, though weary, was the warm, sly one. "Ah well," she said. "I'm very good at making the best of things."

A last ghostly thought of the dead Holloman floated into Landry's mind, and he said, "We'll be married, of course. Will you be faithful to me?"

"Marriage? We'll have to think about that. As for being faithful, well, we'll have to see about that, too, won't we? But I can assure you of this, David: I will always be faithful to myself."

"Witch," he said. Pietro hailed them from the meadow, and Landry knew he had only seconds left to hold her. "When this is over," he whispered, "when I come back, we'll walk by the lake. We'll walk in the sun, and find the perfect stone to sit on, and we'll just sit there and wait until all the bad memories are gone and until a wonderful feeling of peacefulness soaks in like the sunshine."

"I think I'll love that," she said.

Pietro lifted his free arm and waved. Landry stood. There was a bullet tear high on Kavanaugh's trouser leg, an exit wound where a track of blood had mingled with gray cloth. Someone, Pietro most likely, had tied a handkerchief tightly above the wound to stanch the bleeding.

Stefanini and Pietro brought Ugo the last few yards to the grassy bank. "We saw the boat sink," Pietro said. With Stefanini's help, he lowered Ugo into the grass. "Who opened the sea valve? Veterano?"

"Yes," Landry said. He eyed Kavanaugh's leg. "How bad is it?"

"Bad?" Kavanaugh said. He grinned like a moron, happy to be alive. "There's nothing to it. Damned bullet went through meat, in the back and out the front. Didn't hit bone or anything. I've got a free ticket home."

"What about him?" Landry said, nodding down at Ugo. He was surprised to see Ugo's eyes blink open and return the look. From the way Ugo's legs had dangled and his head had drooped during the cross-meadow walk, Landry had thought him to be unconscious.

"His spine is severed, I think," Pietro said. "Where is Veterano? We lost sight of him when the boat went down."

"He didn't make it," Landry said.

Kavanaugh's good humor faded instantly. "Oh hell. What happened to him?"

Ugo's voice, soft and scratchy, came to them from the grass. "What difference does it make? The fool deserved to die." Unable to move anything but his eyes, he looked first at Pietro and Willoughby, then at Landry and Viviana. "You are idiots, all of you. There was a fortune on that boat. Why did you let that old fool sink it?"

Landry said, "You would be wise to keep your comments to yourself, comrade. You have much to answer for."

"I answer nothing to you," Ugo said weakly. "Not to any of you." He tried to look away, but muscles refused to obey signals from the brain. He had to settle for closing his eyes.

Pietro said, "He has lost much blood, I think. I have little medical knowledge, but I have seen it happen to partisans in the hills. The face, like ashes. The skin, dry and brittle."

Freddy Stefanini rubbed his nose. "He'll probably die if we can't rake up a doctor for him somewhere. It's a shame. After all the things he's done, shot by a German like that, he'll most likely end up a hero."

Willoughby stared at the high mountain ridges to the east. "It's too far back across the mountains to Lake Como," he said. "He would never make it. If you have in mind finding medical attention, you'll have to cast about closer. On the far side of the lake, perhaps. Porlezza? That might be close enough."

"Yes, Porlezza might do," Pietro agreed. "But we would have to leave immediately."

Viviana stared at Ugo's round face and said, "It would be a pity if he died without coming to justice."

"Yes, it would be, wouldn't it," Pietro said.

Viviana studied Pietro's expression. Then she put her hand on Landry's elbow and stared at the others, moving in silent communication from face to face. Nothing was said aloud, but her unspoken question was received and acknowledged by each of them in turn. She sat down quietly in the grass and said, "For poor Luisa."

Pietro lowered himself wearily beside her. "For Dante," he said.

Landry sat down between them. "For the Lizard."

Stefanini hunkered down next to X. B. Kavanaugh and began to loosen the makeshift tourniquet. "For Salvo and Piccione," Stefanini said. "Now darn it, X.B., you stop that bleeding. I don't want to make it for you, too."

Willoughby sighed and joined them in the grass. "For Veterano and Gualfiero and il Gallo and all the innocents who perished at the edge of the storm," he said.

Ugo's eyes flickered open. His pupils darted from side to side. "What are you doing?" he said. "Why are you sitting?"

Pietro ignored him and gestured toward the center of the lake. "It does seem a shame about the treasure," he said. "Should we mark this area and come back for it?"

"Let it lie," Landry said. "It's caused nothing but grief for those who have touched it."

"I suppose you are right," Pietro said. He braced his elbows on his knees and gazed out at the still, deep waters. His thoughts seemed far away.

Kavanaugh moaned softly as Stefanini produced a knife and neatly ripped his trouser leg, exposing the wound for what treatment they could give it. Stefanini looked from Pietro to the lake. "Forty million bucks," he murmured. "What a waste."

An even louder moan escaped from Ugo's throat. "You can't do this," he said. "You must help me."

"I wonder if we'll ever see the two shipments of treasure that the Commies got away with?" Kavanaugh said. "What do you reckon they did with it, anyway? Do you suppose we'll ever . . . Ouch, Freddy, that hurts. Take it easy. I don't want to pass out now and miss everything."

Willoughby moved over to help Stefanini with the bandaging.

"I imagine it's all been transported to Milan by now," Willoughby told Kavanaugh. "I doubt you'll ever hear of it again."

Pietro swung his chin around. "He will hear of it. Everyone will hear of it. Too many good men have died for us to keep silent."

Stefanini left the bandaging to Willoughby's skillful fingers and settled back in the grass. "I don't know what good it will do to talk about the missing shipments," Stefanini said. "We've got no proof. All our best witnesses are dead. This bastard saw to that."

Ugo spoke again, in a voice slurred with self-righteousness, a groggy whisper that was hard to understand. "I did only that which was necessary," he mumbled. "It was my duty. I do not regret it."

Pietro grimaced. He looked out across the lake and his eyes took in the still, solemn majesty of the mountains and the warm, brilliant blanket of the sun. "I wonder what time it is?" he said quietly. "Does anyone know?"

Landry squinted at the sun. "Close to two, I'd say."

Pietro smiled without mirth. "Then the peace is almost upon us," he said. "There will be celebration on the lake. Flowers, laughter. People will crowd the streets. What a shame that we must miss it."

They sat quite still for a while, each wrapped in his own thoughts. Ugo lay with his eyes closed, breath coming through lax lips. Viviana stole a look at him and seemed almost to weaken, but Landry patted her arm and she kept quiet. Several minutes passed. Then, suddenly, Ugo's eyelids popped open. "Sandrino," he said. "Sandrino, where are you?" His face was bloodless and his voice was distant.

Pietro, like Viviana, also seemed to be weakening. He allowed himself a corner-of-the-eye glance at Ugo and the spreading red stain in the grass. "Perhaps we should take him to a doctor after all," he said. "The war is over. It's time to put the past behind us."

Ugo's eyes heated up briefly and his voice gained strength. "You are wrong," he told Pietro. "You are all wrong. The war isn't over. The war is just beginning." He smiled at them fiercely, then his eyes dulled and the lids closed. His breath faded to shallow puffs.

For a time, none of them spoke. They sat in a tight group on the grassy bank, staring out at the placid lake waters. The sun burned down on them from a white-hot sky dimpled with clouds. Insects hummed in the silence. A light breeze whiffed in from the north and ruffled the surface of the lake. Landry took Viviana's hand in his own, but her fingers were cold. Far away, from some unseen meadow on the opposite shore, a cowbell tinkled, borne to them on the wind.

Landry could no longer hear Ugo breathing, but he could still see the quick rise and fall of Ugo's chest. Landry closed his eyes and thought of the many friends who would never feel the sun again, of the men and women who had died only one step from the sunrise of peace. Then he tilted his head back, warming himself in the sunshine, and thought of Viviana and the future, wondering what effect, if any, their involvement in this day's activities would have on their relationship. Even more important, perhaps: How would it affect his own ideas about himself? Would he survive it? Or would he, like so many before him, become a victim? He thought about it long and hard and made up his mind. He would not allow it to make a difference. He waited confidently for a feeling of peacefulness to consume him. But nothing happened.

He decided to wait a little longer.

Epilogue

The Aftermath

La commedia è finita! . . .

The comedy is done! . . .
    —Leoncavallo, *Pagliacci*

The entire Dongo treasure, a consignment of bullion, currency and gemstones estimated to be worth some ninety million dollars, disappeared within a week of its recovery from the fleeing Fascist caravan. It was never seen again. Surviving partisans on Lake Como claimed that Communist leaders in Milan siphoned off most of the treasure, while the Communists themselves accused lakeside partisans of the theft. A number of civilian and military inquiries were launched in the years following World War II, but the Italian Communist Party emerged from the war as a strong, unified political force, and few of the investigations were ever concluded. Nevertheless, when the Italian Communists built a new official Party headquarters in Rome shortly after the war—a modern, five-story building that stretched the length of a city block—perceptive Italians promptly dubbed it the Palazzo Dongo, in honor of Mussolini's missing millions.

It is still there, on the Via delle Botteghe Oscure (the Street of the Shady Shops), and it is still known informally as the Dongo Palace. It may be the only concrete evidence of the missing treasure that the world at large will ever see.